Out Of The Mist
To Kings Mountain

A Novel By

Shawn C Roberts

Published by Longhunter Press

Copyright 2018

ISBN 978-1986211154

Forward

My second novel <u>Out Of The Mist To Kings Mountain</u> is a historical novel based on the real-life war time experiences of Rice Medaris, my ancestor.

An act of Congress was passed in June of 1832 to provide pensions for American Revolutionary War Soldiers. The requirement for the benefits granted to the officers and enlisted men of the Continental Line, State Troops, Sailors and Volunteer Militia was clear. The applying veteran had to serve at least one tour no less than six months to be eligible. Later amendments to the law extended the benefits to widows of these men as well. Rice's widow Rachael, applied in Buncombe County North Carolina on the 17th day of August in 1850.

Like my first novel <u>Redskins And Lobsterbacks</u> much of my book is based on the content of sworn pension depositions. You will see in the footnotes throughout the book, references to other pensioners besides Rice. It is my intention to give my books a background based on the known facts of the stories I tell. I also use journals, history books, interviews, and diaries from the time period. With these documents and tools, I know precisely where and what the people in my book were doing. I cannot always know what they may have said and what they were thinking, but I do know what transpired while they were there. My writing style is to fill in the missing dialogue and their thought process as I see them. I also travel to the geographical locations indicated in the story to have a good understanding of the lay of the land. Having done so much research on each person in my books, I have come to understand their personalities as best as can be done in this modern age. I hope that you enjoy my version of these historical figures. Their journey through life is our history. It is sometimes joyful, and at other times heartbreaking, sometime benevolent, and at others cruel, as history has always been. With each turn of a page you will be stepping back in time and I hope you enjoy the journey.

Chapter 1

Rice

The coals of the fire were dying down inside his forge. Not satisfied with the look of his charcoal and black coal mixture, Rice Medaris reached up and pulled the chain that made his bellows whoosh the much-needed air into his rock firebox. With a few pulls of his strong arm, he had stoked the fire back to the desired color and temperature.

Being in his twenty-fifth year of life, Rice had mastered the fine art of blacksmithing, and was beginning to make a good name for himself, here in the Yadkin Valley of western North Carolina. He stood at five feet, ten inches when he was fully erect and not bent over his work. His broad shoulders had been developed from countless downward strokes of his heavy hammer onto a battered anvil. He walked over to his workbench and using his tongs he picked up the last of ten pipe tomahawks that he was working on. He held it there for a moment while he studied the bowl with his deep set blue eyes, He liked the way it looked, it was ready to hold tobacco now.

Turning, he made his way back to the fire and stuck the business end of the weapon into the coals.

"Well Jeremiah, the hard part is all but done now, my friend. All that is left to do is hammer out the blade and you'll be off to Kentucky."

"I'm not off that fast," replied the buckskinner as he stood just inside the door of Rice's shop. "It will still be a week or so before we head for the gap. You know how cold it can be up in those mountains, even if it is the last week of February. Hell, those March winds can stick a cold dagger in you back as well you know."

Rice nodded his head as he pushed a stray lock of black hair off his sweaty brow with his free hand. He reached in and pulled the glowing red tomahawk from the coals with the other. As he walked to the anvil, sitting to the right of his firebox, he looked over at Jeremiah and asked "Who all is going with you this time?"

"Well, let me see, there's me of course, and Samuel Tate along with his boy Robert, and my cousin Thomas McDowell for sure. And hopefully a few more. James Harrod's party [1] of last summer was about forty strong when he laid out his

town. Even with that many he had to abandon it, but he'll be back this summer from what I hear. I will not need that many, for my goals are not the same as his. We will be hunting out in the open and

---

[1] James Harrod 1746-1792. Contrary to what many believe, Harrod established Kentucky's first settlement in what is now Mercer County Kentucky at Harrodsburg. This was a full year before Boone's settlement at Boonesborough in 1775. Harrod was a soldier and surveyor from western Pennsylvania who played a prominent role in Kentucky's settlement.

with us being a small number, it should be easier for us to hide from the savages, if need be."

Rice nodded his head in agreement as he slammed his hammer down on the hot blade, and with eight or nine lighter taps the blade began to take shape. "Do you have the wooden handles made yet?' Rice asked.

"Yes, I do, they are out in my saddlebag," answered Jeremiah. "Are you ready for them?"

"No not just yet," Rice replied. "What about your brothers? Are any of them going along with you?"

"No, I guess not, but I still have some time to talk one or two of them into it before we go. Maybe David will go; he has heard the Boones speak of Kentucky a time or two. You know all of the buzz they spit out about settling out there. Daniel is out there now, down around the Watauga and Holston rivers parlaying for Judge Henderson as we speak."

"What about your father, has he ever spoken about going to the other side of these mountains?"

"No-o-o-" Jeremiah answered, dragging the word out long enough to cast an eye in Rice's direction. "Momma's not ready for another Indian war just yet, she said the last one we had here was bad enough, and I believe father is of the same mind, even if he won't tell her so. It's not like we are completely out of danger here, you know. They know that the Cherokee can fall on us at any time. At least, that is what I tell them when they give me grief about going over to the other side of the gap to Ken tuck.

"Yah, but we don't have to run as far back to the settlements to fort up as those folks over the mountains will, if it gets bad again." Rice replied. "Fort Grider may be small, but it has always held."

"You know, you ask questions in a roundabout way sometimes Rice." Jeremiah said, as he watched a relieved looking Rice set down the finished pipe tomahawk so it could cool.

"Why, what does that mean?" Rice asked through his crooked smile as he pulled his leather apron from over his head."

"You ask about the folks, but your interest lies more with Rachael I believe, so I will give you a direct answer, and put you out of your misery, even though you ask indirectly about my sister's situation. No, she stays right here on Moravian Creek with all the other McPheeters here in Surry County, or Wilkes County, or whatever they finally settle on calling this area."

"They do move the borders a lot these days, don't they?" Rice remarked as he picked up the cooled tomahawk. "Do you want the edge of the blade filed down or do you want to sharpen it yourself?"

"I'll do it myself," Jeremiah replied, "but I would like for you to take a look at the hammer on my rifle. I want you to make me a spare one to take along. After I lost that one over on the Clinch River last fall, I would like to keep one in my stores. Doubt if there are any gunsmith in Ken tuck. Mine is too good a rifle to be used as a club."

"Yes, indeed it is," Rice agreed "I expect that's what the tomahawks are for."

"No, that's not the case," Jeremiah replied as he pulled a long stem pipe from under his bearskin coat. "These are not for hostiles, if Daniel is successful with the Cherokee this spring, they should be in good humor. Maybe I'll have some good trading this coming summer with peaceful Cherokees."

"So, you will be returning a rich man then?" Rice asked with a raised eyebrow.

"Yes Sir," Jeremiah replied "too rich to speak to the likes of you."

Chapter 2

Sycamore Shoals March 17, 1775

Richard Henderson stood gazing out over the rushing waters of the Watauga river on this cold gray evening. He had been here at the old fields of Sycamore Shoals for some time now. It had been an extremely tiring trip up the 23 miles to these rapids he now looked out over. In only three more miles downstream, the river would end where it poured into the Doe. He knew he was not the first Englishmen to stand here, by any means, but what he had accomplished here today greatly overshadowed what all the others had done. The longhunters Julius Dugger and Andrew Greer had waded these waters in the 1760's. William Bean had raised the first cabin only fifteen miles away. And James Robertson the leader of sixteen families had founded the Watauga settlement only four years before, but that too paled to Henderson's feat. His dream of the new Colony of Transylvania was now a reality. He felt it was only a matter of time before he and his partners would become very wealthy men. His thoughts were interrupted, as he heard the gravel and shells lying on the bank behind him being disturbed, as a man approached.

"Judge Henderson, I'm off to my hollow" Joseph Vann announced as he came to a stop. "Those young bucks up there are beginning to feel the effects of your rum. And I, for one don't see the advantage of being around a few hundred drunken Indians."

"I know that feeling myself Joseph, but I cannot afford to take the chance of offending Chief Attakullakulla or the Raven by departing too soon."

"I understand that sir," Vann replied as he shifted his long rifle to his other hand. "'The Little Carpenter' has become one of the elder man" Vann remarked using Chief Attakullakulla's better known English name; "but he may also have some of that fire his son showed today."

"You contained that situation very well this afternoon Joseph, you are a fine interpreter. Indeed, I employed the right man for an important undertaking," replied Henderson as the handed over a purse of coins.

"Well, we will see if that's the case in the coming days I suppose. But, I do believe, that since I have a little of their blood running through my veins, it can come in mighty helpful at times," replied Vann as he tucked away his pay. "I am afraid that that pocked faced Dragging Canoe understood all too well what happened today. I was afraid that speech he made had undermined the whole treaty. He spoke powerful words that almost broke up the council circle. That statement about the Cherokee melting away like snow in the sun, and the shouting about how weak the Delaware have become after their treaties with the white man had a big effect. I still don't know how we got that treaty signed."

"I'll tell you how we got it signed," Henderson replied, "at great expense. At least in their eyes. A few stands of guns and ammunition, four wagon loads of trinkets and supplies, all spread out on the ground made quite an impression, and the feast and rum help as well".

"It was a well negotiated treaty" Vann announced as he ran his fingers along his jawline. "It brought about quite an expansion, an immense area really, all the way from the Cumberland River to the Kentucky River, millions of acres. That deed of yours sure has the right name, The Great Grant. Plus, you got the Path Grant as well."

"Yes," Henderson replied proudly. For an instant there, I thought Dragging Canoe was going to attack me, when he hears that second proposal. Colonel Boone has already gone on ahead to blaze that road. My party will follow him soon."

"I do have one more concern though Judge, what about King George's 1763 proclamation about not settling beyond the mountains?"

Richard Henderson turned and looked at the eastern skyline, pausing a moment before answering "War is in the air over there Joseph. A royal proclamation will be of no matter once that begins."

"And afterwards" Vann asked?

"If the Colonist win, they will want to extend the new country's western boundaries, and if England should win, The King will most likely try to make a peace offering by opening the west. That would help bring his discontented subjects back into the fold. Either way Transylvania [2] was born today."

At the same time Judge Henderson and Joseph Vann were discussing the events of the day, Dragging Canoe found himself

[2] Transylvania never came to be. Neither the Royal nor the American government ever recognized it as a legal state. However it's capital Boonsboro played a great part in the settlement of Kentucky.

looking into a newly lighted fire on the banks of the Nolichucky River. His heart inside his strong chest was so heavy, he had to swallow a lump in his throat every time he spoke. The dark cloud he had foretold of the white invaders, was at hand, and he felt it storming in his heart and mind. He knew he was not alone in his desire to rid his home of the white man. Doublehead and Bloody Fellow, both rising powers in the Cherokee nation, where of the same mind, along with countless other young warriors who were eager for their leadership. Big Jim, [3] a Shawnee warrior, was in attendance and ready to relay the bad news of the treaty to his people in the North.

"Brothers, I feel shame and disgust in my soul tonight. Shame for my old and weak-minded father, and disgust for Oconostota. Some call him 'Stalking Turkey' but I will not. I call him 'Stalking Nothing'. They are no longer men in my eyes, not worthy of being chiefs of our great nation. They should drink the black drink so it can wash away their sins today." Dragging Canoe announced in a low, rumbling voice "But I promise you, soon we will beat our war drums. Beating out an everlasting desire to win back what our fathers gave away today. I would not do what they have done. I will not crawl upon the ground under the white man's feet. May the Great Spirit come into my lodge and tear me into a hundred pieces if I ever treaty with those white devils as my father has done here today."

Doublehead did not speak, instead, he reached over and grasped the raw heart of a dear that was waiting to be cooked. He held it high over his head for a moment, just long enough to get everyone's

---

[3] Big Jim is best known for his part in killing James Boone, the son of Daniel Boone in 1773. This act put an end to Boone's first attempt to settle in Kentucky. Big Jim met his end at the hands of Kentucky militiamen under the command of Benjamin Logan in 1786. Daniel Boone was a witness to his death.

attention. Then he bit into it as though it were an apple. Everyone knew he had tasted the flesh of longhunters before, and was eager to do so again. The ground was about to run red.

Chapter 3

A Duchess for a Brute

When Rice got up this morning he was met outside his shop door by a familiar guest. It was always here after a rainy night like last night had been, and it lingered around his new place of business as though it wanted to be his partner, usually until around noon. Everyone who lived in this mountainous region knew this particular guest well, for this floating mist greeted everyone almost daily. The fog was not as thick today, but it was here nevertheless, and it put a deep chill into Rice's bones on this early spring day. However, his bearskin coat took good care of him, keeping the cold at bay, he thought as he ran his blue eyes over the landscape outside his open doorway.

Rice had skinned the pelt from a large black bear he had killed last fall, while building the chimney for his forge. The big old fellow had lost his fear of man over time and his new-found courage had led to his undoing. Rice had little choice but to put the animal down, for no one would come to a blacksmith to have a shoe a fitted to their horse with a bear running around close outside. He had kept some of the bear meat but it was a little on the greasy side, not so good as beef, but it had helped to get him through the winter. Hopefully, he would not have to depend on eating as much wild game this coming year if he could start a new herd of cattle like he planned. Having already inspected his Pennsylvania rifle before opening the door, Rice stepped out into the mist with his gun in hand.

Within a few steps he was greeted by his two hounds, Brute and Duchess. They gave Rice reassurance that there were no Indians about. Brute had a keen sense of smell and could always tell when someone approached Rice's Shop. He could pick up their strange sent well before they ever cleared the forest and walked onto the land Rice had cleared around his new homestead. Duchess was just coming out of her puppyhood, just a little over a year old. He had taken her in as a companion for Brute now that they had moved out here, not wanting his longtime companion to be lonely. She was a beautiful dog. Her coat was mostly white, with a few black spots on her back. She had a solid white face and loving golden eyes. She was quite a contrast to Brute, who was a large hound completely black except for his tan underbelly. You could see the age creeping into his face, a few white hairs had appeared around his mouth this spring. His battle-scarred nose and split ears revealed that he was not a dog to be trifled with, by neither man nor beast. Rice lowered his hand and Duchess met it with a cold, wet nose and a warm tongue, as she licked his hand. Then he turned his attention to Brute, running a hand down the dog's side while squatting down beside him, Rice again looked out over his cleared land and said "Go ahead boy, see if anyone's about."

At Rice's command, the hound took off at a fast pace, running around the property, nose to the ground.

"Go on and help him out," Rice said to the female, "it's time for you to start picking up some of this stuff yourself girl."

With no more encouragement, she too ran out into the mist and quickly disappeared behind Brute. The last thing Rice could see of her was the little black twist of hair on the tip of her white tail.

Rice lowered his head and let his own eyes roam around the grounds. His view began at the corral; seeing nothing, he turned his head toward the center of the clearing where he would soon build a cabin for himself. Sleeping inside the shop had kept him out of the weather, it was a roof over his head, but it had none of the comforts of a home, like the one he had grown up in while still a child in the care of his father and mother. Next, he turned his attention toward Warriors Creek and walked over to the top of the small rise that commanded the lay of the land. When he reached its eminence, he looked down towards the small waterfall, and saw the two dogs approaching him, having finished their scouting of the grounds. He gave each dog an encouraging and approving pat.

Then he turned to the east feeling as sure as he possibly could that no Cherokee were about planning to burn his shop while he was gone, or possibly steal his horse from the corral. Word had traveled throughout the North Carolina backcountry about how successfully Richard Henderson's treaty with the Cherokee had transpired. He hopes that maybe the hostilities between the two races would be lessened this year. Peace had always been elusive here in the back country as far back as 1753 when all of this mountain range was part of Rowan County. And even further back to 1700 when the Cherokee had driven out the weaker Catawba's, a rivaling tribe.

With that in mind he turned his thoughts and steps towards the trees. It was just a good stretch of the legs through the forest to his destination, the McPheeters homestead. He trekked up one side of the ridge then down the other to Moravian Creek. Being on foot, maybe he could bring down a deer or elk on his way over, if one was nearby. Jeremiah would be leaving tonight on his travels to Kentucky, and

Rice wanted to wish him a fond adieu. In addition to being Rachael's brother, Jeremiah had been good to Rice this past year, good enough to become Rice's best friend. As he reached the tree line he turned back, and motioned for Duchess to come up behind him and take her place beside Brute. Then, Rice entered the trees with thoughts of Rachael's long black hair on his mind. Today should be a good day.

Chapter 4

A Sweet Breeze

It was nearly two o'clock by the time Rice reach the McPheeters family homestead on Moravian Creek. He had taken a well-traveled deer trail that had become the route he and the McPheeters used to visit each other. Maybe someday it could be widened with a few swings of a great many axes. County roads where in the near future, and a planned bridge near Moravian Falls would be a great help when completed. No deer or elk had appeared on his way over. They were becoming scarce with all the new human activity, but a tom turkey made the mistake of taking flight in front of Rice; having been kicked up by Brute's approach. Rice always hated arriving empty handed and thanks to this bird's poor judgement in its haste to escape, it had provided Rice with a respectable gift. He set the bird down on the ground as he reached the clearing where Charles McPheeters had cut away the forest a few years before. He untied one of the two ropes from around his waist and called Duchess over to him where he quickly tied one end to her collar and the other end to a pine tree: knowing all too well that if she saw him tie Brute first, she would never come to him of her own will. Brute, on the other hand, always came when called, and in all honesty, Rice hated to tie up his old, but still powerful dog, because he minded so well. But Rice never trusted the McPheeters dogs to stay away from Brute. It wouldn't bode well for them if they ever decided to pick a fight with Brute, because he would certainly kill one before Rice could pull them apart. Once Brute had a lock on an opponent and had the taste of blood he would never let go, that was the only command of Rice's that the dog would not submit to. When Rice walked away Duchess pulled at her rope trying to break free, wanting to continue on with her master, but to no avail.

"Look at him sitting there, behaving like he should!" Rice scolded turning back to the two. "You're just going to choke yourself. Do yourself a favor girl, and watch how a smart dog behaves."

Having done all, he could to secure his dogs, Rice started the remaining walk to the McPheeters cabin. Rachael's father was smart enough to clear away all of the trees, bushes. or anything else that might provide an attacker within gunshot range with any cover. This precaution would give his family time to fort up inside the cabin, and plenty of time for the defenders to shoot down a good number of any attackers on their approach. At one time the McPheeters clan could hold off almost any attack, but their dwindling numbers were once again about to decrease with Jeremiah's departure. Four of Charles's son, and two of his daughters had moved away after getting married. Now, David would be the only son left, with Jeremiah gone to Kentucky. It would seem strange with only David, Charles, his wife Mary Ann, and their youngest daughter Rachael left here on their riverside farm. The farm itself, like all the others in the Yadkin Valley, was not the most bountiful but its beauty was beyond compare. The grass still had a yellowish tinge, but soon it would be green. When the redbuds and dogwoods began blooming, in a few weeks' time, their colors would put an end to all this brown and grayish landscape.

As Rice's eyes were roving over the ground, the back door of the McPheeters cabin opened, and a female figure draped in a brown gown and white linen blouse under a pale blue outer weskit, like the ones all the Scottish woman wore, stepped into the sunlight. She waved a yellow scarf high above her head in greeting. Rachael started to walk towards the tree line and soon broke into a quick trot. As she picked up her pace, her hair began to wave in the breeze. She moved with great ease and grace across the field. She was tall and athletic and moved with the dignity of a very fine lady. She may not have been born into a family of great wealth or title but she possessed all the qualities, in abundance, that any lady would need.

Now that she was only a few feet away, Rice, like so many times in the past, couldn't help but admire her beauty. Her dark eyebrows arched over her perfectly set brown eyes; her full pink lips and high cheekbones matched the wonderful lines of her nose and jaw line. The low-cut neckline of her blouse revealed smooth youthful skin above what little cleavage a modest woman of her caliber would ever show. Rice had drifted off to sleep many a night with visions of Rachael in his mind, and now she had given him another one to remember her by.

"How are you on this fine day?" Rice asked as he came to a stop taking her hand into his own.

"Well enough, I suppose," she replied smiling as she watched Rice wet his lips as he looked into her eyes. "I saw you tending to your hounds from our window. I thought you might grace us with an appearance today."

"So, you have been watching for me most of the day then, from your window I suppose," Rice teased as the two continued on toward the cabin.

"Yes," she answered "However you are aware that we always keep a watchful eye upon the tree lines. Besides the rest of Jeremiah's party was arriving today as well."

"Yes, I knew that," Rice continued "But you did not greet them with the same enthusiasm as I was granted, I hope."

"No, not quite' she laughed "You know very well I always anticipate your callings"

"I hoped as much" Rice replied proudly.

The two walked on the rest of the way to the house in complete silence, neither saying a word to the other. Rice watched her walk along, as she tied her scarf around her delicate neck leaving a neatly tied bow that she situated on her left shoulder. She glanced over at Rice's far hand that was gripping his rifle at its mid-stock. Then she slowed her pace and stepped behind Rice to inspect the size of the bird hanging over his shoulder. She reached for it as they neared the back of the cabin. He untied it from his shoulder strap and said "mind your gown; for you are without your apron."

"I know as much, Rice Medaris. I, for one, am able to keep my garb clean" she teased holding the turkey away from her hemline. "Maybe you should heed your own advice in the future." She then disappeared into the doorway from which she had earlier appeared; leaving Rice stretching his neck back over his shoulder, trying to see the backside of his bearskin for any blood that the bird might have leaked onto his coat.

He laid his rifle barrel across his shoulder thinking it could only be a few drops and continued on around the side of the cabin. 'Rachael is amazing,' he thought, fashionable enough to wear that yellow scarf but yet practical enough to begin to prepare the bird for a future meal. She would make a man very content. It would be a lucky man who could win her hand. Rice was confident that he was her leading suitor. Their courtship had proceeded very well this past year but not every one of the other men who were admirers of hers were willing to concede a young lass of her abilities and charms. John McFall certainly had not. Rachael had politely declined his advances last Christmas, but here he was, standing among the party of men heading to Kentucky. Rice knew enough about him that he was certain that McFall was not going to be a member of that party; Jeremiah would never stand for it. The men were standing in the sunlight among their horses between the cabin, and the McPheeters small stable. Jeremiah was down on one knee under his horse tightening the girth of a packsaddle with an annoyed expression on his face. When he rose to his feet, he turned to his antagonists, McFall, who was sitting on a trunk that was waiting to be mounted onto the saddle.

"I'm very aware of the King's proclamation John. I just choose to pay it no mind" he laughed.

"Boys you shouldn't be going on this adventure" McFall replied coming to his feet. "You just can't keep on acting as though the King's laws don't apply here in the backcountry. It may be popular with some around these parts but I'm telling you nothing good will come of this. It will be a fruitless waste of your time and efforts".

"Our time and our efforts" replied Thomas McDowell peering over his horse's back. "Why are you here anyway John? You have known for some time that our minds and ambitions are set."

"Just trying to keep the peace." McFall answered, raising his hands in the air. "I just want you all to know there are men in this valley that are keeping an unwritten list of seditious men."

Samuel Tate reached down and picked up the trunk that McFall and been sitting on, and with one quick motion he flung the trunk up onto the horse's back, intentionally hitting McFall's shoulder in the process.

"I have also heard talk John. Some say you are one of those men keeping a book. Did I hit you with that trunk? I thought I hit something or other."

Rice could see that John McFall, a large, young, and powerful man had taken great offence at Tate's actions. The blow to his shoulder had knocked him off balance and caused him to stumble onto his side, no doubt taking some skin in the process. Rice saw the fire rise up in McFall's eyes as he placed a hand on the affected shoulder. McFall swiftly placed his other hand on the deer antler handle of his knife. But before he could pull the weapon from its leather sleeve his eyes caught sight of Rice's. He stood there for a moment feeling all eyes on him. Then he removed his hand.

"Maybe you should head on home John." Rice suggested breaking the silence.

"You would like that wouldn't you?" McFall replied "I know what you are up to," he said as he looked into the open cabin door where Rachael was standing, listening, having heard the mood outside turn for the worst. "Samuel didn't intend any harm. Did you Samuel?"

Samuel didn't reply, he just let out a single moan that could have passed as a chuckle.

McFall, trying to keep his composure looked back at Rice, and continued his attempt to get out of this situation, without destroying what little cordial relationship he still had with the McPheeters. "Rice, you mind your own business. I'm a guest of Mr. McPheeters and Rachael, not yours. You have no say as to when I may come and go in their home.

"That's right" Charles McPheeters announced, walking out of his stable door with his son David a few steps behind. "It's my say and none other's". The head of the McPheeters household did not say anything else as he continued his walk between the horses. Silver and gray had appeared in his beard and hair the last few years, but he was still capable of handling any situation with ease and diplomacy.

"John you are a friend of the family and you are welcome here any time, but I believe Rice has a point here. These boys are just as set in their ways as you are in yours. You have said you piece. We know that your intentions are good, but maybe you should go on and leave before someone says something out of the way that can't be taken back. Relay my good wishes to you father, John Alexander, on your return home. You know he and I were some of the first men to set foot in this valley. He is a good man."

"Yes sir, my father is a good man, and he knows how to raise his sons as well. I'm proud to be his name sake. I'll take my leave at present and present your good wishes to him."

John McFall took Charles's outstretched hand into his own and gave him a handshake in parting. He turned, and walked over in front of Rachael, and removed his tri cornered hat, and said his goodbyes in a low tone, so no one else could hear him. When he had finished, as the others watched, he walked to the cabin's outer wall, picked up his rifle and walked away. As he entered the tree line Jeremiah placed the last trunk upon his pack horse. Rice walked up and began to help tie down the load when Jeremiah looked at him with concern.

"Rachael made it very clear back in the winter that she had no desire to become John's wife. We had all hoped that he had accepted her wishes, but now I see that he has not. You keep a watchful eye on him Rice. You too David." Jeremiah told his younger brother who was tying the reins of the pack horse to the back of Jeremiah's mount.

Don't worry about him," Charles said to his son. "You keep your thoughts on your own well-being. Kentucky is no place for men's minds to be wondering, take good care of yourself son."

Jeremiah took his father's hand and said "You know I will. Is Mother coming out?"

"No son, you know how she is about goodbyes."

Jeremiah shook his head and motioned for Rachael to come to him. He gave her a kiss on the cheek and whispered, "Tell her that I love her, won't you?" Rachael nodded her head, wrapping both of her arms around his neck. Jeremiah broke away and pulled himself up into his saddle. He reached out and shook David's hand saying "See you next spring brother, we will have a thousand pelts by then and maybe some of Richard Henderson's land as well." As he let go of his brother's hand he knocked David's hat from his head, like he had so many times in the past. He tapped his horse's side, and with a grin, rode away.

Later that evening Rice and Rachael found themselves back at the tree line. Duchess was lying asleep in the last rays of sunlight, tuckered out from fighting her leash. Rice reached down and unleashed Brute as the dog sat on his hind legs. He rubbed the back of one of the dog's long ears and said "Look among the trees ole boy, but do not go too far." As the dog ran off into the forest Rice turned back to Rachael, he could see very plainly that she was deep in thought, worried about something.

"What's the long face about Rachael?"

A small smile broke across her upturned face as she looked into his eyes. "You read me so well Rice. It's like you have a window to see into my soul that no one else can see through."

"I must confess that my eyes linger on your form anytime I am in your presence. If any man could see into your soul, it would have to be me." He reached down and took her hand into his and said. "Jeremiah knows the ways of the woods. This is not his first long hunt."

"I know, but nevertheless it's still not easy to see him go. I suppose I have a lot of mother in me. She is so much better at hellos than farewells".

"I was somewhat surprised that she stayed inside when he departed," Rice replied "Anyone could see by her mannerisms, that she was visibly upset by his leaving, after they were gone."

"That's just her way." Rachael replied as she glanced back at her home in the distance. "I better be getting back," she said looking up into Rice's eyes.

"Before you go, would you tell me what John said to you on the porch as he was leaving?" Rice asked.

Rachael tilted her head ever so slightly, recalling the scene in her mind, and breathed a sigh. "He apologized, but it was not a sincere apology. What he was saying was appropriate, however the contempt in his eyes belied his words. I have relayed to him long before today, that nothing intimate could ever be between us." She squeezed Rice's hand and said "I told him my heart belonged to another, but I said nothing to him today. I just nodded my head in acknowledgement of his words without saying anything."

She released his hand, and as she turned to walk away she blew Rice a kiss and said, "Father is watching from the house."

Rice stepped away and untied Duchess as Brute ran out of the trees to join his master. As the three entered the woods, Rice lingered in the shadows of the setting sun until his love was safely under the roof of her father's home. Only then did he take his own first step on his return journey home.

Chapter 5

Splashing Footsteps

The moonlight cast a pale bluish glow over the campsite were Jeremiah and the rest of his party had stopped to camp for the night on March 27, 1775.The water from an unnamed creek was still and clear and tasted good going down. For Jeremiah everything seemed to be a little bit better here in Kentucky. Maybe it was the sense of exhilaration and danger that made his senses seem so heightened. The constant threat of death made him enjoy the smallest aspects of life. Their journey had been going well until a few days ago, when they were introduced to the type of violence they would have to endure in order to settle this land. A few days out, his small party had the good fortune of coming up on Daniel Boone's road cutters, who were blazing the Wilderness Road, as they were dabbing it, for Richard Henderson. The two parties converged just on the northern side of the great Cumberland Gap. This meeting had given Samuel Tate a great deal of relief, for he felt it was much safer to have his young son Robert, who only fifteen years old, along now that more men were about. While they were still in the settlements Samuel had thought everything was fine, but now that they were deep into no man's land, he was beginning to wonder if he should have left the boy behind.

Boone's ability to progress while traveling with a large number of able-bodied men, had given everyone a false sense of security, until three nights ago when Captain William Twitty, a fellow North Carolinian, was killed along with his slave Sam. Those two unfortunates were bedding down for the night when a sudden volley of Indian fire poured into Boone's Camp. Everyone else dashed out of the firelight and into the dark woods. A few more shots were exchanged as the attackers ran into camp with tomahawks and scalping knives in hand. Thomas McDowell, felt that his shot was true, even though no war painted bodies were found after the ambush to prove his claim. A little over an hour later, Daniel Boone had led Jeremiah and the rest of the road cutters back into camp but the war party was long gone, along with a few horses and Captain Twitty's scalp. Felix Walker [4], another member of the party had been badly

---

[4] Felix Walker 1753 – 1828 said of Captain William Twitty 1719-1775 "We placed ourselves under the care and direction of Capt. William Twitty, an active and enterprising woodsman, of good original mind and great benevolence,

wounded, but had crawled off into the underbrush and had not been found by the Indians. But his destiny was still unsettled. His wounds were very bad and very few gave him much of a chance to see another fortnight. No one slept the rest of the night, fearing another attack. When the sun rose the next morning, two graves were dug and words was said over the dead. Soon afterwards, the job of cutting the road was again underway.

This morning Jeremiah and his friends, along with two other men, Salomon Gore and Ben Glasgow, had volunteered to be the day's hunting party, and were to rejoin the road cutters in the morning with fresh meat.

"Another cool night," Jeremiah announced as he rubbed his hands along his upper arms, trying to keep warm.

"I wouldn't say cool, it's downright cold out here cousin," replied Thomas as he watched Robert Tate rubbing the bottom of his bare feet. "It may snow tonight. But after that fire gave our position away the other night I can live with a little frost on my nose."

"Captain Twitty sure can't" Jeremiah replied in agreement.

"How are your feet tonight son?" asked Samuel as he sat down next to his son on an old moss-covered log.

"Not good Paw, that red skin is peeling off. It's painful."

---

and although a light habited man, in strength and agility of bodily powers was not surpassed by any of his day and time, well calculated for the enterprise." In 1816, Walker was elected to the US Congress representing North Carolina.

"You got to keep those moccasins dry son. You won't be able to walk if your feet keep on being wet like this."

Salomon Gore walked over and stooped down and peered at the soles of Robert's feet. "Mine are bad enough, but not that bad. I am afraid they soon will be if I don't get them dried off. We have got to strike a fire and dry out our moccasins, that's all there is to it."

"I don't know about that boys," said Jeremiah, "a fire could mean our end. Maybe we should think this thru before we do something rash."

"You can chew it over for a spell I suppose," replied Gore as he walked away.

Thomas also looked at Robert's feet, as Samuel spoke up after a few moments of silence. "I just don't believe that attack the other night was by a very large war party. They left too soon and didn't come back for us afterwards. They saw how big a party we are. It should be safe. Maybe they are gone for good"

"Could be, and maybe all our dangers are not all out in these woods Samuel," Jeremiah replied "I know we need to attend to our footwear, but as for a fire, I don't believe a fire is wise."

Nodding his head Samuel seemed to agree. "Maybe we can hang them up and if we are lucky the wind might dry them for us tonight." `

As Jeremiah and Samuel stood talking, there was movement on the other side of camp. Jeremiah heard the sound of steel striking flint. Glasgow had kindled a fire with a few twigs and dead grass, and with a couple of downward strokes of flint on steel, Gore had it burning. Soon a makeshift rack was over the flames with six pair of moccasins drying above it.

Doublehead was riding along the southern end of the creek bank in front of sixteen mounted warriors, when his nose picked up the faint scent of cherry wood burning in the night air. He slowly pulled the reins of his black mount to a stop. Without a word he raised a leg and slid to the ground. Taking his lead, the rest of his war party did the same. Bloody Fellow ordered five of his Cherokee warriors to lead the horses back the way they had just come, not wanting a single nicker from the animals to alarm the campsite up ahead. Not knowing the strength of his enemy, Doublehead drew an arrow from his quiver, and notched it in his bow. He had his long rifle slung over his shoulder. He was not about to let the flashing pans of his brave's rifles reveal their position to a superior force in the dark. A few of his braves were young, this being their first war party. Boys he had watched grow into young men; men that he was becoming closer too by the day. Both his views, and their views were very much the same in these trying days. Treaty or no treaty, this was their land and they intended to keep it . They had shown him great respect and in turn were earning his respect by the hour, and that was not easily done. He was not going to lose them so early in this war, even if the White Eyes did not yet know a war had started. Silently, he began to stalk his prey. If he was outnumbered, he would use his bow and retreat into the night. If not, the longrifle would quickly follow the arrow's lead.

Jeremiah and Thomas had taken to the trees on the north side of the camp, not exactly happy with the decision about the fire. Here, they were out of sight from the flames. On the night of Twitty's Defeat, the attack came from the north. So here they sat acting as guards for the camp. The Tates had taken the southern end. But the sight of Gore and Glasgow tending to the fire, warming themselves, had drawn the father and son back into camp over an hour ago. "I'm going to check and see if mine are dry, they have got to be by now" Thomas said to Jeremiah in a whisper.

Having watched Thomas creep back into camp, and remove his moccasins from the rack, Jeremiah came in to remove his as well. Thomas walked over and sat on a log, leaning his rifle against an old, dead tree trunk. As he was pulling a moccasin over his toes he said. "As much as I hate to say it, we better stomp out that fire."

As he pulled the moccasin over his heel an arrow flew into his back.

The coal black arrowhead had gone deep into his kidneys. He jumped to his feet as he yelled "Indians!" but a few steps were all he could muster before falling to his knees. Shots rang out as Gore and Glasgow sprang into the darkness without rifles or footwear. Samuel pulled his son into the darkness with one hand while grabbing his rifle with the other. "Run through the creek boy, you will leave no tracks that way"

As Robert splashed into the water, Samuel fired off a shot. Then he ran in the opposite direction, hoping to lead the pursuing Indians away from his son.

Jeremiah, having already taken one shot to the arm, raised his Kentucky long rifle with his one good hand, the other arm useless and lying limp at his side. He cocked the hammer of his weapon back with his teeth, simultaneously killing a warrior that was about to lift Thomas' scalp, with a shot from the hip. Dropping his gun, Jeremiah ran toward Thomas, hoping to pull him into the darkness. But Doublehead crushed that hope with a shot to Jeremiah's stomach. The two cousins lay there together, side by side, as the Indians gathered around them. Thomas quickly sat up and pulled Jeremiah up too, so the two could lean against each other, while gritting his teeth at his attackers.

In a sarcastic tone of broken English Bloody Fellow remarked, "Make peace, your God" as he tapped his leg with the side of his tomahawk.

In great pain, while wrapping his arms around his wounded belly, Jeremiah looked up and replied "No need, we did that long ago. Do your best, you damned savage! At that, Bloody Fellow and Doublehead's tomahawks fell upon the two young men beside the waters of what would now and forever be called Tates Creek.

Chapter 6

Laying a Foundation

Rice struggled as he walked out of the cold water of Warriors Creek. The round seventy-pound stone that he was carrying was slippery in his arms. The fact that it was wet and hard to hold made it all the more difficult for him to gain his footing as he stepped onto the bank. This morning's work had already equaled a normal full day's labor, and it was still just noon. He dropped the stone onto an already heavily laden sled filled with smaller stones. Most of these he had picked up from the dry creek bank, but none of them had the flat square shape of this monstrosity. It was just the right size, and it's nice flat top was exactly what Rice needed to place on the last corner of his new cabin's foundation. The new twenty by ten-foot cabin would finally get him out of the blacksmith shop. It would be small, but big enough for him and a future wife. Some families nearby had as many as nine or ten people living in cabins no bigger than this one would be. If all his plans for the next few years could somehow come together, the next house he built would be a large two-story frame, maybe with glass window panes.

As he walked over to his two draft horses, Bob and Queen, that were waiting to pull his sled, Rice began to calculate how many more stones it would take to build the cabin's chimney. He could go the fast and easy way by building it out of small wood sticks and mud. But that would not last very long and he wanted this cabin to hold up well over the years to come. When at last, the frame house would finally rise up, he planned to keep this cabin as a detached kitchen. Having the kitchen away from the main house would help keep the house cool, it was also safer, there was no need for a grease fire or a flying, popping spark to consume the entire new house in flames.

Rice popped the reins over the horse's backs and watched as Bob slowly began to pull the sled towards the cabin site just up the hill, not far from the shop. Then he gave Queen an extra tap across her back, because she was not pulling her fair share of the load. Today would bring an end to the foundation and tomorrow he could start felling the trees that would be needed to raise the walls. That, he was looking forward to.

All he had at this moment, was a squared off rock wall, two feet high, which was yet to be completed. But once this last load of stone was placed, the logs were cut, and the bark stripped off, the wooden walls would rise quickly. Nothing smells quite as good as fresh cut wood, and the inside of the cabin would smell pleasant, at least until he burned up a meal or two inside the fireplace.

As the sled came to a stop, Rice saw the hair on Brute's back began to rise and a small flash of teeth appear from under a raised upper lip. The dog was growling in the direction of the tree line. Rice reached down and quickly picked up his rifle and shouldered it to its firing position as he waited to see who would emerge from the shadows of the trees. Within a few breaths, he lowered his rifle as a line of mounted men came into view. If all of these horses needed shoeing, the foundation would have to wait another day, he thought to himself.

The lead rider of the six-man party was a huge man, near forty years of age, all of six-foot-tall and pushing three hundred pounds. Yet, despite his bulk, he moved with the light-footed ease of a much smaller man. He slid from his mount's back to the ground in one smooth fluid motion. He placed his hands behind his back and began to raise the heels of his black boots from the ground with the tips of his toes bouncing up and down a few times as he watched Brut set on his hind quarters at Rice's command.

"May I take your mount Colonel Cleveland?" one of his men asked as he reached for the horse's reins, but stayed in his saddle.

Benjamin Cleveland had settled on the northern end of the Yadkin River with his father-in-law back in 1769. He was a man of recklessness, with daring habits. It was said that in his youth, he never passed on an opportunity to play cards or bet on a horse race. And he never allowed the brown jug to pass without getting his fill first. But in recent years he had become more and more involved in politics and was deeply against King George's attitude and the politics of the English Parliament towards the thirteen colonies of North America. Rice had heard of Cleveland, but had yet to meet him face to face, but he knew exactly who he was when he heard the words of Cleveland's loyal attendant.

"What may I do for you today?" Rice asked as he sat his rifle down.   "A little bit of farriering business," replied Cleveland as he pointed to a pack horse at the back of his string of horses. "Jack, bring up that poor animal so Mr. Medaris can take a look"

"Colonel Cleveland, I'm surprised you know my name," Rice replied as he approached the group and took Cleveland's hand into his own. "I don't believe we have ever met."

"True" answered Cleveland "But you did know who I was. Maybe I can put two and two together as well as you can. But I must admit to the fact, that the McPheeters telling me about your blacksmithing abilities was a great help in the matter."

As Rice bent down to raise the horse's hoof, Cleveland looked at the foundation of Rice's cabin and said, "That is quite an undertaking for one man. Do you plan on building that cabin all by yourself?"

"At the moment, Yes," replied Rice. "But I will need some help when it comes to raising the log walls."

"Could be I have just the man you need," Cleveland volunteered. "Jack here is looking for some work. Maybe you two can come to some sort of arrangement. We are heading home and that will put Jack out of work for now."

Rice stood back up and said "I have a shoe that will fit that hoof nicely. I believe it's already hammered out up in my shop. This will be a quick fix for you Colonel. As far as your man Jack there, all I can give him is a roof over his head and the same food I eat as payment. Maybe we can trade hours if he needs some smiting done in the future."

"Sounds fine to me," replied Jack.

"Tell me Colonel," Rice asked "Are you at liberty to say why you and your men were at the McPheeters place?"

"Grisly business I'm afraid. I was the bearer of bad news. Their son got himself killed in Kentucky. Telling bad news is one part of my duties I wish on no man. Damn Indian savages.
I'm afraid Judge Henderson has opened up a hornet's nest over the mountains and this is just the first of many stings we will be feeling."

With a stunned look on his face. Rice asked about the rest of the party.

"The Tates are doing well as far as I know, but regrettably Thomas McDowell also fell" replied Cleveland. "We are off to Quaker Meadows to relay that sad news. I can't say I know his family, but Joseph being the head of the McDowell's surely will know."

Rice quickly went to work on replacing Colonel Cleveland's horse's shoe. It fit just as he thought it would, and with a few tack nails he had it hammered into place. Colonel Cleveland reached into his vest pocket and pulled out a coin and flipped it into Rice's outreached hand.

"I assume by the pace of your work that you are off to see the McPheeters family?" Cleveland asked. "How well did you know Jeremiah?"

"Well!" Rice replied "Well enough that I can't stay here, I need to be giving my condolences to the family."

"What about Jack and your arrangement?" The Colonel asked.

"Well Sir, that will have to wait for another day." Rice replied.

"It looks to me like you have to attend to your animals before you go. That will take some time. May I suggest that you let Jack do that for you today? It would be wise to have another able-bodied man around in these times anyway. I can vouch for his character," assured Cleveland. "All of your belongings will be here on your return".

"All right Colonel" replied Rice "We can give it a try. However, I do hope that you do indeed know this man as well as you say."

Chapter 7

An Empty Coffin

The mood was very solemn at the McPheeters cabin when Rice arrived. Mrs. McPheeters, the former Mary Ann McDowell, sat in her rocking chair, not quite able to muster up enough strength to put the old rocker into motion. As Rice looked at the grieving women sitting beside her fireplace, he wondered if it was the same chair she had rocked her dead son to sleep in when he was a babe. She was holding the family Bible in her lap letting the ink dry where just a moment ago she had recorded Jeremiah's death. She had not said a word since Rice had arrived. At first it had given Rice an odd feeling that maybe he should have stayed away a few more days before coming over. However, Mr. McPheeters had put Rice's fears that he was intruding to rest by saying "No one at a respectable Irish wake, would ever turn a good friend away when he came to the door with hat in hand." Mr.

McPheeters was also glad to have another man in the house. His son David was off over the trail to inform his sibling's, expressly his two brothers, Jonathan and Joseph, about Jeremiah's demise.

Rice was amazed at how well Rachael seemed to be taking the news. She was catering to her mother's ever need as though their rolls were now reversed. Rachael waited on her mother as though she herself was the head woman of the household, but still being mindful not to overstep her bounds, by fluttering over Mrs. McPheeters too much. Every now and then he would make eye contact with her, and Rice could see Rachael fighting back tears. She would swallow down the lump in her throat and quickly regain her composure. On the other hand, Charles was nothing like his tight lipped wife. He was grieving the loss of his son with the help of some Irish whiskey. He had tapped his store of wooden casks twice before the sun had gone down. But, now that it was dark, he was out pacing Rice two to one of the smooth tasting barley malt. His face was starting to turn a bit red and his temper was becoming more fiery with every drink.

"I will tell you one thing Rice," he proclaimed in a loud voice "once my boys get back here, we will be off to Kentucky and teach those godless heathens to dread the day they ever laid a hand on my boy. We will play for blood. No hand for a hand or eye for an eye this time; it will be ten eyes for one. You can come along if you want. I see no fear in you when I look your way."

"No, you certainly will not" Mrs. McPheeters said loudly, finally ending her silence. "Do you really believe that the four of you can kill enough Indians to make a difference?"

"Yes, I do! Besides, once Hunting John hears of this you can be assured that all of the McDowell clan will be out for blood as well," Charles replied. "We will have more than enough to avenged our boys."

"If he is smart Charles, he will know that all he will do by going out there will be digging more graves for his other sons" Mary Ann argued back. "Remember Charles, vengeance is mine sayeth the Lord."

Charles stood up from his chair at the head of the table, and looked down to the floor for a moment. Then he turned for the door and with a few steps he reached out and grabbed its wooden latch. Pausing again for a few seconds he looked back at his wife. "How do you know I am not the tool the Lord will use to carry out His vengeance Mary Ann?" Turning away, he stepped outside into the cold night air slamming the door behind him. Mary Ann rose from her rocker and laid the black leather-bound Bible on a small table. She left it resting, still open, so the pages would not smudge the fresh ink. Silently, she followed her husband out of the house leaving the door open behind her. Rachael stood at the threshold and watched as her mother walked over to her husband, taking his hand into her own. Rachael's eyes lingered on her parents for a moment, and as she shut the solid oak door, she began to speak. "Looks at those two, Mother is coming out of that trance she has been in. Papa is strong, but he needs his wife like most men do in times like these."

"What about you?" Rice asked as he walked around the table. "You are bearing this burden well, but I sense you need a comforting shoulder to lean on too my dear."

Rachael walked to him and buried her head in his chest and said "I do, I'm so glad that you are here Rice, just stay close and I'll be alright."

Rice placed a steady hand around her waist and said "I'm so proud of you Rachael. You are handling a very stressful situation here. No woman could do better. I know you were very close to your brother."

"Yes, I am, or I was, I should say. Odd speaking of him in the past tense isn't it?" she said. " I expect it will get better after the burial. But Lord knows I have a tearful time coming. It's a pain deep in my heart pressing like a heavy stone upon me. But I can't relinquish myself to those feelings just yet. Maybe when the rest of the family arrives, but not now, not just yet." she said as she began to sob quietly. And, as a light rain can become a flood, she began to cry violently. Rice held her close as her shoulders began to shake and jerk with her every breath. Then, after her weeping began to fade away, she pulled out of his embrace, wiping her eyes with a linen handkerchief. She smiled a sad smile at Rice as she pulled out a chair from under the table and sat down, giving herself a much-needed rest.

"Feel better?" Rice asked as he sat down at her side, leaning over and resting his head in his hand and propped up elbow.

'Yes,' she nodded.

"Did I understand that you said there is to be a burial? Is Jeremiah's body here?" Rice inquired. "Are the Tate's bringing him back home?"

Letting out a long breath Rachel shook her head, no. "Mother wants a place to remember him by. They plan to put some of his belonging in a coffin. She even wants a headstone so she can plant flowers by it. At first, I believed she was going a little crazy, but now I like the idea myself. Papa is going to make a coffin on the morrow. That way he won't be forgotten any time soon. I guess some tears never dry."

Chapter 8

Fort Grider

Frederick Grider was an older man, in his late sixties he supposed, maybe even in his seventies. He never knew the exact date of his birth, because his father never told him what day he was brought into this world. Frederick and his brother Martin, who was just as ignorant of his birth date, believed that their father Joggi never knew himself. Their mother had died when they were still young boys, in a house fire, while still living near the German border in Runenberg Switzerland.

They theorized that she must have been the keeper of the family history and it died along with her.

Joggi Grider, a German, who had married a Swiss girl, and after her death, he felt lost without her. Not wanting to return to his own war-torn country he decided to leave the old country behind altogether, by sailing out of Rotterdam on the ship, *Princess Augusta*[5]. He arrived in Philadelphia along with his two sons on Sept 16, 1736. Like most other German men of his time, he loved the Alps, so he moved his family to the high mountains of the North Carolina backcountry so he could be reminded of his old home. When he died in 1754 he could still call himself a true mountain man.

Frederick still spoke with a German accent, but Martin had always said that just because their father was too stubborn to learn English,

---

[5] The Princess Augusta was built in 1710. The length of her gun deck was 73 feet 8 inches; keel, 57 feet 7 ½ inches; breadth, 22 feet 6 inches; depth, 9 feet 6 ½ inches; 155 tons, 8 guns; and she carried a crew of 40 men.

that it was no reason for them not to. So, the two had lost most of that thick accent over the years but some of it lingered. Often in times of danger Frederick would invite settlers to fort up with him, and after they would leave they would call his home Ft. Crider instead of Ft Grider, because of his accent. His son Fed on the other hand had none in his voice, just as all of Martin's children had none in theirs.

Frederick also shared the same sad history as his father. He too had lost his wife in a fire, but it had not been an accident. She fell to the Indians while Frederick and Fed were out hunting a few years after the French and Indian War.

He swore that his family would never be that vulnerable again, so he built a stout blockhouse instead of rebuilding a defenseless cabin. The site he chose was just a few miles west of Hibriten Mountain, which marks the end of the Brushy Mountain range. It was situated upon a small eminence with twelve-foot-tall picket walls made of oak logs, about one foot in diameter. Its walls were fitted with portholes for defense. Besides enclosing the blockhouse, the walls also enclosed three-quarters of an acre of land with a running spring on one end and a barn on the other. Cannon fire could easily blow its way through the walls but musket fire could do little damage to Frederick's family and friends inside.

That was one aspect of life Frederick had no shortage of. He might run low on supplies, but never on family. Fed was always nearby, being his only child to live to adulthood. But Martin's boys were around just as much now, since he had died back in Virginia. Martin Jr., the oldest of Frederick's nephews, and the next in line to John, had arrived at Fort Grider last year. And soon, now that Martin was gone, his other two sons, Jacob and Valentine would arrive too.

Jacob rode his wet horse up to the barred door of Ft Grider where he pulled his mount to a stop. He reached out and rapped hard upon the oak wood with his clenched fist. "Open up in there Fed, we have come to get ya boy."

As he turned his horse, the dogs inside his uncle's stockade began to bark. "That should get them up Val" he said as he slid off his mount, sinking a few inches into the mud.

"Is that you out there on that horse Val?" Fed asked, pointing his long rifle out of a porthole.

"Yes, it is cousin, none other than me, myself" replied Valentine, still mounted.

"I thought as much," Fed said as he unlatched the bar and swung the stout gate open. "Jacob always was the one playing in the mud when we were boys, looks as though he has not changed much."

Val nodded his head 'yes', as he looked through the rain at his brother. Laughing, he put his horse into motion and rode on through the gate, heading towards the barn that stood just to the right of the blockhouse. "Good to see you Fed."

Jacob extended his hand and took Fed's into his own, greeting his cousin with a hearty handshake. "I remember those times well Fed. You were in the mud as much as I was. That is, when you were not pouring molasses on the cats."

"Oh yes, I remember that!" Fed replied as he pulled the gate back in, laughing out loud. "Your maw had me washing and grooming that poor cat the rest of the day or at least until your father let me stop". By the way, you have my sincere condolences on your father's passing. He will be greatly missed"

Jacob nodded his head 'yes', and then he slapped Fed on the back, saying "Come on, let's get out of this April rain and into that dry barn'.

As the two walked through the fort yard, Jacob raised a hand to the side of his mouth calling out, "Hello in the house." and before they reached the barn doors, Frederick stepped out of the blockhouse in front of John and Martin, who were following behind their old uncle. But as the older man began to walk toward the new arrivals, the two younger men outpaced him in their haste to greet their brothers, who were now inside the barn. As the three entered the barn handshakes and slaps were made all around, in greeting. John handed Val a brass and glass candle lit lantern, while taking the reins of a horse with the other.   John began to unbridle his brother's horse as he asked "did y'all get Paw's affairs in order?"

"Just about" Val replied as he hung the lantern onto a wooden peg "Some of the bigger stuff that he wanted y'all to have, we have stored away for you, but all of the livestock has been sold off. We got a handsome price for them I believe, but we have other news to relay."

"What's that? "Martin asked, as he cupped his hands around the hanging lantern, trying to keep them warm from its heat.

"Shots have been fired up around Boston" Jacob said as he raked off some of the mud that was on the side of his boots on the bottom plank of a stall. A lot of Lobsterbacks were killed. King George's taxes are not very popular up there. Looks as though full out rebellion has arrived in Massachusetts.

"Really?" asked Frederick, "well that does not surprise me, but it doesn't really matter much down here. We don't buy much tea and paper. Do we boys?" The Cherokee are our worries, not the King of England.

Chapter 9

Ringing out

Rice let the axe handle slide smoothly through his hands as he made his next swing. When his blade made contact with the ash tree, it knocked another chip of wood free, sending it flying into the air. He tightened his grip to keep control of the tool just as it bit into the hardwood. When he pulled his blade from the tree, Jack drove in another hard chop from the opposite side of the trunk. They were in perfect timing with one another. The sound of their labor rang out through the woods as if it was music. Yet, there was a friendly, unspoken competition going on between them. Both were skilled with an axe and it just seemed natural to race one another, even if they were both hacking away on the same tree. They were becoming quite a good team, they had felled two dozen trees since Rice's return from the McPheeters.

When he was over on the other side of the ridge with Rachael's family Rice had little time to ponder what was going on his side of the ridge. The whole family was grieving and he was very engaged in tending to their needs. He was needed those first few days and he was happy to be of some service. But at night he did worry a little about Jack. Even Rachael's presence and beauty could not totally put his mind at ease. She was his main reason for going there, that he would admit to himself, but to no one else. Yet, even if they had not been courting, Rice would still have felt an oblation to go, because of his own friendship with Jeremiah. He hoped Charles knew that, he knew Rachael did. But when he had reached the headwaters of Warriors Creek his mind began to return to his own homestead. He was wondering if he had made a grave mistake in leaving a stranger on the place. Colonel Cleveland had vouched for Jack McCalpin, but Rice was still relieved to see that all was well and accounted for on his return. His worries of thievery and betrayal where now a distant memory. Jack had earned Rice's trust. It is easy to be trustworthy when someone is around. But temptation can overpower those of low standing when they have free run, without any supervision, to keep them honest. Rice did not intend for his absence to be a test of character, but Jack had passed it anyway. The ringing axe's stopped as the tree began to fall to one side. The crackling sound of snapping wood was all that could be heard in the forest until Jack called out "timber" with a satisfied look on his face.

"One of that size sure can make the ground shake" Rice announced as he looked at Jack after the tree's earth-shaking fall.

Jack just nodded yes. Then he swung his axe down again, cutting off one of the tree's smaller limbs with one blow. Jack was a strong young man in his twenty's. He stood five feet eight with a wiry body build. Rice could see that his new friend could handle himself well, if need be. He was muscular enough to be a hard man to put down if a situation called for it. Yet, he had a good nature, but something seemed to be digging at him at times. However, Rice did not ask what it was. He felt it would be rude to ask a question like that. Even if you knew a person for years, it might be awkward. And Rice had just met this man. Jack would tell his story when he felt the time was right anyway, Rice supposed.

Rice walked over to the shade of an old maple tree where he had placed his rifle and some water. He pulled the plug from a crock jug and took a drink as Duchess woke up from one of her many naps. He reached out and patted the dog's head and leaned up against the bark of the tree as Jack approached. Reaching out Jack took the jug from Rice's hand. "You know Rice, if my plans had come to be, I would have been building my own cabin instead of yours."

"How so?" Rice asked, as he sat down on the ground, hoping that Jack was finally going to tell his story.

"I purchased a tract of land from a man back in Virginia. Two years' worth of labor. It was all I had to my name beside my horse and gear. He told me that this land was on the waters of Kings River, about twenty miles west of Salisbury."

"I never heard tell of a Kings River" Rice replied.

"And you never will unless you are addressing Aquilla Price!" Jack answered angrily. "I was gullible, stupid even. Looking back now, I see it was a mistake to buy land out of the colony without ever seeing it. He was a smooth talker and I took his word to heart. He seemed to be a trustworthy man. Well dressed, wealthy and educated. I never dreamed that a man as rich as he, would steal such a small amount of money from a poor man, such as myself. Every indication led me to believe that he was a fine gentleman. He is one of the King's officers, well connected, but a crook. You can't always tell by a man's appearance, Price taught me that.

When I got out here and realized that I had been taken for a fool, I looked up Colonel Cleveland hoping for some justice. I told him my story and he said that was not the first time this has happen out here. I wanted to go back and take Price's head but the Colonel talked me out of it."

"How so, what was his reasoning?" Rice asked, "why protect a son of a bitch like that? That was far more than an insult. Duels have been challenged for far less."

"He surmised that there was little I could do. Price has a large estate in Frederick County," Jack expanded. "With him holding public office I have little chance to win in open court. Everyone on that jury would be a wealthy landlord. They would take care of their own and if I took the law into my own hands I would surely swing. Price is very loyal to the crown and Governor Dunmore will do anything to keep the loyalty of the men who still favor the Crown. But I sure would like to get my hands on Aquilla Price one more time. I could wring his scrawny old neck, I guess I could stand for a duel, but I doubt if his feet would hold for one."

"I can't say I would blame you if you did," Rice replied, "maybe he will get some frontier justice someday."

Shaking his head 'no' Jack said "I doubt it, but I sure would like to sick a mean ass dog on him someday. You would loan Brute out to me wouldn't you?" he asked with a wicked smile. Anyhow, that is how I got hooked up with Colonel Cleveland. He took pity on me, I suppose."

"What about some of Judge Henderson's Transylvania land?" asked Rice.

"Maybe," Jack replied "But I'm not ready to trust another rich man, not just yet anyway. Besides, I had my heart set on the Carolinas from the beginning. Something will turn up around here sooner or later, God willing."

Chapter 10

Liberty

Rice and Jack stood in the shadow of Hibriten Mountain looking at the closed gates of Ft Grider. As the two peered out over the clearing, wondering why the gates were shut at midday, Rice motioned for Brute to stay with the horses they had tied up in the trees behind them.

"Frederick must be gone," Rice announced a little disappointed at the sight of the closed doors. "It's always open when he is here. I believe that we have made a wasted trip today. He has the best horse flesh this side of Salisbury. I sure do hate not getting a chance to see them."

"Well let's make sure no one is here before we go" Jack replied as he stepped into the clearing bringing his rifle down off his shoulder.

Rice followed suit as he walked along, scanning the sloping landscape around the station. As he went, he began to notice changes around the property. A plot of land close to the fort's wall had been planted this spring, and was well maintained. A crop of corn was popping up through the ground, so the station had not been deserted. Yet Rice was still disheartened to see the fort's outside corral empty. Maybe someone had already been trading with Frederick and taken the biggest part of his animals. Not hearing any noise coming from inside, Jack turned around and began to walk backwards, feeling a little wary, wanting to put himself on a more watchful guard of their backside. "There is no sign of an attack from what I see," he called out to Rice, "But caution is always a good rule".

"Amen to that!" replied Fed as he lowered his British fowler, a smoothbore flintlock, about fifty yards away from the two approaching men. "I spotted you boys from inside, through my porthole. From that distance, I could not make out who you were. So I slipped out the back door and came around through the orchard to get a closer look. I saw you first," Fed continued as he pointed at Jack "but when I saw you, Rice I knew all was well. Who is your friend there?" he asked inquiring about Jack.

Rice place a hand on Jack's shoulder and replied, "A friend and good man to have around, Jack McCalpin. You had us spooked with the gate being shut."

"Being cautious," explained Fed. "Come on inside, Paw is showing some hides. I suppose he is who you want to see. But one of you should go back and bring in your mounts, they could disappear without a guard."

"I'll see to them" Jack volunteered as Rice and Fed walked through the gate that had been swung open by none other than John McFall.

As the two walked in, McFall kept a surly eye on Rice.

"Still a little sour I see," Rice whispered as he looked at his adversary.

"You seem to bring out the worst in that man"" Fed chuckled under his breath, after the two had walked out of earshot, "he is the reason the gate is shut."

"I would shut it to keep him out, instead of in," Rice teased.

"Aw, he is not that bad," Fed replied. "He's sweet on Rachael and you seemed to have won her favors. If it was not for that, you would still be in good standing with him I dare say. A few of the men around here took an eye to Ellen before we wed but in time they cooled. He will too, in time I expect. Besides, he's buying furs to take to Charles-Town."

"That is all well and good in your case, but something tells me that our differences may not play out that well. His Tory leanings put even a greater strain on our standing."

That is why I'm trying to stay clear of all this talk of sedition. Neutrality is the path for now Rice. You would be wise to remember that."

Rice just nodded his head 'yes', as he pondered which side of the approaching war Fed would be on. Rice's own feelings on the subject were made up. The Cross Creek settlement, along the Cape Fear River, had given Rice pause this spring. A great many of the Scotch traders would not sell salt unless you took an oath of allegiances to the King. Politics should not keep a man from feeding his family, and if those Highlanders were any indication of what the Tories would be like, Rice was for an independent nation as long as a new and fairly balanced government could be forged. Kings never had the best interest of their subjects at heart, but a legislator could be held in check with elections. Laws should be passed by men, not by just one man who had little comprehension of what it was like to live on this side of the ocean.

Politics soon left his thoughts as his gaze took in a wonderfully handsome, reddish brown horse that was trotting at a fast gate around the rails of the fort's inner corral.

"You will make me a happy man Fed, if you will say that bay is for sale" Rice said.

"He is", Frederick replied as he approached Rice and his son Fed, "so you are tired of riding around on that draft horse of yours."

"Yes sir," answered Rice "That I am. I hope we can come to some kind of understanding about him."

"Well, I'm afraid that is not up to me" Frederick said, pointing to McFall. "That one belongs to John, so you two will have to iron out the details, but he is for sale I understand."

"What about it John, will you sell him to me?" Rice asked, trying to hide his disappointment at learning that McFall was the owner.

McFall walked over to the fence and leaned over and grabbed the horse's bridle pulling him up close. Then, he began to rub the stallion's neck. He paused before answering Rice's question, making Rice suffer in anticipation of what he thought was sure to be a very stern no.

"His breeding is everything anyone would want in a high-quality Barb," he finally answered.

"So that's the breed," said Jack as he tied down his own horse having made his way inside the fort. "A Barb?" He resembles mine in many ways, Rice. He would look fine on your homestead."

"That is, if John will let him go," Rice replied, hoping that McFall would let the horse go to Rice, even if he did not like him very well.

"Yes, Rice you can have him, that is if you have my price," McFall answered as he let go of the horse. "I have another that is his equal back at home. This one's not in his prime just yet. Still a little wild, but next year he will be an outstanding mount." Turning to Rice he said "I know we have had a rough patch in our friendship, but I am man enough to let that stay in our past, if you are."

"I have no doubt about that issue, John. If I thought you harbored hard feelings toward me, I would not have asked you to sell me the horse. I accept our circumstance, just as you say they are. But you still have not quoted your price."

"Make me an offer"

Rice looked at the horse and estimated him to stand at 15 hands. He looked back at McFall and said "Forty-five pounds."

"Rice, he is every bit of 15 hands" McFall replied "I need sixty."

"How about fifty pounds and a bundle of buckskins I have over there on the back of Bob?"

"If they are in good condition we have a deal. Let me take a look at them."

Both men walked over to Rice's draft horse where the buckskins were tied to his back. Rice pulled the rawhide tug that held them on the horse and set them on the ground so McFall could get a good look at the pelts. McFall was taking his time as he picked up each hide. He would look at each side and even went so far as to smell each one as well. As he sat them back down he placed them in two different piles. Rice could not see any difference between to two, but he did not protest the fact. He wanted the bay badly and he was becoming anxious, so he started a new conversion to settle his nerves.

"Fed said you was the reason the gates were shut, but he never said why. What did he mean?"

McFall stop going through the pelts and said "Well, they closed the gate because of the news I brought in last night. The rumor is that Governor Martin[6] is giving black powder and lead to the Cherokee by way of Richard Pearis [7] and Alexander Cameron [8,] the Indian agents. Like I said, it is a rumor, but I do know that down in Charles-Town the Cochran Magazine was broken into by some Whigs. They pilfered eight hundred stands of small arms, all of the cartridge boxes and even some cutlasses. The war may already be going on up in Boston, but it will soon be here too."

"Powder to the Indians," Rice replied looking over at Jack with disbelief. "What is he thinking? That news is not good for Tory or Whig."

"I agree," McFall said as he went back to the pelts. "But those ruffians down in Charles-Town have no right to steal the royal militia's supplies either. We cannot have armed mobs roaming the countryside. Feelings are running high on both sides. Some have turned to their own forms of justice. A few cases of tar and feathering have occurred. It might not kill a man, but it is bad a business. Some reports are even saying that a thousand pounds of that very same powder was shipped to the middle towns of the Cherokee by William Drayton [9]. We all know how big of a Whig he is."

---

[6] Josiah Martin 1737-1786 was the last Royal Governor of the Province of North Carolina.

[7] Richard Pearis 1725-1794 was an Indian trader and loyalist officer. He was trading with the Cherokee as early as 1753 in partnership with Nathaniel Gist.

[8] Alexander Cameron 1720-1781 was a British Indian agent among the Cherokee. Cameron was highly honored by the Cherokee often referred to as, The Beloved Man.

[9] William Henry Drayton 1742-1779 was a plantation owner, lawyer and Revolutionary Patriot, a member of South Carolina Committee of Safety and a delegate to the Continental Congress.

"Both sides want to keep the Indians on their side," Jack spoke up shaking his half empty powder horn. "And here I am about out of powder, and you are telling me it is going to the Cherokee, instead of into my horn? That is one dangerous way to woo a savage."

"That seems to be the case," old Frederick said, joining the conversation. "But you must admit John, it would be a lot better for all of us if that powder stays on the side of the Whigs. There aren't any Lobsterbacks for them to fire that powder at in these mountains. On the other hand, if the Cherokee rally for the crown they will be after us here on the frontier for sure."

"Well Rice, we have a contract, the horse is yours" McFall said not answering Frederick's statement. "You can keep that pile." he said pointing to his discard pile. "They are not worth much."

"Thank you, John," Rice said as he shook McFall's hand to seal the deal.

"You got a bargain today Rice, but once those damn Indians gets that powder in their hands, that may not be the case. I may have sold him off cheap today, but it's better to get something now than wait for Dragging Canoe to steal him out from under my nose and get nothing later on."

"I sure hope you're wrong about Dragging Canoe," Rice replied "I suppose you're gambling on Cherokee powder and I'm betting on Whig powder to stop them. Does the bay have a name?"

"No," McFall answered. "That is up to you; I just saddle broke him."

"Have you been studying on a name?" Fed asked, looking at Rice.

"Yah, Liberty" Rice said with a smile.

McFall took a knee and as he began to tie up his pelts he said, "Damn Rice, I sure hope I don't regret selling you that bay someday."

"Now why would you regret having all of Rice's hard earned money?" Martin asked, having just walked in the fort's front gates with his brothers Val and Jacob Grider. 'I'm certain that Rice wore out ten hammers working to saving up all that coin last year."

McFall picked up his pelts and swung them over his shoulder. As he carried them to his pack horse he said. "Don't worry about our dealings Martin. I know what I'm doing."

Within half an hour John McFall rode out of Fort Grider with a string of five pack horses, fully loaded with last winter's pelts, on his way to Cross Creek. Everyone watched as he rode away into the mountains without saying anything. But as soon as Val shut the gate, and barred the door, Jacob broke the silence.

"I will bet you boys all that I hold dear, that was the last time we ever deal with John McFall. He is Tory through to the bone. Next summer we will be shooting at that sour bag of bones."

"I sure wouldn't take that wager," Martin replied as he turned to Rice. "And I tell you something else. If the Tories are unleashed on us next year, John will be knocking on your door first with cruel intentions, and he will be after more than just that horse."

Chapter 11

These Walls

After returning from Fort Grider, Rice and Jack recommenced their work on the cabin. It took them a week to split the logs with chisels and wedges. Jack would hold the chisel while Rice struck it with a three-pound sledgehammer. Then the wedge, which resembled an ax blade, would be placed into the groove left by the chisel. In turn, it too, would be hammered down into the log, dividing it in two. Once the logs were split in half, they were much easier to handle, but they still had to be squared off by chipping away at the bark on the remaining sides. It took almost three hours per log. With all of this swinging away the two men had become something of artists in their own rights. The groves and cut marks they left in the wood from their ax blades gave each finished log a beautiful appearance

The draft horses had done their share of work as well, pulling the logs to the cabin site. Sawing the logs to the desired size and length was just as taxing a task as was notching each corner, so that the log walls would fit well together, once they were stacked up on the stone foundation of the cabin.

Rice was very pleased with the cabin's progress. He and Jack had raised the four walls up onto the foundation eight logs high, reaching a height of ten feet. It was hard, leg wobbling work, but very satisfying. The first six feet were done by hand, with one man on each end. But the last four feet was too high for them to reach from the ground. So, they devised a way to reach the desired height by placing two stout, round poles on the top of the latest secured log with the other end lying on the ground. Then all they had to do was slide the four remaining logs up the makeshift ramp to the top.

The square logs slid up with a hard push, but would not roll back down after being flipped over thanks to having four sides.

The chimney had slowed the pace of placing the log walls. This was because at each level Rice would stop on the cabin wall to build up the chimney, keeping them at the same height. This would help one to support the other, and ensure that the chimney would not lean to one side.

Today, they would finish building the gabled roof in a purlin roofing style, again using notched logs placed horizontally. If all went well by nightfall they would be nailing down the hand split hickory shingles that Rice had cut last fall. Rice could see the results of his and Jack's labors, and was extremely pleased with their progress. To help speed matters along, additional help was expected today. John Grider, one of old Frederick's nephews had arrived last night.

Grider was concerned over what type of influence all of this additional gunpowder would have on the Cherokee. With all the other Grider men at Ft Grider, he felt that he and his long rifle would be of better use here. He had volunteered his protection, because he rightfully knew that Rice and Jack would be sitting ducks perched up on the roof with only hammers in hand. Rice's rifle was of high quality, but it would do him little good if it was not in his hands. And the same applied to Jack as well.

To look at John you would not think that he could be of much use in battle. He stood at about five feet six, weighing maybe one hundred and forty pounds. His thin legs that showed under his hunting shirt and above his leggings, were not that stout looking, and the same could be said for his arms and shoulders. But his weathered face, under dark hair that sometimes hung over his blue eyes told a different story altogether.

John Grider never moved without his rifle, and deer skins always hung from his pack horse. Even this spring, all the talk of an Indian uprising could not keep him out of Powell's Valley. He did not say much, being somewhat reserved Rice noticed, but his conduct revealed a man that would stand at the gates of Hell and not back down. Rice was a little surprised at John's offer to stand guard over them while they worked, but Fed assured Rice that this was a common trait in little John Grider's strong character. And if need be he. like all the other Grider's, would be a fine Indian spy.

He had risen with the sun this morning, grabbed his knapsack of jerked meat and corn bread, and without a word, o walked off into the surrounding fog covered landscape, disappearing with his rifle, into the trees that lined Warriors Creek. If it had not been for Brute's keen sense of smell and watchful eye on the creek bank, Rice would have never known where John had positioned himself to watch over the workmen, which would soon include Charles McPheeters.

Charles was supposed to bring his son Joseph, who Rice had yet to meet, and although Charles didn't say that he would be bringing the female members of his family, Rice was sure he would. Since David had traveled to the capital in New Bern, the women would be all alone if he did not bring them with him. This gave Rice hope that he could steal a moment alone with Rachael before the day's end.

It was nearly ten o'clock before the McPheeters family finally arrived, riding out of the trail that led from their home. All were on horseback, Charles leading the way with the women riding sidesaddle in the middle and Joseph bringing up the rear. Both men were armed with long rifles, and Rachael had a pistol stuck into the holster of her saddle.

"That is one fine looking cabin you have got there Rice," Charles announced as he dismounted from his horse. "That is not bad for a first effort."

"I appreciate that sir," Rice replied. "How was the ride over?" he asked, looking into Rachael's eyes.

"Pleasingly well," she said, as she dismounted with a smile. "It sure does look wonderful. I like the way you have put the windows in the front. One is a little higher than the other."

"Well, the first one was tough. You should have seen Jack and me arguing over how to go about shoring up the sides." Rice explained. "After that first window was done, the rest were a lot easier to finish. The one in the back wall went up real fast compared to ones out front.

Putting up my shop last year was a good experience, I learned some tricks on it. I made a few mistakes on its construction that I did not repeat this time around. I predict by next year, when I start my grist mill down by the creek, I will have become something of a carpenter and undertaker [10]. Come on inside with me Rachael, nothing smells as good as fresh cut wood."

She wasted little time in following Rice through the doorway, leaving the rest of her family behind as they penned up their horses inside Rice's corral. She walked about the dirt floor with an inquisitive expression on her face. She came to a stop in the back corner of the one room cabin. She placed her hand upon one of the cracks between the logs. Closing her eyes, she breathed in a long breath, smelling the wood's sweet aroma. Then she asked Rice, "No floor boarding?"

"Not for now," Rice replied, "but next year for sure" he answered.

"There is a water powered saw mill in Salisbury," Rachael suggested. "I would prefer to have wooden floors. They keep the damp night air out. Don't you agree?"

"That is a matter for the master of the household to decide," Mary Ann McPheeters said to her daughter, as she stepped over the threshold. "Or his wife, I suppose. Mind your manners young lady.

---

[10]   In the 1770's what is known today as a building contractor was then called an undertaker.

But I must admit Rice, I for one would not want my daughter. or my grandchildren, for that matter. living on a floor that could never be cleaned properly." She turned and cast her eyes about the unfinished walls, and took notice that the cabin doors were yet to be hung.

"It is nice Rice," she continued "but when you chink the walls, don't use too many rocks in the mud. Charles did that; it will fall out sometime afterwards and your Misses will be sweeping it up all the time," she concluded as she wrapped her arm around Rachael's waist. She walked over to Rice after releasing her daughter, and patted his shoulder and said "lay those floorboards as soon as you can Rice."

Then looking back at Rachael, she said "Come on dear let's walk down to that little waterfall at the creek to converse a while."

Rice watched the two women as they walked out of the cabin's doorway, feeling he and Rachael had just won Mrs. McPheeters approval for any matrimonial plans they had planned. But then Mrs., McPheeters stopped and made one more observation. "Make sure you hang a very strong door. What you have inside your home is precious; everything outside can be replaced. But what you cherish inside of these walls can never be replaced."

No sooner had the two walked away than Joseph, Rachael's brother entered the room. As he walked in; all light was blocked from the doorway by his overwhelming size. He stood well over six feet. His features resembled Jeremiah in almost every way except size, the same dark complexioned, handsome looks of a determine frontiersman. He presented his hand in a warm manner of greeting.

"The folks tell me that you and Jeremiah had become fast friends in my absence. I know Rachael has been smitten as well. If you have earned their trust and friendship I see no reason to believe we can't do the same."

"I must admit I have taken a liking to the McPheeters" Rice replied as he released his hand from Joseph's grasp.

"They are good people" Joseph teased "Let's get to work on that roof."

Chapter 12

Rendezvous at Mulberry Fields

Mulberry Fields was abuzz this June morning. Rice, like most of the other men, and women in western Surry County had come to this valley snuggled among the rolling hills and high banks of the Yadkin River for this rendezvous. The bottom contained hundreds of acres of land that ran all the way down to where the smaller Reddies River ran into the Yadkin. It was becoming an ideal place for assembling in the wilderness.

Moravians had acquired land here as early as 1754 from the Earl of Granville, but few had stayed because of fear of Indians, and the French. Instead they settled in Salem. A group of Baptists had built a meeting house here last year, but not having an ordained preacher it was still not a full-fledged church and the congregation suffered from the lack of one. Mulberry Fields was growing, having a few families settled along the river bank. However, the one family Rice wanted to see was yet to arrive. He had gotten little sleep last night; always keeping an eye on the road, but it was of little to no avail. Rachael never showed.

Just weeks before, Colonel Ben Cleveland had turned down an offer to be an ensign in the newly formed North Carolina Continental Line. Instead, he accepted the Colonel-ship of the county militia. He had called for a rendezvous here at the home of his brother Robert, who like Rice, had just built a new cabin this spring.

Rice and Jack had arrived last night, having slept out in the night air. The limbs of a black oak tree had provided a good substitute roof. It had kept some of the dew off their blankets and heads. Val Grider had picked the spot for the rest of the Grider family, who in turn invited Rice and Jack to join them. All but Fed had chosen to attend the rendezvous. He was still clinging to his neutrality, having stayed back at the fort with his growing family. But unlike Fed, Colonel Cleveland left little doubt as to where his loyalties lay. He was a Whig through and through. But to Rice's astonishment there were men like Gideon Wright, who was just as strong a Loyalist as Cleveland was a Rebel. Rice was also worried about the McFall brothers who had arrived with Wright. Arthur and George, the brothers of John were just as harden Tories as he was. If they had partaken of their brown jugs as much as the Grider's had last night, there was bound to be trouble.

Compromise was not the best quality of Colonel Cleveland, or Gideon Wright. It would be a challenge for both men to hold their impulses in check. With the outbreak of war in the east, tensions were growing high around the camp. The militia had become an Indian fighting force exclusively, since the end of the French and Indian War. The defense of the frontier was the responsibility of both sides.

The Cherokee might be able to distinguish Tory from Whig if they were so inclined, but maybe not. They lived so close by, they knew many of the white traders involved, and a few of the settlers as well. But the Shawnee, on the other hand, would not know who belonged to which side. Their raids were going deeper into the southern parts of Virginia, only a few miles away from the Carolina border. They would show mercy to no one. This gave Rice some hope that all would go well today, out of necessity. It would be in the best interest for both Whig and Tory alike, to prevent all of the Indian tribes, including the Cherokee, the Creek, and the Shawnee from attacking on this side of the mountain.

Another reason for staying civil was the addition of all the women and children attending. Neither side would try any mischief with wives and sweethearts so close by. The fairer sex always enjoyed drill days as much as the men. It gave them an opportunity to see each other and let their children meet people outside of the family's inner circles. Being on the frontier they may not have a village green to socialize in, but they had drill days like today.

Rice had risen from his sleep to the sound of a crowing rooster this morning. Robert Cleveland had just two birds left; one black, the other a dirty white leghorn hen out of the flock he had brought out this spring. Wolves and wildcats had thinned his stock of poultry considerably. The two stayed close together as they pecked and scratched around the wagons of the sleeping, visiting families. The hen made the mistake of walking too close to one of Gideon Wright's sleeping dogs. The barking of the dog and the squawking, and flapping of the fleeing bird's wings drew most of the camp's attention. Everyone seemed to get a good laugh out of the chicken's escape. But Rice heard a snide remark escape Wright's lips. "Look at that layer ran and fly away" he cried to the McFall's. "I tell you, she sure as hell is displaying her Whig upbringing, 'eh boys?"

With Ben Cleveland still inside his brother's cabin, no one from the Whig side pushed the issue, but Val Grider shot a hard glare across the yard in Wright's direction. But before Val could open his mouth, his brother John stepped in front of him, blocking whatever colorful retort Val was about to unleash.

"Hold your tongue Val," John said as he pressed his hand into his brother's chest. If anyone is to make an ass of themselves, let it be them, not us. It's all that rice malt they drank last evening. You know firsthand how that soured stuff can do all of your talking for you if you indulge too much. It will wear off soon enough."

"We will see." Val replied as he sat down between Rice and Jack. He reached over into John's haversack and pulled out a piece of cornbread before proclaiming. "You may have stopped me from chewing them up over there, but I dare say you will not keep me from my morning meal."

"Don't eat that old dried out hunk" Martin said as he stood nearby, leaning on his upended Kentucky longrifle. "All of these fine-looking women around you are cooking up a storm! And you're about to eat that stuff instead?"

"He'd just as soon go ahead" Joseph teased, walking away into the stirring camp "He's way too ugly to charm one of these sweet ladies out of a breakfast anyway."

"Go on then, you won't do any better than me" Val replied, grinning as he swallowed down his first bite. But then his face turned serious as he nodded towards Gideon Wright's small group. "Don't stray too far though, we may need you yet."

Martin gazed across the campground taking in all of the faces in the crowd. He had become familiar with most, but there was one young lad who kept drawing Martin's attention. He was always moving about, watching and listening, but seldom talking to anyone. When he did talk to anyone, he spoke well but revealed little about himself. His bright red hair looked unkempt, as though the boy had no idea as to how to groom it.

"Do any of y'all know that lad over there" he finally asked. "He seems to me to be out of place. I have been watching him since before dark last night. He is a strange one for sure."

"No, He is a stranger to me," Val answered with squinted eyes. "Why are you afraid of him? Don't worry, if he gets any closer I'll protect you. He sure is a hard looking one ain't he?"

Rice had an envious grin on his face. Watching the four Grider brothers bantering back and forth at one another brought back memories of his own siblings. Sarah, his sister was the youngest and the only girl, so she received her fair share of ribbing, but mostly she was overly protected by her brothers. As for the boys, Massey, John and himself, they had kept their poor mother hopping. She had the burden of raising them all alone after their father had passed into eternity back in sixty-seven. They were still all in their teens, and it was the hardest trial Rice had ever had to deal with in his entire life. But he was soon drawn from those fond and dark memories as he heard the rap of a drum being played from Robert Cleveland's front porch to officially start the day.

Rice swooped up his rifle and trotted off with the other assembling men. Colonel Cleveland was walking along the length of the cabin's porch. The sound of his black leather boots pounding with every step he took as he paced the boards. He drew everyone's attention when he came to a stop in the center of his men. Old Roundabout, as he was affectionately called by his supporters, was dressed appropriately for the occasion. His attire was not overstated, he did not wear a sash or shirt with ruffled sleeves. His dark blue coat was not quite the color of a Continental officer, but it resembled one. Its buttons were made of brass but plain, with no design or insignia. Nor did he have epaulettes on his shoulders. Beige trousers matched the color of his vest, giving him something of a military bearing. His felt tri-cornered hat sat snugly upon his head; decorated with a gold and black cockade, doubtless, made by his wife. He looked like a man of authority, but not someone who was beyond approach. He looked just as he should, a man of the people. And he was just that, in the last election he was voted into office as the Justice of Surry County, as well as the chairman of the Committee of Safety.

As the men were falling in, Rice found himself in the back row of the unorganized militia. He, Jack, and the Grider's made up the first Column, along with three other men up front. As all the men began to fall in, Rice realized that he was as well prepared as any of them for duty. He had not said so, but he was a little nervous, not having ever drilled before. But the conduct of the others caused his anxiety to lessen. No one was standing at attention. True they were in rows, but none had the posture of a true soldier. Within seconds men were talking in the ranks and telling jokes. One man would have his gun in the fold of his arms, and the next would have his slung over his shoulder. Some had the butts of their rifle sitting on the ground or the tips of their toes. One older fellow did not have a gun at all, just an old cutlass stuck in an old rust covered scabbard. But all chatter subsided at the beat of the lone drummer.

"Gentlemen, may I have your attention?" Cleveland began "I am very pleased to see such a great many of you here today. As most of you recall, this time last year I stood before this body as your Lieutenant. All of us were under Colonel Walton who had a mere 80-man force in his command. This year the full command has fallen into my lap and I pray to be equal to the task at hand. The times are dire and the safety of our citizenry is in much peril. Even the most optimistic among us have to recognize that we live in unstable times. We will need more men this year, eighty is too small a number. The Cherokee have always been our most threatening cause of concern. But circumstances can, and do, change. Yes, in the past Indians have stolen our horses, and even killed loved ones. They will always be a threat. But I fear, as many of you do, that a new and much larger threat will come from abroad. Armies from foreign lands may march upon our farms and even into our very homes. I feel it is essential that every able-bodied man of age should be ready to defend his, and his neighbor's, hearth and home. In troubling times, we must do the hard work" Cleveland said with a clenched fist. "A draft must be implemented at this time. The wheat must be separated from the chaff. Every man must take an oath of allegiance."

Gideon Wright broke into a sarcastic laugh as he walked up the front steps of the porch. "Well Ben, I must say you sure have taken to your new position like no other, a duck to water so to speak. Samuel Adams must have your ear, or he yours. What in the King's name are you talking about? An oath of allegiance! An oath to who? Foreign armies? From where I ask? France?" he shouted, answering his own question. "They have been gone for years. Spain, perhaps?" he shouted turning back to the militia. "Why, they seem to be content with all the sand and mosquitoes in Florida. They are yet to settle the lands across the Mississippi River. Why would they ever attack us?"

"The British is who he speaks of!" Jacob Grider yelled stepping forward.

"Exactly!" Gideon Wright yelled back, pointing his finger at Grider. "And you, sir are a British subject. The Redcoats are not a foreign force. They are the King's men. Our very own Army, sworn to protect us all. Swore to protect you, sir."

"Not me," Joseph McPheeters screamed as he stood in front of the rest of his late arriving family "Where was the King's army when those damn godless heathens killed my kin. The crown doesn't give a damn about us out here. If he did, one of his armies would have wiped out all of those redskin's years ago. Every acre across those mountains, he lets them keep, not you or me."

"That is crazy talk" Arthur McFall cried, taking Wright's side. "That will all work itself out in time."

"Maybe in our grandchildren's time" Rice replied as he stepped up beside Joseph. "I for one believe we will not have to wait that long."

"You won't have to wait that long if I bash your cockeyed brains out!" George McFall threaten with the upraised butt of his rifle.

Arthur McFall and Jack both stepped in front of the enraged loyalist. But before Jack could get a punch in, Arthur, grabbed his brother's arm and pushed him back a few feet. "Get yourself under control George. There is no reason for blows today, we are just talking."

"That is the bastard blacksmith that stole John's girl away for him. We owe him something"

"Maybe John does, but you do not" Arthur answered under his breath. "It is not your place, besides we are outnumbered."

Gideon Wright looked at Colonel Cleveland with fire in his eyes, saying, "See what all of this treasonous talk has done Ben? You just can not be doing this anymore. Any oath taken by us against this King will cause trouble. It is high treason; a hanging offence. Did James Pugh not teach you people anything? The Regulators lost at the Battle of Alamance, and the Whigs will too. All your talk of separating wheat from the chaff, you should consider another proverb, 'You will reap what you sow'. Remember all you Scots, the English took our homes in Scotland. Can you not see that they will do the same here if you rebel?"

Colonel Cleveland stepped down from the porch, pulling his pistol from his brown leather belt. He pointed it at a table sitting at the far end of the porch. "That gentleman, is where you will sign up for the draft. If any man refuses to do so, then I say he will forfeit all rights and privileges the militia would have provided to him and his family. Choose well, your life my sway in the balance." Then he turned to Arthur McFall and said "Arthur, even though you are on the wrong side here today, I truly see you as a good and decent man. I can't say for certain why you stopped bloodshed by· stepping between those boys a moment ago, but I believe you did. I'll remember your deeds if the situation ever arises. You may need our assistance someday, even if you don't believe so now."

Then turning his large frame toward Wright, he pointed to the tree line and said "As for you Gideon, I strongly recommend that you follow the path of the old Israelites by taking your refuge in the wilderness."

"Aye" Joseph announced loudly "for if you stay, we may just show you the true meaning of an old song dear to my heart Arthur McBride [11]."

Rice watched as all of the loyalist departed from camp. Nothing more was said between the two groups. But George McFall did not need to speak to get his message across. As Rachael stopped by Rice's side, McFall stood at the edge of the tree line. Looking back at the couple he raised his thumb up under his chin, making a cutting motion across his throat.

"Did you see that Rice?" Rachael gasped.

---

[11] Arthur McBride also known as "Arthur McBride and the Sergeant" was a very popular protest song in both Scotland and Ireland. Its origin is from the 17th century. The song is a narration of an unnamed man who along with his cousin, Arthur McBride are approached by a British Army recruiter named Sergeant Napper, and his Corporal Vamp, and a little wee drummer. Once rebuked the Sergeant threatens to use his sword on them. The two cousins retaliate by using their Shillelagh walking clubs to beat the Sergeant and his men as well as relieve him of his pouch of money with no respect to his bloody back.

"See what?" Rice replied, lying to her for the first time.

"You saw that as plain as I did! We need to be careful of that bunch. Come on," she said pulling at his arm. "We need to tell Papa about this. He will know what to do."

As Gideon Wright led his men away, he paid little attention to the lad bringing up the rear of his column. The redheaded Cherokee spy, Bob Binge, [12] or 'The Bench' as some called him, made sure of that. He had spoken little the last two days but had learned a great deal about the whiteyes' plans for the coming summer. He could see very easily that they would soon be divided, at each other's throats even, hopefully a splintered and weakened shell of their past selves. As the column entered a canebrake Binge stepped behind a dying chestnut and with a snarl of his lip, he bid the fool's good bye. With good weather and no one to slow down his swift young legs, he would be back across the Blue Ridge Mountains in no time at all. A hero to his true people, for he could sit among the enemy as easy as a wooden bench, unnoticed but hearing and seeing all.

Chapter 13

Oh, To Be Yours

---

[12] Bob Binge 1762-1794 would go on to become one of the most feared Cherokee to ever step foot in the Blue Ridge. A son of John Binge a white trapper and a Cherokee maiden; he was very intelligent and took great advantage of his Caucasian appearance. He would lead raids as late the 1790's. Only death could keep him from the warpath. Simon Girty was probably the only other man who could rival Binge in putting fear into the early settler's hearts.

Rice reached down into the cool waters of the Yadkin River and scooped up a handful of pebbles that always decorated the river bed. They were blue and green, worn smooth by the rolling current of the water. He had often admired their beauty in the past, but not today. Today he had picked them up just to keep his hands occupied. Without giving them, any thought he dropped them back into the river. He was lost in prayer and in his own thoughts, not considering the stones at all. He had been pondering his situation for some time now. He had been praying to God for guidance for weeks, but the time for action was coming to an end, as was the rendezvous. After the loyalists had made their dramatic exit from the drilling grounds all had gone well. He and the others had marched and drilled a few hours, until noon. Colonel Cleveland made an additional plea for the draft and received no objection from the remaining ranks. It took all of an hour for everyone to sign or make their mark on the draft rolls. Drilling had continued another hour afterwards until Colonel Cleveland dismissed the militia, allowing Rice some time to reflect on today's events. But the only vision that Rice kept seeing from today's happenings was George McFall's threatening gesture. It was beyond contempt, it was hateful rage. Why would a man hold such fury against a couple he hardly knew? Maybe he thought by challenging Rice he could possibility back Rice down; belittle him in front of Rachael, hoping she would return to his rejected brother, or just maybe the entire McFall family would take up for John, no matter what the situation; brothers to the end even if he was in the wrong. But the one feeling that Rice knew was good and true was his love for Rachael. All the McFall's in the world could not stop that. God had spoken to him and he felt that now was the time to prove it to the world as well. He picked up his rifle and made his way across the drilling field to where Rachael and her family were. As she was standing by her mother's side, their eyes met, and without saying any words he took her hand into his and led her to the river bank.

"I need to tell you something" she said as they came to a stop under a sycamore tree. "George McFall scares me to no end Rice, he will do us harm at the first opportunity."

"Why do you think that is?" Rice asked with an inquisitive look on his face, hoping she could shed some light on what he had been wondering about.

Rachael sighed as she looked out across the water, pausing a few seconds before answering. "He is sweet on me, I suppose. He and John even came to blows once over it. Now I don't want you to believe that there was any affection between us, because there was not, for my blood runs cold at his very presence. Wait, I must amend that. At one point in time I did take a liking to John, but it was short lived. I have told you as much. I just want you to know where all of this hostility is coming from. Please don't hold this against me. I want you to know that my acquaintance with both was proper. And not based on romance, just a slight friendship in John's case and not even that in George's."

"I realize that," Rice reassured her, taking her hand into his "if I thought otherwise I would not have been pursuing your hand so diligently this past year. My heart sees no flaws in you Rachael. I feel only love and affection. But after his actions here today, I do feel some concern. I have complete confidence in the ability of your father to protect you, but I want that task to fall to me now. If you love me half as much as I love you, marry me, here and now, this very day."

A tender smile crept over Rachael's face as she leaned into his chest. "Oh, to be truly yours," she said. "To have your lips on mine, to share in all, with the man I love. Why would I ever refuse? Only the stopping of my heart could cause me to do so."

She looked up into his deep blue eyes, placing her hand on the back of his neck. She gently pulled his head down to meet her acceptances kiss. They lingered in their embrace for a short moment, lost in their passion for each other. Her eyes grew large as she broke free from Rice's grasp. "We must wait for the morrow. It is customary to wed before the noon hour Rice," she said giggling. "I have always dreamed of a December wedding, but now I no longer wish to wait that long. But, the ceremony must be performed before noon, that I must have. And I must dress of course. I will not stand before God and everyone else looking this drab. You still need to ask for my hand from my father and I need to talk to mother. And you need to find someone to marry us."

"I know as much," Rice, replied softly. "Colonel Cleveland is the county Justice. He can perform the vows, and even provide the needed license. We should be able to use the meeting house for the ceremony. And you are correct, we must have the ceremony done to your liking. My proposal may have been somewhat unvarnished, not the most romantic, but I promise, your wedding will be properly done."

"Yes, it will," Rachael agreed "I promise you that too. There are enough ladies here to help see to every detail. Mother and I will attend to our part, you just fulfill your portion. But there is one thing that I disagree with what you just said. Your proposal may have not been well planned but it was heartfelt. I felt the romance in it very strongly. I'll always remember this tree," she said looking up into its branches. "This is where you fulfilled my fondest dreams."

Rice took her hand and kissed it in parting. As he pulled away his heart leapt with joy. But he had little time to bask in it. He had to make his way to the cabin of Robert Cleveland to find Old Roundabout before he broke camp. All of his and Rachael's plans would be for naught if the only man able to wed them was gone. He hoped Ben would be as enthusiastic in carrying out his duties as Justice of the Peace as he was in commanding the militia. Rice was sure Charles McPheeters would certainly approve his and Rachael's purposed union. That would just be a formality, and it could wait until he had informed Colonel Cleveland that his services would be needed one more day.

Chapter 14

A Blessed Day

It was June 18, 1775, and Ben Cleveland stood at the head of the long aisle in the Meeting House. The podium that he stood behind was small in comparison to his stature, for he was uneasy in the pulpit. He felt unworthy standing where an ordained man of God should be. He glanced at Rice, hoping that the groom would be just as unsettled as he, but it was not the case. Rice stood coolly as he waited for his bride to enter the ribbon draped doorway. His appearance suited the occasion fairly well, considering the fact that he had come here to drill with the militia, not to marry. His black britches had brushed out very well this morning. Jack had supplied a grooming brush from his saddlebag. The two had a good laugh cleaning the garment with a horse's brush, but no one was the wiser now that the task had been completed. Martin had a clean pair of white stocking in his stores that he had loaned to Rice for the ceremony, yet that paled to the gesture made by Robert Cleveland. His contribution was a fine maroon frock coat decorated with brass buttons and white lapels.

Jack, nor any of the Grider's for that matter, would ever say so, but Rice did indeed look handsome standing in his wedding attire.

Feeling even more uneasy in front the wedding guest, Colonel Cleveland stepped out from behind the podium, leaving the pulpit behind. He looked at Rice and the assembled guest. Then remembering how at ease he always felt at his political speeches in the past after an amusing joke, he gestured back to the pulpit with an outstretched arm. Once he had the room's attention, he proclaimed with a whimsical smile, "My hypocrisy only goes so far". This amused the congregation to no end. Everyone there knew his reputation for having a short fuse, and he took advantage of that well-known fact. Now, feeling more at ease after breaking the ice the Colonel continued on. "Before the bride enters I would like to say a few words. First of all, I want you to know this will be my very first attempt at joining a couple in matrimony. I have forewarned Rice of this fact, however he still wanted me to continue, but I must admit in Rice's defense, if I had a beautiful young bride, such as his lovely Rachael, I too would not want any delays on my wedding day. But please bear with me if I misspeak while delivering the vows. I know very well a few of you boys out there would love nothing more them to shame me by pointing out any mistakes in my performance. So, hold your tongue back there William Perryman[13]. Today is not your day, Sir."

"I would never embarrass or disgrace the bride like that," Perryman laughingly replied "But afterwards, when we gather outside to celebrate, now that's another matter Colonel You will be fair game then, Sir."

Cleveland raised his hand and said "Fair enough William. But remember, I very well may have the last laugh on the matter."

---

13 William Perryman 1759-1854 Was in the Rev. War and had sever encounters with the noted Tory, David Fanning. After the war Perryman would move to Russell County Kentucky. His Rev. War pension number is M804.

At that moment, Rachael's father Charles entered the room. He looked and sounded like any proud father as he addressed the onlookers. "The ceremony will begin in a few minutes, and Rice you certainly will be pleased when you see our Rachael, my son." He turned back to the door as he motioned for Colonel Cleveland and Rice to follow him outside

Rice's mind was racing as he allowed the Colonel to exit in front of him. He hadn't seen Rachael all day and was anxious for her to appear. At her request, Joseph had ridden out last night to retrieve Rachael's best gown for her wedding. That long dark ride was the perfect wedding gift in her and Rice's eyes, and proved that her brother's love knew no bounds. He was back early this morning, and on his return, Rachael had been swept away, out of view.

As Rice stepped into the sunlight he caught his first glimpse of his intended. Her long black hair was braided and coiled atop her head with a single curl falling on each side of her glowing face. Mrs. McPheeters had woven a wreath of flowers from the blooms of the white crimson eyed rose, a favorite mountain flower of Rachael's. As she had placed it on Rachael's head she gave her daughter a final kiss and smoothed her hair and straightened her gown. The gown was a light, pale blue, the same color as the sky above. It was decorated with a small white flower pattern that matched the nosegay of wildflowers in her hand. The sleeves of the gown were long, running the entire length of her arms. They were accented by a fall of white lace that just covered the palms of her hands, but left her fingers in full view. Her slender neck was graced with a black onyx necklace, a family heirloom that had come from the old country decades before.

Rice stood tall as she took her place by his side, locking her arm in his. A deep feeling of pride burned within his heart. He knew that today was a blessed day indeed.

"I told you that you would be pleased" Charles repeated as he looked upon his daughter.

"This will be last time you will ever bear my name child, but remember my dear, you will always be my daughter. He reached up and brushed her cheek with his fingertips, like he had so many times in the past, before saying, "Always remember, no matter what may befall, you have a family to come home to. That goes for you as well Rice, you don't even need to ask. He then looked to Colonel Cleveland and said "Lead the way Sir."

"Just one more moment Colonel" Rachael requested as she flung her arms around her father's neck. Undeniably proclaiming her love to the man who had seen to her every need her entire life. She leaned into him and whispered into his ear, "Thank you father. I have always felt your and mother's love, but you have been my favorite. I know I should not dare to say such a thing, but it is true. You taught me to follow my heart and trust my instincts, even if it's not always prudent to speak my thoughts."

Charles had no words to reply. He just nodded his head as he wiped away a few tears.

"Come on you two, if we stay out here any longer I will not be able to perform my duties. Who would have had ever thought that I would be sobbing over a wedding." Cleveland replied choking back his emotions. "And Rice, there is no need at all for anyone to hear of it."

"Yes sir," Rice assured the Colonel "I'll take it to the grave."

Having received Rice's assurance, Colonel Cleveland entered the meeting house first. He was followed by Charles, who was next in line, as protocol required of the bride's father. Both were followed by the soon to be married couple.

As the colonel flipped through the pages of his Bible to find his mark, Rachael gave her mother a reassuring nod. Her radiant appearance told all present that she had no reservations on becoming a wife, or taking her last step into womanhood.

"Who is to give this young woman away today" Cleveland asked in a loud, strong voice?

"Her mother and I" answered the proud father. "May the good Lord bless this union." He then kissed his daughter's cheek and slowly turned and sat beside his wife, Mary Ann.

"Very well then, we may proceed," The colonel replied "I do believe that this is a proper verse that applies well for the occasion. It is from the book of Genesis." Old Roundabout coughed to clear his throat as he shifted his weight to the other leg. But then, like a preacher of old, he spoke the words of God.

"Then the Lord God said, "It is not good that the man should be alone; I will make him a helper fit for him." Now out of the ground the Lord God had formed every beast of the field and every bird of the heavens and brought them to the man to see what he would call them. And whatever the man called every living creature that was its name. The man gave names to all livestock and to the birds of the heavens and to every beast of the field. But for Adam there was not found a helper fit for him. So the Lord God caused a deep sleep to fall upon the man, and while he slept took one of his ribs and closed up its place with flesh. And the rib that the Lord God had taken from the man he made into a woman and brought her to the man. Then the man said, "This at last is bone of my bones and flesh of my flesh; she shall be called Woman, because she was taken out of Man." Therefore a man shall leave his father and his mother and hold fast to his wife, and they shall become one flesh."

As the colonel finished reading he looked up from the pages of his bible; pausing a few seconds as he cast his attention to the groom. Then with a serious demeanor and in a sobering voice he said.

"Rice, take her hand into your own. Do you, Rice Medaris take this woman, Rachael McPheeters to be your wife before all here, and before the Lord. Do you promise to honor and value her above all other women, putting no other above or before her? And to treat her as the Lord would want a godly man to honor his wife."

"Yes, I do" Rice replied, never breaking eye contact with his bride.

"Very well then" Cleveland said turning to Rachael but softening his tone.

"Do you Rachael McPheeters take this man before you, Rice Medaris as your lawful husband? Will you care for him in good times and bad? Will you submit to his wishes as long as they are proper and Godly, and yet offer a helping hand as well as cherish him above all others?

"Yes, I do," she said softly.

"Well then," Cleveland announced proudly as he shut his Bible." By the power vested in me, by the soon to be overthrown Governor of this Colony, I hereby proclaim you to be husband and wife, before God and all others present here today, or not. Amen."

Chapter 15

Mistook for another

Jack was having a hard time falling asleep. He could not sleep any better than Rice had in this terrible excuse of a bed. So, he got up, shirtless from the hard mattress, to stretch his aching muscles. As he pulled his shoulders back arching his sore back, his eyes moved across Rice's shop's floor to where Duchess always slept. Being true to her nature, she never stirred; dead to the world and as useless as ever.

Pale moonlight was glowing in the open door so Jack made his way over to take in what he hoped would be a star filled night sky. He placed one outstretched hand on the wooden frame of the doorway and drew in a deep breath of the night air. All seemed quiet tonight, nothing like it had been those last few nights after the wedding. The McPheeters and most of the Grider's had hung around giving the newlyweds a rousing shivaree, but they were all gone now. Jack himself, would be leaving in the morning. He had been told by Colonel Cleveland about an abandoned homestead over on Deep Gap Creek. Old Roundabout believed it could be had for a cheap price, since most everyone was afraid of Indian attacks in that area.

The land was on the other side of the Blue Ridge, but still inside the county lines. It would be one of the most exposed and vulnerable cabins in the whole county. It would certainly be a huge risk, but well worth taking Jack believed.

As he looked at Rice's finished cabin across the way, a smile appeared on his face. No candlelight was burning inside tonight. He was sure that Rice and Rachael were enjoying the pleasures of marriage in the enveloping darkness. With the other wedding guest finally gone, he was sure that tonight would be their first true night together. Brute was lying outside the locked door of their new home, with his nose pressed against the crack. The dog wanted inside and Jack wondered how long it would take the old hound to become jealous of Rachael, if he had not already done so.

Then looking toward, the other side of Rice's property, Jack heard his horse, Ringtail, began to necker. He was moving about in a panicked state, along with all of Rice's other animals in the corral. He and Rice had seen a wildcat lurking around for a few weeks, yet neither one of them had been able to get off a shot before the cat disappeared. Jack hoped to put an end to that tonight. He turned for his rifle, but before he could reach his weapon a brown seed sack was thrown over his head from behind with such force it pulled him to the ground. It was quickly followed with two hard punches to his face, dazing him.

"I told you it would work" Jack heard a voice say as he was returning to his senses.

"A man will always come out for his horse, it works every time, I tell you" the voice continued as Jack was pulled up from the ground to his feet. Quickly a rope was wrapped around his shoulders and he was being pulled out through the doorway.

In a low voice one of the assailants whispered to his partner "Watch out for that damn dog. Once we are down by the creek its waters will muffle any sound we make. Rice, if you want that dog of yours to live you should hold your tongue until then. I'll kill that damn mutt and cut your throat from ear to ear."

As Jack was being led across the waters of Warriors Creek, he realized that whoever had kidnapped him was under the impression that they had Rice, not him. Jack felt sure that if he revealed his true identity, his captors would most likely kill him on the spot. Then they would surely go back after Rice and Rachael to carry out whatever scheme they had planned. With that in mind, Jack stilled himself, and cooperated with his captors. Once on the other side of the creek Jack was again knocked to the ground by another hard blow. While lying on the ground, he could smell the smoke and hear the popping from a nearby fire. He was mad at himself for not smelling it earlier in the night, even if it was across the creek, a short distance from the farm. He heard the splashing of a third man crossing the creek on horseback. With the help from the firelight, he was able see the shapes of the men through the weaving of the thin bag.

"Is that the right one?" the rider asked.

"Yeah that's him! It's not every day a man gets paid twice for the same horse, is it boys? But that day is coming" he said smugly.

"John McFall, I knew that was you." Jack replied not able to hold his tongue any longer. "I hope you rot in hell for this."

McFall laughed as he looked at his brother George, who had dismounted from Rice's horse, Liberty. "Not know who you speak of," lied McFall. "We be Over the Hill Cherokee," he said in a broken dialect in his attempt to fool Jack into believing he was speaking the Cherokee language. He muttered a few lines of made up nonsense to the delight of his fellow 'Indians'.

"You can act the fool all you want John, but I know who you are. That's just gibberish. You can't speak their language" Jack cried out as he kicked out blindly in McFall's direction, but missing his mark.

"No need for all of that now," replied George "We are not horse thieves. We buy our mounts. Your payment comes from the Tar River my friend. After we are done with you Rachael will forsake you for sure."

Hearing those words, Jack realized that the McFall's had no idea about Rice's and Rachael's marriage. They had not yet received word of their union. However, that made little difference in the predicament he now found himself in. The fire had not been kindled to cook on, it was to heat the hot tar that they planned to pour over him.

John McFall turned towards the fire and took the pot of tar off the rod that was supporting it over the flames. Turning quickly towards his victim to pour the contents over Jack's head. But unknown to McFall, Jack saw him coming through the fabric. Lunging to one side Jack ducked his head from under the pot, but the tar still pored over his shoulder and back, burning its way down his spine. Biting his lower lip to keep from screaming, Jack jumped to his feet as McFall smiled, crazy eyed in delight at the pain he was inflecting. He slung the rest of the tar from the pot, splashing the last of it on Jack's chest, neck and under his chin. In desperation Jack dove for the cool creek water, in an attempt to relieve the pain. But George grabbed his arm causing Jack's leap to fall short. but some of the tar stuck to McFall's hand burning him as well.

"Damn, that is hot as hell" he proclaimed, shaking his hand as Jack finally rolled into the water. John dropped the pot and yelled to the third man, "Cunningham! Shoot that bastard before he swims away."

As the Tory raised his rifle to shoot, Rice fired a shot from the opposite side of the creek. The ball entered Cunningham's chest killing him before he could fire at Jack. Surprised by the shot, both McFall brothers darted into the darkness. John leaving his rifle, and Liberty behind in his haste to escape. Rice rushed into the water pulling Jack to his feet as Brute splashed across the water and entered the tree line in pursuit of Jack's tormentors.

"Who was that" Rice asked angrily as he removed the bag from Jack's head?

"The McFall's replied Jack. "They mistook me for you".

Chapter 16

A Bitter Dose

The sun had come up on this terrible morning, but no one had taken any notice of the fact. Rachael and Rice had been tending to Jack by candlelight. Rice had put his razor to good use. Its six-inch blade pulled off great gobs of the tar. But he was using the dull, back side of the razor instead of its sharp edge.

Even though he was very careful, occasionally a layer of Jack's skin would roll off with the tar, leaving behind only the thinnest underlying pink layer to cover his flesh. Rachael would take her fingernails and pick off the smaller pieces. It had taken all night but at least now the tar was off. Rachael had cut long strips of white linen from a bolt of cloth she had received as a wedding gift from her mother. She had wrapped it around his chest and shoulder to stop the seeping of the burns, but there was not much they could do for Jack's pain. Jack seemed to use that pain to fuel his outrage that men could commit such barbaric acts against each other. Now the three of them set at the table in the center of Rice and Rachael's new home.

"What should we do now?" Rachael asked looking at Rice. "We can't just let this pass without consequences."

"That fellow outside lying by the creek bank surely understands what consequences are," Rice replied. "But I know what you mean, it's a bitter dose. He's not a McFall."

"He was a Cunningham" replied Jack as he raped his knuckle on the tabletop. "I heard as much last night. But I still have not had the chance to get a good look at his face. Did you recognize him from anywhere?"

"He's not from around these parts," Rice replied. "What about you Rachael? Have you ever heard tell of any Cunningham's around here before?"

"It doesn't ring any bells," she answered "Still he's of no relevance now. The identity of the dead may help us later on, but not now. We need to report this to someone. John and George are still out there, free as a couple of birds."

"Colonel Cleveland?" Rice asked with a raised eyebrow. "Or I could try to track them down on my own. I do feel somewhat responsible for this."

"No," Jack replied. "They did what they did. You are not responsible for their actions. Besides, we already know where they are going, back to their Pap's place. I can ride with you to the Colonel's. We will overwhelm them with greater numbers that way anyhow. The Colonel will have more men to help out, and that way it will be legal as well."

Standing up from her chair Rachael reached for her small straw hat that hug on a peg driven into the cabin wall. "I like that idea, we can be there by nightfall."

Rice ran his hand over his jaw, squeezing his chin between his fingers and his thumb, as he looked at his wife. Then laughing as he spoke, he said, "Where do you think you're going?"

"Why, with you two!" Rachael replied as she tied the ribbons of her hat under her chin. "I'm not staying here alone with those marauders running about the countryside. They may be back tonight anyway. And I'm not a child that you're taking back home to my family whenever trouble comes knocking on our door. If they burn this cabin tonight, I will not be inside it. I will be with my husband where I belong."

"That is fine, you are right," Rice replied raising his hands into the air. "I'll tend to Cunningham's body and the horses afterwards. Come with me Jack, maybe we can figure out who it is in the daylight. And Rachael, you can pack some food for our ride over." Jack chuckled for the first time today, as he picked up his rifle ever so slowly. He was moving stiffly, but moving all the same. "Well Rice, you may have a young bride," he proclaimed "But I can see she is not one to be trifled with."

Rice proudly shook his head, 'yes', as he gazed over at his wife. This was his first opportunely to see Rachael in a bad situation, and she had handled herself very well. He already had little doubt, but this episode proved she was the partner he wanted by his side to stride through life's many trials.

Still sitting, Jack paused for a second before speaking again. "Maybe we should haul that body with us to Cleveland's. Someone just might know who he is over there. Besides if this was my place I would not want that scoundrel buried on my property."

"Yes, we should do that," Rachael replied "I really do not want any reminders of what happened to us here last night."

Chapter 17

We'll Set Things Right

Even though the daylight was about gone Rice could still see the potential of Colonel Cleveland's estate. Like the Colonel himself, it too went by the name of Roundabout. It was so called, not for the size of its owners' stomach, but for the beautiful bend in the Yadkin River where it was situated. Here, inside this u-shaped curve, Cleveland had settled with his family. The main house of the estate, a large two-story log dwelling, was snuggled inside this bottom surrounded by beautiful hills. Several out buildings graced the grounds. The Colonel's original small cabin now housed a few slaves, a couple hundred feet from the big house, but was still within eyesight of the river. A stable, two barns, a corn crib, and sleek, fat livestock roaming the grounds all surrounded by split rail fences gave Roundabout a grand appearance.

Newly lit candles flickered just behind the glass window panes of the Colonel's home as Rice's small party dismounted from their day's ride. Rice reached out with his hand and caressed Rachael's cheek and lips as Jack pretended not to notice the kiss that followed. But when Rice handed over his reins over, Jack rolled his eyes and shook his head. The expression told Rice that this was not the place or time for romance, even between new lovers. Rice nodded his head getting Jack's point, but said in reply "I know, but it's not easy to restrain myself now that she is really mine".

Jack smiled, shaking his head as Rice turned and made his way to the green door at the front of the house. He had seen movement inside through the window, but he still rapped on the door to announce his presence. Rice stepped back a few feet as the Colonel swung open the door with pistol in hand. After a quick evaluation of his guest, Cleveland lowered his weapon. Placing one hand on Rice's shoulder, he led the newlywed to the outside corner of his home.

"Rice," he said jovially, wearing a big grin, "If you are here to learn what to do on your honeymoon I can't help you with that."

"No sir" Rice replied shaking his head after a small chuckle, "that is not the reason for our presence I'm afraid. Jack has been attacked, and we need your help in the matter."

"Attacked! By who?" demanded Cleveland.

"This is one of the scroudrels." Jack replied, as he raised Cunningham's head to show the Colonel, from where the body was slung over Queen's back. The man's cold body was turning hard, as rigor mortis was starting to set in.

"Why, I know him! That's Pat Cunningham, he is one of George McFall's fools," Cleveland announced through gritted teeth as he reached into his pocket. "By the looks of him, we will have to bury the bastard in a round coffin if we don't get him off that horse soon."

"The only coffin he'll get is the cold ground he will be laid in," Jack replied.

"Was John there as well?" Cleveland asked as he fired up his pipe."

"He poured the tar." Jack answered "all over my side and back.

"Tar!" Cleveland exclaimed as he approached Jack in the dimming light. "Are you whole boy? I've heard tell of men being laid up for weeks after a tar and feathering. 'It must have cooled off somewhat before they got to you."

"Believe me when I say, it was hot enough," Jack replied as he raised his hunting shirt to reveal his bandages. 'Rice and Rachael did a good job with the burns. But I must admit this cockeyed ride over here today was none too pleasant."

"I am sure it was not," the Colonel replied shaking his head. "Do not misunderstand me Jack, I was not trying to belittle your wounds. It was meant to be a compliment to your fortitude. I understand that it had to be a hard ride, and it is one ride I am happy you were able to make. We will set things right on the morrow."

"We believe they are back at their father's place," Rachael announced. "Most likely they have run back to their hidey hole like the rats they are."

"Did their Paw or Arthur either one have a hand in this?" The Colonel asked.

"No, just John and George," Rice answered.

"Well I should hope not, that is good to hear," Cleveland said. "I just don't understand how all of that man's boys, other than Author, turned out so badly. John Alexander sure did spawn more than his share of bad seeds. But my thoughts go right along with yours Mrs. Medaris. That's where they will be all right, no doubt hiding under their beds as we speak. I am somewhat surprised though, that it was not you they were after Rice. John did not make it a secret that he wanted to wed your Missus. Author has that beautiful wife of his own, with all of that flowing red hair. I always believed that ate at John and George a little bit, but that's neither here nor there, I suppose."

Cleveland motioned to his open doorway, inviting the three in with the gesture. "Come on in and rest your bones for a spell. We will have some supper here in a little while"

"Yes Sir," Rice replied gratefully. "We can use the time to hash out a plan of attack".

Ben Cleveland looked at Rice with a stoic expression and said. "Boys, there is no need for grand plans in a situation like this. We will simply ride straight over there in the morning and grab those two scallywags by the ears".

"And hang them by the necks," Jack added, cutting off Cleveland in mid-sentence.

"No, we'll have none that." the Colonel answered. "We have the law on our side and all they have is a tar covered pot sitting in their yard for the world to see. That will not make much of a defense in my humble opinion. But that is enough talk for now. Please, Mrs. Medaris, do come on in and rest awhile."

"Gladly" Rachael replied "I'll be needing it from what I understand. The McFall place is a hard ride from what I've been told".

"True enough, but that is one ride you will not have to take young lady. My hospitality goes far beyond tonight's stay. You may remain here at Roundabout until our return."

"I thank you Colonel for your fine offer, but that will not be necessary. The ride will be no more difficult than the one I endured today.

The Colonel looked at Rice with an expression that said, 'I need your help'. Rice understanding all too well, reached out and took Rachael's hand and led her to the end of the Colonel's porch.

"Rachael, the Colonel knows you can handle the ride. What he is saying is that this is as far as you can go, my dear."

"I'm the cause of this whole mess, Rice whether we like it or not. I feel I have to see this through just as much as you or Jack. Everyone says Mr. McFall has a good, level head. Maybe I can talk to him and he in turn can bring this mess to some kind of conclusion."

"No Rachael, you can't go any further. You speak as though this will all end peacefully. It may not. What if there is shooting? What if the McFall's get the upper hand? You would be at their mercy. What kind of a man would I be if I led my wife into such a hardship? I love your fire my dear, but you must stay behind".

"He is right Rachael," Jack said "We could no more take you any further than we could have left you back at the cabin alone. Believe me, I know firsthand what those men are capable of. Please, for your own safety, you must stay."

Shaking her head, no in obvious disappointment, she closed her eyes. When she opened them, she looked squarely into Rice's and said "Very well, but I'm not happy about it. I declare, sometimes I wish I had been born a man."

"Well I for one am overjoyed that you were not," Rice proclaimed as he pulled her close. "Thank you my dear for understanding. This will be for the best."

Chapter 18

The Compromise

John McFall dropped an armload of split hickory next to the fire that he and George had lit earlier in the day. They were tending to their still, and were about to run the mash through for the second time. The white smoke from the fire rose high in the sky every time a gust of wind blew down thru the hollow.

It would swirl around their copper pot and up and over their heads high into the mountain air. Most of the time they would run the mash through a third time, but not on this day. This batch was not for them anyway. What they made for family and friends always got that last loving touch that made their whiskey go down so smooth. But Indians would not know the difference between two and three runs John supposed. Why should they do the extra work, if this was going the Cherokee? John got the idea while at Cross Creek on the way to sell his pelts. A trader there with a big load of pelts had told him that once a brave was hooked on sprits, an easy trade would soon follow. The two brothers planned to load two pack horses with kegs of their home brew and head to the middle Cherokee villages this coming winter. But now that they had lost Pat they would need a new interpreter to take his place.

"I still can't imagine where that shot came from," John said as he turned to George. "Maybe it was his brother Massey".

"Or one of the Grider's" George suggested. "They are getting as thick as thieves. But whoever he was, he sure in hell could shoot. I say Pat was dead before he hit the ground. Damn John, I can't believe you were dumb enough to leave your rifle behind like you did. Are you sure it can't be traced back to you somehow?"

"No" John snapped back angrily. "I'm getting weary of hearing that. If I have told you once I have told you a hundred times. I don't carve my name into the stocks of my rifles like some do. Besides the only reason you still have yours is it was still in your hands when he fired. If you're so brave way didn't you fire your gun. After all, whoever fired that shot was empty then."

"There could have been more than one, or he could have had a second shot already primed in another rifle. I sure was not going to wait around and see," George answered.

"No, but you question my actions for not taking the time to find my rifle in the dark, don't you?"

"Damn it to hell John, I just don't want it to come back and haunt us later on." George said matching his brothers tone. "Hell, we didn't get the horse back or nothing. And now we're a man short. I still say we should go back and kill him sometime soon."

"In good time," John replied as he dropped a few sticks of the hickory on the fire. "Rice isn't stupid; he'll have his guard up for a while. When he falls back to a normal routine, we'll be there".

Maybe so, but what's keeping him from talking in the meantime? He might not have seen us, but he knew who we were."

"Knowing it, and proving it in a court of law is not the same, now is it George?"

"We will see about that," Rice announced as he stepped around a two-hundred-year-old chestnut with the muzzle of his rifle pointing at John.

"No, we won't!" Jack interrupted, pulling back the hammer of his rifle. He lowered the weapon straight at John, who fell to the ground cowering and trying to get out of range of the gun that Jack had aimed at his head. "They didn't have a trial for me back at the riverbank and we ain't having one here now. Get ready John, I'm about to blow your head plum off"

"No Jack, we've already talked this over. This is going to be done legal," Colonel Cleveland said as he pushed Jack's rifle down and away from John with his free hand. "You boys could not have done a better job of letting us know where you were. If the smoke was not enough, the smell of the mash sure was." Colonel Cleveland replied as he covered John with his own weapon. We knew you two would be here at your Pa's, but it sure was hospitable for y'all to light that signal fire for us."

"Pa get up here!" George yelled, as he turned towards the creek bank that sat in the distance. Then he coolly pushed away Rice's rifle that was now covering him. "You have no call for this Cleveland," George accused, looking over Rice's shoulder at the Colonel.

"Not according to these boys," Ben replied "you can't go around tarring people without expecting some kind of consequences."

"We don't know anything about anybody being tarred" John replied coming back to his feet. "I have not seen Rice Medaris since I left Fort Grider"

"It wasn't Rice, it was me that you jerked that bag over, your sorry bastard" Jack said, tapping his own chest. "Who do you think shot Cunningham? You two had the wrong man all the time.

You were real big men until Rice put that ball through your henchman. After that, you didn't stick around long enough to even see that you had the wrong man, or even gather up your belongings."

All conversation stopped as John Alexander McFall walked into the fray with a bucket of water in each hand. His long gray hair flowed free under his tri-cornered hat. He sat the water down, and pulled a pistol from his belt. Then sitting down on an old, dead stump he pointed it at Jack. "Boy," he said in a calm low voice. "You need to cool off while the Colonel and I hash this out."

"Nothing to hash out John Alexander," Ben answered. "We are taking your two boys here to Mulberry Fields, plain and simple. But they will be under my protection while in my custody. You have my word on it."

"Taking my two splendid sons," their father said sarcastically, letting all know his disappointment in them. "And afterwards? What then?" the head of the McFall family asked as he crossed one leg over the other. "My other boy, Arthur, told me the last time he and George were at the meeting house they were ridiculed for standing up for the King. Why would it be any different this time? These two may be my blight, but they are still of my blood."

"They will be treated fairly. You have my word on that as well. Your boy Arthur has the same level head as his father," Ben replied. These other two, not so much, but if John and George will submit to my charge as he would, they will be safe until the trail. Where is Arthur anyway?"

"Around somewhere close I suspect, John Alexander replied as he glanced around the tree line. "It's true they don't always show the best of judgment, as Arthur does, but with due respect I could say the same about you Ben. Everyone here knows of your temper when things don't go your way."

"Do I look like a hot head now?" Ben asked.

"No, but you are still in control or at least you think so" McFall answered. I'm sure Arthur has you in his sights by now".

"And I'm sure one of the Grider's has him in theirs" Rice said looking up to the top of the surroundings hills. "Martin and John are fine woodsmen."

"Could be you are right," John Alexander said with a smile. "But we won't have to find out if Ben will agree to take them to Salisbury instead. I will not hand my boys over to a group of Whigs. I'll only let you have them if it's Salisbury, and not your own backyard. Are you willing to compromise or not Ben? If not, this next hour will be bloody".

Ben looked around at the faces of the men who stood watching him. He was silent a few seconds, and Rice could tell the Colonel was mulling the situation over in his mind. Then turning to Jack, he said "Once the truth is told, I don't see how the outcome could be any different in Salisbury." He approached John Alexander who was still sitting on the stump, and dropped two pair of irons at his feet. "I can go along with that, but it is not because of the threat of Arthur."

"I know," the old man replied as he picked up the irons. " Ben, I have another request. Let me have a word with them alone before you take them. I don't even know what this is about just yet."

"As long as you stay in view," Ben replied, "but you put those irons on them."

Rice looked on as the two parties split to confer. He could not tell who was the most upset with the compromise. The McFall brothers, who were still conjuring up lies to bolster their defense to a doubtful father, or Jack who was none too happy with the new turn of events. He had listened to Colonel Cleveland's reason for accepting John Alexander's request for the Salisbury court. Yet he still did not like the idea of someone else holding the McFall's fate when there was such an abundance of hanging trees at hand. However, Jack knew what was truly at the heart of this matter, and he wanted to add a little fuel to that fire. He looked John McFall squarely in the eye and said. "Hey John, did you hear the good news? Rice and Rachael are man and wife now. Got married in front of all their friends and neighbors. Did it up right and proper, even had Colonel Cleveland here do the honors. I just thought you would like to know that!"

Chapter 19

Salisbury

For Rice the trek from the McFall homestead to Salisbury was surreal. He was at the root of this crime, but yet unbelievably, not its victim. The two brothers denied their guilt with every step they took. Strangely, John seemed undaunted by the news of Rice and Rachael's wedding. But, there had been one brief initial expression of rage that soon disappeared, leaving this vacant nonchalant look of unconcern. He could have been one of William Shakespeare's actors, but Rice knew that it was eating at him. That made him very dangerous. How would he react once that rage returned? George seemed more concerned about his own fate and the upcoming trial. He was constantly telling and retelling his alibi to Martin and John Grider, who were acting as guards. Blind accusations he kept repeating which infuriated Jack to no end. He could hear George referring to the bag that had been placed over his head that night. Not only was George lying he, was mocking his victim with his alibi.

But that all ended when John Alexander caught up with the party telling his sons to shut up and be quiet. He was not alone either, Arthur rode up as well. But instead of slowing their pace, they rode on ahead of Colonel Cleveland's party. At the pace they set, they would arrive at Salisbury a few hours before the Colonel's party. This gave Jack some pause, wondering if Arthur and John Alexander had planned an ambush up ahead. The East West trading path presented several spots that would give them a good advantage, especially between Cabin Creek and the Yadkin. Yet Colonel Cleveland did not seem concerned. As much as Ben looked down on John and George, he respected the McFall's father and their brother Arthur. Rice, however, was inclined to agree with Jack on the subject, and told the Colonel so. What he had seen of the McFall's actions in the past, had shown that character in those two was sorely lacking. But Ben assured Rice and Jack that all would be well. He pointed out the fact that John Alexander was unarmed and the two culprits were in irons under the watchful eyes of Martin and John. Rice thought Arthur would consider an ambush a cowardly act. Besides, he was a free man with no charges against him, so the Colonel had no control over him. He could not hold Arthur if he wanted to. Still with all of Colonel Cleveland's assurances, Rice's concerns did not die down until the party rode into Salisbury.

Rice, still leery of Arthur's whereabouts, tried to spot the missing McFall as they came down Corbin Street, but he was nowhere to be seen. The town itself was not very active, until they reached the Common. A few men were watching eight or nine head of cattle that had the customary free range of the public grounds. Children were running about tossing and catching wooden hoops out of the air with long sticks. Women were watching their children play under the young oaks, which had only been planted within the last ten years. However, as their small party rode down the street all eyes turned to the McFall's. It was not every day that men were led into town with irons on their wrist. As Rice and the others dismounted their horses, Arthur appeared, pushing his way through the gathering crowd. He approached with his father, John Alexander, as Martin and Jack pulled the two prisoners off their horses. Jack did little to help John keep his balance, giving him a hard jerk while he was still atop his horse. Some of the crowd gasped as John fell on his shoulder but most just laughed. John jumped to his feet quickly, in another rage but soon cooled at the sight of John Grider's rifle pointed at him, but not before saying "You will pay someday for that McCalpin."

"Maybe so, but not today, this is your time for payment." Jack replied.

"Can't you restrain you men better than that, Ben?" John Alexander said as he looked at Cleveland, who was tying the reins of his horse to the hitching post. "There have not yet been any trials, as far as I know."

Ben did not respond he just turned to the Grider's and said "Come on boys the jail is a little down the street here. Bring them on. Jack, you stay here with Rice, we will be back directly. After I dispose of these two with the jailer, I'm going to have a few words with my barrister William Kennon. [14] We will meet you two over at Steele's Tavern afterwards."

Jack watched as the four men made their way across the street towards the jail. Rice watched as well for a second, but soon turned

---

[14] William Kennon 1735-? Was one of the original signers of the Mecklenburg Declaration of Independence. A Colonel in the Revolutionary War and was on the Rowan County Safety Committee.

his attention back to John Alexander and Arthur hoping he could hear their conversation.

"Did you see either one of them?" their father asked.

"Yes, both, thanks to Gideon Wright," replied Arthur, as he and his father walked away to keep their conversation private.

"Gideon Wright!" Jack said turning to Rice. "Well don't that just beat all. I knew Arthur was up to something. If Wright is going to have a hand in this, things could turn sour for us.

"I don't see how," Rice replied, "We have a strong case. They will spend a few months in the goal. I expect they may even receive a branding on the foreheads, or possibly on their hands as well. The next time they see daylight they will think twice before they pull another stunt like this again."

"I hope you're right Rice," Jack said as he placed his thumb under the strap of his powder horn. "But I know there is a greater amount of support here for a loyalist then there would have been back at Mulberry Fields. We'll find out soon enough I suppose."

Chapter 20

Steel's Tavern

Rice and Jack sat at a long table inside the tavern belonging to Mrs. Elizabeth Maxwell Steel. She was a very pleasant lady, always putting on a happy face to the townspeople, despite the fact that she had buried two husbands. The first, Robert Jackespie was scalped and killed near Fort Dobbs by the Cherokee back in 1760. However, her loss did not stop her from finding a way to support herself and her two young children. She purchased town lot number two in the North Square where she opened this tavern. She enjoyed a good standing among the citizens of Stanbury, and her neighbors were pleased for her when she met and married her most recent husband. William Steele. Mr. Steele had passed last year after suffering from a stroke while working behind the bar.

A heavy heart is slow to heal, and she shows her grief on occasion, mostly at night, but rarely in the daylight hours when her responsibilities kept her busy. So, she once again, is the sole proprietress of the most popular tavern in Salisbury.

As Rice sat at an oak table, his eyes fell upon the portrait of King George hanging on the wall. It hung inside a very handsome gilded gold frame. It was placed in a prominent spot, in the center of the wall, just above a small table that had a pewter pitcher of rum and matching mugs on it. Ten years before, this would have been a prized possession, but now it was something of a liability, the cause of several disagreements between her customers, Rice imagined. Maybe that was why she had a rifle and powder horn hanging above the portrait. The big end of the horn almost covered the King's face.

The door leading out of the kitchen squeaked as Mrs. Steel popped her head out and asked "Will you two lads be taking a meal today?"

"Yes. I believe we will," replied Rice.

As Mrs. Steel withdrew back into the kitchen a fat hound, shot out the very same door. It trotted over to the table where the two men sat and cured up next to Jack's boots. Pushing his chair back from the table, and with a grin on his face Rice leaned under and looked at the fat belly of the dog,

"Oh, don't pay him any mind. He keeps my floor fairly clean," Mrs. Steele said as she entered the room. She had a tablecloth draped over one arm and a loaf of bread on a plate in her other hand. She sat the bread on the corner of the hard-wooden surface of the table. Then, as she spread the tablecloth over the other half of the long table in front of the two hungry men she laughed as she said, "He does really well for himself when we have children eating. Little ones get as much on the floor as they do in their tummies"

"I have no doubt," Jack replied, rubbing his hands together in anticipation of the coming meal.

She reached under her apron and pulled out a knife and stuck its point into the freshly baked loaf of bread, leaving only the handle sticking in the air. Then she sat the good smelling bread, and a crock of fresh churned butter upon the white cloth in front of Rice.

"How did you come by that portrait of the King?" Rice asked as she turned to the pitcher of rum.

"That come from England as a present from a person at court", she replied. "Don't worry lads, I only leave it there because of my late husband, God rests his soul. He was so proud of it. It hangs only because William loved it so. And even he only took pride in it because of the stature it afforded. Not for his love of the man that is our King. This is not a Tory establishment by any means, your money will still be in good hands. But mind you now, if you know any loyalists don't tell them I said so," she said with a wink. "I'll be back with a nice cut of roast for you in a moment."

Jack wasted little time in pulling the knife out of the loaf. He was cutting into the warm bread as the front door of the tavern open, and in walked John Dunn and Benjamin Boote, [15] two well-known lawyers of Salisbury with loyalist tendencies.

"I do believe young Kennon is as mad as a raging bull," Dunn said smugly as the two sat down at a table across the room.

"He sure is," replied Boote. "With Mr. **Rutherford** and Lock away at the Assembly, we had a free hand. **Justice** Smith[16] was none too happy either. but there was little he could do. And that backwoods ruffian, Cleveland showed his poor breeding as well. We should have a fine game of nine pens this afternoon. Gideon may be able to supply royal pardons from his pocket, but he rolls poorly. Yes, we will have a profitable day."

At that moment Mrs. Steele re-entered the room with Rice and Jack's food. The sight of the steam rising in the air off of the onion covered roast, dressed with buttered potatoes and green peas, ended the loyalist conversation. As Mrs. Steele sat down the food, Rice saw the anger rising off Jack, almost as much as the steam from his dinner. He too had overheard what was being said across the room. Shakings his head he stabbed his two-pronged fork into the meat and pulled a tender portion free. Then pointing his fork at Dunn with the meat still on the point, he said. "Are you two speaking of the McFall brothers?"

"We are," answered Boote after a few seconds passed "What concern is it of yours, my good man?"

---

[15] John Dunn and Benjamin Boote sometimes called Booth would be arrested before the month of June was out for circulating an oath to the crown. Both men were shipped off to Charleston by the way of Camden where they were imprisoned as Tories.

[16] James Smith was appointed to the rank of Major in the Salisbury Militia, of which Francis Locke was Colonel, and Griffith Rutherford was Brigadier-General.

"They were under our care coming in to town. We are part of that backwoods ruffian's party that apprehended them. Not to mention being the victims of their crime as well."

"Then you harbor ill feelings for them I suppose," Dunn replied looking over his shoulder. "I'm afraid you have wasted your time on the matter. They are already free men."

"How so?" Rice asked.

"Mrs. Steel," Dunn said ignoring Rice question "I see that your fine-looking roast is on the menu today. Two more dishes, if you please."

As Jack stood up from his chair waiting for his answer, Ben Cleveland entered the tavern and walked straight to the two lawyers. Pointing a finger at Boote he said "You sir, are a scoundrel of the first order. How do you sleep at night knowing what you are? What you have done here is an outrage! You can scarcely conceive the uproar this will bring about, you macaroni bugger."

Fear ran up Boote's spine as this towering man stood over him, speaking in what could only be described as roaring indignation. Raising a hand Boote replied, "Sir we are not your enemy, there is nothing personal in our actions today, we are only instruments of the court."

"There was no court!" Cleveland thundered, "They were freed at the jail!"

"Sir, your issue is with the McFall's and Mr. Wright not us," Dunn replied as he stood to his feet. "We are taking our leave".

"Believe me when I say, if Gideon Wright had been at that jail I would have had his worthless hide," Cleveland shouted as Boote and Dunn exited the room for the safer streets outside. "But no, you two wretched scoundrels did his bidding for him instead."

As the two scoundrels hurriedly made their way down the streets of Salisbury, Ole Roundabout turned to Jack and said, "I'm so sorry Jack. I never believed they would walk out of this town as free men. But I promise you this, the next time they fall into our hands, they will be left swinging from a nearby tree."

"Where are they now?" Rice asked.

"On their way home I suppose, slinking back to their hidey hole, like the rats they are." Ben answered. "Martin and John are watching for them on the road going out of town. But I see no lawful course for us to take at this time."

Cleveland walked over to the window and glared out into the street, deep in his thoughts. At that moment he made a solemn vow to himself as he removed his hat from his aching head. From that day forward justice would be served; carried out on the spot. Never again would he concede his authority to another. Some may see this as an overstepping of his power, or maybe even a form of vigilantism, but in his heart, he knew he would be on the just side of the issue. He envisioned many hanging in the coming years.

Chapter 21

The Green Sash

Alexander Cameron, long time British Indian agent among the Cherokee, sat alongside Dragging Canoe as an approaching rain fell across the river, at Mialaquo[17]. This Cherokee village had sat snugly

---

[17] Mialaquo is now under the waters of Lake Tellico near Loudon

on this island safely tucked in the waters of the Little Tennessee River for as long as anyone could remember. From the dawn of time some of the old ones said. The two had been observing four young Cherokee boys blowing darts at an old musty deerskin; discarded by one's mother. Having been the center of attention since Cameron's arrival, the two enjoyed watching the boys at play, and not mulling over the problems at hand, if only for an hour or so. But now as the rain drops began to fall in a heavy downpour, the two men made their way back inside the octagonal shaped council house five hundred feet from the riverbank.

The large room was almost dark now, since its fire had burned down to only hot coals. What little light that came through the hole cut in the roof, to draw out the smoke from the fire, was being blocked by the clouds of the storm outside. The three tiers of benches that lined the room's walls were all but empty. Not like last night, when the room was full of men and women talking over the advice that Cameron had delivered. Cameron was one of the few white men who could be at ease here at Mialaquo. He had been appointed to this position back in 1764 and had earned the Cherokee's trust over all of those years of service. He was even Dragging Canoe's adopted brother. He could walk into any village of the Cherokee nation and be well received, in all safety.

His message last night was direct, and to the point. The King's children were overstepping their bounds. These settlers were not only pouring into Kentucky's hunting grounds illegality, but into the Cherokee's own homelands as well. The Watauga and Nolichucky settlements were in violation of past agreements. Henderson's purchase of Kentucky was unlawful, as far as the King was concerned. The settlers would have to return to their old homes and abandon the bluegrass and cane lands once order was restored.

Tennessee.

The Cherokee had not pushed the whites out of their nation in the past. Partly because of Cameron's presence here, and his words. He had always told them the King would handle his children when the time was right. Patience had always been his council in the past, but not anymore. War was now at hand, and that was all the Cherokee needed to hear.

"When will your father, the King be able to supply the arms we need to drive out the squatters?" Dragging Canoe asked as he placed a hand on a pole supporting the roof overhead.

"In the fall, or the spring at the latest," replied Cameron as he removed his haversack from across his shoulder. "Most likely by the way of Mobile. You know we are now cut off from the east. We will also need an escort to help with the Creek. I for one, am not looking forward to traveling through their land without one. I am counting on you, my brother. You hold their respect like no other."

Dragging Canoe drew his knife from the sheath over his shoulder and said, 'We must act now! The king's children's eyes are looking across the water, not at our lands. If we strike now we can drive them all out like the wildfires in a dry season drives everything before it, or leaves all things destroyed behind it".

"Only with enough powder, my friend," Cameron answered. "You know this as well as I. I too, am ready to strike the war post with you, but we must wait for the right time."

"Who has been calling for more Longrifles for years? I, Dragging Canoe! But your father the king was afraid to let us have them. If he would have done the things I said, his children would have stayed where they should have stayed. They only fear us when we are strong. Your king too was afraid. Afraid we would become too strong for even him. So, now we all suffer for his slowness to act. I will keep the long knives away with what we have now, until you can supply enough to drive them back, even until my death."

"I have no doubt that you will," Cameron said as he placed his hand on Dragging Canoe's shoulder. Death will only fall upon you as an old man. No longknife can take you from this world. I'll deceive the whites with false tales of peace. That should keep them at bay for the time being. But now, I wish to speak of friendship, not war. I have a gift for you. I was going to give it to you last evening but I thought better of it. The few who do not want to go to war would have said Dragging Canoe is bribed easily. They would only twist my gift to you for their own benefit. So now I give it as only a brother would, under only our eyes. Alexander Cameron withdrew a long green silk sash from his haversack. It was over five-foot-long and decorated with gold tassels at each end.

"When I saw this sash I instantly thought of you, my brother. The green represents the color of your homeland. What you fight to protect, as in the green of the great trees and grass upon your soil.

"And the gold?" Dragging Canoe asked.

"Well, you know how the white man covets gold above all else?" Cameron expanded. 'When they see it hanging around your waist they will know you are a great man among you own people, as well as theirs; one not to be taken lightly, but to be feared.

Dragging Canoe proudly wrapped the sash around his waist. He tied it tightly around his black hunting shirt, letting the tassels hang halfway down his legging to his kneecaps. "Dragging Canoe thanks his white brother" the war chief replied. "Soon I will wear it into battle and all will know of the bond between us, for I will say. "This is from my white brother, the great Alexander Cameron, a much-respected man."

Chapter 22

A Tug of War

Rice hammered out the last edge of the four plow points that Colonel Cleveland had ordered. Spring was near and they would be needed soon. January had been as cold as ever, and February was holding to the same pattern, with another ten days yet to come. Still, even with the cold outside, this winter his home was very warm. Rachael's soft body helped to keep the cold out of his bed at nights. Having learned the mysteries of the female form was not only pleasant, but warming. As much as Rice enjoyed his matrimonial bed, it was Rachael's presence in his home that made his heart soar. Her sweet smell, the way her hair flowed down around her shoulders at night, the sound of her feet moving across the floor as she prepared their meals. Marriage was all he had hoped it would be. He counted his marriage a blessing, even with the war going on and the opportunity it afforded wicked men to settle old grudges. The McFall's had not been seen since Salisbury. Rice always tried to keep a watchful eye in the trees around his homestead. It was all the more necessary now that not only the Indians were a concern, but knowing that the McFalls were still free to move about. But as time went by, month after month, his concerns began to fade somewhat, but even so, his watchfulness never wavered. Jack was no longer around to help, having taken his gun to the North Carolina Militia, under Colonel Richard Caswell who was planning to march his army to Wilmington. On the other hand, Royal Governor Martin was desperately trying to keep the Colonel under British control. He had been meeting with loyalist all winter hoping to muster up a militia for the king. Rice's concerns may had lessened somewhat, but he was no fool; alertness was still a priority. With that in mind, he picked up the holster that he always kept hung on the corner of his work bench.

It gave him quick access to the Queen Anne pistol[18] tucked inside if the need ever arose. Its scarred pistol grip and pitted barrel showed its age. Yet his paternal Grandfather Charles, its original owner, had kept it in good firing order. It was the only possession that Rice still had from the balding old man he had loved so much as a boy. Rice also kept the century old weapon in good order. He placed the holster over his shoulder and put on his bearskin coat, that kept the weapon out of view. Always in the past his long rifle would have been within easy reach, but most days lately, he had intentionally left it inside the cabin, for Rachael.

Leaving his hammer on the anvil, he walked out of his shop's doorway, knowing Rachael would have supper ready soon. And there, before him, he saw the only member of his family that was not happy with the new marriage. Brute. He was locked in a tug of war with Rachael. He had the broom she was sweeping out the house with locked in his jaws, pulling with all his might. She in turn was pulling on the handle, just as determined as the dog not to let go.

"Let go, you awful dog," she cried. "You chewed my other broom to pieces, but you're not getting this one, darn you."

"Brute! Let go," Rice demanded laughingly, as he approached the two from across the yard.

---

[18] The Queen Anne was a famous English pistol that was very popular during the reign of Anne; Queen of Great Britain 1665-1714, hence the name Queen Anne.

As the dog let his grip go at his master's command, Rachael stumbled a few steps, her momentum pulling her backward.

"I do declare," she announced as she regained her balance "that dog is so jealous of me he can hardly stand it. He truly despises me."

"Oh, he is coming around some," Rice laughed as he patted the dog on top of his head. "He let you have the broom this time."

"Maybe so," Rachael announced as she pointed her newly won broom at the growling dog. "But let me tell you something Brute. I am here to stay, old boy. Neither man nor beast will ever drive me from my new home. So, get used to it."

Rice's eye grew large as he saw a Cherokee step behind Rachael from inside the cabin door. The tug of war over the broom had given him the opportunity to enter the house undetected, using the back door. Two other braves stepped from around the corners of the cabin, both with muskets pointed at Rice.

The large warrior wrapped a strong arm around Rachael's waist before she even knew he was there. He pulled her up close to his chest, looking at Rice with angry, hate filled eyes. Rachael, with her feet dangling in the air, looked up into her captor's face, but quickly turned her head away to avoid the foul smell of liquor on his breath.

"What is it you want with us?" Rice asked coolly, hoping to plant a seed into this drunken man's mind, knowing all too well that was all he could do. "I see you have no war paint, so your visit must be peaceful".

"Whisky." replied the Indian with a big gaping grin. "McFall say you keep lots of whisky here. Told us to come see you. We come to drink and eat. We may kill you if you say no. That would make McFall happy. Maybe I not kill you, just to make McFall mad" he chuckled. "We not kill this one" he said as he squeezed Rachael tightly "take her back home with us maybe. She make son good squaw."

Brut showed his white fangs as he let out a low growl, and stepped forward towards the Indian who was still behind Rachael.

"You call off dog. Make go," the Cherokee said looking at the enraged dog. "I like warrior dogs, but I kill warrior dog if you do not stop him."

"Heel boy," Rice commanded, as he snapped his fingers.

The Cherokee motioned with his eyes and a nod of his head toward Rice's shop, sending an unspoken command to the warrior at Rice's left. As the warrior turned and ran toward the building, he let out a loud war whoop. Without another word, the Indian holding Rachael darted back into the cabin with her still locked in his arms. Rice, holding his breath, followed the two inside and was in turn followed in by the third Indian holding a gun.

"You must be a smart man" Rice said as he watched the leader of this small band release Rachael. "You speak good English. What is your name brother?"

The Cherokee did not answer, he just stared at the floor a moment as his legs began to wobble. He reached out and pulled a chair away from the table and dropped down with a thud. "Bring food," he snapped looking at Rachael while he banged his flattened palms on the tabletop. Looking up at Rice, he said in a roaring voice, "You sit," as he kicked over another chair from under the table. Rice bent over and picked up the overturned chair, and sat down as the

Cherokee spoke in his own tongue to the third Indian who quickly went about ransacking the cabin.

"Where is jug?" he demanded, once again speaking in English.

"In that chest over by the bed." Rice answered, somewhat surprised that he had not asked about a rifle instead.

Rachael walked across the room and sat a plate of food on the table in front of the drunken man. Her face was expressionless, showing no emotion whatsoever. Only a small strand of her long black hair was out of place, hanging just to the side of her cheek. As the Cherokee grabbed the venison roast from his plate with his bare hands, Rachael pulled a knife from under her apron and plunged it deep into his throat with one quick motion. Rice, in turn, pulled his pistol from under his coat and shot the remaining unexpecting warrior across the room. As the smoke from the shot floated in the air, Rice jumped from his chair grabbing his rifle from the wall. As he turned to the open door he saw the last remaining Indian running for the cabin with a tomahawk in his hand. Rice raised the gun and fired. The shot was true, hitting the warrior in the stomach, above his beltline. Hunching over, he made a few sideways steps before falling to the ground. Rice handed the rifle to Rachael who immediately began to reload the weapon, having already done so to the Queen Anne. Stepping out the door, Rice once again took up his pistol as his mark had regained his footing and was running for the tree line. Not being able to get off a clear shot, Rice took to the warrior's heels. As he ran along, a small limb hit Rice in the face as he entered the trees, just as he pulled the trigger of the pistol. Hearing the shot the brave changed direction, as the bullet sailed over his head. Even wounded, the last intruder was still fleet of foot. This was a race for life. The Indian knew it, as did Rice. Both men had to win.

If this brave made his escape, he would lead another war party to the cabin for revenge. As the two men made their way along the creek bank, leaping fallen logs and moss-covered boulders on their way, Brute ran past Rice and within a few seconds. the dog had overtaken his prey, pulling the Indian to the ground by tearing deep into the brave's leg. Rice finished the job by driving his knife into the brave's chest. With the life all but gone from what Rice hoped was the last of the attackers, he began to run back to the cabin, praying that no one else was about. Three was all he had seen, but there could be more about. As he made his way around his shop he saw that Rachael was dragging the dead warrior out through her cabin door. She dropped his feet as his head cleared the bottom step of the porch. She then ran back inside and as Rice reached the cabin she reemerged with his rifle in her hand.

"What are we to do?" she asked as she handed over the rifle. Rice took her hand and pulled her in close, happy that they were both still alive and unhurt from the ordeal.

"We will fort up inside tonight," Rice answered his brave wife. "At sunup we will start for Fort Grider, if all is clear. This could have been a smaller offshoot of a larger party of warriors. We need to give the alarm. The whole Blue Ridge could be in danger if we don't."

Chapter 23

Moore's Creek Bridge, Feb 27, 1776

Jack was cold, wet and damp and his heart was beating like never before. A silver blanket of fog hung in the air. And in the distance, calls of 'King George,' and the clash of broadswords were heard. Maybe, just maybe, one of the McFall's would step into the sights of his rifle today. He had no way of knowing whether or not they were in the army of Loyalist that lay just across the creek. What he did know was that he was about to take part in the first big battle of the war here in North Carolina. There had been little opportunity so far, to obtain any revenge on his tormentors. Back in December, he missed out on what was now being called the Snow Campaign. Wendell Miller, a German born Captain of the Rowan County Militia had been part in that campaign.

Jack had befriended Miller's son, Fredrick while in Salisbury, and had planned to go along with them, but he had fallen ill with white fever and was too sick to go.

That patriot force under Colonel Richard Richardson had overrun Colonel Thomas Fletchall and Captain Patrick Cunningham's Loyalist militia. Fletchall was captured hiding in a hollowed-out sycamore, and Cunningham was likewise captured a week later but, in a more dignified manner, having been hauled off to Charles town in irons afterwards. What was left of their defeated militia had taken refuge in the Cherokee nations. So, when the younger Miller told Jack that his father was not going on this new campaign, and he wanted a traveling companion, Jack had jumped at the chance. The two had met up with this six-hundred-man Army under Colonel Richard Caswell at New Berne.

The threat coming from across Moore's creek was made up mostly of Scots. The clans of old, were never hesitant to wage war, and so were often at each other's throats. Jack could not understand why these men were willing to bloody their dirks for an English cause. Many of them, their fathers, and their forefathers had suffered greatly under the English yoke and yet, history was going to repeat itself again, for here they were, fighting again, this time for the King of England.

They were under the command of the elderly General Donald MacDonald and his second in command, Colonel Donald McLeod, both veterans of Bunker Hill, and both from clans with warring histories. They were here in the Carolinas to help Governor Josiah Martin recruit a loyalist militia. Martin, much like his Virginia counterpart, Lord Dunmore, had to take refuge with the British Navy out of necessity. But the Virginia governor had been in far more danger, so he was now safely aboard a ship somewhere offshore, while the majority of his men were under siege on Gwynn's Island near Norfolk. A great number of the force opposing Dunmore's men was made up of yet another newly created Patriot regiment from North Carolina. Martin, on the other hand, was aboard a sloop of war, just off the mouth of the Cape Fear River, in the Atlantic. There he could have men of influence come aboard the ship, or meet him at Fort Johnston, which also provided him protection from the rebels. This had kept the royal government afloat in North Carolina, but he could not assemble a militia under those conditions.

MacDonald and McLeod had labored tirelessly on Governor Martin's behalf, and the results of their labors was a twenty-five-hundred-man force, that had mustered in at Cross Creek. Their plans were to march to the coast after the muster, and meet up with British troops at Wilmington. However, disputes in their ranks, and the lack of any British regulars to keep order, as well as a shortage of muskets, had caused mass desertions. Now they were reduced to only eighteen hundred men, still more than enough to win the day, they believed. Victory certainly could be theirs, especially with all those North Carolina Whigs foolishly off in Virginia, chasing Dunmore, instead of staying in their home colony to protect their own.

Having received word of a Continental regiment, under Colonel James Moore blocking MacDonald's path into the city, the old Scotsmen chose an alternate route, down to the confluence of the Black River and Moore's Creek.

Jack's eyes peered into the fog where he saw the gray outline of a kilted highlander approaching the bridge. Not a McFall, but a target nevertheless. The sight of this Scot raising his broadsword, and the sound of bagpipes made Jack's blood rise. A jolt of adrenaline made him forget just how tired he was. He, along with the rest of Caswell's men, had had a hard march from Corbett's Ferry to beat the Tories to this bridge. Their arrival was a great relief to Lt. Colonel Alexander Lillington and his small group of patriots, who had just been stationed here at the bridge a few days before. Earthworks had been dug after their arrival. Old Mother Covington and her Daughter, as their two canons were affectionately called, were placed in the line. But Caswell still had doubts about the position of his Militia. He ordered the earthworks abandoned, and pulled his men back across the creek. New defenses were built in a circular position. The planking from the bridge was removed and grease was applied to the remaining support beams to slow MacDonald's attack. Many believed they would not dare a crossing at all now.

The Loyalist, likewise had had a difficult march here, so much so that the aging MacDonald had to turn his command over to McLeod to lead the forthcoming charge.

Jack pulled back the hammer of his rifle as Frederick announced, "They will be like a bunch of drunks on New Year's when they try to cross that bridge. It will be quite a surprise, eh Jack?"

"Who goes there?" a voice yelled from down the Whig line.

"A friend of King George!" was the replied from across the water.

Shots rang out on both sides of the creek as the battle began in earnest. Jack saw his mark fall after pulling his trigger. He quickly began to reload his rifle as he heard the thudding sound of the enemy's musket balls slam into the loose dirt of the earthwork that he was standing behind. The smoke from his rifle and everyone else's joined with the fog making it much more difficult to see what was happening on the other side of the bank. When he fired his second round he simply aimed straight across, without seeing a target. He just relied on his best guess as to where the Tories where and hoped his elevation would be true, not too high. Whig Captain Thomas Wade ran down the line calling out to all "hold your fire until they cross the bridge. We need to see what we are firing on boys. When you hear Old Mother Covington roar, knock down whatever is left standing."

"Look there," Frederick said, pointing to the bridge with his ramrod, where the highlanders were making their way over the slippery beams. "I wager only a few of those cur dogs will make it across."

But to Frederick's surprise, the attackers slowed their pace after seeing what was causing their difficulties. They took smaller steps, but they kept advancing, most of them keeping their balance. Less and less of them were falling from the ties, and into the cold water below. One made his way across, then another, and another after that. Jack shouldered his rifle one more time as Mother Covington roared her terrible rage. The Patriot gun volley that followed put a timely end to the attack, quickly killing McLeod in the process. The surviving Loyalists fled back across the creek as best as they could. Some were shot while still in the water, others while trying to re-cross the bridge.

Jack licked his dry lips with his tongue as he looked at Frederick. "Victory" he yelled. "They may have been friends of the King, but we sure are not. They have no friends here among us. The British may hold on to Wilmington, but the back country is still ours."

Chapter 24

A Blue Frock Coat

Fort Grider was overflowing with people. It had been a place of refuge in the past, sometime crowded, but nothing like this. After word of Rice and Rachael's ordeal spread through the area, settlers began to pour in with alarming news of their own. Sightings of Indians was a common theme. Both Beaver and Cub Creeks had numerous signs and John Grider had tracked down, and spied on a large party of warriors between the two streams before returning to the fort. They were heading east, but how far and where to, he had no clue.

The overcrowding had come to such a point that the woman and children had taken up all the room inside Old Frederick's home. He, along with all the other men, was sleeping outside in order to accommodate everyone who needed shelter. No one seemed to mind the crowding, it was worth it to be inside the safe walls of the stockade. While the crowding was something that could be ignored, low supplies was another matter altogether. Food would be running low for everyone here within days if the people could not return to their respective homes. Ten fires had burned inside the courtyard last night to keep the men warm. And it would take that many again tonight. Two parties where to go out today, one for firewood and the other to see if the Cherokee were still about. Rice would be in the latter of the two. Old Frederick and Rachael's father Charles would watch over the woodcutters with rifles while Rice and the Grider boys would head out into the woods as a unit of rangers.

Little John Grider was moving quickly across the frozen forest floor leading the way. Val and Martin were on the right flank of their brother while Rice and Fed were on the left. All were on foot except for Jacob who was bringing up the rear on the only horse that was in the party. If ambush and disaster were to fall upon the men he was to ride back to Ft Grider and inform the defenders and help prepare for any incoming attacks.

As Rice was walking along the cold ground peering into the leafless trees up ahead, Fed walked over and whispered "Did Rachael really slit that savages' throat?"

"Indeed, she did" Rice answered with a grin, "as slick as a ribbon. The act even took me by surprise. By killing him, she gave us an advantage that I alone would not have had. If she had not made the first move the way she did, and at the time she did, I can't say what would have become of us."

"Maybe she should be here with us today, instead of you," Fed suggested, rolling his eyes in Rice's direction.

Rice answered silently by cocking his head to one side with a raised eyebrow indicating 'maybe so', but his smile faded as he saw fresh moccasin tracks on the ground. They were moving through a patch of grass that was growing under several walnut trees. The frost covered blades had been snapped off and were mashed down by the weight of a moccasin shod Indian who had passed thru this morning. Fed had not missed the sign either. As he gave out the cooing sound of a dove to get the other men's attention, he picked up a second set of tracks. By the time the other Grider men had reached Rice and Fed, the two sets of tracks they were following had merged into a well-traveled path made by ten or more Cherokee.

Val looked down the beaten path that led east to the Little River. Then turning back to Jacob, he said, "You need to ride back and relay the news that they are still here among us."

"No, I'm going with y'all!" replied Jacob

"Not this time," Martin said, agreeing with Val. "They need to know about this back at the fort. That is why we brought the horse in the first place, and that is why we are here".

"I know" Jacob replied leaning forward on his mount. "Why don't you go instead John? You were out all day yesterday. Here, you take the horse."

John looked up at his brother, and without saying a word he turned and led the others down the trail. Jacob straightened up in the saddle, letting out a disappointed groan as the rangers moved on without him. With a tap of his foot and a slap of the reins, he turned his mount and bolted off back in the direction he had just come.

Within half an hour, the sun was high enough to melt away the frost, but by now Rice and the other were well on their way to catching up to the Indians.

The spacing of the tracks the Indians left behind indicated a party of men walking in short and constant steps. By pursuing at a fast trot, Rice and his friends were gaining ground with every step. The pursuit came to an abrupt end as Fed slowed his pace and came to a stop behind a large oak tree. He pulled back the hammer of his New England style fowler as he caught his breath. As Rice took a knee behind a fallen log he saw why Fed had stopped. The Cherokee had halted their march and were standing in a circle and talking. They were all gathered around one warrior who seemed to be the leader of the party.

The plan from the beginning had been to only observe the Indians, determine their numbers, and see if they were indeed a threat. Rice counted twelve, but unlike the party that had intruded into his home, these warriors had painted faces. This was obviously a war party. Val waved to John and motioned him to crawl up beside him.

John fell on his stomach and slithered over to Val as silently as if he were a snake.

"They are going to hit the James Phipps cabin," Val whispered to his brother.

"I believe you are right." John replied "If James is not forting up at Mulberry Fields, he and his family are just over that hill.

Rice watched the Indians as they broke out of their conference. And just as Val and John had predicted, instead of walking down the path they had been on, the Indians turned up the hill. As they reached its peak they began to spread out   preparing to attack.

"We must intervene, "Rice spoke up. "We can't just walk away and leave that poor family to their fate."

A smile spread over Val's face "Jacob's going to be mad as a hatter when he hears he missed this. Well boys, we will have the high ground, and surprise on our side, we should be all right"

Rice took off up the hill as did the Griders, and as he reached the top the Phipps cabin came into view. It was sitting at the end of the valley, backed up to the hill he had just climbed. No real plan of attack had been discussed, there had not been enough time. It would be frontier combat; every man for himself, to a point. Rice would fight at his own pace, relying on his best skills to stay alive, but still fighting with the rest of the Grider men as a group.

The Cherokee were still in view having hunched down and proceeding slowly, stalking their prey, but paying little attention to their rear. The wind was blowing down the hillside and was helping drown out the sound of the approaching attackers. What the Indians believed would be a great aid in their attack, was about to play a twist on the Cherokee's rear flanks. The wind   muffled Rice's footsteps as well as theirs. He shouldered his rifle, picking a blue frock coat as his target. The unsuspecting Cherokee's head was shaved smooth all the way to the top of his head. Only a round lock of hair, no more than four inches around was left at the very top. His earlobes had been stretched out, and now were pulled back and tied tightly to the back of his neck to keep them from catching on any low-lying limbs. His face was painted red and black to complete his war mask. The stock of his rifle was painted blue to match his frock coat. Rice squeezed his trigger and watched stoically as the warrior fell. The sound of gunfire echoed down the hillside as the Grider's let loose their own devastating volley, cutting the Cherokee's numbers in half. Having been completely taken by surprise, and not knowing how many were engaging them, the surviving warriors fled to the North leaving their dead and dying behind. Rice sprinted down the hill like a madman running from hell. Still not satisfied with his pace he discarded his rifle to increase his speed. He pulled his scalping knife from his belt as his hip made contact with the ground. His body came to a sliding stop as he grabbed the collar of the frock coat. Quickly he rolled the Indian's body over and grabbed the lock of hair with his offhand. Rice heard the scraping sound of his blade running over the bone as he detached the scalp. Looking to his left, Rice saw Val bent over, struggling with the dying Cherokee at his feet. As Rice walked over he saw Val step away from his victim with a look of disbelief on his face. Realizing that something was wrong, Rice looked at the Cherokee for a closer look, but not wanting to get too close, a wounded bear could still do damage.

"Damn you Brian Downey" Val said as Rice suddenly recognized the Cherokee for the white man he was. Rice had shod Downey's horse last spring. He was a quiet, affable man who never spoke of politics, often rumored to be an atheist but nothing to indicate a nature like this.

"You were with that dog, Thomas Fletchall, weren't you?" Val asked, tapping the barrel of his rifle against his own leg. "Been a lot of talk of y'all raiding alongside Dragging Canoe, Cameron's work they say. See where a poor choice in life can lead you. And you people have the gall call us traitors."

Panic filled Downey's eyes as his head began to jerk back and forth. He reached up and grabbed Rice's hand and pulled him down to his side, to say his dying words. As he tightened his grip he looked into Rice's eyes and said. "Rice, for God's sake, don't end up like me, for I can see the gates of hell and the flames are licking me in the face! My soul is lost for sure. Oh God, it's real! Hell is real!"

His grip refused to relax as the life left his body. Rice was forced to pry his hand from Downey's fingers as the dead man stared into horrors only he could see. Slowly Rice stood up and walked away a few steps. He looked down at the fresh scalp still in his hand and dropped it on the ground.

Chapter 25

Annabel

This particular evening, Jack found himself just outside of Salisbury at the small community of Granite Quarry. His host was Michael Braun, a German immigrant who had settled here in 1758. Frederick Miller had talked Jack into attending this pre-wedding party, even though Jack did not know a single soul there. Frederick's sister Sarah, was the intended of Mr. Braun's son, John. Frederick was here acting as his sister's chaperone, but everyone knew there was another reason why he was here. And that was to win the heart and hand of another member of the Braun family. To that end, Frederick was off on a hand in hand walk with John's sister Margaret Braun, Jack was starting to wonder why he had let himself get talked into coming here in the first place. His gun was not needed here. Everyone felt safe after the worst of the Tories were put down at Moore's Creek. Up East in Boston, Massachusetts, General Washington had driven the British out of the city after a long siege.

The Cherokee would not attack a settlement as big as Salisbury now. Rice, on the other hand could use his help this spring. Maybe he would be of better use at Mulberry Fields or even Fort Grider.

As he was sitting on the top rail of the wooden split rail fence that ran around the Braun's stone home, his eyes fell on the blue Continental uniform of the intended groom. He thought to himself that maybe he should go all the way and enlist in the Continental line, and leave the militia behind. Most of the men in the militia had a family, or a woman to come home to when they were not called up. They never knew the loneliness he always felt upon their return home. It would at least keep him with a job. Lately it seemed the only work he could get was something that would only last a short time. The life of a soldier could be his calling he supposed. Shaking his head, Jack turned his attention to the mug in young Braun's hand. A drink would help kill some time while he waited, until Frederick returned, he thought. So, he hopped down off the rail and made his way around the other guest. Most of them could speak English, but some knew only a few words which they used on the occasions where English was required. They preferred to use the language of their German homeland instead. Jack made his way to a table that sat under the budding blooms of a redbud tree. He picked up an empty mug and presented it to the pretty young barmaid that was passing out the drinks to the guest. She filled his mug without a word, and watched as he took his first drink. He nodded his head in thanks to the young lady, as silently as she had poured the drink. She smiled back, a smile that lit up her face and crinkled her clear green eyes.She wore a kerchief, which had slipped back on her head, revealing her long blond hair.. He was instantly smitten by her beauty, and as he turned away he said out loud to himself "She just might be worth the trouble it would take to learn a little German."

"No need for that, good sir, Yes, I speak German, but I also speak English," she replied "So if you are speaking of me, either language will suffice."

Being somewhat caught off guard Jack began to apologize for his remark. "I am sorry Mistress," he proclaimed as he was removing his hat. "If I had known you could understand what I was saying, I would have never spoken as I did."

"Well, if that be the case, I am happy you did not know," she smiled." It is nice for a woman to know that someone notices her every once in a while. Did you think I was another of the Braun's daughters?"

"Truly, I did." Jack answered, enjoying the smile on this lovely girl's face. "If I am mistaken, the mistake is all mine, but one not out of the realm of possibility.

"That, I am afraid, is well out the realm of possibility. You see, I am indentured to Master Braun these last four years."

"So, you have three more years to serve?" Jack asked

"No, only two more months," She said over her shoulder as she filled a mug for another guest. Jack's eyes fell upon her wrist as she sat the pitcher back on the table. His eyes continued up her arm admiring her skin until it reached the edge of her sleeve. The roundness of her breast was the last target for his gaze until he finally returned his look to her green eyes, as she continued on. "My first two years was under a wretched old widow woman back in New Bern. She sold me off to the Braun family. That was a grand day I can tell you. I have not been hungry one day since. She was as mean as a work day is long. But the Braun's have been good to me. They gave me this fine dress that fooled you into mistaking me for one of them."

"That it did." Jack replied as he not only admired the dress, but the beauty in it as well. "So, your freedom is within sight. What are your plans for the day it arrives?" Jack asked.

"I can't say. Not a lot of options for a girl from Ringwold, England."

"I would not say that, Annabel!" Frederick announced as he stepped up beside Jack, still locked arm in arm with Margaret. "You never know what the future may hold, ain't that right Jack?"

"You're not going to get an argument from me," Jack replied. "Mine always seems to be changing. A lot can happen in two months Miss Annabel, and it does not always have to be bad."

"Yes Annabel," Frederick continued, "All kinds of opportunity are at hand. I hear good things about Mulberry Fields' future. Could be Jack here, could be of some assistants to you in that regard.

I understand that Colonel Cleveland is putting up some land for sale on the Yadkin. Maybe that is something you should pounder as well Jack."

Margaret smiled and pulled Frederick away by the arm, and as the two walked away, she looking back over her shoulder and said. "Aren't you the matchmaker?"

"We will see," he replied "I hope for both their sakes that I am. They would be a handsome pair, don't you think?"

Chapter 26

A Murder of Crows

William Hannon had big plans for the day. It was May, corn planting time, and if all went well, by nightfall half of his crop would be planted and the other half would have been plowed. Spring was a nice welcome for his family. The children were smiling more these days, now that the God-awful winter was over. It had been hell for him. The Pacolet River Valley was always cold, situated between the Green River and the Pacolet, in February, but none as cold as the day he had dug his poor wife Sara's grave beside his cabin. The soil was frozen hard that terrible day. Only a pickaxe could penetrate the ground and then only small flakes would break free. Life in the backcountry is hard: even more so on a woman who was the mother of eight. She was simply worn down to a nub. Life was exhausting, and she had no more strength to continue on in this world of hard labor. Her end finally came about two in the afternoon, she had passed out of this life with her bedside surrounded by sobbing children and a grieving husband holding her cold hand.

Yet life must go on, so William Hannon[19] found himself, along with his four oldest children in the far side of his flat bottom land that ran along the river. As his old red oxen reached the far end of the fertile bottom, he pulled the gentle beast to a halt. He glanced back

---

[19] William Hannon's homestead was located in western Polk County North Carolina near the town of Columbus.

across the field he had just turned over, and proudly watched as his two daughters dropped the seed corn on the ground while their brothers follow along behind with homemade wooden hoes in hand, covering the kernels over with a swift downward chop of their hoes[20]. As he tied the reins of his ox to the handle of his plow made of two sourwood saplings held together by thongs of deer hide, he heard the cawing sound of several black crows flitting about in the woods that flanked the bottom. In the far distance, at the east end of the bottom his eyes spotted white smoke swirling out of his cabin's chimney top. Edwin and Winifred must just have kindled the fire for tonight's meal he thought. They were responsible enough to watch over little William and John and tend to the house, but not quite old enough for the field just yet. As he walked over to the river bank for a drink of its clear water, he again heard the sound of even more crows cawing. He looked up into the treetops, but no birds were in sight, even the clear sky above was void of a flock flying overhead. Stopping before he reached the river bank, he quickly turned for his old 50 caliber Hudson Valley fowler that his father had used in the French and Indian War. The weapon was tied to the back of the oxen but before he could reach it the bawling animal fell to the ground in pain as three shots from the woods struck it in the side. Ole Red made a lunge for freedom, but the plow kept him in check. The fowler fell to the ground, and it was the worst kind of bad luck to have the ox fall upon it. In so doing, the fate of William Hannon and his family was sealed. As he fell to his knees with an arrow in his back, he could see that his two daughters were already dead. The Cherokee warriors were still mutilating their bodies, with quick, deadly downward chops of their tomahawks. The boys, being fleeter of foot, were running for the

---

[20] The names of the children working in the field have been lost over time.

cabin, but they too were soon cut off by a second group of warriors It was the last thing he saw, as the light went out of their father's eyes.

Back at the cabin, ten-year-old Edwin heard the dreaded sound of Indian war whoops, and the terrified cries of his dying siblings. "Indians" he yelled to his sister. "You get William and run for the cane break. I'll grab John and try to cross the river." At that, he bolted out the front door with John in his young arms, while Winnie darted out the back door, pulling William by his arm. As she entered the brake that was twenty-five yards from the cabin, she could hear Edwin screaming at the top of his lungs near the river bank. She looked back to see two-year-old John still in the grip of Edwin's hand, but Edwin's other hand was in the hand of a Cherokee. The Warrior made a fearsome strike with his tomahawk ending little John's life. Edwin released his brother's hand and dove into the water and swam to the far bank. As he climbed out of the water, he saw John's murderer enter his father's cabin, with John's small blond scalp clutched in his hand. He watched as smoke billowed out the front and back doors of his home. 'The Cherokee must have taken the fireplace shovel and poured its hot coals over the floor, setting it afire' he thought. Praying that Winnie and William had made it out undetected, his heart pounded as he saw the killer of his brother bolt out the front doorway with a basket of goods in his hand. The Warrior stopped for a moment watching the flames consume the cabin, then letting out one last war whoop he returned to the war party that was now butchering Ole Red.

Edwin fell to the ground sobbing, but still remembered his father's instructions. Paw always said if they were attacked, not to return to the house until several hours had passed. All he could do now was wait. Then, if they were still alive, he would lead Winnie and William downstream to Colonel Earle's blockhouse where they would be safe[21].

Chapter 27

A Tender Hand

Iona McFall stood outside Robert Cleveland's cabin in tears. She had been turned away by every storekeeper and cabin owner in Mulberry Fields. She was angry and upset at being shunned, all because of her husband Arthur's Tory leanings. The McFall name had been almost completely destroyed by her brothers in law's actions. She was devastated by the cruel treatment she had just received from people she had known for years. She had never been disliked before, she had always remained calm and kind when dealing with others. She avoided topics that would agitate. People were drawn to her because of her beauty, but soon found that her heart was as sweet and beautiful as her physical appearance. Her goodness had brought out the best in people, both women and men, even after her marriage to Arthur. Yet now, here she stood, alienated and alone.

Rachael had heard rumblings of resentment for the McFall's, deservedly so in most cases, but not in Iona's. She herself was guilty of spreading word of their bad deeds, for she had seen their awful work with her own eyes. But Iona had done nothing to earn the chastisement she had just received, other than having wed into the McFall family. Rachael had considered Iona a friend before the war, and saw no reason for their friendship to end now because of it. Besides, Arthur was yet to take up a gun in the name of the King, and Rachael hoped, that just maybe his die would not be cast in that direction after all, but only time would tell. She had met Iona two

---

21 Edwin did indeed lead the other children to their Minister Uncle, John Earle's blockhouse in safety. They were the only survivors of the Hannon massacre. All three lived out long lives with William becoming a prominent Baptist Minister.

years before, during her short friendship with John. They had based their friendship on the love they both held for dancing, hats and other feminine joys. And even though Iona had married Arthur, they both had a strong dislike for George, and even John, after Rachael had seen his true nature. Iona had even advised Rachael to break ties with John before the two could got too involved. She had said there was only one McFall worth having, and she already had him.

Rachael and Rice had ridden over to Mulberry Fields this morning to deliver some hay cutting sickles to one of Rice's customers. With her husband, off with John Grider to have a drink and to find the sickle's new owner, Rachael had learned of Iona's presence in town from a gossiping old woman who had proudly announced that she had ran off that awful Iona McFall. Rachael had quickly roamed the growing village looking for her friend, who must be in a great deal of distress. And now, having spotted her, she walked up to Iona and placed a loving arm around her shoulder.

"Iona, how are you dear? It's been so long since we could talk. We need to catch up on one another's doings," Rachael proclaimed in a tender voice.

Iona wiped a tear away from one of her green eyes and said. "I have had better days, that is certain. It is so good to see your friendly face Rachael, but maybe you should not be seen with a supposed Tory, even if I'm not quite sure I am one."

"Nonsense," replied Rachael as she pushed a few stray red hairs back under Iona's straw hat in an effort to comfort her friend. "If they don't like seeing me conversing with a good friend, they can just look the other way."

Iona took Rachael's arm and led her around the corner of the cabin. The two walked until they stopped at an old oak tree where they both sat on the ground under it's cool shade. "I appreciate the gesture, but these are uncaring times. Why, Rachael the Cleveland's would not even sell me a small pair of scissors. Arthur had hoped if I came in alone I could buy a few things, but I guess not"

"If that is all you need, Rice can make you up a pair in no time" Racheal exclaimed.

"Oh, my goodness, that's right," Iona said grabbing Rachael hand. "You too have entered into matrimony since we last spoke. You and Rice have been the subject of many a spiteful conversion over at John's since he got word of your marriage. How has it been, is Rice as devoted to you as much now as he was before the wedding?"

"Yes. Very much so. I dare say with just as much devotion as Arthur as shown for you." Rachael answered while patting her friend's hand.

"I would hope not, hopefully he can muster up more than Arthur has." Iona laughed. "Thank you, Rachael, I needed a good laugh. If our station here remains as it is, the McFall's may have to go to Cross Creek, where the real Tories are for our future needs. It's hard to believe, but this could be our last meeting for a good long while. The folks around these parts may force us to the King's standard."

"Oh, I pray not" Rachael exclaimed. "However, if that is the case, you will have your scissors, and you won't have to wait on Rice to make them either. You just sit right here while I go up to the store. They will sell me a pair for sure, and you and I will have the last laugh at their cold-hearted expense."

As Rachael made her way back to the Cleveland's cabin determined to buy the scissors, she began to realize that the war in the backcountry was not only going to be waged against the British regulars, but also against the Colony's own citizens. Furthermore, it would not only be fought with musket and sword.

Cruelty could inflict pain, without a single shot being fired. The weaker of the two sides would be persecuted by the stronger. Mercy and kindness could very well be the first casualty of the war. She hoped the Whigs would always be able to hold the upper hand and keep the Tories in check. If men like the McFall's and Gideon Wright could gain power, it would be her family in need and not Iona's. But she did hold out hope, that just maybe all of those battles being fought up north, would end the war before it raised its ugly head here in the Carolinas.

Chapter 28

Just Out of View

Rice reached and grabbed the iron poker he always kept by his firebox. He stuck it inside one of the red-hot links of the chain that he was forging. After placing it back on his anvil, he tapped it a few more times with his hammer, to round out the oversized hoop link that would be the chain's end into the correct shape. It was fifteen feet long now that the last link was finished. It's hook on the far end was cool w, and soon this end would be as well. He left it hanging there over the anvil to cool as he walked out of his shop. He made his way up to the cabin and walked inside its open door. Rachael was nowhere to be seen inside. Neither was Duchess, who by now was truly Rachael's pet and on longer Rice dog. She always shadowed Rachael's ever move. Maybe the two of them were outside in the garden he thought as he stepped outside, passing through the cabin's back door. She was not at the henhouse, Rice and seen a basket of fresh eggs inside on the tabletop, so he knew that she had already been there today. After checking that she was not gardening either, he continued on out of the yard's boundary and into the tree line that ran alongside Warriors Creek. The closer he got, the louder the sound of the water running off the rocks and down the falls became. As the water came into view Rice spotted Duchess lying asleep beside an empty kettle by the creek bank where Rachael liked to wash the laundry. However, today there was no basket of clothing accompanying the kettle, just Rachael's brown butternut dress draped over the top of the kettle with two dry towels folded on top.

Her shoes were neatly placed beside it, with one of her white stocking stuffed down inside each shoe. He knew that he had found her in a compromising situation, because this was the favorite bathing spot of them both. He was somewhat surprise that she had done this by herself. Even though the trees shielded this view from the house and grounds, she was shy about bathing here, and had never swam here alone before. She was still not at ease enough to stand in the waist deep water under the falls, but there was one large boulder that was as big as their cabin sitting in the middle of the creek. He knew she had to be on the other side of it, just out of view.

He reached down, grabbing both towels in his hand, and with three giant leaps found himself on the backside of the bolder. It was lowest on this end so all he had to do now was crawl up to the top and he would have quite a view. He kicked off his boots, pulled his blouse over his head, and slowly made his way to the top on his hands and knees. Placing his chin on top of his clasped fingers, he gazed down upon his topless wife standing in the water. Her hair was still dry, at least on top, but it was so long that it flowed down her back and into the water. Her back was turned to him, as she kept her eyes on the far bank feeling confident that any intrusion would come from that direction. Slowly, she began to turn his way reaching down and cupping her palms full of water. As she raised her hands and arms to wet her face, the smooth roundness of her breast was within his full view. At that moment, Rice was thankful to God for creating something this beautiful and sending her into his life. He watched, silently, as she raised one leg and placed it on top of a small stone, just under the water. As she bent over to wash her leg, Rice dropped a small pebble into the water from above. Its splash drew her attention to the ripples it formed. Pulling her arms up over her breast, she squatted down into the water up to her chin, as she called out Rice's name.

He quickly replied, not wanting to put any more fear into her heart than he already had. "If I had known you were going to cover up so quickly I would never have dropped that stone into the water."

"Land sakes Rice, you put the fear of God into me" she said looking up at him, still submerged in the water.

"Stand back up for me, and put your hands back on top of your head, like you were a moment ago my love."

"How long have you been up there? And I will do no such thing!" She replied smiling.

"Why not?" Rice asked still looking down from above. "Are we not man and wife?"

Rachael did not answer, she just slowly stood back up into the sunlight and posed as he asked. She stood there for a moment staring up at him, until finally he reached over and picked up a towel and dropped it down to her.

"Why give me the towel now?" she asked as she held it to her chest.

"You look cold down there" he said as he rolled over onto his back. He raised his hips off the stone, pulling his trousers down his legs.

"What makes you think the water is cold?" she asked, tossing the towel away on top of a dry boulder protruding out of the creek.

"On account of my two girls are standing up at attention." Rice replied referring to her erect nipples.

On hearing Rice's explanation, Rachael fell back into the water and began to swim away. She tossed him her most winsome smile saying, "If that is the case, then why don't you jump in and help me warm them up? Besides, why do you think I brought two towels instead of only one?"

Rice smiled and without hesitation, jumped off his perch splashing into the water below. As his head broke the surface Rice turned towards her, and pushed his feet off of the bolder he had just leaped from, propelling himself towards his wife.

"All right then," he said as he pulled her into his arms. "Never let it be said that I failed to helped a lady in need". As he delivered his first kiss, his only thought was that it was indeed nice to be young lovers, and of one heart with the other.

Chapter 29

The Coming Storm

Isaac Thomas [22] was a worn and weary man. He was sick and tired of being stuck in the middle of an approaching storm. Suspicious looks were becoming an everyday occurrence not only from his own people, but from the Cherokee as well. Being an Indian trader in times like these had brought his allegiance into question more than once. He had been among the Cherokee for 45 years, and had even taken one as his wife so the Whigs suspected he had Tory leaning. On the other hand, Alexander Cameron had flat out told him that his fate would suffer if he ever doubled crossed the British. Even Dragging Canoe was debating whether or not to keep a white man around who could possibly act as a guide for a militia that could destroy every Cherokee Village in the mountains.

Alexander Cameron was the one who had gotten him into this mess. The pay was good at first, but now Thomas was not so sure it was worth getting killed over. He had his eye on a spot of land on the Pigeon River where he planned to make one last settlement, [23] but only a live man could do that.

His troubles all began when Thomas delivered a dispatch to William Bean and Captain John Carter of the Watauga settlements at Sycamore Shoals on the first of June. The document listed the Cherokee Nation's demands. The settlers were to leave behind their leased lands and return back to the Yadkin Valley within twenty days or suffer the same fate as the William Hannon family. Isaac also

---

[22] Isaac Thomas 1735-1818 had established his reputation trading with the Cherokee in the vicinity of Fort Loudon about 1755.

[23] Isaac Thomas did settle on this spot. It is today the city of Sevierville Tennessee.

relayed the news that some white hunters had been killed in Powell's Valley. Their detached scalps having been the centerpiece at a war dance back at Chilhowee, to the delight of Dragging Canoe and even Old Abram, another war chief whose tolerance for the white man was beginning to run thin. If the settlers did not obey these demands, one thousand to fifteen hundred warriors would descend upon Fort Caswell [24].

And what thanks did Thomas receive for being the bearer of this bad news? A court appearance before Captain John Shelby, resulting in sixteen days under lock and key. Thomas had received enough support from Captain Carter and a few others to be cleared of sedition, but after surviving such a narrow escape, he had half a mind to wash his hands of the whole deal. Why should he risk his scalp for unappreciative people? But his friend and fellow trader Thomas Moore had counseled him saying it was in his best interest to keep the Indians at peace. He was beginning to see the wisdom in that counsel, especially now that word of an up and coming British officer, by the name of Charles Cornwallis, had reached the Shoals. He and his men had rowed up the Cape Fear River to revenge a British sloop, *The Falcon*, after Whig militia had fired upon it from the river bank. The tall Londoner soon overran Brunswick Town. The display of British power had overwhelmed many patriots, causing some to react rashly. Hence, the annoying court-martial that Thomas had just endured. Now that Thomas had been cleared, Captain Carter had sent a return letter with him, back to the Cherokee, asking why his red brothers would now wage war on their good friends here at the Shoals. He also asked for more time, proclaiming twenty days was just not enough time to move all of his people out of the settlement.

---

[24] Fort Caswell named after Gov. Richard Caswell was built between 1775 and 1776: Now known as Fort Watauga to avoid confusion with Fort Caswell a Civil War fort on Oak Island in North Carolina.

Thomas knew this was just a ploy by the Captain, but he would still deliver it back to the Cherokee anyway. Tensions were high on all sides, and Thomas could feel the presence of onlookers on his return trip thru the forest . He was sure he had been followed by an Indian on his way to the settlements, no doubt a spy ordered by Dragging Canoe. After a few miles had passed behind him on the return trip. 'The Bench' made little effort to conceal his presence, confirming Isaac Thomas' suspicions. But it also put the envoy at ease, because the red headed Indian would have never shown himself if Thomas was still under suspicion. The jail time must have helped his image with the Cherokee. Years spent around the Cherokee had convinced him that there was something very wrong with Bench. When he looked at you, he had the look of an attacking bear just as it lowered its ears before charging. Thomas was not the only one to see this, even the Cherokee knew that this young man had inner demons. Some in the nation thought it could be put to good use, but others were not so sure.

Bench was not the only person Thomas met on the trail back to the Indian villages. Tories roughed up by Captain Shelby where fleeing the Watauga settlements out of fear. Cameron had offered relocation to western Florida the year before, and some was praying that offer was still good. A few were forced to take an oath to establish a British free state by Shelby, but they felt that would be of little matter once Dragging Canoe laid Fort Caswell to ash. That feeble document would burn along with the fort's logs. The Bench had sent runners into Chilhowie to announce Thomas' return, as protocol required. Thomas was happy the Bench had done so. He was already late due to the sixteen-day delay and the last thing he needed was a Cherokee nation upset over bad etiquette. He hoped Alexander Cameron was still there so he could turn the reply over to him instead of Dragging Canoe. If not, he would seek out the beloved women, [25] a cousin of the Canoe and an old friend from his and her childhood. She was known to have a good head on her shoulders. As the village came into sight, one more thought came to Isaac Thomas's mind. The next dispatch would not be carried by him. After all, he was not the only Indian trader among the Cherokee. let Nathaniel Gist dirty his hands some.

Chapter 30

Nightmares

Rice rolled over violently throwing the quilt that was wrapped tightly around his neck off of his shoulders downward onto the foot of the bed. It was still very dark inside the cabin but he saw movement out of the corner of his eye. He sprung up from his sleep as swiftly as he ever had in the past; as though he was dodging a charging bull. In one frantic motion he pulled his rifle to his shoulder bringing it to bear on his adversary just across the room. As his eyes began to focus to the firelight he realized all he had seen was his own reflection bouncing off Rachel's pewter pitcher that was sitting on the table close by the fire. He propped his rifle back up in its corner before sitting back on the bed. He lay back down beside his wife,

[25] Nancy Ward 1738-1822 Wife of Kingfisher of the Deer clan. She had been educated by Moravians as a young girl which had given her somewhat of a favorable view of the Caucasian race. So much so that her second husband was an Irishman named Bryant Ward. Although known mostly as a great advocate of peace her first claim of fame was her brave actions at the battle of Taliwa in 1755.

feeling a little silly that he had startled himself. He ran his fingers across his chest, watching his reflection bounce back off the shiny pewter, as he remembered the dream that had just awakened him. It was blurry, like most of his dreams were; but he wanted to recount it before it faded completely away. He took his hand and rubbed his forehead with his fingertips. The pressure felt good above his closed eyes, causing the dream to reappear in his mind.

It began just as he was now, with he and Rachael lying in bed. War whoops had awakened him. Through his window he could see an overwhelming war party just outside the cabin. They were painted black from the chest up as they danced around a ceremonial fire. Then somehow, he was outside standing beside the burned-out ashes of the fire, but the Cherokee were gone. When he looked back at the cabin it was small and far off in the distance, miles away it seemed. Rice felt the fire had been a well-planned trick to get him away from the house. As he was running back to the cabin he could hear screams coming from inside. But with every step he took, the cabin seemed further and further away. It was at that moment in the dream, he realized, that he awoke from the nightmare, just moments ago. He rolled back over on his side, placing his hand on Rachael shoulder giving her a gentle shake "Rachael, are you awake?" he asked.

"Yes, about half," she replied sleepily. "You woke me a while ago talking in your sleep."

"What did I say?" Rice asked.

"I can't say for sure" she replied. "It was more like wails and moans than words: just gibberish. A bad dream?" she asked.

"More of a nightmare," he replied as he swung his legs over the edge of the bed, sitting back up. "Why didn't you wake me?"

"Mother always said never to wake someone up from a dream. She said it was bad luck to do so. Some even say it can cause a nightmare to come true."

Rice stood up and walked over to the window and peered out into the darkness as Rachael asked him what his dream was about.

"Nothing to speak of" he replied "You know how crazy my dreams can be."

Racheal reached down and pulled the quilt back up under her chin before letting out a long sigh. "You dream a lot more these days it seems to me. Ever since you and the Grider's came back from tracking down that war party at the Phipps cabin; does that haunt you any?"

"Some, I suppose," he answered, "but I think you are the cause of my loss of sleep more than anything else," he teased. "We'll speak of it in the morning. Why don't you go on back to sleep; I'm afraid I'll be up for hours before sleep comes back to me tonight."

"That sounds agreeable to me," she said softly "Good night again my dear, I do love you so."

As he looked back out the window, once again Rachael's words were running through his mind. Dreams coming true were nonsense, he thought to himself, but then he remembered one of his father's old tales about how his own father had once foreseen a horse giving him a bad fall in a dream, before it actually came to be a week later. Maybe it was time to fort up for a while at Old Fed's. At least for a few days until it became clear what the Cherokees were going to do. Rice felt the fears and rumors of coming attacks were well warranted. A little prudence could not hurt in times like these he surmised. Maybe that way he could get some measure of peace at night, but Indians was not the only concern on Rice's mind. The

McFall's were still out there, and revenge was becoming a common theme here in the Carolinas. Like so many of his neighbors, Rice had heard the horrible story of one such case.

At the age of twenty, William Cunningham [26] had originally been a Whig. But after a dispute over ownership of a horse, and having received the wipe for his foul language towards his Captain, who of course, was the same officer that wanted the horse, he had a change of heart and joined a Loyalist Militia. Upon hearing of his desertion, Patriot Captain William Ritchie had ridden to Cunningham's home and beat his crippled brother to death. That not being enough restitution, Ritchie had laid the rod to Cunningham's aging parents. In turn, "Bloody Bill Cunningham" had traveled by foot to the Ninety-Six district of South Carolina and promptly murdered Ritchie in his home. While Rice knew he had not wronged the McFall brothers, it was possible that in their twisted minds, maybe he had. Hoping he was wrong, he feared the summer of 1776 was not going to be peaceful.

Chapter 31

Something Is Amiss

Rice and Rachael had been inside the safe walls of Fort Grider for weeks now; using a very small tack room as their

[26] Captain William "Bloody" Bill Cunningham would go on to be one of the most feared Tories in South Carolina.

temporary home. Once again, the Grider's had offered protection to whoever asked for it and they had plenty of takers. But not as much as in the past; some had gone over to the newly constructed Cathey's Fort. [27] It was further away, located on the Catawba River near Turkey Cove, but it was larger and some thought it was worth the extra risk to travel that far. Others, like Rice's in-laws had simply stayed at home, a decision that troubled Rachael greatly in an already trying time. Rice, however, was doing a good bit of blacksmithing at Old Fed's anvil. He had been paid well, mostly in coin but also with pelts and even with tobacco in some cases. But that work had dried up over the last few days, and Rice was getting tired of fort life and was considering maybe it was time to return home.

As the moon popped over the treetops outside the fort's walls, Val and Martin was sitting around an open fire. They were cooking a large pot of pork smothered in wild onions. Cornbread was also being prepared inside a smaller blackened skillet that the two always used when out in the woods. Rice stood nearby taking in the good smelling aroma as it rose from the pot. As much as he hated to admit it the Grider's were quite good cooks, but that never stopped Rice from saying otherwise. He walked over to the fire, and leaned over the food turning his nose up and shaking his head in a manner that left little doubt of his opinion of their efforts. "Good luck with that boys, hope it stays down this time. The way that stuff looks it could make a man a little green around the Jacks. Hey, is that a tumble bug floating around in there? Oh, don't tell me! I don't want to know if it is or not. I'm heading on in to get something edible to

---

[27] Cathey's Fort was built by William Cathey in what is today the small township of Woodlawn- Sevier, McDowell County, North Carolina. Some have credited George Cathey as its founder. Cathey's Fort would become an assembly point for campaigns against the Cherokee for the rest of the war.

eat. Rachael should have my supper done by now" he said with a satisfied grin.

As Rice was making this way across the fort's courtyard he could hear the two brothers mumbling to themselves behind him as he was walking away. "It truly is a blessing that poor girl took pity on you Rice, and consented to your request of marriage. For we will never indulge your sour palate ever again. Someday you will regret your words tonight when you belly is rubbing a hole on your spine and that wife of your is not around to fed your sorry ass."

Rice just laughed as he walked away. "That may very well come to pass,1 but not tonight boys" he replied.

But then, before he could reach his and Rachael's cabin door he heard John Grider call out "to arms, to arms" from his post at one of the portholes by the fort's locked gate. As he was peering out into the moonlight he spoke again. "I can see them better now. Looks to be two people out there, and they are riding up on a single horse. Still can't tell if they are armed or not just yet."

As Rice manned his post and raised his cocked rifle to his shoulder, He squinted his eyes to focus through the pale light, on the approaching horse. With each step the animal took, the face of the rider became clearer and more familiar. "Stand down boys, it's Jack with a young lass, believe it or not. Open the gate and let them in John," he announced.

As Jack rode in the open gate, he looked down at John and said, "Swing her shut fast John, something is amiss out there tonight." Then, looking at Rice, he pitched his rifle to his friend who snagged it by its stock in midair.

"What's concerning you Jack?" Rice asked as he watched Jack slide from his mount to the ground.

Jack reached up and place both hands around a young woman's waist to help her dismount, before answering the question.

"We came in from Salisbury, and we saw some odd goings on at a few cabins along the way. The first one was at Gideon Wright's Place. A tall pole had been raised by the house. The bark was all peeled off, and a white scarf or maybe a sash tied at the top with the ends flowing in the wind. I kept our distances as we rode by, after that affair at the muster this spring. I thought it queer at first, but we saw another one at John Mason's. Then one at John Folk's place as well."

"All three, Tories to the end." John said looking at his brothers.

"Aye, they are," Jack replied. "That is why I swung around the McFall's. We rode high up on the ridge, but I still saw the pole by the house."

"Father always spoke of the French using pass-over poles back in the Seven Year War." Val said as he walked to his father's door to tell him the news.

"Pass-over pole?" Jack asked "What does that mean?

Rice looked at his friend, handing him back his weapon and said, "Whoever has a pass-over pole, is allied to the British in this case. The savages can't always tell who is a Whig and who is not. This way, when a war party comes to a homestead they know who to attack and who to pass by."

"That is what I thought." Jack replied as he placed his free arm around his companion's waist, pulling her close.

"Well Jack, are you making introductions or are you going to make us endure a long night of wondering who you're traveling companion is?" John asked as he eyed the handsome woman leaning into Jack's embrace

Looking at Rice, and then back at John, a smile parted Jack's usually solemn lips before he replied, "This, my dear friends is Annabel, my newly wedded wife. How 'bout them apples boys? See, not all the news is bad tonight."

"I should say not," Rice replied as he took Annabel's hand in greeting. "I was wondering what was holding you up. Now I see why Salisbury was so appealing. Welcome to Fort Grider Mrs. McCalpin, and if Jack has no objection, you and he are welcome to stay in our cabin tonight. My wife will be wanting to hear all of the details of your and Jack's courtship, so she might just as well hear it from your lips as mine. I would most likely not get the right details anyway. "

As the newlyweds were led to Rice's small room, Martin and Val broke into song, singing "The Mousetrap." Not because the two possessed great voices, but to welcome Jack and his bride with a friendly jest.

"Of all the simple things we do

to rub over a whimsical life.

There is no folly so true as a vain wife.

We're just like a mouse in a trap

or a rat caught in a gin

We sweat and fret and try to escape.

And rue the sad hour we came in."

Chapter 32

Fellow Compatriots

Ben Cleveland was back at the McFall homestead and his temper was at the boiling point. "Son of a bitch" he muttered through gritted teeth. "Jack, that is indeed a pass-over Poll. By the almighty, either it's coming down, or I'm hanging the whole damn lot as the redskin loving Tories that they are."

Overhearing Cleveland's rant, Rice reached around to his hip and grabbed his powder horn hanging down from his left shoulder. He gave it a shake to make sure it still had powder inside. Years ago, he had lost the contents of his horn when its wooden plug somehow came unplugged from its tip. That day he was just out hunting. But today, the way Colonel Cleveland was talking, would not be the time to be short on powder. Trouble had started early this morning when 'Ole Roundabout pounded on the gates of Fort Grider. He was accompanied by ten of his men and they were on their way to Fort Caswell. But once he was told of the pass-over poles that Jack had spotted, his destination changed. Cleveland was becoming a hard man, still fair, but his patriotic fires were making him a man you did not want to deal with if you were still holding to the king's old ways. He had already hanged a Tory by the name of Jackson this spring, for burning Whig cabins. Jackson would not talk after he was captured. It was not even clear if Jackson was the man's first or last name. He remained tight lipped to the end; even as the noose was placed around his neck. "We may not be able to make him talk in this world," Cleveland had said, "But God will in the next." Lines were being drawn all over the back country and everyone knew what side Ben Cleveland was on.

With a kick of his powerful legs to his mount's sides, Cleveland led Rice and the rest of his men down the hill and into the McFall yard. A single horse was tied to the hitching post in front of the cabin's open door. "Alexander McFall!" he called out at the top of his lungs. "Come out here, we have business to conduct."

Jack dismounted and pulled the hammer back on his rifle, as everyone heard the sound of heavy boots walking across the planked flooring just inside the door.

"He's not here, "said Arthur as he stepped outside his father's doorway into the waiting mob. "What's the meaning of this?" he asked, as he placed a haversack over his right shoulder. He held his rifle in a nonthreatening manner in his other hand, as he looked into the eyes of an extremely agitated Ben Cleveland.

"That pole," answered Jack, not giving the Colonel enough time to answer.

"Where is your father?" Cleveland asked cutting off Jack, and once again taking control of the conversation.

"Escorting my Iona to Cathey's Fort, but I do not see how that is any of your concern. You do understand that we are no longer welcome in these parts don't you?"

"What about the pole Arthur?"

"George and John put it up last week. They came in with word of a coming attack. Say what you will Colonel, but if putting up that pole to save a man's family is a bad deed I'll take the consequences every time," Arthur announced boldly. "Besides, the union jack is not flying on top of it, now is it?"

"It just as well could be. If you have a pass-over pole you are allied to the British. Everyone knows that Arthur," Cleveland said grimly. "Someone is going to pay for this and you are the only one here to hang."

Arthur reached into his vest pocket and pulled out a folded piece of paper as he said "So you are hanging Whigs now are you Colonel?" Not every family around here is in complete agreement about this war, like yours seems to be. Like I said we are not too welcome here, so I'm off to the Catawba to join Captain Reuben White and his rebels. We plan to take a few Cherokee scalps. I was fighting the Indians before this war began, and I do not plan to watch them run roughshod over our homes now, if I can help it. This is a correspondence signed in White's own hand, accepting me into his fold. I am sure you are acquainted with all of your fellow compatriots communications. I don't agree with everything that the Continental Congress is saying, but they are right about the Indian situation. So for now, I'm a Whig, same as y'all are.

Cleveland took the letter from McFall's hand and read it without saying another word. He took his time reading it over intently as everyone watched. John Cleveland was already tying a noose on the end of his rope and seemed ready to carry out his brother's threat. But with each line Cleveland read you could see disappointment creep onto his face. Rice was not sure how all of this was going to play out, but he was praying for a peaceful conclusion. If Arthur was being truthful Rice saw no reason for him to swing.

Ben looked up at Arthur, then back to the letter. As he began to refold it he said. "Very well Arthur, this seems to be in order, and it may have saved your neck, but that damn Pole is coming down. And as a member of Captain White's Militia, it is your duty to chop it down. Get an ax and proceed."

Arthur took the paper from Cleveland's hand and smugly placed it back into his vest pocket. He looked up at the pole and said, "Very well, I will do as you say Colonel, but I don't see the point."

With all eyes on him, Arthur walked to the left side of the cabin and pulled an ax from an oak chopping block. With a few swings of the ax, the pole soon fell to the ground. He wiped away the sweat from his forehead with the backside of his arm, then stepping back in front of the open doorway, he flung the ax inside, letting it bounce across the floor flipping end over end with a clatter of noise that seemed to release some of his anger. He spun around and locked the cabin door, using an old rust colored padlock, wordlessly mounted his horse and rode away. As he disappeared into the distant tree line Jack looked at Rice and asked. "Do you believe him?"

"Yes I do, and like he said, we all are a bit leery of the Indians. But what will he do once, and if, we have them under control? Who knows? He did say, "For now I'm a Whig," but what about later on if a British officer comes recruiting on behalf of the King? We know where his brothers stand, but the jury is still out on him. I guess only time will tell."

Overhearing the two, Colonel Cleveland walked his horse over to where Jack was standing and said "Slippery bastards those McFall's, but I am still not sure about that one. Arthur could be redeemable, but those two others?
Not worth a tinker's damn. He never said a thing about John and George's whereabouts. If I was to wager I would say they are with Gideon Wright's boys."

As Jack pulled himself up into his saddle, Rice asked the Colonel "Would you have really hanged him if he had not had that paper?"

Cleveland straightened himself on his mount and leaning forward, he looked straight into Rice's eyes and explained. "When I'm speaking of military or lawful matters I will never say anything that I do not mean; at the campfire, maybe. But not when on duty," Cleveland said coldly. "Yes, that letter did a great service to Arthur today. But I will tell you this Rice, if that was either John or George a pardon from George Washington himself would not have saved either of those two scoundrels."

Jack, having now remounted himself, looked at the colonel, grinned and said, "I'm glad to hear that Ben. I was starting to lose a little faith in you. It's a damn shame those other two were not here to test that rope of your brother's. I wager it would have stretched their necks good and long."

Cleveland's chest rose as he drew in a long breath, and Rice was not too sure this was the time for Jack to be speaking so casually to the Colonel.

"John McFall is on the thin side, a worthless windbag," Ben announced, looking at his younger brother John. "but George's fat arse is almost as big as my own I dare say. He would be a true test I wager, so keep that hemp rope dry, and for God's sake don't let the weevils gnaw on it. When we place the noose around his worthless neck, we don't want it to snap."

Everyone laughed as Ben pushed his hat back a little revealing a smile, but then he looked at Jack and said. "I did not say that in total jest, boys. We'll get that bastard before this is all over."

Chapter 33

A Bloody Fellow Indeed

The afternoon sun was hanging high in the sky on this first day of July. And a loud calling locust, perched high in the top of a black walnut tree announced to all that it was going to be another hot day. Bloody Fellow stood above the waters of Smokey Creek looking at his own reflection bouncing off the God created mirror. His war paint was painted in such a manner that it was meant to send a shiver of fear running up his enemies' spine at just one look from this warrior. His upper body was completely black, as was his face. His war paint was made from ground charcoal mixed with animal fat. He had done this because he was already a battle tested warrior and black symbolize that he had proven himself in battle in the past. He had painted three yellow lines in a downward course from his chin to the hollow of his throat. The first meant that only words of death would be spoken by him this day. The second to symbolize high intellect, and the third to show that he would not die today in battle, for he still had a long life before him. He also had two red stripes running across his face made from red clay. The top one spanned from one ear to the other, crossing his eye brows on its way across. This let all know that only war was on his mind. The lower stripe began at the bottom of his earlobe. It too ran to its counterpart on the other side of his head, by going directly over his broken nose. This symbolized his youthful power and energy, even if he were no longer a young man. Red had yet another meaning too, that of blood. So, he put red tear drops on each cheek to show that blood from his victims was about to flow, and the only option his prey would have was tears of sorrow. As he waded out of the water and climbed up on the bank his eyes quickly darted back to the trail of a scouting party he and his fellow warriors had been tracking all morning. He surmised that the Quaker Meadows area would be the best spot for his ambush. The John's river would be an ideal spot to take them by surprise. If Bloody Fellow and his men could run at full speed, and if they took an old buffalo trace that his father had shown him in his youth, they should be able to get ahead of the white eyed rebels. As he and his warriors ran along the trace, his thoughts drifted back to the days before the breaded whites ever showed their ragged faces here in the Carolina backcountry. Then, he could hunt in relative safety, barring any Shawnee hunting parties that had roamed too far south. In the past, on rare occasions, a French trader might be seen, but once the English traders rolled in, life changed for the Cherokee. As a teenager Bloody Fellow was somewhat fascinated by the Europeans, but that all changed when his father was killed in 1761. Major James Grant[28] was a veteran of the French and Indian war and the very same man who was now in New York still battling for King George. However back in sixty-one, during the Anglo Cherokee War, he was still in the South. And when his army shot and killed a lone warrior on the Catawba River, he had made Bloody Fellow an enemy of the white man forever. On three separate occasions today, while on the days run, he had passed old camping grounds that his father and he had frequented in his youth. This only enraged the Cherokee more and when his war party reached the river his blood was up and his anger was at a fever pitch. His knowledge of the landscape, and the speed of him and his men had paid off. His plan had worked, for he had arrived with visions of victory running through his head. He visualized a musket ball from

---

28

Major Gen. James Grant had served as Governor of East Florida from 1763 to 1771. During the Revolution he was highly involved in the battles of Bunker Hill, Long Island, White Plains and Brandywine before being shipped off to the West Indies.

his weapon killing his adversary as he came out of the river. He would rush forward with his father's old war club in hand. He had always done this in the past and he found it to be helpful. Not that his visions always played out as the battle took place in reality, but it did put him in the right state of mind for combat. He twirled the war club anxiously in his left hand by its wooden handle as he waited. The handle had been replaced a few times in the past, having been broken in battle, but its sharpened blue stone was still as hard and handsome as the day his father had cut its groove all those years ago.

As he looked at the road on the opposite bank, the silence in the air was broken by the sound of approaching horses. The lead rider stopped at the water's edge as his mount lowered its head to take a drink from the river. The rider looked back over his shoulder and said a few words to his six companions but Bloody Fellow could not make out what was said. Yet that was no matter he thought as he pulled back the hammer of his musket. After peering across the ford for a moment Matthias Barringer led his men across the John except for one. The party came to a stop as they waited for **Philip Frye who was now in mid-stream** to cross. Bloody Fellow paused for a short moment before discharging his musket. The ball's flight was true to its mark. As Frye's horse stepped on dry ground Barringer fell from the saddle dead, likely not even hearing the shot. The Cherokee rushed forward, following their war chief's lead, having also delivered a volley of their own. They quickly finished off the wounded. Bloody Fellow bashed in the cheek bone of one of the Whigs as he vainly plead for his young life. He wiped the man's blood off his father's battle ax by passing the blue stone over the dead man's vest. Stepping over to Barringer he pulled a scalping knife from his belt. Frye was the only member of the party not killed, but his horse was shot and it barely made the tree line before it fell dead in the woods. Frye crawled for cover to the same tree that Bloody Fellow had fired from. He watched from its branches as Barringer's hair was ripped away. Then the war party stripped the bodies of the dead of their wearing apparel. Terrified that he was about to be discovered, Frye cowered as low as he possibly could. He could hear the horses being gathered, and the wild voices of the Indians as they began to talk among themselves in celebration. War cries were shouted, and then gradually, silence returned to the river bank. Frye slowly rose to his feet, dazed and bewildered that he was alone and still alive, with the corpses of his friends as his only companions.

Chapter 34

Massey Calls

The wicker bottom of Rice's chair popped as he squirmed and sat studying the strange letter that had come to his hand today. No, this cannot be, he thought as he stood up. He held the paper behind his back and paced back and forth across the floor as Rachael watched from her seat where she sat, sewing the ticking closed on a duck feather pillow.

"Why are you pacing again, perhaps you are just practicing you drills for the militia?" Racheal asked teasingly, attempting to get her husband to stop and confide what was troubling him to her. "I do wish you would stop that" she said before biting the thread from her finished handywork.

Looking at his wife, but not really listening to what she had just said, he handed the letter to her and asked "Does this sound like you brother in-law to you?"

Rachael took the letter from his hand and sat down in the same old and worn chair that Rice had just sprang from. She opened its two folds, looking at Rice, who was still pacing about in a continuous circle around the room. "Go and set on the cot. I will never be able to muster up enough concentration to fully understand this if you can't be still. This tack room is way too small for all of that. Forting up is getting old. I'm missing home"

Rice sat down on the rope corded cot as she asked, and Rachael began to read.

Dear Brother

Hope you are well for I need your asistantis As you well know the Tories are playing much havak here in Chatham County. My herd of cattle is disapearing nightly. I stand watch over them as best as on can. But even I canot stay up all hours of the night. If you would stay a fortnight to stand guard I would be beholding for I may not have a hoof to my name if you should do your brother an injustice by staying away. Not the fasts but the best and safest route would be by way of Cane Creek not Salisbury and Trading Ford. Come soon.

Your very distresed brother Masey

Rachael waved the letter up and down with her wrist as she looked at her husband through a frown and said. "Massey never wrote this! One, it is too cold to be by his hand. Not one word about the family; you know he always has news of your family. And two, all of the misspellings; He is always very particularly about his wording. This looks more like the penmanship of a young boy, not a correspondence that Massey would have written.

"Or an imposter." Rice replied. "And why Cane Creek and not Salisbury? Tories are the only ones not safe in Salisbury these days.

Remember in his last letter how he spoke of Brother John becoming a quartermaster in the North Carolina Line. How his two brothers were so proud, about us getting married and about John's appointment. And then there is only one letter s in his name. Still, the biggest tell of all is the fact that he sold his herd to John and the Continentals, according to his latest letter back in April."

"I have that letter here" Rachael announced "The Indians may burn out our home but not my bible." She walked over to a work bench and removed her bible from a wooden box that was protecting the Holy Book inside. After pulling the letter from its pages she sat down next to Rice and the two of them had no trouble comparing the two letters. "Definitely not written by the same hand" Rachael announced. "Someone wants you at Cane Creek. It's either John or George."

"Or both of the McFall's" Rice agreed.

"Well, you are not going; it could be some kind of ambush. They must believe we are halfwits to not see through their poor plan."

"It could be someone else, but I think not," Rice replied. "It would not be much of an ambush if a man knew what he was walking into. If he had a few men along, maybe like Jack and some of the Grider's, the shoe could be on the other foot so to speak."

Rachael frowned, while looking at Rice and said, "Why take the chance husband? We already know that letter is nothing but a ruse. Why would I sew up a stone in my pillow? It would only hurt my head, so why do it?"

Rice stood up and walked to the table where Rachael had left her pillow laying. He pressed his hand deep down into its softness and said. "You may not drop a stone inside, however if one was already there, you certainly would remove it, if it was causing pain to you and your loved ones would you not? It would be nice to remove ours, I know that."

"Yes, it would," Rachael replied "however you could just simply flip the pillow over to the soft side and ignore what was on the other. But I see that I'm just wasting my breath. My words are falling on deaf ears here, I can see that."

"No, not deaf" Rice answered "I'll consider your request. You very well may be right, caution can be wise at times, but letting a lingering problem continue to fester could prove to be fatal."

Chapter 35

Wet Firelocks

The sky was black over Warriors Creek even though it was just after noon. John Grider hunched down low as a flash of lightning bolted overhead. He even went so far as taking a knee as the following boom of thunder bellowed out down the hollow. Val smiled at Rice "Storms make brother a little jumpy."

"Damn right they do!" John snapped "If you had seen old Dash you would jump to."

"An old dog," Martin explained looking to Rice. "Hit by lighting under the very same tree he and John had treed a coon in, a few years back. Killed the dog and burned John's left hand in the process."

"That poor hound sure did smell," Val said as he turned up his nose. "Stunk like a burned turkey Maw forgot to turn over the fire. Ain't that right, John?"

Will you two dumb asses shut your mouths? If I can hear you two clucking out that nonsense you know anyone else can. This ain't a bloody rabbit hunt. You don't see Jack flapping his jaws, do you?" John hissed as he turned his attention back down the hollow. Rachael's little brother David, leaned over to Rice and said in a whisper, "Val reminds me some of Jeremiah."

Rice smiled and nodded his head in agreement as the men continued down the creek bank. David had come into Ft. Grider this morning and after seeing the false letter and hearing of this spying trek, he had talked himself into a spot in the party. Rachael was doubly upset with Rice. He was not only going off on this foolhardy trip, to whatever was waiting for them at Cross Creek, he had also allowed her younger brother to go along as well. David was joining up with Captain William Moore's militia the next time they were called up, so Rice told his wife that this would be good for David. He tried to sooth her fears by reminding her that he couldn't learn from anyone better than the Grider's and Rice, himself, how to handle himself in the woods, but in all reality, David was already a skilled woodsman and needed no help.

Rice also knew that John was right. Now was the time to behave like rangers, and not as if they were out hunting supper, but the Grider boys were speaking softly in the thunderstorm. It would take mighty big ears to hear their whispers.

The entire party was in a much better mood after checking on

Rice's home this morning, baring John's fear of lighting. They were all relieved to find that his cabin was still standing; they knew it had been at risk. He and Rachael had been forted up with the Grider's for some time now, and they very well could have been burned out. While he was there, he took the time to find Bob and Queen. He had been forced to leave the two gentle giants behind.

There was barely enough room for the horses already quartered in the fort, without Rice adding to their numbers. He could only take one horse with him, and that had to be Liberty. The two big work horses had been roaming the grounds around the cabin and grazing at will in his absence. He had been worried that they might founder themselves, if they ate too much grass while he was gone. Life was getting tedious back at the fort and if this trip to Cross Creek turned out to be a wild goose chase, he was planning to return home as soon as possible, so he could take better care of his livestock. Jack and Annabel were welcome to return with them if they wanted, until they decided where they would settle. Rachel and Annabel would enjoy each other's company, and Rice knew Jack would be ever ready with his gun if one was needed. Two more rifles could never hurt.

The wind began to blow harder and a few drops of rain started to tap on the thick leaves overhead. And as the rain picked up, the leaves could no longer hold the weight of the water pooling on then. The rain was falling through the canapé to the ground. Rice, like the other men, covered the pan of his rifle with an old shirt that he pulled from his haversack, then placed a leather strip over the cloth trying to keep his rifle dry. Damp powder was of no use to anyone. But if this turned into a downpour the leather and cloth would do little good. John, having taken the lead looked at the sky before waving his arm and leading the men off the beaten path to an old camp site of his. He led them down a small hill to where he had once built an old lean-to. As Rice and the others crawled under the moss covered roof the storm began in earnest.

"It's been two years since I've been in here" John said out loud to the group. "I'm somewhat surprised that it is still here."

Martin pointed out the fact that a few of the logs had been recently replaced by tapping the handle of his tomahawk on the fresh wood chippings on two of the newer log ends.

"I did not do that," John responded "I quit coming here when the ginseng ran out. 8Me and Jacob dug all of the best roots back in '74. I know I have not been back and neither has he, as far as I know."

"Well I for one am grateful that someone has," Val replied "I don't think it was injuns but who can really say? Maybe Jacob did it before he left to help build Davidson Fort. Think our rifles will still fire?"

"Mine will," Jack said as he looked over his lock. "But I am replacing what's in my pan. It's a mite damp. By the way it looks out there we could be here quite a long spell, and I want old sweet lips in good firing order."

"Well, I for one am happy that you have now entered into matrimony. Jack" Val said. "I worry about any single man that calls his gun 'Sweat Lips'. How about you boy got any names for that 50 caliber there in your lap?" Val asked, looking at David.

"No, I can't say as I do," David laughed.

As Rice was tucking away the priming powder that he had just replaced in his pan, he looked at his brother in-law and said "Well David, I suppose you and Jack are members of this group now. They are taking pot shots at both of you."

After about an hour of waiting, friendly banter, decision making, and planning, the wind outside the lean-to died down again. Rice and the others broke camp as a dry lot, and where once again back on the trail to Cross Creek. Jack, along with Rice took the lead at the front, on this uphill leg of the trip. The Grider's fell to the rear, after being the point on the previous march as was the customary practice of the group. Rice was glad that Old Sweet Lips was present. Jack may have had an odd name for his gun but he was a damn good shot with her. The stream was running at a higher, swifter pace, from all the runoff the storm had dumped and was now emptying into its waters. The sound of the rushing water was making it hard to hear any other sounds that might be coming from the surrounding woods. This made Rice much more observant.

He came to a stop as his eyes picked up the movement of a deer's white flag to his left. He raised his hand signaling the others in the party to stop. Then he heard the whistling snort the white tail deer was blowing in an effort to intimidate whatever he was looking at. The buck was concentrating its gaze to the east and was yet to realize that he had a party of rangers marching up on his rear. This was a rare occurrence, since bucks are hard to walk up on, without them seeing the approaching party first. Rice paused as he continued to watch the buck drive its front hoofs into the ground, making a loud thud with each powerful stomp. Finally, the animal's feet could no longer hold, and it dashed away to Rice's left. He gave its sudden departure sharper attention, for he knew that someone or something other than himself and his friends had first drawn its attention. Rice heard the clicking sound of the hammer on Val's rifle, as he pulled it back into firing position. As one, they all saw a lone Cherokee warrior moving slowly through the woods. He was soaking wet from the storm, his hair still damp and his blue hunting shirt sticking solidly to his skin. He was armed with only a bow and arrow, having slung his rifle over his shoulder. His gun was now most likely useless, having gotten wet in the storm. Not having the benefit of a lean-to, this warrior was now down to his secondary weapon. John tapped Val on the shoulder as he pulled his tomahawk from his belt. The two brothers exchanged a few whispers before John began to crawl low to the ground towards the warrior, as Val in turn did likewise but in the other direction. Seeing that his two brothers were moving into position, Martin reached down and picked up a twig as Rice watched. As the Indian approached, Martin snapped the twig sending the snapping sound crackling through the air. As the Cherokee paused, Val stood up in plain sight drawing the painted warrior's attention. As he pulled the string back on his bow to deliver a killing shot, John rose to his feet unseen by the warrior. Val and Martin's diversion tactics gave John all the time that was required to deliver a perfect throw of his tomahawk. Its blade landed squarely between the Indian's shoulders. He made two staggering steps backwards as if he were trying to reach the handle of the tomahawk. But all he could do was get a fingertip on the instrument of his death.

Rice pulled his knife as the warrior finally fell and with one flick of his wrist he cut the gun strap from the dead man's shoulder. John quickly removed the tomahawk from the body as Rice examined the rifle. He looked at David and proclaimed "He was the point of a war party, and they all are going to have wet firelocks by the look of this one. We will cut them to ribbons."

"Damn right" David replied "This time they will be running the gauntlet boys."

"Well at any rate, they will be upon us within minutes" Rice answered with a smile while placing a steady hand on his brother in-laws shoulder. "Keep your head now David. Just let the game play out."

"But do we ambush or let them pass?" Jack asked as he watched John remove the scalp.

"Depends on their numbers," Martin answered. "We will have to wait and see what comes our way. Ten or less, we take them, if more then lower your heads boys and let them pass. Remember, no one fires if they outnumber us. "

Rice, Jack and David each took a tree as the Grider's crossed over the path, dragging the corpse by its feet. They quickly disappeared into the tree line and took up their own fighting positions, planning to give the Indians the illusion that their attackers were greater in numbers, being fired upon from all sides.

Using the upper side of his arm Rice wiped the sweat away from his forehead. As he was doing so, David came into view. He had a look in his eyes that Rice had never seen on him. You could see the hardened expression of revenge all across David's face, and the hope that just maybe, he was about to slay the killer of his brother. Rice hoped that maybe this would indeed be the case, but he also knew the odds were slim. There were thousands of Cherokee warriors in the mountains to the west. With hundreds more in Kentucky, but he would never say it to David. If a victory here today helped bring closure to Jeremiah's death for David, then so be it.

Once again Rice turned his attention back to the path, as he too cocked his rifle. A painted buckeye shrub drew his eye as it was parted by a young warrior. He twisted his shoulders and hips as he silently stepped through the shrub's green leaves. He slowly raised a hand to the side of his mouth as he mimicked the call of a crow. He paused for a moment, waiting for his dead point man's reply, Rice supposed. He stood his ground until he heard the false reply that John sang back to him. As he moved forward into the clearing, the warrior was joined by another member of the Deer clan; messengers of the Cherokee, and their best and fastest runners as well. The new arrival bent over for only a second as he drew in some fresh air to replenish his heaving lungs. Soon the two were joined by six other runners in intervals of three minutes. As the lead runner remover, a canteen made from a gourd from around his neck David looked at Rice and silently lipped out a question "What do we do?"

Rice raised the palm of his hand and slowly lowered it to make a calming gesture as if to say, "be patient."

As the gourd was being passed around, after each warrior had his turn for a drink, Rice looked at the far tree line hoping to see what the Grider's were about to do. As far as he was concerned it was time for David to exorcise his demons on these runners. He was willing to wait as long as the Indians stayed where they were, but once that lead runner gave the first indication that the race was on again Rice was going to fire. He felt sure that John and his brothers were thinking the same, and making sure that no other runners were on the trailhead, and had not yet arrived. But with each passing moment it was evident that this was the whole group, and not a small part of a larger party. Much like the whites, once the runners had stopped they had begun to inspect their firearms. They began to speak to each other and even though Rice had no knowledge of the Cherokee language he could tell they were complaining about the soggy powder inside each of their rifles. Finally, the lead warrior slung his rifle back over his shoulder and stepped up on a pale brown sandstone boulder. He gazed down the trail that Rice and the others had just walked up. Shaking his head as though he was still concerned about his missing lead runner, he made another attempt to contact his friend by again mimicking a crow. This time when no reply came, he pulled a war club from his belt. Turning to the second runner he squatted down and softly spoke to who Rice surmised was the second in command among the Indians. They spoke just for a moment as the others gathered around. The leader then turned back to the rest of his companions and ordered them to pull their weapons as well.

Rice and David glanced at each other, both realizing that the Cherokee were beginning to show some concern about the situation. Rice pointed to David and with his trigger finger he made the squeezing motion. David nodded and took aim on the runner still perched on the sandstone.

As he squeezed off the round his mark was knocked off his perch as if he was being pulled by a rope. Rice likewise hit his target killing the second warrior. Smoke hung in the air across the way from where the Grider's all fired simultaneously. All but one of the runners were hit by the devastating volley. He had quickly dived under a bush and scrambled away a few feet on his hands and knees. As the whites began to reload the runner jump to his feet and dashed back down the trail he had just come up. Jack, being the only one not to fire in the initial volley, leaped onto the sandstone boulder where the leader, that David had just killed, had stood. As he brought Sweet Lips to bear his sharp eyes homed in on the bronze shoulders of the fleeing runner. As the Cherokee ran, he would change his course, cutting back and forth. He was trying desperately to make his path unpredictable and hard for Jack to get a clear shot through the outlying tree limbs.

"Take him." Val said as he was pulling out his ramrod from his newly reloaded rifle. "We can't afford for him to slip away."

"Hmm" Jack grunted still looking down the barrel of his rifle. He paused a few more seconds as he held the rifle ever so steady. Then he pulled the trigger delivering a two-hundred-and-fifty-foot death shot directly under the left shoulder. He slowly rested the butt of his rifle on the sandstone as he blew down Sweet Lip's barrel to clear out the smoke, and any residue of black powder that might still be stuck down her barrel or touch hole.

"Sweet Lips indeed!" Martin announced, looking down the trail at the dead warrior.

"Well, so much for Cross Creek and the McFall's" Rice said looking at the others. "If these boys are relaying dispatches back and forth between war parties, we will never get through."

"Could be that was McFall's plan all along," Val replied as he picked up a war club from a dead hand. That way Dragging Canoe's braves could do the killing for them. I would not put it past those bloody bastards, their treachery knows no bounds."

"Maybe so," Rice agreed. "Come on, let's take what we can off these boys and hightail it back to the fort before we are overrun by a war party that we can't handle. The whole damn country could be crawling with redskins by nightfall."

Chapter 36

No Rest for the Weary

Isaac Thomas once again found himself rushing through the woods with a massage from the Cherokee. However, this time it was not from the whole Cherokee nation, it was a message of warning from Nancy Ward to her White brothers and sisters. Four days ago, on July 7th while under the cover of night, Nancy had pecked on Thomas's cabin door at Chota. She had learned that Dragging Canoe was about to drink the black drink, which meant that he and his warriors would march northeast at daybreak. Both red and white families would suffer losses if nothing was done. This was no great secret to Thomas, for he had eyes and ears as well. He knew this day was close at hand because Dragging Canoe had become even tighter lipped around Thomas after his return from Sycamore Shoals this spring. Everyone at the Cherokee capital knew Cameron and Dragging Canoe were making plans. Still he was shocked to hear the rest of her news. Dragging Canoe was just the center prong of a war fork that was about to be struck into the western settlements. While he was to attack Eaton Station [29]Old Abram was planning a

_____

[29] Eaton Station was built by Amos Eaton by Reedy Creek near Kingsport Tennessee in the spring of 1776.

simultaneous attack on Fort Caswell at Watauga. And if that was not enough, The Raven was leading the smallest prong of this force into the western settlements of Carter Valley to overrun it as well. So, as dawn broke the next morning Thomas, along with a few friends, set-out to relay her message. All knew very well if they were caught their lives would pay forfeit. In the beginning, they took the Great War Trail, but soon they had to abandon the path for the cover of the trees, to avoid the gathering warriors who were organizing their march from the different villages along the trail. They had even seen Old Abram himself. This had slowed the messenger's pace, but greatly increased their chances of getting through to the settlements.

As Thomas and his two companions, Jarret Williams & William Falling, reached the Nolichucky River they came up on the sight of Fort Lee, a new fortification still under construction by a party of men. Upon hearing the news the leader, John Sevier, was hesitant to abandon the fort for the safety of Fort Caswell. Maybe he did not trust a man of Isaac's appearance, for he wore leggings with a breech cloth, moccasins, and a hunting-shirt of buckskin; looking very much like an Indian himself. Even hearing that the warning had come from Ward and not Isaac, Sevier still showed little concern, but most of his men took the warning to heart.

Feeling as though he had done his duty Thomas headed on to Fort Caswell leaving Fort Lee to its fate. Upon reaching Fort Caswell, Thomas was received in a much better light by James Robertson, who immediately raised an alarm and began preparations for the coming attack. Dispatches were sent East with a call for help, but few believed they would arrive in time to make some differences. After an hour of rest and a meal of fried squirrel, Thomas again took to the woods to spy on the approaching Indian force. There would be no rest for the weary today .

Back in Salisbury, another man of importance was penning letters. His name was General Griffith Rutherford, an Irish born immigrant who had landed in Philadelphia as an 18-year-old youth. His parents, having perished on the voyage over from Ireland, had made him, by necessity, extremely self-reliant. A veteran of the French and Indian War, Rutherford had fought at the 1758 Battle of Fort Duquesne, an old French fort now the sight of Fort Pitt. Then moving south to Rowan County North Carolina, he was posted at Fort Dobbs only to be besieged by the Cherokee in 1760. It was there that he cultivated his hatred for all things Cherokee. And in 1761 he unleashed that hatred upon the Cherokee as part of James Grant's devastating expedition into the Cherokee homelands that had hardened the heart of Bloody Fellow so badly. Now that the Revolution had begun, Rutherford had taken his French and Indian War experience and turned it into an appointment to the post of Brigadier General of the Salisbury District Militia. Although the Cherokee had yet to make a full-scale advance in the settlements, Rutherford was sure the "Red Bustards" as he called them would, as soon as the British supplied them with enough provisions to do so. The attacks of this spring would look like Child's play he insisted. Rutherford suggested in his letter to Colonel William Christian of Virginia that the two of them should join forces.

They could, no doubt, be the instrument to inflict the final destruction of the Cherokee Nation, as it was known. If this war was to be won each Colony's militia would need to work together, just as the Continental Army was doing up north. The Cherokee may have been able to dominate the Creek Nation, but they would never be able to handle a united America. If Dragging Canoe could not see this, Rutherford was more than happy to show him the error of his ways.

Chapter 37

The Prize of Cathey's Fort

Iona McFall peered out into the darkness of Turkey Cove. She was lonely here at Cathey's Fort without Arthur, but she was still happier then back at Mulberry Fields. Instead of being shunned she was a welcomed member of the community. Some here knew of her brother's in-law's Tory leanings, but with Arthur being out with Captain White's militia, no one seemed to care. Hers was not the only family with brothers on both sides. She was a little nervous about Jacob Grider staying around, now that the fort was complete. But to his credit he never spoke of John and George. He had been civil to her father in-law, but he had kept his distance until John Alexander had left Iona here by herself. Once the head of the McFall clan had gone back home to protect his homestead, Jacob did approach Iona wanting her to introduce him to the Rippetoe family. He had taken a fancy to Elizabeth, the youngest of that family's daughters and Iona was more than happy to make the introduction. She did say she believed the girl was too young for him, but he reassured Iona that he knew that, but was willing to wait a few years if need be to start a courtship. All he wanted now was a proper introduction so he could speak a few words to her. Once that the introduction had been made, Iona had taken her leave.

Tonight's sky was beautiful with a crescent moon hanging above. The sound of tree frogs sang out on the cool night air, and the glow of lighting bugs along Cove Creek was more than inviting to Iona. Being shut up inside the walls of a fort for such a long time could become overwhelming, smothering to one's very soul even, and the temptation of an evening stroll along the Catawba was more than she could resist.

As she stepped out of the fort's gate, she heard laughter coming from a nearby fire. A group of hunters talking about this morning's hunt she supposed. Then she heard one call out "Don't stray too far Iona." Feeling that the hunter had overstepped his bounds, she turned the opposite way as another round of laughter broke out. 'The gall of some men!' she thought, 'using her given name as though he were a suitor trying to win her hand'. Sometimes men would try to plant a seed into married women's minds in case her husband might fall, hoping they could be the next man in the young widow's life. Arthur's return could not come soon enough for her. Doubly so now with John Alexander being gone.

She could hear the water from the river, which was just beyond the trees up ahead. She turned and looked back at the stockade, just to keep her bearings. The fire looked small, now that she had walked so far down the bank. She took a fan out of her apron pocket, and as she was out spreading it to its full width she let out a small groan. She felt a sharp pain deep in her side as though she had been stung by a bee. But how could a simple bee sting feel so powerful that it had somehow taken her breath away? As her knees buckled, confusion and bewilderment overcame her. Her sight was blurred and fuzzy, and she was feeling faint. She could not understand why she had the bitter dull taste of blood in her mouth as she lost consciousness.

The war chief Moon could hardly contain himself as he retreated back through the trees he had just crept from. He had seen red hair in the past, but it was always on a man, like that of The Bench's. Not this trophy of long, flowing, red hair from a woman. He would hang this scalp inside his lodge with pride and he was sure he would be the envy of many a Cherokee warrior, who would never have an opportunity to display such a prize.

Chapter 38

The Corn Picker

The shade from Hibriten Mountain was now spreading over Fort Grider and in doing so it had cooled the July heat considerably. Rice was standing at his post inside the walls. He was on the north rampart looking out of a porthole. It had been a long, anxious day standing here, but necessary nevertheless. As of this morning sixteen men and women stood guard around the fort's walls. Fed had spotted a lone warrior about noon, but the fleet footed Indian had quickly disappeared into the apple orchard, not allowing Fed enough time to fire his British Fowler.

All that Rice had seen today was the constant swaying of the golden tousles of corn that and been planted this spring just outside the walls. The ears were still not fully developed on the silk's end of the cob. Only the grains on the butt end was large enough to eat. Still it had been a long time since last summer. So, the first few rows of corn had already been picked over and eaten anyway. With two full acres having been planted those first few rows would make little different to the falls harvest. Besides, everyone always took advantage of this month's long period while the ears were still soft and juicy. When the kernels hardened, the rest would be milled into cornmeal in the fall, but on this day, it had given cover to the Indians. He had heard a few war whoops called out after a few pot shots had been fired into the small fort's walls. None of those shots had wounded anyone. So far Fort Grider had been blessed.

"Rice," Rachael called out looking up at him as she approached the wooden platform her husband was standing on. "Here take my hand and help a lady up" she said as she placed a foot onto the ladder that lead to the top of the fort's wall. Rice did as she had asked and helped her up with a pull of his hand.

"What is the talk on the other side?" Rice asked as he looked to the southern wall.

"Same as over here," she replied as she took her place by his side. "Lots of frustrated comments and worried faces. Fed's Wife, Ellen has marked up some lead balls by chewing on them. She says it will do more damage that way; Annabel has followed her suit and is planning on reloading for Jack if they do attack.

Those shots are unnerving, but Val and Martin are trying to keep the other's spirits up with bold talk."

"Well, they can back it up" Rice said as he looked back out into the field. "What about Old Fredrick? What has he said about our plight?"

"He is confident that all will end well. He keeps saying there are only a few of those devils out there. It's his belief, that they just want to keep us bottled up inside the fort here so we can't send help to any of the other stations to the west. He said The Little Carpenter did a lot of that back in the last Cherokee War."

"That same thought ran across my mind as well. John too, is of the same opinion" Rice confessed "I sure thank the Lord we are not down Sycamore Shoals way or over in Kentucky right now."

Rachael reached out and took Rice's hand to draw his attention back to her and away from the cornfield. "Tell me the truth," she told him, wanting an honest answer, but somehow loathing the thought of knowing the reality of their situation. "How many would it take for them to get inside?"

Rice hesitated before answering. He knew that his wife was a strong-minded woman that deserved an honest answer, she had earned that much by taking a spot here on the wall with her rifle in hand.

"Don't tell any of the others that I said this, but if they try to burn us out; no more the fifty," Rice explained. "If they charge us all at once, after a burning wall has fallen in we might be able to get off two, maybe three shots apiece. Say we kill two each, that would still leave twenty-five once they got in. We might be able to outlast them here inside, but our numbers would be greatly reduced." Taking her hand, he continued on "I did not sugarcoat it, but remember this sweetheart, David did kill Goliath."

Rachael shook her head ever so slowly and replied "If God is for us, then who can ever be against us?"

"That's right," Rice agreed "but like Old Frederick said, I don't think that many are out there. If there were, why not go ahead and attack? But on the other hand, that hillside over there does bother me somewhat. If they have longrifles as good as some of ours,

they could pick a few of us off from it's top" Rice concluded as he looked back out of his porthole.

"Look!" he whispered having spotted movement below. "There, at the end of the patch. Just beyond those German green tomatoes that Fed always grows."

Rachael gazed through her own porthole and saw a Cherokee crawling low, and moving slowly through the green leaves. He was stupidly picking some ears off of the corn stalks while lying on his stomach. With each pull of his hand the shaking stalk announced his presence in the field. Rice leveled the sight of his rifle on the warrior's' neck as he rose up to take hold of another ear. Slowly, Rice squeezed the trigger. The report of the rifle drew everyone's attentions to their side of the fort.

"Do you need us over there?" John called from across the way, knowing all too well if a full-fledged attract was in motion, the fort's defenses would need to be shifted to that side.

"No" Rice replied "but their numbers are one fewer."

Not taking her eye off of her own line of vision into the cornfield, Rachael said with a playful, yet hopeful smile, "That means they only have forty-nine left, Rice. We are safe for sure now honey, don't you think?"

"Hopefully so," Rice answered with a serious smile as he poured more gunpowder down his barrel.

Chapter 39

A Sight for Sore Eyes

John Grider had darted out the gates of Fort Grider this morning well before dawn. He had departed by way of the cornfield, keeping low until he reached the orchard. Once inside its cover, he sprinted along under the trees limbs until he reached the true forest. He had traveled almost three miles before he felt it was safe to hunt. The fort's meat supply was running low and an elk or deer could replenish its provisions for a few more days. He shot an elk in the hindquarters from the bottom of this hollow. He felt the high ground around him had muffled the report so the Indians could not

locate his whereabouts. He had proceeded to butcher the best cuts of meat; he could only carry so much back the fort by himself without the benefit of a horse. As he was packing away the last portion into the last of his three haversacks he heard the sound of approaching horses just yards away. Placing his rifle upon the back of the elk carcass, he hunkered down low and took what cover he could behind his kill in what little time he had.

"Don't shoot John" a voice called out as a horse came into view.

A rush of relief washed over John. As he stood up he looked at Colonel Cleveland and let out a long sigh. "Good Lord, you boys are a sight for sore eyes. I heard shots fired an hour or so ago, so I was thinking you boys were Injuns for sure."

"Well, I can see why, what with all the sign we saw along Beaver Creek" Ben proclaimed as he and his men gathered around John. Those shots you heard did come from us. We spotted a Redskin a couple of hollers over. He has danced his last war dance, 'eh boys."

"We've been pinned up for a few days by those bastards. Rice got one from atop the walls but other than that, nothing has happened" John explained as he watched two of the militia men sling the rest of his elk up on a pack horse. "We never have seen more than two together at once. Colonel, I say the sight of you and your men here will break up their little siege."

Ben turned in his saddle and called for another packhorse to be lead up from the rear of his column. Then looking back at John, he said "Let's ride over to the fort and see if they are still about."

"Oh, they are still about. I got close enough to hear two of them talking in their savage tongue as I left out this morning," John replied as he mounted up. "But looks like they were too busy to spot me. How did you come by the news we were under attack Colonel? We have not sent out any runners."

"We had no clue as to your situation. I've been out trying to round up enough men to go out after that damn Gideon Wright, it seems that son of a bitch has hooked up with another Tory by the name of Roberts. They have been doing all kinds of mischief up around the Virginia border. I was coming to call on you boys for help.

But I see now y'all have more pressing issues to deal with here at home. Still, I believe with my men here, and what y'all have at the fort, we can vanquish both in no time."

"Maybe so," John replied as he set his horse in motion. "But I don't see a lot of our boys leaving loved ones behind, to go off after Tory's up Virginia way, if the Cherokee are raiding in full strength. We may be needed to go down to Fort Caswell at Watauga".

"John, If we head off down there without tending to that bastard Wright first, men like George and John McFall will have free run of our homes while we are gone" Ben explained. "I know either way it's taking a chance, but if what you say about the Cherokee being small in numbers is true, then the Tories are the worse of the two evils for the time being."

John didn't answer, he just kept riding back for Fort Grider. He knew it would be useless to continue the debate with Ole Roundabout. Right now, the Cherokee were the ones knocking on their doors, not the Tories, but Ben was coming to the fort's aid, and that was what they needed right now. He knew Ben had the power to draft anyone into his militia that he saw fit. It would be best to keep quiet for now and not push the matter, but he also knew there was no way in hell he was going off to Virginia while Dragging Canoe was on the warpath here.

Back at Fort Grider, Rice was still manning his post with Rachael by his side. Early this morning, after John had slipped away, a lone Indian summoned the fort from the top of the ridge. "Go back to New Burn and do as you father the King says" was his massage. "If you stay you die under our war clubs" he had cried. As Rice was about to shout out a reply, Rachael beat him to the draw by unleashing a shot of over two hundred yards in distance, that sailed just over Chief Moon's head. The Indian fell to the ground before scrambling to a nearby oak. He then stood up and continued his verbal assault. "See, you no hit the great Moon. You will die now like all of those dead back at Turkey Cove" he lied. "See my voice is true" he proclaimed as he waved Iona's scalp from behind a tree for all to see. They all rot in the sun as you will soon ."

Having heard enough Rice, also discharge his rifle. The lead ball struck close to Moon's head; so close that the flying bark from the tree splintered off into Moon's eyes and forehead.

The proud chief dropped the scalp and began to rub his eyes for a short moment, trying to get them to refocus. As his sight began to return, he called out one last time, but this time in his own language, no doubt cursing the marksman who had nearly blinded him for life[30]. However, his threat of doom failed to come to pass, as hour by hour the sun rose higher in the sky. But, Moon would have been proud if he had known that his claim of the fall of Cathey's Fort did unnerve some. Everyone here knew someone there. The Grider's, with Jacob

---

[30] James Harrod put an end to the Moon's raids in 1780, when he and a party of Kentuckians ambushed a war party led by the Cherokee chief on the Wilderness Road. Harrod was the one who made the killing shot. He also took the Moon's scalp, his sash and silver medallion from the body as trophies.

being stationed there acting as one of the fort's spies, were not saying much, but you could tell that even they, the tough-skinned frontier veterans, were concerned. Adding to their woes, was the fact that John was still out in the woods, somewhere alone.

Val was keeping his eyes on the dirt road that led out of the trees in front of the stockade, as Martin was climbing up the ladder. Val did not say anything as Martin leaned his back up against the logs, and slid down into a sitting position. He was silent as he sat down crossed legged beside his brother and pulled a warm meat pie out from under the towel he was holding, Val spoke up. "Fed's Ellen has been cooking again I see."

"Indeed," Martin replied "She asked me to bring you this one, and it's something of a miracle that I got it here without breaking the crust with my finger to take a sample. She can cook even if she is a little moody at times."

"I can overlook her ill temperament as long as a meal this good is attached to the end of its provider's hand" Val said as he broke open the round pie crust with his knife to let it cool. "Is this the last of our meat?'

"Until John gets back" Martin replied, as he raised up off the boards to take Val's place along the upper wall of the stockade with his rifle in hand.

"So, you are still confident about him getting back safely then?"

"By God, it will take more than that bunch out there to get John's scalp," Martin answered coolly. "But I must admit I got a little spooked about that speech that red-assed Moon, gave about Cathey's Fort. He got that scalp somewhere. John is way too fleet of foot to fall in their hands out in the open woods, but Jacob, inside an unproven fort with someone else calling the shots, could be another matter altogether. I cannot deny that his boast is preying heavy on my mine."

"Yah me too," Val said still looking out over the wall. "And I tell you something else; when they give up this siege, I say we need to give them a visit. I, for one, am tired of looking over my shoulder while they pick us off, and then return to their homes in safety. We can attack to the West, just as easily as they can to the East."

"Amen to that." Martin said, watching his brother take his first bite. "What's good for the goose."

Chapter 40

The Battle of Long Island Flats

Dragging Canoe was rushing forward with as much speed as his horse could muster. Shots had been fired up ahead where he had ordered twenty scouts to reconnaissance the area that lay between his force and that of Eaton's Station. His battle plans depended on a quick decisive strike on the whites, and that was now in jeopardy. The Cherokee offensive up the Holston River thus far had gone as planned. Fort Lee had been abandoned by the God-awful whites and was now lying in ashes. After his warriors, and those of Old Abram, had set it to the torch, the two Chiefs split their force, as previously planned. Old Abram was now well on his way to Watauga, as was The Raven on his drive into Carters Valley by the way of the Great War Trail. Sub chiefs, like the Moon, were taking small bands of warriors up into the Brushy Mountain range of North Carolina to keep any reinforcements from there in aiding the settlements here in the East Tennessee Valley. However, the whites had somehow gotten word of the invasion. All of the outlying cabins were deserted.

Maybe they were going to make a last stand here at the ford beside long island[31].

Dragging Canoe pulled his mount to a halt, as a young warrior of the Deer clan came running towards him with a report of the skirmish. As he sat atop his horse, he was outraged that the youth took a few second to catch his wind. It seemed like an hour to the Canoe. "Speak now," he barked.

"We were deep into the ravine where the flat land starts" the warrior said as he pointed back in the direction he had just came. "They fired at us from behind the trees along the flat's edge. The wolf was killed outright, but we pushed on and fired our own rifles. We then charged into the smoke from their carbines with our war clubs. The dogs then ran away."

"How many dogs?" Dragging Canoe commanded.

"No more than us," was the reply.

Dragging Canoe quickly spun his horse around and yelled at the top of his lungs. "stay mounted and attack from horseback. The White-eye are running, come let us scalp them."

With the order given, two hundred Cherokee warriors rushed into the open flats with all their fury, and there waiting for them, was Captain James Thompson and one hundred and seventy other men. They were divided into five companies commanded by Captains James Shelby, William Buchanan, William Cocke, John Campbell, and Thomas Madison. Unbeknownst to Dragging Canoe earlier in the day under the advice of Captain Cocke, the militia had marched

---

[31] The island is about four miles long and stands just above the point where the north fork of the Holston flows into the main branch of the Holston River southwest of present day Kingsport, Tennessee.

out of Eaton's Station in two columns to meet the Indians out in the open, where they believed they had a better chance to stop the invasion. What Dragging Canoe believed to be the whole of the militia in full retreat, was only a small number of men in an advance guard out spying, just as the Cherokee were.

Thompson had his company in the middle of the battle line, and was planning on making his stand where he was, but one of his scouts informed him that the Indians were on horseback. This gave them the greater advantage, so Thompson began to fall back towards Eaton's Station, with flanking company's on each side of the main force.

As Dragging Canoe's horse reached the middle of the flats his heart raced at the sight of a running buckskinner. He bellowed out a blood curdling war cry and dashed after the fleeing man with his war club raised high above his head. As he was about to overtake his mark the buckskinner rolled to the ground and came up on one knee, now facing Dragging Canoe. He coolly squeezed off a shot that tore into the upper thigh of Dragging Canoes right leg. The ball went straight through the flesh without striking bone but it did kill the horse that the Canoe was on. Both animal and man alike, came to a crashing halt. The war chief tried to stand to his feet but the hard fall of the horse had broken the bone in his wounded leg. He could not maintain his balance and fell back to the ground in total disgust. He pulled a pistol from his gold sash and waited for what was in store for him now, either rescue or death.

Seeing that the battle was now most certainly going their way, Captain Shelby's company fired a volley into the charging Indian's ranks. Many of them had dismounted to meet the whites in hand to hand combat. Justin Moore, one of Shelby's men dodged a flying tomahawk [32] that a huge warrior had thrown at him. Having already

---

[32]   Alfred H. White donated this tomahawk to the Historical Society of Tennessee on January 6,

emptied his gun, Moore charged into the big buck with a six-inch scalping knife in his hand. The Indian reached out for Moore's arm in a bid to stop the thrust, however his reach was short, only managing to get his hand on the blade, which cost him his thumb as Moore sliced it off with an upward jerk. Still not conceding the issue, the warrior pulled his own knife with his off hand. The two struck blades, this time, doing no damage to the other, but the Cherokee was slower to defend himself, leaving an opening for Moore, which he took by driving his blade in the wounded warrior's stomach ending the encounter. As Moore looked over the field he saw that the battle was now over. The Indians had collected their wounded, including Dragging Canoe while he had been engaged with his big adversary. They were now departing the field in total defeat, ending the battle of Long Island Flats,[33]but there were still two other war parties in the valley.

Chapter 41

Walked Away

The yellow blooms of a black-eyed Susan were swaying ever so slowly in the wind as Iona stumbled slowly along Cove Creek. She was not sure how long she had been walking or even if she was heading in the right direction back to the fort. She could not even remember coming to, but the sun was up now. Her dress was hard and stiff; having stuck to the side of her body where she had been stabbed. These two facts told her that she had lost hours and maybe

---

1860. Moore's Christian name is not known today therefore I added Justin to help the story.

[33] The Battle of Long Island Flats was fought on July 19th or the 20th of 1776. Both dates have been recorded as the day of the battle. At any rate this battle was costly for the Cherokee; not only did they lose thirteen men killed but also forty wounded including Dragging Canoe.

even days while she was unconscious. The blood-stained cloth most likely did save her life having stopped her bleeding by sealing the wound for the time being. She had a tremendous headache that roared inside her head and was distracting her thought process. Her vision was fuzzy and blurred in the bright sunlight. Having lost her hat, she raised a hand over her eyes to block the sun. She looked all around the countryside hoping to regain her bearings. However, she just could not bring her eyes to focus in on anything more than twenty feet away, but her hearing was fine. She could hear water running nearby, but not any sounds that could be heard coming from a settlement such as a blacksmith's hammer ringing, a cry of a peacock or the bark of some playful dog. She slid back to the ground in a sitting position as another dizzy spell buckled her wobbly legs. She sat there for a moment, sure now that she had walked miles in the wrong direction. Then totally exhausted she laid back into the wildflowers.

"Arthur," she whispered, praying that somehow, he would come to her rescue, but knowing he was far away, and had no way of knowing of her struggles. In her desperation and pain, she could swear that she heard him calling her name. 'Wishful thinking', she thought as she passed out again.

Yesterday, Arthur McFall had returned to Cathy's Station to reunite with his young wife, but she was not there he had been told by William Cathy. She had not been seen for the last three days and Jacob Grider and two other men had been out looking for her.

"Just two men and Jacob?" Arthur asked incredulously. "What about the rest of the men here. Are they all sick or just plain damn cowards?" he demanded to know. He whirled and climbed back atop his horse, shouting for the gates to be opened, departing Cathey's Station on very bad terms with all there, having refused help from anyone inside the post. Even after he was told that in the time she had been missing, search parties in great numbers had been out looking for Iona; even to their own peril. However, the consensus now, by most here, was that the poor girl was either dead or cared off to the Over-hill villages by the Cherokee. Her straw hat lying next to a bloodstained patch of grass was all that the search parties had found. All had been done that was possible to be done, but they understood that time was a factor and her's had run out, he was told. Once tensions between the settlers and the Cherokee had settled, maybe he could find her and a ransom or an exchange could take place.

Arthur would hear none of that talk and departed alone. He had come upon a woman's trail at nightfall last night and he knew that it was hers. She had broken the square heel on her right shoe back in the spring and he had replaced it with a round one making her tracks very distinct, but he lost it in the darkness as night had fallen. Last night as he lay awake under the stars, he wondered if the loyalist would have handled Iona's disappearance any differently than they had back at Cathey's. All sorts of wild thoughts of what had happened to her ran through his mind as he set out again on his search for his wife this morning, but all of those thoughts left his mind as he finally spotted her in the far distance. She was sitting in a patch of a black-eyed Susan, but she had slid down into them and was now completely out of sight as he was called out her name.

Was she hiding from Indians or possibly she had mistaken him for one of them. Either way he was not going to approach her until he found out. So he took a knee to blend into the high orchard grass that was around him. He waited a half hour there watching the tree lines for any movement that could be a threat. And just when he finally believed it was safe to approach her, she stood up and started to walk away from him at a slow and halting pace.

Finally, Arthur stood up and dashed across the field. The closer he got to her the more he realized, by the way she was walking, that his wife of two years was definitely injured. He ran up to her he wrapped his arm around her and gently sat her back down on the ground. As she looked up at him he could see how badly wounded her head was. The Moon had not just scalped the small round spot on the top part of her head; he had ripped it off from ear to ear. The whole top of her skull was exposed. The only hair she had now was on the very back of her head just above the neck and just a little above each ear. Her beautiful red hair would never fall over her shoulders again. His mouth dropped open in shock and he slowly began to step away from her, in disgust.

"They have murdered my beautiful wife," he whispered, cruelly turning away from her.

"No Arthur, they have not," she said in a weak voice. "Thanks be to the Lord that you have found me," she said reaching up to him.

"Your hair Iona, your glorious red hair is gone. You are no longer the beautiful woman you once were. You are no longer my wife either. You are dead to me. Do you think I could ever sleep with something that looks like that" he yelled pointing at her head? "They have killed you for sure".

Iona reached up and touched the top of her head for the first time since the attack. In all of that time she had not realized the full extent of her wounds, her mind was in such a haze. Her eyes grew large as panic rushed over her. "I'm still your wife" she cried "There is more to me than just my hair!".

"No Iona, I'm doing us both a favor. You are dead to me now, but I will remember you as you were, rather than as you are" he said as he turned and walked away.

"For God's sake Arthur, give me something to eat and drink before you go!" she begged trying to stand. "You monster, you never loved me! Only part of the time, when I was in your bed. Remember my cries Arthur, they will haunt you till your dying days and beyond. You may believe nobody's watching, but God sees all. Run you coward, run, but whenever you close your eyes I'll be there. My voice will call out to you. Voices carry over time as well as distance."

Coldly, Arthur looked at the ground while he spoke, "Shut up, you're dead." he said again. "They have killed my dear Iona and left me with this."

He doggedly walked away without a backwards glance, leaving his wife to die in a deathly wilderness divorce.

Chapter 42

Encouraging Words

Ben Cleveland plopped his mug of rum hard down on his host, Old Fed's table top. The force of the blow sloshed a good amount of the golden liquid on his wrist. The palm of his other hand followed suit, splashing even more rum over the rim of his mug. "If I could be so bold boys, this could be the beginning of the end. This settles the matter, Gideon and Roberts it will be" he said. "Joseph you have made my day."

Much debate had been waged back in forth since he and his men had ridden into the gates of Fort Grider this afternoon. No bones about it, Cleveland was dead set on going after the Tories up near the Virginia border. Old Fed was not so sure, he felt it would be unwise to traipse off after white men while the Indians were on the warpath. Not even a slab of John's good tasting elk could quiet the men as they ate the roast from their wooden plates. Rice was sure that if he told Ben, that he had just eaten a rat, Old Roundabout would have never missed a beat in his argument. He was so engaged in the conversation he had no memory of what his taste buds had told him. Ben was becoming more and more agitated, because he was gaining little, to no support from the defenders of this fort. Rice had been holding his tongue for the most part, but he too was taking the same view as the Girders, but that had all changed at sunset. Joseph Vann had made his way up from Fort Caswell with the news that the Cherokee raids had failed miserably. Not only had Dragging Canoe been beaten, Old Abram had been as well. Bonnie Kate Sherrill [34] was outside the fort's walls as the attack was made. In the defenders haste to slam shut the fort's gate they closed it too soon, and in the process, had left the long legged Kate outside of the fort's protection. With a hailstorm of bullets and arrows flying about the young lady's supple frame, she made a mad dash for the fort's wall, determine to scale the walls before her, or die trying. As she made her leap of faith, John Sevier reached down from over the top of the fort's ramparts. Between the height of her jump and the strength of his arm, she cleared the wall unscathed. The attack was then beaten back and Old Abram withdrew his braves to a safer distance, and besieged the fort. One more rush was made by the Indians the next day in an attempt to set Fort Watauga ablaze, but it too failed. Two days later, the Indians had not been seen again, giving hope to those inside that maybe the attack was over. So James Cooper and Samuel Moore slipped out of the fort to investigate. As the two reached Gap Creek, Cooper was shot and scalped and Moore had disappeared. Most likely he was now a captive, at best. Also, William Bean's wife Lydia had been captured on her way to the fort the same day that Cooper and Moore had been attacked. Old Abram had hoped for much more carnage than Cooper's death, and Moore and Mrs. Bean's unknown fates. Only the Raven on his drive into Carters Valley had done any real damage to

---

[34] Bonnie Kate Sherrill 1754-1836 would become the wife of John Sevier on Aug,14 1780.

the settlers. He had killed dozens, burned many cabins and destroyed most of the valley's crops. Dragging Canoe's campaign only had Fort Lee's destruction to crow about, and in all truth that was a hollow victory, because it was deserted at the time.

"Come on boys" Ben continued, "The Cherokee are heading back to the Overhill villages to lick their wounds. Sevier and Robinson have had their victories. Let's have ours now against Roberts and his band of bastards."

Rachael was standing behind Rice as he sat at the right of Colonel Cleveland. She was listening to every word of the conversion and as Ben ended his plea she wasted little time in stating her opinion.

"Colonel, Rice and I have been away from our home a long time now. Why should my husband, now that we finally have an opportunity to return home, go off after this Roberts fellow?"

"Well Rachael, all that Rice needs to do is look at you and wonder what would have happened that night the McFall's attacked y'all's home. Imagine that Gideon Wright was there that night, along with another forty or fifty men, maybe even a hundred. Rice would be dead, along with Jack, and forgive me for saying such a terrible

thing, but rape and torture would have been your fate. A cabin in flames with you inside, while flames licked at your pretty face. And for you other men here with children, who of you would like for their young eyes to witness such an atrocity. Roberts has done all that I just spoke of." Ben tapped his fore finger down on the tabletop to make his next point as he looked back at Rachael. "Gideon Wright is at this very hour with Roberts as an understudy. That my dear, is what he will bring to all of our homes if nothing is done. Once Roberts and Wright are hanging by a rope we can all go home and sleep a whole lot safer in our beds at night. I'm just asking for a few days, no more than few weeks. If we do this, it could be the end of our troubles for a good long while.

Rice placed an arm around Rachael's waist and pulled her close and said "We will be back soon and then we will go home in complete safety afterwards."

Racheal appreciated Rice's comforting words: but she also remembered that Jeremiah had spoken with the same tone at his departure. And she knew all too well how that had turned out, despite his encouraging words. Yet deep down in her heart, she like Rice and all the others here, knew that Ben was right. The Tories needed to be dealt with.

Chapter 43

Many A Slip Twixt the Cup And The Lip

The split rail fence that lined the burnt-out Montgomery County, Virginia homestead was knocked over. Horses must have been stolen from the pasture, Rice thought to himself. The cattle had been shot where they stood. Two of the cows had been butchered but the others were just killed to punish the owners. Roberts was truly a cruel man to any Whig that fell in his path. The carcasses were yet to bloat in the hot August sun, and the heat coming from the cabin's charred foundation was still hot. This could only mean that Colonel James Roberts and his band of Tories were not far away. As Rice looked down at the ground, he pulled Liberty's rains back to settle the young horse's nerves. Just as he had surmised, the tracks of four horses indicated that they had been driven out of the gap left in the downed fence.

Liberty's hind foot hit the downed rails as Rice slapped his reins to follow the fresh trial before him. The New River ferry was only an hour away and he knew he had little to no time to waste. Being the scout for Ben's Militia, he knew that, in all likelihood, he was no more than two to three hours ahead of Cleveland and the rest of his men. Rice also realized that he could only follow the Tories so far, as their numbers were too large for him to engage alone. He only hoped to see if they were headed up stream or down, and then he would turn back and relay their whereabouts to Ben. This was not the first cabin ravaged by Roberts that Rice had seen on this northward trek. Four others had received the same treatment. They, like this one, had been set to the torch with nothing left of the owners to be seen in the Tories wake. As Rice rode along, he ducked down low in the saddle letting Liberty demonstrate all the best quartiles a fine speed horse should have. The horse was fast, and Rice enjoyed the ride with each stride Liberty took, but when the trail forked all of his speed came to a halt. Which way to follow? Roberts had split his forces. For no reason Rice took the ferry route. If Roberts had not gone that way, then just maybe Gideon had. As he reached the hilltop overlooking the ferry he rode Liberty under a wild cherry tree's low limb to stay out of view. Gideon was not among the men strolling around the ferry's landing. Rice had never seen Roberts before, so he had no way of knowing if the Tory colonel was among the men. They seemed to be in no hurry to cross over. Many of them had unsaddled their mounts, a fire had been kindled, and a cook was tending to a meal. 'Time to head back,' Rice thought, but as he was turning around, a lone Tory down below jumped on his horse and was riding up the ridge that stood between him and Rice. As the rider was making his way up the hill, Rice rode down into the waters of a small creek to hide. As the Tory rode by, Rice dismounted into the muddy water to keep his head and shoulders out of view. Mud had stuck to liberty's legs and underbelly as he had slid down the bank. "Damnation!" Rice thought. "That will take a good hour of grooming tonight." Pondering his next move, Rice rode back up the bank, adding more mud to Liberty's coat on his way back to the cherry tree, and there he saw that no other riders were following the first. 'A dispatch courier,'' Rice thought as he again reached the road, leaving the tree behind. Rice took his time on his pursuit, walking Liberty at the same speed as the rider ahead. The carrier was out of sight now, but this did not concern Rice very much, as it allowed needed miles to pass between him and the ferry.

He needed distance so the reports from his or the dispatcher's guns would not announce his presence to the Tories back at the river. Confident now that the two were well out of hearing range, Rice pulled his pistol from his holster, and unleashed Liberty after passing passed a bend in the road. Within a moment the Tory was back in view, and still had no idea that he was being followed. Perhaps gunplay would not be needed to capture this man after all, Rice thought.

"Woah up there" Rice called out as he tucked his pistol back into its saddle holster 'The colonel has another urgent dispatch for you to relay."

Hearing Rice's request, the rider pulled his horse to a stop. Neither side wore any uniforms to distinguish themselves from the other, so with his ruse being successfully played out, Rice casualty trotted forward and within a few strides Liberty came alongside the Tory's horse.

"I have it here in one of my saddles bags" Rice lied as he swiftly pulled his pistol, leveling its barrel at the Tory's chest.

"What is the meaning of this? Where are you taking me?" the shocked courier asked.

"Back to that cabin you boys burnt" Rice responded coolly.

"Why, was that slut one of yours? She was rather sweet, but no quim is worth the effort that you are going through. Didn't anybody tell you that boy? They all have one, you know. You will not get the satisfaction of chastising me for the likes of her I dare say. There is many a slip twixt the cup and the lip." Enraged, Rice flipped the pistol, catching the barrel in his hand and brought its ball handled grip down hard on the rapist head delivering a staggering knockout blow in the process.

"Doubtful," Rice said softly "Doubly so for a hogtied man riding across his horse's back like a bag of rotten potatoes.

The ride back was a hard one for Rice's captive. True to his word, Rice had tied the scoundrel over the back of his horse. And with his belly draped tightly over the saddle, the Tory's innards jarred heavily with every step of his mount. He had complained of his ill treatment, but Rice ignored all his complaints Still,

this bastard simply would not shut up. Rice could not understand why this man refused to be quiet and not incriminate himself. He kept bragging about his conquest of all of the lone wives of Whigs he had enjoyed. How he had, unknown to Roberts pulled his last conquest away from the mob and her children into a corncrib. How she had fought to keep him off, but lacked the strength to save herself. How easily he had ripped open her jacket and stays. How the sweetest of quim was that taken by force. The panic on her face when she realized she was fighting a losing battle. Maybe he was trying to entice Rice into untying him so he could try an escape before punishment could begin, maybe he was just stupid, and still lost in the thrill of his detestable deeds, or too insane to understand he was digging his own grave. Either way Rice could not take any more of what was spewing out of the foul mouth of this man. First a gag was placed around his mouth but he soon chewed his way through the yellow checked cloth. At that, Rice went back to what worked best.

Another blow from his pistol's butt finally ended his consent babbling. It was dark by the time they arrived back at the burned-out cabin site. Ben was setting beside a fire with a middle-aged woman and four children. As Rice rode into the yard she saw his prisoner. She calmly stood up and adjusted the neckline of her shift. With the memories of his captive's statements still fresh in his mind, Rice looked at her ripped, soiled, white skirt. The faded blue neckline of her jacket had been re-sewn with a black thread. The stitches made in haste to repair the garment as quickly as possible. The needle and thread, no doubt supplied by Ben since her home was in ashes.

She gazed at the Tory for only a moment with little expression on her face. Then looking at Ben, ever so solemnly, she nodded her head, turned her back, and walked off into the night, guiding her children before her as they walked away.

As Rice dismounted from Liberty, Ben untied the reins of the Tory's horse that Rice had tied to the back of his own saddle to lead it in. Ben picked up a lantern and led the horse up even with Rice and handed him the reins.

"I got this one riding away from their camp at the ferry" Rice explained "He has a dispatch tucked in one of those saddle bags.

"Have you read it?" Cleveland asked.

"No, didn't have time to."

"I see" Ben said as he grabbed the unconscious man by his long dark hair. He then pulled the man's head up in order to see his face. "Has he talked any?"

"Too much for my taste," Rice replied.

"That explains the knot on his head and the swollen eye I suppose," Ben said as he released the hair.

"I can explain that Sir"

"No need, I have a good idea as to why." Ben said as he opened the saddle bag. Rice took the lantern from Ben and held it as Ole Roundabout read the dispatch.

"It's nothing" Ben said as he wadded the paper up in his fist "Just instructions from Roberts to his wife on what to do back at his plantation. I'm relieved that it was nothing so important that it would keep this bastard from swinging. Did he tell you what he did?"

"Yes, but I'm somewhat surprised by her reaction" Rice said looking back into camp. "She was so calm. It was not the reaction I was expecting."

"Her husband is off with the local militia and she does not want anybody else to know what she had to endure. She said she saw you ride by this afternoon, but she was reluctant to reveal herself. She had nothing to mend her dress with at the time. Once we got here and she showed herself, I took her aside and put two and two together as she told her story, but not until after she made me swear an oath not to repeat what had happened. The only reason I'm telling you is the fact that you already know what as trespassed. You do understand what I'm saying don't you Rice?"

"Yes, Sir I'll take it to the grave, but he will not" Rice said pointing at the Tory. "We need to gag him or he will tell all, at the first opportunity. He takes a misplaced pride in repeating his actions. He will talk just to unnerve her one more time if he can."

"If that is the case, we'll just have to do what has to be done ourselves, before he has that chance," Ben explained as he began to untie the condemned man from the saddle. "This rope should snap his neck with no trouble at all."

Rice placed another gag into the rapist mouth before he pushed the body off the horse's back. The short fall from the saddle awoke the man as he hit the ground. Colonel Cleveland and Rice quickly pushed the man back up on the horse's back, but this time with his hands tied behind his back with strong rawhide tugs. Rice walked along beside the prisoner looking him in the eye as the Tory tried to stare him down. As Ben was leading the horse out of view from the rest of the camp, Rice realized this man had yet to grasp the fact that he was about to meet his end. He still had that cocky look on his face and it did not set well with Rice.

Taking the rope in his hand Rice began to tic a noose at the end, never breaking eye contact with the Tory as he did so. "Should we let him have any last words Colonel?"

"I think not." was the reply. "From what you have said Rice, I believe he has already done enough talking. Ahh, that limb should do the trick.

All of the defiance that the condemned man had just shown, suddenly vanished as Rice tossed the noose over the indicated limb. Ben grabbed the sleeve of the Tory's work shirt in an attempt to pull him down low enough to place the rope around his neck, but he was met with a wild. desperate resistance. Rice, having already tied off the rope, jumped on the horse's back to help put the noose over the furious man's head. It took all of his strength to do so as the Tory lounged his head backward in an attempt to head butt Rice, but he only made contact with Rice's shoulder, as the noose finally found its way home. When Rice had dismounted Ben asked, "Did you ever get this sugar sticks name?"

"No, I was too mad to ask, and he never volunteered it."

As Ben was leading the horse forward to tighten the rope, he looked back up into the man's face and said "I suppose we'll never know. Some people are not worth knowing."

"Wait, I want a moment!" called out a strong voice from the darkness. "I want to see his eyes. That is what he kept telling me as he was having his way."

As the lady of the house walked forward, Rice saw the rage he had expected from her when he and the rapists first entered camp. She could no longer conceal her hatred. Here in the darkness,

she could have her revenge in almost complete concealment. "What did you call me? A van neck I believe. Well this van neck is going to show you there is indeed many a slip twixt the cup and the lip. Another one of your favorite sayings, I believe."

Then she just stood there watching as all hope drained from her attacker's face. He was frantically looking around for help, but realizing none was coming, he quickly turned to Ben and began to mutter under the gag as loud as he could in an effort to get the Colonel's attention.

As Ben reached up to remove the gag he said "Well a few words now won't kill us I suppose. Whatever you have to say, say it quickly!"

The Tory licked his upper lip and said while looking into Ben's eyes "Let me go and I'll tell all I known. We got word from Richard Pearis that the Cherokee are going to attack your settlements. So, we started this raid to draw y'all away from your homes to make it easier from them. You need to cut loose on your chase of Roberts and return home as soon as possible. At least that is what I would do if I was you."

"Old news." Ben replied, "They were defeated last week, now it's your time."

As the condemned man began to cuss, Ben roughly replaced the gag back in his mouth.

"I could listen to you lie all night, but supper calls." Ben announced as he again took the side of the horse's bridle. As the prisoner's eyes rested a hateful gaze back onto his victim, she returned one in earnest. Without breaking eye contact she said "Go ahead Colonel Cleveland. Send that whiskered thing to hell!"

Rice watched as the horse moved out from under the man struggling in the grip of the noose. It was a slow death, for the rope was too short to break his neck in the fall. His legs kicked about wildly for a long moment until he finally choked to death. She held her fist clenched tightly behind her back, showing no sympathy, as he slipped off to his just reward. Finally, she broke the silence as she looked at Rice and said, "Thank you for bringing him back, I needed to see that."

With an appreciative nod she looked over to where Ben stood waiting, and said "That was quite adequate, You sir, have done your duty well tonight. I will think of him no more, as if he were a piece of dung wiped from my shoe."

Chapter 44

The Call of Sheep

This morning, Colonel Cleveland had broken camp well before sunup. He knew it would be a difficult ride to the ferry. The sky was overcast with no moonlight to brighten the way and no stars were visible. The horses moved slowly down the narrow road, staying on the path only because they could see the faint outline of the front rider in the darkness. In the lead was Rice, flanked by Jack on one side and John Grider on the other, both holding tin lanterns to keep them from straying off the road. They had gotten the lanterns from Val and Jacob, who had led the first leg of the pursuit. Ben knew it was dangerous to the light bearers, for if Roberts had posted sentries along the road, they would be the first to draw fire from the Tories. Rice had told Ben that no one had followed the dispatcher at his departure, but Ben quickly pointed out that there had still been enough daylight and time for Roberts to do so, if he had decided to after Rice had ridden away last evening. The ferry was situated on low lying ground downhill from the ridge that Rice had spied from. Now that they had reached their destination, the candles and lanterns were snuffed out and returned to a pack horse at the end of the line. The morning air was quite, the wind was yet to stir and all was silent below. Rice was sure the man next to him must hear his heart beating from the excitement in his chest. The sun was yet to rise over the northeastern hill across the still waters of the river. Time seemed to have come to a stop. The wait seemed long to Rice, but he knew that it had actually been short in real time, and his eagerness for the coming charge was slowing the sands of time only in his head. He had always hated waiting, but there was little choice here in this darkness. The Tories had let their fires burn out overnight and that had been a good decision on Roberts's part. Ben had said if there was a fire still burning anywhere, that would be the charging point of the attack. Finally, to Rice's relief, the sunlight broke the crest of the hilltop, and with it the air was instantly filled with the sounds of the forest awakening. Insects began to stir, filling the air with their buzzing. Leaves were being rustled by the day's new wind and a family of gray squirrels had ventured from their nest, and were starting to cut into the acorns from a hickory to Rice's left. A thick morning fog hovered over the bottom below, keeping the Tory camp well out of the militia's sight.

Jack tapped Rice's tomahawk to indicate for him to keep it handy as the men began to descend the hill. The heavy fog could easily make this a hand to hand fight. Rice pushed his rifle over his shoulder, letting it hang there by its strap. He took the tomahawk in his right hand, and just for good massager pulled a knife, from under his wool sash that he kept wrapped around his waist, with his left.

The first burned out campfire that Rice reached was void of any men. No tents or blankets lay on the ground, just ash from the night before. With every step Rice took, it became more evident that Roberts had already crossed over the river. As Rice reached the river's edge, he saw that the ferry's rope had been cut from the other side, and its barge had floated adrift downstream, landing on the far bank in a bend of the river. A few boats were left on this side of the river, but they had large holes knocked into their bottoms. The ferry's owner walked up to the riverbank and stood between Rice and Val as he said "That son of a bitch Roberts did that to make his escape. A Tory spy saw y'all's camp last night, as well as a hanging. He rode in and reported your presence to Roberts. It sure did spook him. He did not have a whole lot of fire left in his belly after he heard that report. His feet could not hold, so he made it impossible for you to follow him over the water. Damn, it will take me a good week to get things back in working order around here."

As Rice slid his knife back into its holster, the mocking sound of a sheep's bah was called out from across the water to taunt the Whigs, by a lone member of the rear guard of Robert's force. He then laughed just as loudly, and disappeared into the woods before John Grider could respond with his rifle.

"Is there any other way across?" Ben asked in disgust, not taking his eyes off the far bank.

"Not for miles," the ferryman answered "I'm afraid the fox has sprung the trap today Colonel. James Roberts[35] is one wily critter."

Chapter 45

Silhouettes

"Stop squirming around," Racheal said looking at her husband with her lead pencil in her hand. "You'll have your freedom in a moment. I declare you are as bad as a boy getting his first haircut."

Rice exhaled a long breath while trying to sit still at his table. His eyes focused on the blackened silhouettes that graced the cabin's walls. Racheal was quite talented at drawing profile portraits of her family. Both of her parents had sat for her and she had even charmed Jeremiah into posing a few months before his death; now a prized possession, after his passing. She and been drawing silhouettes for years. First by tracing sunlight shadows of her subject on paper attached to the wall then coloring the tracing in with black but it was sometimes hard to capture the proper size because shadow can be distorted if the distance between the subject and the wall was too close or too far away. However, that no longer was an issue for she had mastered her art so well she could simply freehand the portrait to

[35] James Roberts was quite active in the war. He and his Tories where mention in many revolutionary War pensions by the men he had fought. Roberts was born in Kent, England. He was in Dunmore's war of 1774 at the battle of Point Pleasant. Because of his Tory leanings, his land in Montgomery County, Virginia was confiscated on July 5,1776. In 1779 his land in Surry County, North Carolina was also confiscated. However, in 1780 he got back his Virginia land.

any size she desired. Once the portrait was finished, she would glue it to a piece of wood for display, as well as for safe keeping.

As he had been sitting here Rice's mind was still trying to come to grips with the fact that Roberts' Tories had escaped. Maybe that was why he could not sit still. Ben was quite disgusted with the outcome of the pursuit, and a lot of those ill feelings were souring within Rice as well.

"There!" she declared setting down the pencil "You have your leave sir."

Rice rose from the chair and walked down to the other end of the table to study his image. Placing both of his hand on her shoulders, he bent down and laid his cheek next to hers. "I must say Rachael, that is without a doubt the best-looking subject you have ever captured. I never realized I was so handsome my dear. No wonder you pursued me so diligently" he teased.

"Well I must admit that I did correct most of your flaws. It can be quite startling to admit that one's husband has such a weak profile." Rachael bantered back.

"Thank you my dear, for attempting to teach me some humility," Rice whispered into her ear just before he kissed her cheek. But as he drew away after the kiss he said, "However, I doubt that your attempts will ever take. You are wasting your breath, for I am indeed a truly flawed. man."

Racheal rolled her I eyes and announced "You are rotten to the core Rice Medaris, but I do want to thank you for doing this. I wanted to draw it before you left again." She said somberly changing the playful mood between the two of them.

"I know" Rice answered "Why else do you think I finally gave into your request for the sitting? My wish though would be that I had a pocket sized one of you to carry inside my waist coat instead. I must find someone who can capture your likeness for me. Could you do one of yourself?"

"Not hardly!" she replied with a laugh. "Maybe someone at the next rendezvous at Mulberry Fields could pen one.

"Or perhaps Salisbury" Rice replied "I must have one soon."

"Is Rutherford about ready to muster" Rachael asked?

"I believe so," Rice answered. "We need to break the Cherokee's will to make war while they are still weak from their latest defeats. It has to be soon."

And soon it was to be, for General Rutherford had that very night issued the call to arms, ordering his expedition into motion, and Rice was more than willing to accept the General's call to rendezvous at Davidson's Fort.

It was the largest muster Rice had ever witnessed in all of his days; nothing like the gatherings in the past at Mulberry Fields. Not a man was absent from the rolls and there were several new faces buying time as they all waited for Captain Silas Martin[36] and his men to arrive from Salisbury. It was late on a muggy Saturday night, the 16th of August and Ben was still in command; at least until they met up with General Rutherford. He had been using this time wisely,

---

[36] Captain Silas Martin of Surry County, North Carolina took part in the siege of Charleston. On the morning of June 28, 1776 according to the Pension application of Absalom Nixon of Christian County, Kentucky .Pension, # W3033.

reorganizing the men into new companies. Rice had little to do in the matter, because he was to stay with the men from Fort Grider who were yet to fall into the ranks. They would join the army as it passed the fort in the coming days.

Jack and Annabel were here as well. They, like Rice and Rachael, were planning to size up the approaching army, to see if its numbers were what they were hoping for. The decision of what to do with the women was in the balance, depending on the strength of General Rutherford's call to arms. If they were wanting, the wives would ride along to Old Fed's fort for another forting-up that would have to be endured without their husbands. This was something Rachael shuttered at the thought of. She and Annabel both wanted to stay back at her and Rice's cabin with the dogs and livestock. They both had handled themselves well at the siege earlier in the year, and saw no reason to believe they would be in any danger now that the Cherokee were on the run, and the Tories having been disbursed as well, besides her father was only a few hours away. If something came up or a call of alarm came, they could ride over and stay with her parents. Rice was hoping the two would consent to stay at the fort again, but he understood their reluctance to do so.

Robert Cleveland had invited all of the women and children that were present to spend the night under his roof. There were several of them, so many that the Meeting House was already overflowing. But Rice and Rachael declined, choosing instead to cuddle under their engagement tree so they could enjoy one more night of each other's company. They were joined by Jack and Annabel, and soon a fire was kindled, and after some small talk the two couples each took a side of the fire for their own. The men lying with their backs to the flames and their arms tucked around their wives. Rachael rolled over and took Rice's hand into her own and looking into his eyes softly said, "Another night together."

"And another reason to remember this tree," Rice chuckled.

"I do love our tree," she replied. "What do you suppose those two over there are whispering about?"

"Sweet nothings I would say, the same as us. You know, I am already missing you."

"Me too," she said squeezing his hand hard. They did not speak anymore, just a soft rub of each other's noses followed by a kiss good night. Soon afterward, the firelight faded and they fell asleep in each other's arms.

Rice rose before the sun, and as the dawn began to break he stoked the fire with a stick, stirring up what was left of the coals from the night before. Bacon, which Rice was convinced made everything better, might just take away some of the soreness from his back, and be a pleasant surprise for his still sleeping wife once she awoke, he thought.

"Can't sleep?" Jack asked, setting up.

"Guess not," Rice replied as he dropped the bacon into his spider iron skillet. "The first of many a night outdoors I suppose, better get used to it".

"Aye, it will be," Jack agreed, "And the last with a soft one by our sides as well," he said looking at Annabel. We have had too many evenings like last night, too many for a certainty. Once this is all over, Annabel-girl and I will move into our own cabin. Ben has made me an offer on that tract of land across the Yadkin. You know, over the mountain peak. We talked it over last night and we both agreed. It is time for us to put down roots, so to speak. Annabel and I that is."

"And the Cherokee?" Rice asked?

"God willing, they will be gone by then," Jack said, tapping Sweet Lips' stock in his hand. I mean, that is why we are here.'

Rice nodded his head in agreement as Annabel rose from her sleep. "Annabel" he asked over the popping sound of the frying bacon "Do you possess the hand and eye to produce a Silhouette of Rachael for me while we are away?"

"Yes," she said." if you possess the supplies to do so. I used to draw the Millers when I was with them. It will be a pleasant pastime for us ladies while you two are away. Better than listening to the other women packing tales."

"Ah, that will be grand Annabel. I thank you for your willingness to do it for me. Here, have a strip of bacon to start your day" Rice replied behind his smile. "That always helps when the day is new."

"See Rice, I may not be the best at acquiring land, but by God I can pick a bonnic wife" Jack proclaimed proudly as he wrapped a loving arm around his beloved.

"Well Rice, it looks as though you got you wish," Rachael stated boldly. "I would even dare to say that the best place to make such a drawing would be back at home, wouldn't you say. Safe inside the strong walls you two supplied, and not at Fort Grider with all of those old men and boys fluttering around two young brides. I will set for Annabel, but only there."

'I suppose so," Rice agreed after a long groan "but Jack has a say in the matter as well don't you think?"

"So, they need a "by my leave" do they?" Jack said standing tall, basking in the fact that he was the center of attention. "So, this is what men of power feel like when making a decision." he said in jest.

But then he turned to the women and the playful look on his face disappeared, and his expression sobered. "If I know Rice, he will agree with me on this matter. If Rutherford has the manpower everyone says he will have, you two have my blessing to stay at the cabin.

"Agreed," Rice announced "We should have a good gage by the Salisbury turnout, I just pray that this is the correct decision."

Chapter 46

The Audience

Patrick Ferguson's posture, though extremely slender, was very elegant as he stood under an ageing oak on The Long Walk[37] . He had an air of confidence that few thirty-two-year men possessed. He had the reputation of a man of good taste and style and most of all of being very intelligent. He was known to be the best of friends to those he cared about. A man who would come to a friend's aide even at the worst of times. He was a man of great moral fiber, his only vice being the fairer sex, whose company he enjoyed immensely, with that aside, honor and his name where often companions.

He had the good fortune of coming from one of the better families in Scotland. His ancestry included the names Murray, Stewart, Douglas and Cunningham. His lineage could be traced back to the victorious Robert the Bruce, the King who had freed Scotland.

---

[37] The Long Walk is a grass covered avenue of elm trees at Windsor castle. It was commenced by Charles II in 1680. A carriage road was added by Queen Anne in 1710. King George III added a pond with gardens. He used it as a playground for his children and to entertain guest in the summer.

Ferguson had the benefit of being educated at the Royal Military Academy in Woolwich. He was a member of the Royal North British Dragoons, "The Scots Greys". He had served in the Seven Years' War in Prussia, only to be stricken by chronic synovial tuberculosis of the knee. He was sent home to recuperate and once he was well, had wasted little time resuming his military career, despite his new limp from that illness. He was soon stationed in the West Indies where his regiment restored the King's authority during The Black Carib Revolt[38] on St. Vincent. After the revolt was contained, he purchased a sugar plantation on the island of Tobago. He was a well-traveled man that had already witnessed a lifetime of experiences. Maybe that is why the redhead stood so coolly here today on the grounds of Windsor Castle. Patrick Ferguson had that light in his eye.

But on the other hand, so did King George III. He could tear apart the most hardened of men with only a word when he wished. He often made sport of the very best of the nobility and took joy in doing so. But the King had an interest in weaponry, and was eager to see Ferguson demonstrate one of the new breech loading rifles he had just made in Birmingham.

Although not a gunsmith, Ferguson, had been working on improving the Frenchmen, Isaac De La Chaumette's 1720 design of a breech loading rifle. Ferguson's version fired a standard British carbine ball of .615 caliber, the same as the Brown Bess. Yet it was three pounds lighter and much easier to handle. But unlike the Bess,

---

[38] The Black Carib Revolt was a conflict on the Caribbean Island of St. Vincent in the years of 1772-73. The Caribs were descended from the original population of the eastern Caribbean who had intermarried with runaway black slaves. The leader of the Revolt was Joseph Chatoyer a chieftain of the Black Carib. Under his leadership the Carib would force Great Britain into signing a treaty; it was the first time Britain had been forced to sign an accord with indigenous people in the Caribbean.

Ferguson's rifle had a swiveling trigger guard. Once the trigger guard was turned it lowered a screw in the breech low enough to drop in the charge and ball. It was a very quick loading weapon. This was Ferguson's opportunity to have his design placed into every British armory around the world. However, he also knew that the King was slow to forgive a mistake. This shooting demonstration had to inspire and make a lasting impression or Ferguson would never see the King's court again.

So here Ferguson stood, in the shade of an old oak tree, eyeing the round table that was set before the King. All he saw on the tabletop to drink was tea. The King rarely drank wine, and being as frugal as he was, there was none for his guest. So, Pattie, as his family and friends called Ferguson, pulled a flask from his vest to wet his dry lips. Not that he could partake from the king's table. The table was dressed with some of the Kings favorites, beef, lamb, pigs head, root vegetables such as beets and turnips, and fruit. Brown bread with butter was also on display next to a simple steamed pudding. All was set for the King's appearance. Ferguson even had one of his rifles on display next to the King's chair.

Ferguson gazed down the row of trees to seven well placed targets ranging from 100 to 300 yards away. The wind was still; a perfect day for a marksman to prove his worth. His gaze was broken by the sound of the King's approaching party. Not only the King, but also Queen Charlotte was attending the demonstration. Ferguson had hoped Lord North [39] would be attending as well, but he was yet to be seen. Lord Townshend had already seen the rifle and liked it so much

---

[39] Frederick North, 2nd Earl of Guilford 1732 – 1792) was the acting Prime Minister of Great Britain from 1770-1782. He is the father "OVER" of the Intolerable Acts that was meant to punish the American Colonies after the Boston Tea Party and was a dear friend of King George III.

he had arranged this meeting today. North would be another feather in Ferguson's hat.

The King was dressed in a red waistcoat that had black cuffs around the wrist. Both coat sleeves had four gold buttons sewn onto the fabric. He wore a blue sash under the waistcoat and over a white vest. His tricorn hat was black, braided in a handsome gold trim. The Queen's hair was bound up high on her head. She had several strands of pearls intertwined with her auburn hair. She had a blue silk choker around her neck and it was adorned with a teardrop pearl that was the size of her thumb. A fox fur was draped over her gold satin gown, to keep out the chill of the cool English air. Her eyes were green and her nose was oddly turned up. She was not a great beauty but the King was very devoted to his Queen. She was the mother of his eleven children [40] and she had a wit that he enjoyed. It was said he had never taken a mistress, unlike his father who had taken many.

As the party gathered around the banquette table, the King looked at Ferguson who was bent in his bow. Still bent from the waist with his hat in his hand, Ferguson was executing the etiquette that such a situation required. His eyes were still focused on King George's boots when his Majesty spoke. "Satisfaction has become a rare commodity these days. I sincerely hope that today you will break this unacceptable trend. Proceed."

Patrick Ferguson had every intention of doing just that. He again bowed to the King and said "As you wish, your Majesty."

He then turned downfield and exhaled a long breath. He quickly shouldered his rifle and taking aim at the closest target, pulled the trigger. Before the smoke had cleared allowing all to see that the

---

[40] Queen Charlotte would bear fifteen children to the King in her lifetime.

first shot was true, the marksman had already reloaded and fired again, hitting the second target. With a quick turn of the trigger guard the third round was in place. Like the other two shots this round also found it's mark. The King looked very satisfied as Pattie hit the last four targets in rapid succession. He had struck all seven and in less than one minute.

"You sir," the King announced "are going to the Americas. There, you will show those grossly repugnant Whigs the error of their rebellious ways. Revolt, hostility and rebellion will cease under the guidance of your teachings. Now tell me, Mister Ferguson just how expensive is this weapon of yours?"

Chapter 47

The Wager

Rice found himself climbing up the hill that faced the western side of Fort Grider. He was nervous, and not quite sure how he had gotten into this argument, but here he was. Little John Grider was his only companion on this mission; a trustworthy witness to what was about to unfold. As the two reached the hill's eminence Rice looked up to the top of Hibriten Mountain before looking back to the fort. "If I miss I'll never live this down" he thought. He let out a breath and looked back at the Fort. What he saw below was a crowded stockade, at least on the northern interior of the fort. The men of Salisbury had indeed turned out well. In such numbers that Rachael and Annabel were confident enough to returned to the cabin on Warriors Creek.

Every man below was looking at an old ragged brown frock coat. A target that Old Fed had placed on a cross made of hickory sticks, to settle the debate.

"No shame if you miss. That is a tall order for any marksman" John said looking down.

"Well, if I don't hit it I'll never hear the end of it."

"True, but if you puncture that hemp; you will be praised for sure."

Rice smiled as he placed a round patch of blue silk over the muzzle of his longrifle. Then he placed the ball onto the silk and drove them home, down the rifle's barrel.

"Now, that is smart" John said as he rubbed his whisker covered chin. "That will give you a few more yards.

"That's the idea" Rice replied as he withdrew the rod.

This had all started this morning as Captain Martin was drinking his morning chicory. As he was emptying the bottom of his pewter cup his eyes spotted this hillside over the fort's walls just above his cup's rim. "One fieldpiece" he declared "placed on that hill could disable every man, woman and child inside the walls of this place and the enemy would not even damage the fort's walls in doing so," he proclaimed. "Win the prize without destroying it."

[41] William Lenoir would go on to settle near Fort Grider at his home, Fort Defiance. Lenoir would become one of North Carolina's early Statesmen. The town that bears his name would grow around the sight of Fort Grider. The town of Lenoir is now the county seat of Caldwell County North Carolina. William Lenoir's journal is one of the most detailed accounts of General's Rutherford expedition of 1776.

Henry Sumter, an ageing hunter and Veteran of the French and Indian War, spoke up and declared that in his youth all he would need was his long rifle and a wind free day, like today, and he could perform the same feat without the benefit of a cannon.

"Hell you say," replied William Lenoir [41] a newcomer to Mulberry Fields and a man who was looking to making a name for himself in Rutherford's Army. He had just this day accepted the appointment of first Lieutenant under Ben, and was feeling his oats. "I would like to see such a shot, why not show us how you did it all those years ago?"

"Old and fuzzy eyes my boy, but I could do it back in the day. How about it Fed, you have been here as long as anyone. Have you ever been fired on from up there?"

"No" answered the fort's founder. "I doubt if anyone has ever thought to try. I would guess that any shot fired from that range could harmlessly be caught by a bare hand, because the ball would be so spent. No harder than a hailstone falling."

"Well, let's see then," Sumter cried out. Captain Martin Sir, I see a few kegs of rum on some of those pack horses of yours, and I'm a hoping that at some point you will let us men have a turn at the jug on this campaign. Is that the case, Sir?

"It is," replied Martin.

"Well Lenoir my boy; will you wager you're first ration of spirits on the outcome of a friendly contest between you and me?"

"Sure" Lenoir said without hesitation. "You have already said you can't see any more.

"Oh, I can still see" the old hunter replied, "Not like I use to, and not well enough for a shot like we are speaking of. But I can still see well enough to know it is possible" Sumter proclaimed, pointing an old boney finger at Rice. "I hear you parted a few hairs here a while back."

"Well yes, but not at that range," Rice said somewhat surprised to be drug into the fray.

"I don't know about this" Lenoir said coming to his feet "I have yet to see Rice bare down on anything with that rifle of his."

"Well now," Jack said coming to Sumter's aide; "are not you the one who said a shot like that could not be made? Besides, Rice is a Blacksmith by trade, not a hunter. You should jump at such a bet."

Like Jack, all of the Grider's began to rib Lenoir to accept the challenge. Rice was not so sure they had that much confidence in his skills with a gun. From the way they were elbowing each other and by the looks on their faces, Rice was fairly sure they saw a good opportunity to tease a friend. Especially if he failed before the whole fort. Either way they would win, bragging about their friend's marksmanship or playfully dragging his name through the mud if he missed.

Ben was enjoying the scene just as much as Captain Martin and the Grider men were. "John," he said "Go with Rice if you please, my boy. That way when I relieve Silas of the burden of toting such a heavy purse, he can be assured that the shot was truly fired from the top.

So off Rice and John went, and now was the time to see who would be drinking whose rum in the days to come. Rice propped his hip up beside an oak to steady his aim. He could see the frock coat between the wishbone sights of his rifle. He held it there for a moment as he let out a breath, then he squeezed the trigger sending the shot to call.

"I swear Rice!" John called out in a shocked loud voice. "I saw that frock coat move."

Rice was not so sure. The smoke from his pan was still heavy in the air and it was hard to see if his shot was true. But as the men below rushed to the coat and a loud cheer began to float up onto the mountain Rice knew that Lenoir's cup would be on the dry side of this wager.

Chapter 48

Davidson Fort

The departure from Fort Grider and the march to Davidson Fort had been fairly smooth and uneventful. On Monday, an easy crossing of the St John's River was made. On Tuesday, more Militiamen were waiting at Quaker Meadows, the home plantation of General Charles McDowell, a 2nd cousin of Rachael's. The General was not at home at the time, being away on military matters. However, two hundred pounds of black powder was alone with three dozen head of cattle and even more men. The General's mother, Margaret acted as hostess, feeding the men the best she could from the plantation stores. That night a powerful Presbyterian sermon was given by Rev. James Hall from the second book of Samuel. *"So, I stood upon him, and slew him, because I was sure that he could not live after that he was fallen: and I took the crown that was upon his head, and the bracelet that was on his arm, and have brought them hither unto my Lord".* The sermon was intended to inspire, and even to console, a man's soul if needed. Rice knew where he stood with the almighty. His conscience was clear at the moment and he intended to keep it that way. War could bring out the worst in men and Rice was sure he was on the right side of this conflict. Yet he was not going to allow anyone to lead him onto a path to darkness while on this expedition. King Saul's past and the Cherokee's future may have their similarities, but the Cherokee's fate was still in doubt.

Rice was pleased with the army's progress as was Ben, and everyone else for that matter. They had yet to meet General Rutherford, but they could already tell this was not a man who was complacent about the details of his campaign. However, even with the best of planning, a few things went awry. Seven steers were lost near Buck Creek Wednesday afternoon, and John Grider complained of night sweats and weakness in his legs on the way to Davidsons. Friday, near the Catawba, the militiamen saw the reason for this army's existence. There was a lot of damage done by the Cherokee and the Tories alike. Burned-out cabins, fresh graves, and plenty of old Indian sign. This did little to dampen the men spirits, if anything it boosted them. William Sharpe, who was to be Rutherford's aide, also joined the march with even more men.

Davidson Fort [42] was located just a day's march southwest of Cathy's Fort, with both being about the same in size and design. Davidson had been built just this spring by four brothers, John, Samuel, William and George Davidson for protection against the Cherokee raiding parties. But at the time, they had no way of knowing that 2700 men would be here today, about to make amends.

It was nightfall when Rice and the rest of the Surry and Rowan County militias arrived. Rice had never seen so many people at one time in his whole life. This group definitely made the turnout at Mulberry Fields seem small. It was as if every Whig in the Carolinas was stationed here at the new outpost. Camp fires surrounded the fort's walls by the dozens if not the hundreds. The sound of all of

---

[42] Davidson Fort is today the town of Old Fort in McDowell County, North Carolina.

these men talking to each other carried far on the night air. It was as if they knew they were far too strong to worry about being attacked.

Rice looked out over the outer grounds of the fort. Out there somewhere was Rachael's brother, Joseph. He had been spying between Cathey's and Davidson's all summer. Rachael had penned him a letter and Rice wanted to deliver it as soon as possible. As he was scanning the men's faces for his brother-in-law Martin and Val walked up by his side.

"Seen Joseph yet?" Val asked.

"No." was the simple and tired replied. "What about Jacob, have you seen him yet? He is down from Cathey's is he not?"

"That he is" Martin said walking away "If you run up on him send him to the east corner of the fort's outer wall. John is stretched out over there, sick as a dog. Jack is already looking for him on the back side of the fort for us."

"Will do" Rice assured the brothers as they stepped into the sea of men. In all the time Rice had known the Grider's not a single one of them had ever even hinted at being unwell. John was surely in bad shape if he was laid up at a time like this. This was a historical moment and everyone here knew it. John lived for moments like these. Men were proudly showing off newly acquired rifles and tomahawks to each other. Every blade was being stroked over a whet rock; stories of each other's hardships were being told of this summer's raids. And the tone that these men spoke in let everyone within hearing know that this was no laughing matter. Men in their sixties encouraging boys in their teens. Rutherford's Army had a confidence that would make any officer on the seaboard a happy man, no matter what color his uniform, but Rice could already see that some were going to be unruly. Rutherford and his officers would have to hold a tight rein in the coming days in order to keep control. Rice knew that Rutherford had no lost love for the Cherokee, but he had a reputation of being a man that would not let his dislike for something or someone cloud his better judgment.

Rice thought that if Dragging Canoe could have envisioned an army of this size about to overrun his country with vengeance and so much hatred in their hearts, the Cherokee would have never attacked the settlements this spring.

Rice continued to weave his way through masses and finally he saw Joseph standing among some buckskinners. They were watching as a single Catawba warrior trotted out of Davidson's open gate and disappeared into the night.

"I was under the impression we were going to kill us some redskins on this push into the mountains" Rice said to announce his presence.

"Yes, but not one of the General's runners, off to see Williamson [43]" Joseph replied. "See that buck's tail hanging from his hair lock; that's meant to distinguish our Catawba's from the Cherokee. Maybe on the way back though, after we don't need 'em anymore. Who would care then if one turned up dead?" He chuckled, but not so as to let Rice know if he was kidding or not. "Good to see ya Rice. It's about time you boys from back home got down here."

"You been here long?" Rice inquired.

---

[43] Major Andrew Williamson 1730-1786, was a Scots immigrant who hailed from the Ninety-Six District of South Carolina. He was the commander of the South Carolina Militia that would take part in The Rutherford campaign. Williams had been fighting the Cherokee since the 1760's. He was the Whig commander at the first battle of Ninety-Six in 1775 what today is known as the Battle of Fort Williamson.

"Just a few days, came down with Rutherford from Cathey's."

"So, he is here too?"

"You can rest assured of that. The General has been planning this the better part of a year now. He is feeling poorly, but a little gout is not about to slow him down now" Val said as he walked out and around Joseph.

"Val!" Rice shouted "You need to find John. He has come down with something himself. It's so bad that your brothers are out looking for you, but John is lying back at that corner of the wall" Rice said as he pointed back to where John lay.

"Damnation! Val exclaimed shaking his head "Is he shot or stabbed?"

"Neither, just sick with the sweats, and he is very weak as well." Rice said as Val trotted away.

"Well there go the Grider's" Joseph said in disgust. "The General will pull any man from the ranks that might bring a sickness into camp, and any men that's been too close to him as well. Once he finds out about this, all of them Grider boys will be stuck here. If I was you Rice, I would steer clear if you want to claim any scalps in the days to come. Mark my words, they will be stationed here to man this fort while we are out killing us some Indians."

"Are you sure about that?" Rice asked, leaning in closer so no one else could hear.

"Oh yah, he left ten or so back at Cathey's. The pox won't stop this invasion, nor hell or high water for that matter."

"He ain't got the pox" Rice said trying to insured John's place in this army. "He probably just ate something that was a little tainted."

"Most likely," Joseph agreed "but that will not matter to Rutherford. The Cherokee are going to pay dearly and Rutherford is going to be the one handing out the Lord's wrath on them bastardly heathens. You can talk till you are plum tuckered out, but it will not change the General's mind on the matter. Come on, I got a lean-to on the other side of the fort. We should get some sleep tonight, for on the morrow we will be heading into the mountains. Rutherford has said as much himself. He was just waiting for you boys to get here and now that you are, we'll be off at dawn."

Rice was tired and with a wave of his arm, he let Joseph lead the way to his sleeping quarters for the night, but once he found out where it was, he would track Jack down before stretching out for the night. Rice hoped that Joseph was wrong about the Grider's but if he was not Rice was going to make darn sure that Jack would not suffer the same fate as they. He needed to be told what Joseph thought. Rice wanted his friends with him on this coming march into the wilds, and if the Grider's were forced to stay behind, Jack was his last close friend here, other than Joseph. If Rice was to fall to a Cherokee warrior he wanted a friendly face by his side to be able to tell his story once the army was back home. Rachael deserved that much.

Chapter 48

The Bond

The night air was cool on Rice's neck as he sat under Joseph's lean-to. Jack was fast asleep, worn out like a young colt after his first race, at least that was how he described how he felt before dozing off.

Joseph had wondered off into the surrounding camp having said that his blood was up too much to sleep. Rice was feeling the same, but he was taking advantage of one of the two candles that Rachael had packed in his haversack. He thought he might as well use it now because Rutherford would certainly ban their use once the Army was into the Cherokee homeland. Cooking fires would be necessary but not candle light. And with the Grider's staying behind, Rice was sure that one if not more of them would be heading back to Feds in the next few days to relay the news about John worsening condition. They would gladly carry Rice's letter home to Rachael. He paused for a moment, not quite sure how to open his letter.

He realized this would be the very first correspondence he had ever written to his wife; so why not begin with it that way.

    My dearest, sweet wife Rachael,

    As I sit here outside the walls of Fort Davison, looking into the darkness I must make note that this is the first time I have ever taken pen in hand to correspond with you. It's odd not having you by my side. It is a hardship I dare not speak of to any of my fellow comrades, so I will relay it to you now. In the daylight I do not dwell on our separation but once darkness falls your sweet face haunts me in camp. Soon the mountains will be between us but I felt they already were that first night I was away. But I know that our love for each other cannot be stopped by something as small and trivial as a mountain. Although we cannot physically touch each other at the moment, our bond one for the other can never be breached in this world, or the next I dare say. You are a part of me as surely as any limb on my body. I do love you so. I just wanted you to know that.

    Some may see my writing tonight as silly and a waste of time and paper but they do not have the joy of possessing a bride as wonderful as I do. They will never know the pride I hold in my heart every time I hear your name spoken and they could never feel an inkling of what I feel when you are so close in my arms. So now that I have once again spoken that you are the best part of my life I will lay down my pen but not before saying once more. I love you so and I will be seeing you soon,

Your Adoring Husband, Rice

Chapter 49

Who Gives a Good Damn?

That very same night John McFall wiped his sweaty forehead with the sleeve of his hunting shirt. It smelled clean and fresh having been washed just yesterday afternoon by a young Cherokee girl.

She had been sharing his bed ever since he had been here at Kituwah [44] the old Cherokee mother town. Her long black hair was lying over her bare breast as she slept, but McFall saw no beauty in her form.

He rubbed his eyes, trying to forget the dream that had just awakened him. He was not sure if it was a dream or a nightmare, but the vision of Rachael was haunting his sleep once again. He could lay

[44] The village of Kituwah was near the Tuckasegee River in Swain County North Carolina. It was close to modern day Bryson City. Today the valley is empty, just farmland and if you look close you can still see the remains of mounds left by the Cherokee's ancestors of the Mississippian culture from over 4000 year ago. The land is now owned by the Eastern band of the Cherokee Nation having been purchased in 1997 by the tribe.

with hundreds of women but no matter how attractive they were or how much they may resemble Rachael, they could never fill the hole that was inside his heart. 'That son of a bitch', he thought, thinking of Rice, 'poisoning her mind the way he did. She should be by my side, not this Indian girl'. He gave the sleeping girl a kick trying to relieve the pain that always seemed to accompany his thoughts of Rachael, but the act did little to tame his madness.

Having become use to McFall's wild dreaming, she rolled over putting her back to him. Still half asleep she pulled her knees up to her stomach as if she were a small ball, a new twist to her sleeping habits. Being smaller, she would be less of a target.

Peering into the overhead darkness of his hut, John knew that Rice had wronged him and he still had not gotten any satisfaction on the matter. The hatred ran deep in his marrow. If I could only get her away from that devil I could win her back he thought, as he placed his clenched fingers behind the back of his head. One night of her in his bed, would be all that he would need. He would show her what kind of man he really was. She may resist at first, but soon she would come to know the pleasures that only he could provide for her. He still held out hope that somehow, somewhere Rice Medaris would get his damn throat cut in this war. It would only be fair. Maybe even by my own hand McFall prayed. 'I need a Tory victory back home to put them rebel bastards on the run, instead of us', he thought. He had made plenty of strong bonds here, with some of the Cherokee, while trading with them over the last few years. But being here was getting old, no matter how well they treated him. Tomorrow morning, he would rise and dress in his Indian garb and head back home. Maybe Gideon was back by now with a stronger militia, and together they could take Quakers Meadow. "Vengeance is mine", he had heard somewhere, maybe in the Bible. He twisted the words in his head, believing they were meant for him. With a victory like that, I can then simply take what is rightfully mine, he thought. The way it should have been all along. A homestead with her and a growing family; that would win back his father's favor as well, McFall theorized. He would be even a more respected man then, more than he already was among the Tories. And as for what the Whigs thoughts, who gives a good damn?

Chapter 50

A Snake In The Garden

Yesterday Rice, Jack and Joseph along with 2400 other men marched out of the open gates of Davidson Fort. Rutherford left about 300 of his militiamen to guard the new outpost and among that number was the Grider's. John was just too ill to go, and Joseph's words rang true about his kin being stationed at the fort as well.

Rutherford had led his army across the Blue Ridge east of Black Mountain at Swannanoa Gap, just before coming down alongside the Swannanoa River. There he made camp for the night. A herd of beef cattle had been driven along in the rear of the procession. They would supply meat at night in the coming days. At dusk, the pack horse train arrived in camp, completing the first day's Westward push.

It was now Monday morning the 2nd day of September and Old Roundabout was to lead the way, along with the rest of the men from Surry County. The goal of the day's march was to reach the French Broad River, if at all possible. Rice and Jack were among this group, but another company had been attached to Ben's command for the day to bolster his numbers. Captain Michael Henderson of Rowan County was not pleased to be a subordinate to Ben, but he had little choice in the matter. Rice was not pleased with the makeup of the day's march either, his was more of a personal reason than a military one. Arthur

McFall was among the Rowan men and Rice was leery of anyone who carried the name of McFall.

"Look at that son of a bitch" Jack muttered under his breath. "If my wife was lost to those damn savages I would not be sniffing around the women of Davidson's Fort the way he was the other night. He does not care one single hoot about Iona I say."

"Yah he talked a sad story for a while, but once he won a gal's sympathy he tended to stop talking about Iona," Rice replied as he glanced across the camp to where McFall stood beside one of the two small cannons that the pack train had been pulling the day before.

"You boys know Arthur?" asked a buckskinner who was packing his haversack with some jerked meat. "Sounded as though you do, I tend to agree with you about that one. He is a snake in the garden, as the song goes. He rode into Salisbury a while back and I made his acquaintance inside Steele's Tavern. Said he had been combing the countryside for his stolen wife. Said she was taken by Injuns. Seemed odd to me that he was looking around Salisbury instead of down here where the Cherokee live. Now I ain't one to brag," the buckskinner continued "But I can hold some licker with the best of them I'll tell you. I have put more than my share under the table. And to give the Devil his due, Arthur can as well, but not quite as well as I can. One-night a while back, it was well past the witching hour and we were the last two still in the tavern. That is when the cup finally got the better of him. He began to cry, and normally that is when I take my leave of a crying drunk, but I thought his first story was not as truthful as he played it to be. So, I put up with him till the tavern was closed for the night. We walked out into Corbin Street and he fell on his ass crying about abandoning his scalped wife to die in the wilds all alone. He finally passed out after that, and I put my boots to good use, leaving that scoundrel where he sat."

Rice stood there for a moment, stunted that Arthur would do something like that. "What?" asked Rice "Are you saying he did find her after all, only to abandon her afterwards? Are you sure?"

"That is what he said. You can never tell if a man is telling the truth or not once he is that far gone, but if I had to bet on it, I would say he was telling the truth. Back at Davidsons the other night, he said he was talking nonsense that night. I let on as though I had no recollection or faculty of what he had said either. But I say he knows I do. He keeps a watchful eye on me most of the time; just like he is now. See how he is staring as we speak?" the Buckskinner said as he turned his back to McFall.

"I don't like for him to know that I know he is watching me all the time. I tell you boys he either left her to die or still worse, he killed her himself and laid the blame on the Injuns. Well, I better fall in with the rest. See you boy's latter."

As the buckskinner walked away to join the rest of the Rowan County Men Rice asked Jack who he was.

"Jonathan Huff," Jack answered. "He is one of the Galbraith Falls [45] men."

"Is he trustworthy?" Rice asked as he shouldered his rifle.

As Jack looked at McFall still staring at them from across the way he said, "Never have caught him in a lie yet, but I really don't know him all that well. But I will say this, we know what we just heard is not out of the realm of possibilities when it come to a McFall's charter, now don't we."

---

[45] Galbraith Falls would later fall in Battle; dying at the Battle of Ramseur's Mill North Carolina on June 20, 1780.

The next day, after breaking camp, the morning march had passed in relative ease. Ben had placed the Scurry men next to the river to march along the shoreline on the path that the Cherokee had blazed years before. Henderson and his men had been in the rear, staying back a few hundred feet. And behind them would be the rest of Rutherford's force. But in an effort to throw a bone to Henderson, hoping to keep him content, Ben had let him place a few spies from his ranks along the western flank. This would not only pacify Henderson, but also insure that no attacks would befall the point of the army. Arthur had been one of the spies picked by Henderson, so he had been out of sight all morning to the delight of Rice and Jack.

The mountain countryside was truly breathtaking and Rice had taken notice of its beauty. Chestnut trees six feet around towered into the blue sky above, ferns covered the forest floor and whenever the wind rustled the treetops above, acorns fell to the ground like rain. However, Rice was not taking anything for granted with an enemy nation coming closer with every step and with it would be danger. He was watching the far shoreline of the Swannanoa as Jonathan Huff and Captain Henderson ran passed him. Rice watched as the two ran down Ben to have a meeting. Rice strolled up next to the men to be privy of the conversion.

Henderson began "Jonathan here is of the opinion that there could be a spot of concern up ahead. He saw a lot of signs here a month ago."

"I'm sure he did Michael, but the further we go we are going to see that everywhere. We are marching into their very heartland. We cannot slow down at every threat. The general made that plain last night when he gave me my orders. Speed is what he wants. What's you point?"

"Just be advised" a red-faced Henderson snapped before addressing Huff. "Jonathan, go out and notify the Spies what you have told us."

As Huff ran off into the woods Ben reminded Henderson who was in command for the day. "Henderson that is a foolhardy order. Those boys out there already know we are in Indian Country and if they don't they are too dumb to be scouting spies in the first place. If that be the case you should have picked better men for the job! We are not stopping until we reach Warriors ford at the French Broad."

Henderson's temper was growing with every word that Ben spoke and the two had become the center of the men's attention. In a rage he spoke through gritted teeth. "I'm going back to tell Rutherford about your lack of concern"

"Yes" Ben interrupted "You are going back, but you Sir, will be doing so as a relieved officer."

"To hell you say!" Henderson objected. "By whose authority?"

Suddenly, the sound of distant gunshot was heard, and as the men reacted to the shot the argument died down for the moment.

"See, I told you as much. We are under attack, and you Ben Cleveland have led us right into it by not taking my word."

Coolly, Ben took a tree as did the rest of the men. "Easy boys, one shot does not make a battle" he said while looking off into the trees. "We will hold here until one of your Spies reports back."

"Or we are overrun" Henderson said, cocking his Brown Bess.

Rice likewise shouldered his rifle as his eyes picked up the movement of an approaching man. He had someone slung over his shoulder lying limp and motionless as though he was already dead, or unconscious at best. The men all gathered around as Arthur McFall laid Jonathan Huff on the ground. Dead. Shot through the neck.

"How many are out there McFall?" Henderson asked,

"None, not a redskin anyway, before he died in my arms he told me a militiaman from our line got spooked and shot him on his approach. He then ran off after seeing what he had done. Jonathan said he had no clue as to who the shooter was, but it was one of us, according to what he said."

As the men were standing over the body the two captains fell back into their argument. Ben had blamed Henderson for the mishap only to have Henderson deny any wrongdoings. As the two were becoming more engaged and became the center of attention once more, Jack walked over to where McFall had sat his rifle up against a tree. He picked it up without anyone seeing and quickly blew down the barrel of the rifle to see if it was now empty. The weapon was still loaded, for the air inside was still tight and did not whistle out of the priming hole. Rice was the only one who saw what Jack had done and he also knew why he did it. Did Arthur just killed the only man who knew about Iona? He had had time enough to reload if he had pulled the trigger. No one would be the wiser if he had. Maybe he was telling the truth, but Jonathan Huff's [46] words from last night come back to haunt Rice as he looked at Jack's skeptical face. "He keeps a watchful eye on me". And "He is a snake in the garden."

---

[46] Jonathan Huff's death was recorded in William Lenoir's Journal of the Cherokee Expedition and also in the Revolutionary War pension papers of John Rounsavall # S9091.

Chapter 51

I Still Owe You One

Huff's death put an end to the day's march. He was laid to rest where McFall had dropped his body. The Rev. Hall gave a moving benediction that many attended, including McFall. But Rice saw something in Arthur's eyes that was somewhat off. Sure, he was there but somehow not there either. Some might see it as indifference but to Rice he looked like a man who was trying not to look guilty. He kept his hands behind his back, clutched into one another. His head stayed bent with his eyes fixed on his own feet. His feet held but his upper body swayed a little. Once the Rev Hall's service was finished, he was gone.

The Next morning the army rose with the sun. With its warm rays falling on their backs they continued on with the march towards the Middletown's. They marched over Huff's grave as they left. This would hide the presence of the grave and insure that the Cherokee would not disturb his last resting place.

The fording of the French Broad River was the day's challenge. Joseph McDowell, along with four hundred men stood guard while the crossing was made. [47] That night another camp was made at an unnamed creek that was named after General Rutherford that very night by his officers. On Wednesday, they walked alongside the widening Pigeon River. It waters splashed hard on the boulders that lined its rough banks. The rigid mountain terrain was now slowing the marchers pace, but that had been expected, and did not hurt the army's spirits in any way. On Thursday, the Rowan County men had taken the point. This allowed Rice and the rest of Cleveland's men an

---

[47] This crossing place became known as The War Ford. It is near the Biltmore Estate in Buncombe County North Carolina.

opportunity to get some rest. They still had to march at the same pace but not having the burden of being the army's eyes. They could at least get some mental rest, if not a physical one.

Rice and Jack were very skeptical about McFall's tale of Huff's death. Unlike Huff, they made it a point to avoiding being alone. In addition, if McFall took to the trees while on the march, they would not follow directly behind him, making sure to keep other Militiamen between them. It was hard enough fighting the Indians, but now they had to watch one of their own, and maybe some others as well. But yesterday, on Friday things had changed. At nightfall Bill Alexander[48], one of the Mecklenburg men, had seen five Indians rushing off in the distance, and he swore that one of them had red hair. He had wisely waited for reinforcements before advancing into their deserted camp. In their haste to escape, the savages had left behind a 45 cal. Smooth bore musket. The five Cherokee spies were heading into the other villages with word of the coming attack. If they were not overtaken today, all chance of surprise would be lost. Surely McFall would realize that if this army was to survive, every man would be needed from this point on. Arthur was much more intelligent than his two brothers, John and George. Surely, he would be wise enough to put personal grudges aside for the time being.

Ben was chosen by General Rutherford to track the fleeing Indians with a ten-man party of Ben's own choosing. Rice, Jack and Joseph along with seven others had marched off last night, as soon as the order was given. Ben had a faint hope that the Cherokee would foolishly kindle a campfire in the darkness, thereby announcing their whereabouts. But that hope disappeared as time passed the midnight hour.

---

[48] William Alexander, Revolutionary War Pension application number is S6496. He was born in Bucks County Pennsylvania.

The Bench knelt down on one knee as he struck the steel to his flint. A spark arced, lighting the ball of flax that lay at his feet. He quickly fueled the fire with a handful of dry twigs. Then bending down, he puckered his lips and blew into the heart of the fire to increase the flames. He looked over his shoulder into the darkness confirming no one was around. He placed a few larger split logs of dead elm on the fire to guarantee the fire would burn deep into the night. The elm would send out an inviting smell as it's smoke floated into the air. He picked up his rifle and backed off, confident that his bait was well set. Doublehead had told a story many times in the past, of how he had killed four Creek warriors years before using this same method. If it worked once, it would again The Bench believed. As the fourteen-year-old walked away from the fire and into the Indian battle line he stepped proud, for this was his plan, and the older warriors had decided to follow it.

Rice walked slowly along a dark path. It was a rough narrow path no more than two feet wide at places. Low hanging limbs from above and rocks down below needed to be stepped around and over. And if he missed one in the dark a slap in the face or a stumped toe would painfully announce them if not detected. Ben was directly ahead of him surrounded by lighting bugs that glowed in the dark. Rice watched every step that Ole Roundabout, took just as Ben was watching Joseph's, who was ahead of him.

Rice slowed his pace as he picked up the faint smell of a fire. He looked to the East and saw nothing, but the smell seemed to be coming from that way. As he was peering into the trees, Jack walked up and whispered "I smell it too."

Rice snapped his finger, and at its sound Ben stopped in his tracks. Without a word Joseph doubled back to the others and whispered "Fire".

They all waited a few minutes without speaking until a small glow in the dark was seen to the East. All they could hear was the sound of night crickets chirping and the faint sound of the running waters of Richland Creek [49].

"Too late to be cooking at this hour," Ben said, shaking his head. "I feel treachery in the air. Why a fire now, and not earlier?"

"It's a trap," Rice agreed.

"They will not be by the fireside, but in the dark just beyond the light," Joseph replied.

"Let's go lads. Just stay out of the glow of that fire!" Ben said with that devilish grin that Rice was coming to love.

Rice moved slowly in a hunkered down position. With every step his heart pounded with anticipation of what lay ahead. He was once again taking the war to the Indians that had hurt so many, including his wife. As the approaching men came within one hundred feet of the fire they split into two groups of five. Ben to the left with Joseph among his group, while Rice and Jack took to the right with the others. Both parties were looking for any sign of the true location of the waiting Cherokee. Rice was impressed by the false camp's appearance. It looked occupied from where he stood. Maybe they were giving the Cherokee too much credit. Was this a real camp site that showed the Cherokee's sloth? Across the way the sound of a snapping twig broke the night air and brought Rice to a halt. The flash of a pan from the same position across the way gave away the Cherokee position. The loud sound of Ben's rifle opened the skirmish and was soon followed by the bark of Joseph's weapon as well. War whoops rang out after a Cherokee volley. Rice shouldered his rifle as two dark figures approached in a full run. His shot was true as the

---

[49] Richland Creek is in Haywood County North Carolina.

first warrior dropped to the ground. Shots rang out all around as he dropped his rifle and pulled his tomahawk as the second warrior crashed into him. They rolled about on the ground, each grasping at the other, but neither able to strike a hard blow, because they were so closely gripped to each other. Finally, Rice was able to place a foot under the Indian's chest and with one strong kick the Cherokee went flying into a tree trunk landing hard on his back. As Rice came to his feet, The Bench spun away from the tree in a quick motion and disappeared into the dark. Jack was also in the grips of a struggle with a third Indian. They were rolling about under Rice's feet with the painted warrior coming to rest on top of Jack's chest. But Rice's tomahawk ended the struggle. Jack pushed away the corpse and reached up for Rice's sash. He pulled the old Queen Anne out from under the blue cloth and discharged it around Rice's hip. A new warrior had entered the struggle and was about to stab Rice from the rear, but Jack ended the threat with a shot from his knees. As Jack rose to his feet the smoke was still hanging in the air from his life saving shot. Rice placed a thankful hand on his lifesaver's shoulder and thanked Providence for the day that Jack McCalpin was born.

"Damn" Jack said as he wiped his forehead with his blooded hand, "I still owe you one."

"What are you talking about Jack? You just saved my hide. We are even my friend. If anything, I'm in your debt. You would have taken that savage that I just hawked if you had the time to finish the task".

"Oh, how you forget," Jack replied raising an eyebrow. "Remember Pat Cunningham back at your place? I still owe you one".

"You two can debate tallies later," Ben said as he walked up. "We lost two of those devils down by the creek. Any get away on this end?"

"One, that I saw" Rice replied pointing to the south "He lit out yonder way after we tussled."

"How hard is it to track down a red headed Indian in the dark" Jack asked as he picked up a lock of red hair that Rice had chopped off while he was in the struggle.

"Unlikely," Ben answered as he took the severed lock of hair. "They have most likely split up by now anyway. Like leaves in the wind. Besides we can't get too far away from the army. The General will be moving fast now that the Cherokee know that we are here."

As Ben handed the lock of hair to Rice he said, "You know, Bill Alexander said he saw a redhead amongst them bastards. I though his eyes were getting the best of him, but I guess not. Here Rice, take this with you. It will be a topic of conversion for years to come once we get back home."

Chapter 52

The Prodigal Daughter

Jacob Grider looked over at his brother, John, from atop his mount, as they rode along the trail that General Rutherford's army had left.

"Not a word," John announced. "Not from a single one of you!"

Martin and Val smiled at each other as they brought up the rear of the four-man party. John was doing better, having recovered from his untimely illness for the most part, although he still had a lingering cough. they were happy to see the fight back in him. Early yesterday morning they had ridden out of Davidson Fort, trying to overtake the General before he reached the Cherokee towns. If they rode hard the next two days they figured to overtake the army ahead.

"Don't be so sour John," Jacob said. "Ain't nobody here blaming you. We will be in their midst soon enough with them marching at foot speed, and us on horseback. You should still be able to rip off a scalp or two before fall. That is. if Martin does not outrun you to get to them," he teased.

"Weak or not, I can still outfight, out cuss, out drink and outrun any one of you!" John replied, breaking into his deep laugh.

"But all that aside, it is nice to be out in the Good Lord's world again. The air up here just does a man good somehow."

"Beats being cooped up inside that stockade," Martin agreed.

"Yes, the only enticing attraction back there was sweet Beth" Jacob added.

"I believe you are truly smitten by that gal," Val teased, "So much that you don't even remember where we just came from. She is back at Cathey's, not Davidson's, you love sick dunderhead."

"I know what fort she is in, I was just speaking in generalities," Jacob fired back "But you are right about me being smitten, she's as pretty as they come, and she has a sweet nature that anyone with half a brain would be drawn to."

"Yes, but will her father see any redeeming qualities in you?" John teased his brother.

Jacob pulled his horse to a stop to gain his brother's attention, "I believe John still as a touch of the fever or maybe he is cultivating a new-found sense of humor."

John just smiled, and kicked the side of his horse, without trying to defend his newly found wit. As the other three rode away, Jacob fell behind. He pulled the plug from his leather canteen and took a quick drink of water. As he was putting the plug back into the canteen's spout, he saw movement from the corner of his eye, a rapidly shaking rhododendron bush, despite the fact that the air was very still. He dropped his horse's reins and quickly shouldered his rifle. As he slowly walked his horse towards the rhododendron, with his gun at the ready, his brothers' saw that he had spotted something. They quickly doubled back to his aid. Without waiting for them, Jacob raised his leg and slid off his saddle, still pointing his rifle at the bush. Within a few steps, he was on the trail of a barefoot phantom. He took off at a hard run, once he got a glimpse of a dirty blue clothed figure darting away into the distance. With his greater speed, he was soon able to see the fleeing person ahead of him, but not too clearly. Whoever it was, it looked like a young boy dressed in women's clothing. As Jacob finally outran his quarry, he took hold of the person's thin arm. He almost lost his grip, he was so surprised to hear a frantic voice call out in great distress, "No Jacob! Just let me go!"

Iona McFall pulled away as Jacob released her arm. She fell to the ground and scrambled into the hollow of a dying tree, a place of shelter that she had adopted as her poor home. She pulled her tattered apron over her scaly scalp trying to hide the shame she felt. "Don't look at me!" she cried in a sad, weakened voice. "Ride away! Just go and let me be Jacob! Everyone else has."

"Oh Iona, we thought you were dead!" Jacob exclaimed, as he took a knee in front of her hideout. "Please, come out of there so we can tend to your needs. There is no need to shy away from us. We can help if you will just come out of there."

He slowly reached out and gently placed a hand on her shoulder. But she pulled away, and crawled even deeper into the hollow of the tree, pressing her face against the cool wood, clearly self-conscious of her appearance. She did not want to face her would be savior, she just wanted to disappear.

"Who is that?" Val asked as he ran up ahead of his other brothers.

Jacob turned back to his brothers and stood up to face them. Without asking, he pulled off the black scarf that Martin always wore around his head. The scarf still held its hat like shape, with its neatly tied knot still in place. He pressed a finger to his lips before squatting back down to Iona's level. He offered it to her knowing full well why she was acting the way she was, for he had seen the scar left from her scalping. "Here," he said. "Iona, put this on and come out. I promise you we would never hurt you."

As she took the scarf from his hand, he stood up and led his brothers a few feet away. "It's Iona, and she's been almost completely scalped. She is scarred something awful. We need to give her a moment to settle herself."

"Are you sure?" John asked. "She sure does not look anything like Iona did when last we saw her."

"Believe me it's her, without a doubt," Jacob replied somberly.

Wanting to see for himself, Martin slowly approached the tree's opening and said in a soft voice "Come on out Iona, we will get you back to your husband by tomorrow night. Once you are home, all will be well. Arthur has been looking for you for weeks.

This ordeal is all but over now. The hard part is behind you. It is time to go home. You were lost, but now you have been found."

"No!" Iona cried, as she crawled out of the tree. "I'm afraid my hard days have just begun. Arthur has shunned me once. No, I never want to see that man ever again. Once was enough. I'm not going to let him turn me out twice."

As she came to her feet, she tried to straighten her gown and stays as best as she could. It seemed that the scarf had somehow become her shield, and she had taken strength from it. She was frail and thin, but after the initial shock of being found had sunk in, she found she was able to face her future.

"No, never Arthur! If you must take me back, then take me to Mulberry Fields. There I can regain my wits and strength. When I first saw you fellows back there I panicked, but it is clear now. I see the way ahead for me, and it is Mulberry Fields for now."

"Are you sure that Arthur has seen you out here"? Val asked. "Maybe you got a little bewildered and just dreamed it. Pain and hunger can play strange tricks on one's mind out here."

"Oh no," she replied with a quivering lip. "your hair Iona, it is gone. You are dead to me.' That is what he said. I'll never forget his words. He left me to die here with nothing to eat but whatever crawled by. But I did not die. I wanted to, at first, but not now. Now all I want is for whoever sees me to think of his cowardice. I want every step that he takes in public to be a walk of shame for him. I may have to carry this scar, but it will pale to the one he will have to bear. You say I was the one lost, but now am found. Maybe so, but no one will ever kill a fatted calf for him once they hear my story. He will come to regret the decision he made that day. I'll see to that. He may have been able to walk away, but no matter how far he goes he cannot walk away from himself."

Chapter 53

A Call of All Is Clear

Rice stood on the Tuckasegee River in awe. He was amazed at what he saw in its low waters. The Cherokee were still very much his enemy, but they were becoming a respected one. Not everyone would think of building a fishing weir out of stones like the one he was standing on. Sure, he had seen weirs made of sticks and nets in calmer waters. But to build weirs out of stone that would never wash away in a fast-moving current was very inventive. And that was what the Cherokee had done here. The trout trapped inside also told him they had to be close to the village that bore the same name as the river. Would they have one miles away from their home, and not close by?

He took a few more steps, hopping from stone to stone, a feat that could never be made if they were slippery from being wet or when the water was high, when he reached the dry bank he looked back over his shoulder to see the rest of Colonel Francis Lock's men crossing the river. This morning General Rutherford had split his forces and Rice, along with the rest of Ben's militia, was now under Lock's command. Rutherford had done this to keep at least some of his men in the war while he was waiting for Major Williamson and his South Carolinians to join his ranks.

The village, according to New River, [50] one of the Catawba scouts, was just around a bend in the river. He had also advised Lock

---

[50] New River was born around 1725 into the Catawba nation. He was

that the river bank was most certainly being watched by the inhabitants of Tuckasegee [51] So instead of following the bottomland that ran along the river, Lock had ordered a march over a small mountaintop. It's top overlooked Tuckasegee, very much like the ridge back at Fort Grider from which Rice had made his now famous shot.

The uphill march was made with great difficulty, even with New River leading the way. It was steep and rocky and no one could call out any directions to help the men behind because of the fear their voices would be heard in the village below. Slowly, Rice made his way to the top and was one of the first to reach its summit. Bill Alexander, the same man who had spotted the Indians back at Richland Creek a few days before, came up beside Rice. He pulled the stopper from his canteen and offered Rice a drink just as a shot was fired. The lead ball broke Alexander's ankle, causing him to fall to the ground. A second shot knocked the canteen from his hand, but caused no other damage to Bill, only rupturing the vessel. Rice dropped, unhurt, to the ground. While lying on his belly, he shouldered his rifle, but only saw smoke floating in the trees. Joseph and Jack both ran to Rice's side and delivered a volley into the smoke without any real target to hit. War whoops were heard as the Indians fell back down the mountainside in retreat. William Lenoir ran after them, and Rice jumped to his feet to join the chase. Another Cherokee

---

slowly making a name for himself while acting as a scout for the Whigs. His first foray into the war was under Colonel Richard Richardson during the 1775 Snow Campaign. His skills as scout, hunter and leadership of his fellow warriors would become legendary in his own time. Sadly, his fame has now faded. As for his name He killed a prominent Shawnee warrior on the New River, in the 1750's and earned his name from this event.

[51] The village of Tuckasegee was located near present day Sylva, North Carolina. Tuckasegee in the Cherokee language translates to Turtle Place or Place of the Turtle.

volley flew past as Rice began his charge downhill. He could hear the sound of hot lead smacking into the bark on the trees that surrounded him. As he stepped behind a tree, a spinning tomahawk flew past Rice's right shoulder, and he heard a painful scream as it hit its target.

New River had delivered a perfect strike. It had pierced the shoulder of the only Cherokee to hold his ground, an aging warrior who was too proud to run away from his last battle.

Rice drew a long breath and slowly let it out as more militiamen made their way into the fight. One was Arthur, but he gave Rice little notice as he ran by. As Rice once again stepped into the open, he quickly spotted the green hunting shirt of a Cherokee, wearing black and white war paint, and a single turkey feather hanging from his rifle stock. He was no more than fifty feet away when Rice pulled the trigger of his own longrifle, but as soon as the weapon discharged Rice knew he had missed his mark, the shot had flown over the warrior's head. Rice had not allowed for the steep downgrade when firing. He once again took a tree to reload, and adjusted his aim, determined not to make the same mistake with his next volley. He bit into the stopper of his powder horn and pulled it free with his teeth. The taste of black powder was still bad, he thought as he spit out the plug. Arthur was next to Rice and he too was reloading, but he was further along in the process. All he had left to do was withdraw the rod. As Rice was ramming his ball home Arthur peered around his tree and shouldered his rifle as a voice called out. "No! Arthur! it's me!"

Rice, now reloaded, watched as Arthur withdrew back behind the tree without firing.

"Rice!" the voice called out again, "come on, it's all clear down here."

Rice stepped into the open, thinking that Jack had somehow made it past without him noticing. What he saw once he stepped into the open, was the red polka dotted forehead of John McFall. From the bottom of his jawline to the top of his cheek, he had black war paint smeared across his face. The tip of his nose was red, and his hate filled eyes were peering down the barrel of his musket, aimed squarely at Rice's chest. He squeezed the trigger, only to have the flint not spark as it hit the frizzen of his flintlock.

Rice dropped to his knee while raising his rifle to firing position. As he was about to shoot a bump from his right diverted his aim, causing his shot to veer to the left of John's head.

Arthur had knocked Rice off balance as he ran quickly by to assist Ben, who had finally pulled his large frame up the mountainside. He was engaged in a hand to hand struggle of his own. Arthur tackled Ben's warrior around the waist, and pull him to the ground. Once freed, Ole Roundabout drove home a killing blow from a battle ax to the Cherokee's head.

Rice looked back for John, but he had used the time his brother had given him to good advantage, having disappeared into the trees. Angrily, Rice pointed his rifle at the other McFall brother, but he could hardly kill the man who had just saved his commanding officer. He could only grit his teeth, and vow keep his guard up in the future, as the skirmish came to an end.

"Easy," Jack cautioned as he placed a hand on Rice's shoulder. He reached down and lowered Rice's gun, which was still pointed at Arthur, using a slow steady motion, saying "I saw it all. Arthur could have killed you, but he didn't. Keep that in mind. A blow from a tomahawk would have worked as well as that nudge."

Rice knew all too well that the bump had been no accident, but he had overlooked the fact that Arthur did have him with an empty gun in his hand. He didn't much like it, but Jack was right; Arthur could have killed him, if he had wanted.

Colonel Lock walked around the field of battle with his sword in hand. He stopped at the corpse of the older warrior that New River had slain. He took the tip of his sword and turned the Cherokee's head in order to see his face.

"Nobody of consequence," he said as he pulled back his sword. "Where is Dragging Canoe, or any other war chief for that matter?" he asked. "They have to know we are here by this time," he said, looking at New River.

" I not know" replied the Catawba "but close they must be."

"What are your orders Francis?" Ben asked as he gazed down into the village below.

We will take full advantage of the fact that we hold the high ground. An uphill attack at this late hour is unlikely. The village of Tuckasegee will stand another night. But God help it tomorrow. We will tend to our wounded for now. New River, you go down and spy around the village, and report back."

As New River began his downward descent, Rice and Jack watched the Indian disappear into the greenery. Turning their gaze, they looked down into the village below. It was centered around a two-hundred-year-old Sycamore and two large rounds houses. One was likely a council house, Rice supposed. A dozen or more smaller round houses were spread out with about an equal number of rectangular house. The latter had openings under their eaves to let a breeze blow through. The ground itself was ten to twelve feet above the waterline with a floodplain across river. This assured that the village would be safe from floods during times of heavy rains. One portion of the bank had been dug away, allowing access to the river for drinking water, as well as a launching point for canoes into the water.

It was a beautiful view with the sun setting behind it. And on any other day Rice would have taken more notice, but not today. He was indifferent to the village's beauty. He was still frustrated and dismayed by how the skirmish had unfolded.

"Did you see who that red faced, polka dotted warrior was?" He asked looking at Jack.

"I did. It was himself, the bastard" Jack responded. "I should have taken that shot over your head when you had taken to your knee. I was just behind you, but I did not shoot for fear of you standing back up at the wrong time. I heard his call. You are way too trusting in battle Rice."

"I know," Rice answered. "It was a poor showing on my part. But if not for Arthur's interference I would have split that bastard's head."

"Another task for the morrow" Jack replied.

That night Bill Alexander suffered immensely. He sat by a fireside sweating like a poorly tanned pelt, trying to purge any poisoning from his wounds, he said. A jug of rum was his only company now. Earlier in the evening he was more of his hospitable and normal self. But with each drink he took, he became more and more of the mean tempered drunk that he was known to be. His friends were taking bets to see what hour that ugly head would emerge from the top of the jug. William Lenoir won.

The rest of the camp was in a good mood baring Alexander, despite all, the skirmish had been a victory. Eight warriors had fallen to only one of the militiamen, and he was still alive and would most likely survive. Spies were out acting as guards to prevent any unannounced night attacks, and with each passing hour the belief spread that the day's fighting was now over.

Rice was finishing up cleaning his rifle, as the twelve o'clock, 'all is well' call come from out of the darkness. New River was back in camp with word that tomorrow's entrance into Tuckasegee might not be an unchallenged one. The village appeared to be deserted he said, but he did see two warriors enter one of the round houses. He had no way of knowing how many more were inside.

Chapter 54

The Protector

Rice walked out of the trees and stepped into the open meadow that stood between him and the village. He made a quick glance to his left and then back to his right. He was in the middle of the militia's column that was marching towards Tuckasegee. His leggings were being put to good use, thanks to the blackberry briars he had to push through. His eyes turned back to the village as the distance between him and it grew shorter. He checked his firelock to make sure all was well with his rifle one last time. With a few more steps he reached the point where the meadow grass was worn down by villager's feet. A corncrib was the first structure Rice walked past. It was small, about four feet around, standing on legs with maybe twenty bushels of eared corn inside. It was dried, most likely from last year's crop. At that moment, a man bolted from behind the crib in a full out dash for the tree line and his freedom. The Reverend James Hall ended his escape plan with a shot from twenty yards. The Reverend trotted over to examine the corpse to find that his first kill was not Cherokee at all, but a slave belonging to the Tory trader John Scott.

Jack ran past Rice to the first roundhouse they came to as they entered the town and leaned his body against the chinking, beside the door that led inside. Rice did the same on the opposite side of the doorway. The door itself, was an elk skin hanging down over the entrance. Rice took the barrel of his rifle and pushed the skin aside for a quick glance inside. He saw nothing, but heard a quick gasp. He pulled back the flint of his rifle, and stepped inside the round room. On the opposite side stood an old gray-haired squaw, huddled with four children, three girls and a boy. All four looked to be under the age of five. The old grandmother was holding a carved wooden duck head war club. Rice made a few side steps and sat down on one of the four benches that circled the room.

"What should we do about that club?" Jack asked, watching the old woman tightly gripping the handle of her weapon.

"Nothing for now," Rice replied. "Let's let her see that we are not here to kill women and children."

"All right, you do as you please," Jack replied "But I'm going back out. Hopefully there is someone out there that will be a bit more of an adversary than this bunch."

As he exited the room, Rice kept a watchful eye on the old woman. Her face softened after Jack left. Rice wondered what must be going on inside her head. He knew that whites captured by the Indians were sometimes burned. Was she thinking maybe that be her fate as well? She whispered something to the children as she sat down on the bottom row of benches.

Rice kept quiet as he sat there, just watching the children cling to their protector. Then gunfire from outside broke the silence. Rice rose to his feet, holding his open palm out toward his captives, letting them all know that they should stay put. He stepped outside, to see Jack herding even more captives towards the house. Rice held open the elk skin door as the new group of prisoners filed by. They were all either too old or too weak to travel, so they had sadly been left behind by the other fleeing members of the village sometime yesterday.

Rice dropped the skin as the last one entered, but he was not watching them. His attention was focused on an approaching militiaman by the name of John Roberson. His eyes were blazing, wild with anger. He did not speak. Maybe because of the wad of tobacco he had inside his mouth. The fresh scalp in his hand told all too well what his intentions were. Rice stepped forward, blocking the doorway.

"Nothing in there for you John" Rice announced. "Just an old woman and some little ones."

"Little ones? Naw!" replied Roberson. "Maggots maybe. Something to be squashed under foot."

"These are not yours," Rice said, still holding his ground. "They are Jack's and mine. We took them, and we are going to hold on to them until Colonel Locke says otherwise."

"Was what I heard wrong?" Roberson asked. "I heard you take scalps boy."

"Warriors in war paint." Rice admitted "Not some child still too young to talk."

Roberson stood there for a moment as he shifted his weight back and forth from foot to foot. "They ain't going anywhere," he said flatly. "Besides there must be more around here I can deal with." He ended the argument by running off to join a mob that was being led by none other than Arthur McFall.

Rice was relieved to see Robertson end the encounter. He did not know how the rest of the men here would take to a scuffle over one of their own protecting an Indian. He hoped most would side with him, but he was not sure. He turned back to Jack and exhaled a long breath. Jack responded with a nod of his head to direct Rice's attention to his right. Rice followed Jack's glance to see New River standing nearby. The Catawba tapped his bare chest with a closed fist and likewise walked way. His parting left Rice pondering what that gesture might mean in the Catawba culture.

"Torches! Light them up" was the order Ben shouted as he rode up on his mount. He had his rifle butt resting on his thigh, its barrel pointing straight up into the air.

"Rice" he said "Do you have prisoners in there?"

"I do colonel, but nothing to brag about, Just a few old women and some children.

Rice shifted his eyes back and forth between Ben and three men running past, holding torches. Soon the village's meager food stores would be consumed by fire.

Ben looked away while he rested his rifle back across his lap. "This is most disappointing. Where are all of the braves? Well, keep them prisoners safely tucked inside and don't let anyone in until you hear from me or Colonel Lock"

"Yes sir" Rice replied as Ben rode away.

One by one the corn cribs were being set ablaze. Other men were torching a ten-acre field of corn on the far side of the village that had yet to be picked. The destruction of the Cherokee had begun.

Chapter 55

Oconostota, And His Dilemma

Oconostota, the ageing Chief of the Cherokee Nation was sick at heart. 'I have hunted this world many seasons too long' he thought. 'What am I to do? My people. Are they to be cast to the wind or sold into slavery? Chota, his home village, where he was born so long ago. What would come of it? The place he still called home, would be no more. The birthplace of so many great Cherokee would be just an empty field. Worse still, there could be a town of the thieves, with their long beards and pale skin, breaking up the land into small pieces. They act as if man can own the land. Land that Kalvlvtiahi, the one that lives above, meant for the use of all. Who ever heard of man owning the land? It would be like trying to own the air or the sky. No wonder they had crossed the Great Water all those years before. They had come to escape such madness, but they had stayed far too long. The whites had too often fed the worst of the two wolves. Greed was a great sickness deep in their blood, and it had come with them. And now the sickness was almost upon his people.

His old friend, Little Carpenter was lobbying for peace. And Oconostota was starting to lean that way himself. Still, the younger leaders of his nation had too much fire and hatred in their hearts for peace. Maybe they too should remember the old Cherokee parable of the two wolves. Each man has them inside. One evil, the other good. Which do you feed?

Dragging Canoe was calling for another plan of attack, and perhaps he was right. But he was still confined to his lodge, still not able to fight because the broken leg that he had received at the battle of Long Island Flats was so slow to heal. If Bloody Fellow and Doublehead's forces could not turn back the Carolinian militia, Dragging Canoe would be forced go south to the Chickamauga River. He would take whoever was willing to fight, and once his leg was healed, he would return to fight another time. Maybe alongside Alexander Cameron with a British army up from the big waters. The Creek might even fight with them now. Dragging Canoe had said it, but Oconostota had his doubts.

Yet, Oconostota could still remember the long hungry winter days after the Redcoat Grant, had last invaded the Cherokee years before. It had almost killed all the Cherokee. Rutherford would certainly do the same now.

Oconostota had not said it. He had not even dared to say it to himself, but he knew what needed to be done. It all rested in the hands of Bloody Fellow and Doublehead's forces. If they can win a battle the Cherokee will stand firm. If not, he would sue for peace and become a hated man to half his own people. But they would still be alive. Yes, he had lived too long. Would his last years be the most bitter?

Chapter 56

The Tam

Rachael walked up to the front door of her cabin and dropped down the sack full of potatoes that she had just dug. She pulled up a chair and sat down beside Annabel who was peeling a bowl of apples.

Annabel looked up from her work and gazed out at the setting sun. The purple and pink colors were lying low across the fall skyline, just above the mountains. A light breeze was still in the air and the day was coming to an end.

"I was wondering where you were," Annabel said as she picked up another apple. "Not much light left in the day. I have already lit a candle inside."

"Yes, thank the Lord" Rachael replied. "It has been a long day and most likely another cool night awaits us. It will freeze soon. We need to dig the rest of those potatoes before the cold weather gets here and ruins them.

"Tomorrow then," Annabel said in agreement.

The two women sat there for a long while, not saying anything to each other. Being tired from a long day's work helps steal the worries away. Rachael was both weary, and tired. She laid her head against the tall backing of the rocking chair and closed her eyes. She heard the sound of the dogs jumping up on the boards of the porch, and the tapping sound of Duchess's hard toenails moving across the floorboards as she took her usual place at Rachael's side.

"I pray they are well tonight," Annabel said breaking the silence. They could be on the way home by now. It would be nice to feel safe again. Nothing like having a strong warm arm around you at night I always say."

"And others things" Racheal said in a playful voice.

The two began to laugh but suddenly Brute raised his head off the floor and let out a long low growl. Rachael opened her eyes as Brute rose to his feet with white teeth showing and the hair of his back standing erect. The sun had set and it was now hard to see very far into the yard. Annabel stepped inside the door as Rachael picked up the musket that her father had left here for her protection. He was here every other day, helping out and bringing in meat for the household. He always tried to talk the two girls, as he called them, into coming back home with him. Racheal would always decline by saying this was her home now. And that she wanted to be here when Rice finally got home. Maybe that was a mistake, she thought to herself as she closed the door.

Brute was now barking harshly having leaped off the porch but still standing his ground in the pathway that lead the cabin. Rachael placed the musket barrel on the window seal as Annabel grabbed the powder horn and shot bag from its place on the wall. Another shot may be needed and she was getting it ready for Rachael if she needed it. She also placed the candlesticks off the table and set them on the floor of the cabin. This would still give the two lights. but it would be too low to the ground to help those outside see in. This was one of Charles's instructions that he repeated over and over whenever he was here.

"It's not Rice," Rachael said still looking into the dark. Brute does not act like that when he comes in. There I see them" she whispered. They are lingering down by Rice's forge. Two that I can see and it's not Paw either.

"Heal Brute," a voice called out. "Rachael call that hound inside so as he can talk. It's me Val, and my brothers. We have someone here that wants to see you."

"Rice?" Racheal exclaimed.

"Afraid not," Val answered. "But don't fret any, he is fine as far as we know."

"And Jack?" Annabel asked.

"Him to Annabel, no need for you to worry either. Now call off that darn dog."

Racheal happily sat down her musket in the corner of the room. Then she took her fingertips and brushed back her hair from her face. For the life of her she could not think of who would need the Grider's to guide them here. She opened the door and stepped outside and called in the dog. Val walked up alone and propped his foot on the porch's stepping stone.

"Rachael, I hope this is alright with you. Jacob and John are down there with Iona McFall," he said. "She wants to see you".

"Iona?" Rachael asked, looking over Val's shoulder. "Why is she down there?

"She wanted me to come up first. She is a little different than the last time she saw you. I can't tell you why and what has happened to her. She will do that. She needs help and she will only take it from you for some reason. Will you see her?"

Rachael stepped down from the porch and called out "Bring her up. Iona is always welcome here." She stood there as Iona made her way to the cabin. She walked in front of John and Jacob. She was moving slowly but she was walking as always. As she came into view she looked thin to Racheal. Her clothing was worn and ragged and very dirty. Her face was gravely solemn and for some reason she was wearing a Scottish tam.

Racheal started to speak, but Iona pressed a finger to her lips while taking Rachael's hand into her own. She walked past Rachael leading her into the cabin. As she made her way across the room she released Rachael. She did not stop until she reached the hearth. She did not even acknowledge Annabel's presents in the room. Slowly she turned and removed the tam.

Annabel covered her mouth with her hand and made her way out of the cabin to give the two friends the privacy Iona needed.

"Oh, Rachael," Iona said "what am I to do?"

Rachael reached out and placed both hands on her friend's cheeks. She leaned down and gently placed her forehead on Iona's and said "My dear, whatever it is, we will figure it out together. You have come to the right place."

Chapter 57

A Hard Wind

The Cowee Mountains [52] were breathtaking and their beauty did not go unnoticed by Rice as he make his way along its summit. He was surrounded by mountains on all sides. They were covered by a dense hardwood forests, grand and thick as any mountain chain in the world. Too thick, to Rice's way of thinking, for this could be a deadly

---

[52] Cowee Mountains are in Macon County North Carolina.

place. New River's words from last night were still ringing in Rice's ears. The Catawba had sat at Rice's fire last evening. He had simply strolled into the firelight with his war club in hand. He sat down tucking his feet under his calves as he sat crossed legged. A brown oiled cloth was pulled from his haversack and he began to polish the round ball at the end of the weapon. The oiled cloth brought out the reddish color of the wood. New River took pride in the appearance of his weaponry it seemed. But that fact did not keep the scout from speaking as he rubbed away.

"The Cherokee, like most of us have their own way of treating captives" he said in an unconcerned tone while directly looking at Rice. "It would be wise to act in the ways that they would want, to prove one's station among them. Show no fear, for they hate a dog that rolls over on it back and pisses itself. But do not act as though they do not respect your capture. They see that as arrogance, something that is hated as well. Make no request, for none will be granted. A prisoner has no power, and one with no power, should ask for nothing. Your deeds should have only one goal, and that, to be adopted into their nation. That will not be easily done, with us burning their villages. So, you must show yourself as one who is more than worthy. Adoption is far better than a scalping knife or even worse, a fiery death at the stake. A prisoner may escape in a year or two. One never escapes the spirit world."

Rice had taken notice that even though New River had told all those who were around that fire what to do if captivity did fall upon them, but he had only made eye contact with Rice. Maybe, Rice thought, he had already earned the respect of one Redman on this march. New River stayed only a few more minutes after his speech. Not all took his speech to heart, Ben being one of them. Not everyone was ready to take advice from an Indian and New River sensed it. So he walked away as quickly as he walked in. His words may have fallen on deaf ears by some, but not in Rice's case.

Today the wind was blowing hard on top of the Cowee. And as Rice and the others was walking along, a drop of water plopped on top of Rice's felt hat. He looked up the tall cliff face overhead and saw that the water was dripping out of the rock. Drops would fall in evenly timed intervals, and as Rice watched another drop fell. He opened his mouth to let the water drip onto his outstretched tongue. Jack watched as the water hit Rice's cheek instead. He gave Rice a friendly push in the back, to move him along. "No time for games," was all Jack said to his friend, but Rice looked back up and this time he caught the next falling drop squarely on his tongue before moving on.

Within another thirty paces the trail turned away from the cliff and entered into a thick grove of Pine and Maples trees. It was a fine place for an ambush. John McFall was still alive and well, and this spot looked like the kind of place that he would pick, but so had many other spots on Rutherford's trace, as some of the men were now starting to call it. Ben suspected that more ambushes would happen on this march. and Rice agreed. It was nerve wracking just thinking about another ambush. The Cherokee were damn good shots as were the white Tories who were living among the Indians. If you were the man they decided to place a bead on, you very well could be breathing your last. But the army's columns were long, and the odds of any one man being picked as a target were slim, but some unfortunate would be the unlucky one.

A strong gust of wind blew hard on Rice's back, and the sound of the waving trees was all that could be heard. Rice thought if he was to set an ambush this would be the kind of weather to do it in. Your prey could hear very little with all this wind, maybe not even the shots.

"Damn this infernal wind" Rice said as he watched a militiaman fall to the ground about two hundred feet up the path. He did not hear a shot but Rice was sure the poor fellow had not tripped. The rest of the men ahead took to a tree or a rock and began to return fire as a second man fell. Rice took a knee as he was looking into the green nettles of the low hanging pines, but he could see nothing in the thickness of the forest.

"Ambush!" Rice yelled. "Come on."

He rose to his feet and ran into the trees as fast as he could. To his right were Jack and at least four other militiamen. War whoops were being cried from both white and red men alike. He saw two Cherokee from the fleeing force of twenty ambushers stop and turn to fire another volley [53] Rice shouldered his rifle and squeezed off a shot. The ball struck just above one of the warrior's blue breech cloth, into the soft tissue just under his ribs. The man stumbled backwards and fell to the ground. He reached inside his deerskin bag and pulled out a rolled-up ball of dried grass which he used plugged his wound.

Rice poured another charge of powder into his barrel as more shots were being fired from both parties. As he was filling the pan of his rifle with his priming powder, another gust of wind blows out the powder before he could flip the frizzin back into place over the powder. He looked up to see a warrior pick up the one he had just shot and swing him over his shoulder.

Rice tried again to prime his rifle, and this time the powder stayed in the pan. He again shouldered his rifle but the Cherokee were both gone, with nothing left behind but the dead militiaman back on the trail.

---

[53] This small skirmish took place somewhere between Cullowhee Gap and the town of Cullowhee North Carolina.

Chapter 58

The Battle of Black Hole

Major Andrew Williamson looked up into the gray sky overhead. No sun he thought, and no Rutherford either, for that matter. Where in the hell is that man's army? Most likely in the bottom of a gorge just like this one he said to himself. Williamson had been in the Cherokee country for days now. He had woven his army up through Rabun Gap to the Tennessee River and reached the Indian town of Coweecho which he promptly burned. Rutherford was supposed to be there for the rendezvous but he wasn't, and that was two days ago.

Williamson shifted his weight in his saddle as he studied the heavy wooded gorge before him. The advance party of fifty men under Lt. Hampton had not sent back any Catawba runners, so all must be well, he concluded. With a tap of his leg he put his horse into motion and his army behind him did likewise.

Doublehead reached out his hand and broke off the small limb that was impeding his sight. He did not want something as small as this hickory sapling to prevent him from having a good line of fire. He had one hundred and fifty warriors in his battle line. They were all, like him, waiting for the approaching army to walk into their ambush. Across the gorge Bloody Fellow and the same number of warriors were hidden, and just as eager to crush the invaders. "They must be stopped here" was this morning's motto. All of the villages behind them would be at risk if the battle was lost. The plan of attack was simple, surround the army and kill as many as they could. Fire until all the powder was gone then hand to hand if need be. The steep walls of the gorge would act as a mass grave for the whites if all went well.

Lt. Wade Hampton [54] hated all things Cherokee. He was here to kill, scalp, and burn. Revenge ran deep in his heart. His father Anthony and his brother Preston had been murdered on the first day of July this very year, at their home no less, near Fort Ninety-Six. Even his fourteen-month-old nephew had met his end in the massacre, having his head bashed against a tree trunk. Wade was not here alone; all of his surviving brothers were here as well. John, Edward, Henry, and Richard had come along too, and they craved the same revenge he did.

John Hampton looked over at his brother Wade and said, "This is some kind of black hole we are in. With all the shade from the trees and bluffs above us, and then add in the fact that it is so cloudy today, it makes this place mighty spooky." Wade nodded his head, but before he could open his mouth war whoops filled the air. A round of Militia musket fire answered from the rear of where the Hamptons where. Wade slid from his horse's back and ducked behind a tree trunk. Smoke was hanging in the air, and he could not see where the warriors doing the shooting were. He was frustrated that six of his men were already dead, and he had not fired a shot. Finally, he saw a Cherokee warrior. He was reloading his musket, but before he could pull out his ramrod Wade split his head with a lead ball.

"There are hundreds of them bastards," John cried from the cover of a fallen log. "This is a tight spot we're in boys so hold fast.

---

54   Wade Hampton 1751-1835 would not only fight in the Revolution but also in the War of 1812. He was a colonel in the United States Army in 1808, and was promoted to brigadier general in 1809, replacing James Wilkinson as the general in charge of New Orleans. He was defeated at the Battle of Chateauguay near Quebec Canada in 1813 during the War of 1812.

Make good on your shots," he said as he killed his first mark with a shot from forty yards.

Major Williamson was becoming worried. It had been a good hour and a half since he had first heard shots from the battle. Every now and then he would hear a shot up ahead while he was on his approach, but they were becoming fewer. Were all of Hampton's men dead? Were the Cherokee mopping up those who were left over from victory? Was he too, marching into an ambush? Maybe so, but he sure was not going to stop and turn tail, no matter what. He pulled his horse to a stop as he saw the back of a militiaman down on one knee just a few yards ahead. A rush of relief ran over his body as he saw that some of his men were still in the fight.

On hearing the approaching horses, Joseph McJunkin turned to his commanding officer, quickly answering Major Williamson's question, "What afoot?"

"We are holding, but damn low on powder and lead. It's more hand to hand now" he said pointing to a dead warrior who lay just a few feet away. "I just tomahawk his brains out a minute ago. But I think they are low on powder as well, Sir.

Not too many shots coming from their way anymore. And that one there had some powder in his horn but no balls inside his shot bag. I took his horn."

"Have we lost many?" Williamson asked, inquiring about his own men.

"Some, and a Catawba, that I know of" McJunkin replied.

Williamson looked back over his shoulder and called out to his men "If you have a bayonet, fix it and come to the front. The rest of you follow and fire at will.

Bloody Fellow ripped off a scalp from the Catawba he had just killed. He had at first mistaken him for one of his own, but when he saw the deer tail tied into the Catawba's hair he knew better. He loathed that traitorous group of people that would turn against their own race in time of war. As he pulled the deer tail from the scalp and threw it to the ground, he heard a loud cry of huzzah coming from the south. The cry was accompanied by many reports of rifle fire. His heart sank as he realized the enemy had been reinforced. He could stay and die, or retreat for another day's battle. Doublehead was already wounded, having taken a cut in his back. It was time to melt away. Maybe they could make one more stand at the Over the Hill villages, but today was lost. He reached down the picked up the Catawba's rifle and led the retreat to the west.

Wade Hampton held his tomahawk in one hand and his knife in the other. His eyes were seeking another Cherokee to kill but none were left. His tan hunting shirt was now red with the blood of men he had killed. Maybe some of it was his own, but he could not feel it, if it was.

"It's over" he heard someone say. "The battle of the Black Hole [55] is over."

"No, not yet," he yelled in disbelief "It can't be. I still hurt inside."

---

[55]

The Battle of The Black Hole was fought in Macon County North Carolina about half way between the towns of Stiles and Franklin on Sept 19 1776.

Chapter 59

A Heavenly Mound

Rice was becoming something of an expert when it came to sacking villages, as was the rest of Rutherford's Army. New River knew the lay of the land well and was giving the General sold information, and Rutherford used that information to his advantage. Detachments were being sent in different directions to carry out the destruction of every village that New River knew of, no matter how small it was. Robert Brown, an older trader who Rutherford had also been using as a pilot and scout, had been useful but sometime he would lead Rutherford astray when New River was away. Some had said it was done on purpose, maybe to buy time to allow for some to escape, for he had a Cherokee as his woman. It could easily be done, because one mountain gap looked very much like the next. You could cross a stream two or three times a day and it be the same watercourse but look different each time.

The Village of Cawea was the next to fall. Its Strawberry fields were like none that Rice had ever seen before, and no one was there to protect them. Rutherford's horses grazed on the plants as the Village was combed thru by the men. The village had been taken without a fight. Rice understood that the Cherokee's food supply needed to be destroyed, but he also knew that it was such a waste to trample and walk over the strawberries the way the horses and men had. The plants were not all dead, but it would take time for them to recover from the damage.

Nikwasi was the next to fall, but the Cherokee did that themselves. They had burned it before the army had arrived. Smoke had been seen in the distance and by its size, everyone knew that the Cherokee had deprived the militia of the pleasures of striking it to the torch. This was the fruit of Brown's labors. How disheartening it must have been to burn one's own home Jack had said, but they had brought this on themselves by doing the King's bidding. When would the Redman learn that the king's Indian agent's advice was only leading to their own destruction?

Forty pounds of powder was among the spoils, as was twenty horses. Most of these where horse that had been stolen from the army's own stock. It was not unusual to lose a horse in camp at night. The Cherokee must have had more horses than they could handle when they fled. They had chosen to keep their own mounts out of familiarly and affection for their own animals.

Rutherford was succeeding, but sometime the militia would feud among themselves. A fellow by the name of Walton had quarreled with Captain Lenoir just the other day. Even with such actions taking place, nothing seemed to be able to stop the march forward. Even the absence of Williamson's South Carolinians had not slowed Rutherford's pace. Rutherford felt Williamson must also be having his own victories, because he had a well-armed force of his own.

Now, after a twelve-mile march, Quanassee [56] a valley town would be next in line to fall. It was situated on the bank of the Hiwassee River, among its bottoms. A ceremonial mound, [57] thought to be two hundred years old was the center point of the town according to New River. He was of the opinion that the Cherokee would fight dearly for this one, unlike they had for Nikwasi. But he

---

[56] Quanassee is now the town of Hayesville North Carolina.

[57] This mound is now known as Spike Buck mound. Constructed around 1550 AD. A temple was once on its summit but at the time of this battle it had long gone.

also said if no battle took place here, then the Cherokee were already broken and no major battle would take place.

Ben was to lead his men up the river and Rice was again under ole Roundabout's command. It was an easy march. A smooth, flat, well-worn path led their way into the Village. Rice, like the others stayed close to the path's edge not wanting to be an easy target for a waiting warrior. but as they entered the Village all seemed quiet.

Rice looked at Jack and said "They are truly broken. I cannot believe it is going to end this easy."

Ben stepped in between the two and pointed to a longhouse with the tip of his sword. Rice nodded and ran to its door. He looked inside and found nothing but a dying fire with an old dog lying on a deer pelt beside the fire. He then stepped back outside and saw that Jack had propped his rifle up on a small corn crib and was getting a bead on something. Jack did not flinch when a ball flew overhead. He then calmly fired his own shot. Rice watched as the ball crossed the village and struck a brave who fell out from behind a summer hut.

"How many?" Rice asked as Ben emptied his rifle with his own volley.

"Twenty or so, but they are falling back," Jack replied.

Rice moved forward in a crouched position, half of his normal height. He made his way to the base of the ceremonial mound planning to using it as cover. By now the rest of the militia had engulfed the town. Shot were coming and going in all directions. Yet this fact did not keep him from crawling to the top of the mound on all fours. There, when he stopped, he saw he militiaman two hundred feet to his right. He was in a death struggle with an Indian. Neither man had a rifle but both still had a tomahawk. Each man took a swing at the other, only to have the blade deflected. In a low roll the

Cherokee tumbled up and under his opponent and knock him to the ground with a blow to his legs. He quickly rose to his feet and was about to lunge forward with a killing blow to his toppled adversary. Having been disarmed in the fall, the militiaman reached up trying to deflect what would be a killing thrust with his bare hand. He caught the arm as it began its downward thrust. The two pushed against the other with all their strength. Suddenly the Cherokee's arm weakened, as the militiaman looked up into his face. The warrior's eyes narrowed as he coughed up a mouth full of blood.

Rice lowered his rifle as he saw the Indian fall to the side. "Good Lord, it's Joseph" he said as he saw his brother in law regain his footing. Rice had no inkling that the man he had just saved was Rachael's beloved brother at the time of his shot. He was just grateful that the almighty had directed his steps to that mound.

Chapter 60

You Bastardy Heathen

John McFall stepped out of the waters of Warriors Creek, crouched down low. Still bent over, he made his way into the open door of Rice's blacksmith shop. It was empty, other than the horse Liberty, which he had sold to Rice. He walked over to the building's only window and peered out.

'Where is that damned dog?' he thought to himself, as he looked at the Medaris cabin. 'With it being so close to the noon hour maybe he is inside with Rachael. She would surely be preparing the mid-day meal by now. And where is that indentured bitch that Jack wed he muttered to himself. His question was soon answered as Annabel walked out of the cabin with a basket in her hand. He watched as she made the turn around the corner and disappeared towards the garden. She was accompanied by Duchess, but not Brute, much to his displeasure. Then he saw movement down low inside the doorway. The hound had stuck his ugly head out for a moment, only to be called back inside. McFall turned around and sat on the bare floor, as his mind mulled over his options on how to get her away from that hound.

Liberty pawed at the ground and snorted, as he was becoming impatient for the bucket of feed he was sure McFall was about to give him. John's eyebrows rose as the answer to his problem crossed his mind. He stood up and walked over to the horse, pulling his knife in the process. He grabbed the rope that tied the animal to a hitching post and pulled him up close. He did this all while speaking softly, so as not to spook the animal.

"Come here ole boy. Do you remember me?" he said as he jabbed the blade behind the horse's' right ear. Liberty jumped back wildly and let out a scream of pain. McFall quickly returned to his window and placed his rifle on the sill to shoot the dog if he came out with Rachael.

Inside the cabin, Rachael heard the horse's cries. She dried her wet hands and stepped outside looking towards the shop, but then Liberty quieted down. As she turned to go back inside, believing nothing was wrong, McFall lunged towards the horse once again setting him off in a wild panic. This time Rachael did not turn away. As she was making her way towards the shop McFall hid himself in the shadows beside the doorway. He heard the sound of Rachael's shoes as she walked on the loose sand and gravel just outside the door.

She stopped at the doorway as she saw the blood dripping down Liberty's neck. Seeing movement inside, and hearing heavy breathing coming from behind the wall, she turned to run back to the cabin. McFall reached out and grabbed her arm. With all his strength he pulled her inside the door, and pushed her hard against the wall, grabbing her by the throat.

"How could you?" he yelled. "How could you defile a pure and decent bloodline like yours by mixing it with a scoundrel like Medaris?" His grip around her neck was so tight she could barely breathe.

He could see the panic in her face and he began to enjoy the power he held over her, as well as the fear he could see in her eyes. He took his free hand and pulled out the top four pins that fastened her jacket. She tried to push him away, but he was too strong for her to free herself. Her eyes dropped to his hands as he reached down inside her stays. She could feel his rough hands as they groped over her breast. She was feeling faint as she looked up into his gray eyes. What she saw there was a wild man. One who had lost all sense of humanity in this moment of revenge and rage. He pulled at the top of her stays, trying to rip the garment open, but they held firm. Not being able to disrobe her, he turned his attention back to her eyes. And there, he saw that she was about to pass out.

"I want you to see and feel this" he shouted. Reluctantly, he released his grip from her throat, but as she was gasping for air, he pushed her chin up to look into her eyes once more. He saw she had little strength left to defend herself, so pulling her hair back, he gave her a hard and bruising kiss on the lips. In his sick mind he was sure that this kiss would win her over to him. But when he pulled away he saw the hatred blazing across her face. As another rush of madness swept over him, he spun her around and forced her over a work table.

As she fell across it's top, she knocked its contents crashing to the floor.

"Well my sweet," he said, "If Rice can defile, so can I."

Reaching down he grabbed the hemlines of both her petticoat and shift and pulled them up over her hips. She was now fully exposed before him. And as he ran his gunpowder blackened finger up between her legs, Iona drove a knife deep into his shoulder, stopping the rape. His head jerked up as he let out a moan. He turned with such speed after the blow, that Iona did not have time to withdraw the handle protruding from his back. Turning, he reached out for his assailant and as he drew back with clenched fist to deliver a punch, he paused at the sight of his sister in-law. He stared at her in disbelief, for this was the first time he had seen her since she had been scalped in the attack.

"What the hell are you doing woman?" he cried.

"Stopping you. You heathenry bastard." Iona answered, backing out of the doorway. "I always knew what you were John. Now everyone will know."

"You will lose more than your hair if you tussle with me woman. Why would you wrong me? You must have lost your mind when along with your scalp?"

He charged after her and quickly grabbed her by the arm, and with the other hand he punched her squarely on the jaw. As she fell to the ground, from the corner of his eyes, he saw Brute leap from the porch. He ran back inside to get his rifle, and as he entered the doorway he saw Racheal retrieving one of Rice's axes that always hung on the wall. As he picked up the weapon Rachael dropped to the ground behind Rice's forge. As she lay there she heard the rifle discharge outside.

"Oh my God, he has killed Iona!' Rachael thought as she rose to her feet. She stumbled over to the door and there she saw Iona on the ground. Brut was lying dead next to Iona in a pool of blood. Another shot was fired, but this time it came from the cabin. Annabel had missed McFall as he disappeared into the trees across the creek.

Rachael ran to Iona and dropped to her knees. As the two of them embraced in a tearful silence, they could hear Annabel saying "I'm so sorry. I'm so sorry I missed. That damned bastard got away."

Chapter 61

Does Not The Bear Hunt

Rice stood inside the doorway of the hut where he was to spend the night. He was listening to Jack, who was just inside tending to four sweet potatoes and a few ears of corn baking over a fire.

"No meat" he muttered. Why can't they drive some of those fat cows up here from Canucca [58]or Cancceawhoe or whatever they call that damn village'? I swear some of them Fort Davidson boys may munity from the lack of beef around here in recent days."

---

[58] Canucca was a Cherokee village that was used as a base for Rutherford's supply train. It was located two and half miles from down Franklin North Carolina on the waters of Cartoogechaye Creek. Today it is the location of an Industrial park.

"What about the Fort Grider boys" Rice asked with a chuckle, as he watched the Reverend Hall approach up a hill.

"Not this one," Jack replied as he rolled over an ear of corn. "Ole Dragging Canoe is not getting his hands on this lovely top knot of hair any time soon."

"Divine worship in the morning over at the foot of that mound," the reverend announced as he walked on by.

"Yes sir, we are looking forward to it," Rice answered as he turned his head the other way and saw that the meeting of officers was breaking up after it had been adjourned for the night. They were standing at the foot of the mound. Ben was one of the last to walk off, but when he did he made his way to the aroma coming from Jack's labors. As Rice watched Ole Roundabouts approach, he once again made a study of the village. The mound was in the center of the town with a large green in front. The winter houses and summer huts were laid out in a square formation around the green; each house seemed to have its own crib and woodshed. No streets were needed with this layout, the houses were spaced about twenty feet apart in two rows. There was not a fence to be seen, none was needed with all of this open space. The Cherokee could move in any direction with ease. Each house or hut was only ten steps from either the green in the center of the village, or his nearest neighbor's structure. Even the crop land that lay in the rear of the village was close by.

Rice stepped inside and made his way to a Dutch oven that some Indian trader had recently introduced to the Cherokee. He removed the top as Ben sat down on a bench next to the inner wall of the hut. He did not say anything until after Rice had fished out the rather large biscuit from the cast iron pot, but he did remove his hat. As Rice broke the warm bread into four pieces, Ben began to talk.

"Well boys, looks as though we may have missed the big one. Some of our scouts back in the rear heard all kinds of gunfire today. It was miles away best they could tell. Y'all know how sound can carry in these mountains. But Brown was of the opinion that the shots came from a gorge near Wayah Gap. Said he was going to lead us into that very gorge, but mistook the one we took two days ago for it."

"So, his mistake saved us from walking into an ambush?" Jack asked, scratching his whisker covered jawline. "Hell, I may give him my next ration of rum."

"So it seems," Ben answered. "Providence of God's grace. At any rate we will be missing Reverend Hall's massage on the morrow. Sorry about that Rice. I know that you rather enjoy his sermons. We are off to another village at dawn. The Rowan County boys and us will be heading down river around ten miles or so. You boys remember I have been here before. In the spring of '73 it was. I had taken off to Kentucky after pelts the year before. Some young Cherokee bucks stopped us and took everything we had including a fine mount of mine. We were vastly outnumbered and had little choice in handing over all we had. They did give us a bent barreled trade gun. Anyway, I studied over it for a while. Me and good ole William Hightower trooped off down there and got the horse back."

"They hand him over just like that?" Jack asked.

"Oh no," replied Ben. "We had the help of an older chief by the name of Big Bear who escorted us to this very town and the one we are going to tomorrow. Hell, even with his help, one of those damn savages hurled a tomahawk that grazed my hunting shirt. But we got that horse back anyway. Luckily, New River will be with us on the morrow in case my memory fails. He knows every tree and bush in these parts."

"I would like to speak to him again," Rice said as he looked at Ben. "Could you arrange such a meeting?

"Well let's see," Ben said as he stood up and walked to the doorway. " There he is now. I see him across the way talking to Colonel Lock."

 Ben waved his hat back and forth a few times to gain the Catawba's attention, before stepping back inside. "He is on his way over."

Rice picked up a wooden bowl and proceeded to fill it with his bead and Jack's vegetables. His back was turned as the Catawba entered the room. As he turned back around, he offered New River the bowl of food. "Sorry General New River, but we are without meat tonight."

New River stood there for a moment, as if he was in deep thought. His eyes narrowed, but then his lips broke into a small smile. "General New River", he finally said, somewhat flattered by the unofficial title. "Yes. General New River will eat now."

He took the bowl of food from Rice's hand before walking over to a grass mat to sit down. He looked into the fire, and then back at Rice.

"You make that fire?"

"No Sir. We did rekindle it, but it already had hot coals shouldering in it, some Cherokee lass must have made it this morning."

Rice watched as New River sat down his bowl. He was concerned that he had unknowingly delivered an insult. The Indian stood up and walked over to the doorway, but instead of exiting, he picked up a hoe handle that was leaning beside the doorway. With it in his hand he returned to the fire, and proceeded to rake away the top of the burning coals. In doing so he revealed that a fire pit was under the fire. Soon, the top of a clay pot was uncovered, and with a few rakes the entire pot was visible. He flipped the hoe over and stuck the wooden handle into a round hole in the top corner of the pot and proceeded too pulled it from the pit. He poked off the top to reveal a fully cooked roast inside.

"I'll be the son of a suck egg mule!" Jack announced in delight. "Is it good to eat?"

"Yes" New River replied "Cherokee women not as good cook as Catawba woman, but good enough tonight."

Jack's eyes roll up as he bit into the venison, and an appreciative groan escaped his lips as the pleasant aroma and delicious taste of the meat satisfied his hunger. As the men sat around eating their supper, Ben looked at Rice and said. "Well my boy, you said that you would like an audience with New River. Yet you have said little to nothing. Go ahead and say what is on your mind.

"You have words to say? General New River has ears to listen" the proud Catawba announced, letting everyone in the room know that he planned to keep the new title that Rice had just used. "You want to know my heart?"

Rice sat his bowl on his knees, as he looked at General New River. I, sir know why I am here, doing what we are doing. I know why we all our here. We are here to protect our homes and our way of life. But I struggle to know your reasons."

"We Catawbas are here same as you. Our villages have been burned by Cherokee warriors for years. You see our bright skin and wonder why we fight other people of the forest. It is because we hate the Cherokee. They are not our brothers. They helped to make us weak years ago. Our ancient ones still tell the stories of the old days, when we were overpowered by the Cherokee. We have not forgotten. You fight the redcoats. Are they not pale like you? We Indians are a warring people. We fight just like you. We make war before you came to our lands. Why you think we not fight each other now? Cherokee battle us. Cherokee battle the Creek for all my father's father's time. North of the Selewathiipi [59] the Huron fight the Shawnee, and push them West out of what you call the New York's long ago. No matter what tribe, the old always say peace is best, but the young always fight until they win or until all, or most is gone. General New River fights for the old ones that are no more. The young ones who should not be under fear of the Cherokee. But most of all, General New River battles because it is in his blood. Does not the bear hunt? Why would a Catawba chief not be what he is?"

Chapter 62

Into The Fire

Rice stood under one of the tallest beech tree be had ever seen. Its large branches were shading four beaver pelts still stretched inside drying hoops. The skin side of the pelts were still damp from the brains that were used to cure the hides. He ran his hand down the soft hair on the opposite side as he walked by. More spoils for the taking, he thought. His thoughts were cut short as a young Cherokee warrior fired a shot, and a woman and child ran into one of the winter houses in the village located at the mouth of Brasstown Creek and the Hiwassee River. His shot had opened the battle, but it also gave his wife and daughter an opportunity get out of the line of fire that the militia was soon to deliver. The warrior did not try to reload his trade

[59] Selewathiipi, Native American word for the Ohio River.

gun, he just dropped his musket and charged his attackers with a knife in his hand. General New River pulled his tomahawk at the warrior's approach.

Rice watched in awe as New River swung down a hard blow onto the Cherokee's wrist with the wooden handle of his hawk. And as he stepped to the side, the Cherokee's knife fell to the ground. New River stuck the small blade on the back side of his weapon upward, into the warrior's stomach, disemboweling his enemy with one strong pull of the tomahawk. It was a quick, smooth maneuver, done with apparent ease. New River was truly an impressive warrior, he had disabled and killed his opponent in less than six seconds.

Rice fell to the ground unhurt, as more shots rang out from the village. John Roberson cried out in pain, clutching his neck. He quickly crawled behind the trunk of Rice's Beech tree to gain his safety. There, he called out a profanity laced plea for help. Rice looked back over his shoulder to see that Arthur McFall had come to his aid and was tending to the wound. "Good" Rice thought "Maybe they will kill each other."

Another volley was fired from the village, and again the shot passed Rice by, but one struck the wax laced canteen on Jack's hip, but doing no harm to his flesh, only dousing his britches with rum.

Rice rose to his feet and ran to the nearest hut, hoping the Cherokee were still reloading as he ran. His heart was pumping wildly as he fell up safely against the wall.

While he was regaining his breath, he watch as New River pitched a flaming torch up on the grass roof of a summer house just down the way. Suddenly, the barrel of a musket was stuck out of the doorway just feet away from Rice's position on the wall. Without thinking, Rice reached out and grabbed the smoothbore musket. He had no idea who was holding the other end of the weapon, but he did manage to jerk it away from whoever it was rather easily. By now the rooftop of the summer hut was starting to flame up on one corner. As Rice was watching the flames spread across the roofline, a squaw with a child darted out of the doorway right before his eyes. It was a mother who held her daughter of no more than two, clutched tightly on her hip. She was making a panic-stricken dash for the flaming summer house. As she was about to reach the doorway. a lead ball struck the mother's shoulder. They both fell hard to the ground in a tightly bound mass of arms and legs.

Rice ran toward the two, and as he was making his way to them he could see that the mother's arm was shattered. He could also see the pure fear on both of their faces. She was not thinking clearly, he thought. Why would she run into a burning building like that? What he had no way of knowing, was that her fear of capture was far greater than her fear of death.

She said something to him, but he could not understand what she was saying. She finally raised her upper body off of the ground, and as Rice took a knee by her side, she pushed the girl into his lap. Before Rice knew what to do, the mother scrambled up and into the flaming summer house. Rice scooped the child up into his arms, and took her back to the hut that the two had first come from. He sat her down on the dirt floor, but she locked her arms around his leg in a tight grip as he tried to go back out the doorway. She was) frantically calling to her mother, tears running down her little round, tanned cheeks. Rice picked her back up and took her outside just in time to see the burning roof collapse in on the mother [60]. He placed his hand

---

[60] In 1964 The University of North Carolinian uncovered the remains of a skeleton inside a burned house at this unnamed village near the junction of Brasstown Creek and the Hiwassee River. It could not be determined if the structure was burnt by Rutherford's army or not. It may have been burned during the Creek and Cherokee Wars of the 1750s when the two tribes were at war with each other.

on the back of the child's head and pushed her face deep into his chest. He could feel the tight grip of the girl as she clung to the fringe of his frock coat. Looking at Jack with an expression of pity, Rice carried her off to the river bank as the battle was coming to an end. As he reached the bank he looked down at her small hands that were still tightly clinging onto the cloth of his hunting frock. The flesh under her fingernails had turned white from the presser of her grip.

"What am I to do with you?" he asked. "Oh Lord, what am I to do with this little one?"

He pulled her in close while whispering a hushing sound into her ear. He was trying his best to calm her down. This expedition was truly destroying the Cherokee Nation. And some aspects of these victories were hard for Rice to deal with. He had no pity for this child's father. He was a warrior who had raided the Blue Ridge along with the other men of his tribe. Few Cherokee men had clean hands when it came to killing. But this child was another matter. Rice had no plans to hurt her and no one else would either as long as he was able to stop them.

Chapter 63

I'll take her

Major Andrew Williamson and his South Carolinians had finally met up with Rutherford's army here at Hiwassee which was the last of the Cherokee middle towns. They were saluted by the roar of 13 swivel guns as they marched into camp. All of the officers were attending a council of war meeting at General Rutherford's headquarters, the council house left behind by the Cherokee. No doubt many a speech had been presented inside its round walls about the destruction of the approaching whites. Now it was the forum for the exact opposite.

From what Rice had gathered from Williamson's men when he had spoken with them, they too had been burning all that could be burned in the Cherokee Nation. The Cherokee towns of Oconee, Tugaloo, Senca, Tamassee and Keowee had all been put to the torch by the South Carolinians.

Rice hoped this would be the end of this tour. Although it had been a huge success, it was still somehow hollow, without meeting a large army of warriors being commanded by someone of stature, like Dragging Canoe or perhaps even the British Indian agent Alexander Cameron.

Hopefully this could still be a possibility if such an army were found in the coming days, or on the return march home. There was little doubt that this was not the main topic of those attending the council of war being held this evening.

Regardless of all of this going on, Rice was ready to return home. He was missing the company of his young wife., and not knowing what was happening on his homestead was bearing on his mind. McFall was here with other Tories, hiding among the Indians, but how long would he stay, providing he was still alive. And the thought of helpless Cherokee women and children dying in the woods for the lack of food and shelter was always present, weighing heavily on his conscious. More so, with his new found little Cherokee dove running about. She was becoming more at ease, but Rice knew she had to be missing her mother. Could a child of that tender age understand what death meant? Rice was hoping that New River would be of some help with her, but he was keeping his distance. Maybe that was his way of hardening his heart to the Cherokee.

Whites and Indians both had adopted small children into their families. Maybe someone here in camp could be looking for a girl child to rise as their own daughter. A few of the captured women and children had been simply let go. Rutherford did not want the problem of watching over them. And once it was no secret that his army was in the Cherokee nation, he saw no reason to keep noncombatants under guard. There had been talk of having an auction to sell off the prisoners that Rutherford was holding, once the army was ready to return home, but they were few in number. Rice was not going to let this little one fall into slavery. Even if that was what the Indians, as well as the whites did when it came to native prisoners. Jack and Joseph had been out making inquiries to see if anyone was interested in taking the little girl. Rice had already decided that if that person was out there, they would have to prove their intentions were honorable   before he turned her over to them.

Rice watched her as she chewed a bit of steak that he had cut up into small bits for her. He smiled as she made an odd study of the meat. Maybe the first time she had ever tasted beef. He ran his long fingers through his growing whiskers as he watched her continue eating. Then he looked at the men standing in camp. Few had taken the time to shave, or comb a single strand of hair while in the wilds. Including himself.

Maybe a shave would help calm her, he thought. He smiled at her as he pulled a bar of Rachael's soap from his haversack. He remembered how he had teased Rachael, back home, when she put it in the bag. It would be a waste for him to carry it, he had said.

Soon the lather from the soap had softened the whiskers on his jaw. The little girl stopped chewing as Rice ran a blade down his jaw. She came close, watching every downward stroke of Rice's hand. He made his eyes large in an effort to get her to smile, but her face did not change expression.

"I wonder what Rachael would do if I took you home with me?" Rice said, looking into her dark eyes.

She reached up and with a single finger, touched his cheek with her fingertip but still no smile appeared on her round face. Even after Rice smiled, her lips held firm.

As Rice stood up to slide his knife back into its leather sleeve, Reverend Hall, Ben, and a man unknown to Rice joined the two.

"Well here she is," Reverend Hall said as he introducing the girl to the militiaman by placing a hand on top of her head. "What do you say? Is she not a wonder? She could be quite a lass with the proper upbringing."

Ben leaned into Rice's shoulder as the Reverend continued to talk and said, "This ole boy is from Rowan County. Conrad Eckles. His mother was Cherokee. He could be the man you are looking for to rid yourself of that one. Reverend Hall says he's got four boys but no girls, and that his wife doesn't bleed anymore and is past her child rearing years.

"Does he speak Cherokee?" Rice asked.

"No," replied Ben "His father would not allow it. But you can see this man has red blood in his veins. He also has some well-hidden compassion for the Cherokee, but not so much as to cloud his good judgment. I say this could be good for the both of them."

Eckles was smiling as he looked the little girl over. He turned to Rice and said, "I'll take her Mr. Medaris, if you will allow me to."

"What about your wife?" Rice asked "Will she be so kind as to take a Cherokee child into her home and treat her as if she was her own?"

"Oh yes. We have talked about it before. That is one of the reason I'm here. To get us a daughter to replace the one we lost if that occasion should arise, after all, she took me."

"And your boys? what about them" Rice asked?

"They will get the rod if they give her any grief. Look I'm not saying it's not going to be hard. It will be for a time, but she will be loved. And it will be best for her in the years to come. The Cherokee way of life will soon be gone. We all can see that."

"And she will be introduced to Christianity" Reverend Hall replied optimistically. "I have known Conrad for years. Rest assured Rice, he is a good man in charge of a good family. She could not be in better hands. May I suggest that you let him take her now, tonight even. You can watch him for the rest of the campaign. If you don't like what you see you can always take her back. How about it? Will you both agree to that?"

Rice replied "yes", as he took Conrad Eckles hand into his own for a handshake to seal the deal.

Eckles reached down and picked up the little girl and placed her head on his shoulder. He then gave a joyful thanks to Reverend Hall for his help. He then looked back at Rice and said, "Thank you for this. You have no idea what this will mean to my wife. God bless you sir."

As Eckles walked away with the child in his arms, Rice watched her face as she looked into the eyes of her new father. What was she thinking? He could only hope that it would turn out well in the end, but only God could know that.

Chapter 64

We Pretty Much Scorched The Earth.

Rice leaned his back against the welcoming walls of Fort Grider as he slid down on a wooden bench just inside the fort's gate. Almost home, he thought as he took a cup of brandy from Old Fed's hand.

"Welcome home" the ageing founder of the fort said with a smile. Ole Roundabout is paying the bill tonight so take your fill. But not so much that you can't rise in the morning" he laughed. "The night is still young. We broke open a keg on hearing of y'all's return. I was planning to treat you boys myself but Ben insisted on paying. He said it was his way of rewarding y'all. So, tell me Rice, how was it out there?"

"Not entirely what I was hoping for. I had envisioned that it would be something like the Battle of Point Pleasant[61] that those Virginians had with the Shawnee up north. We never got that big of an engagement, but we hurt them, hurt them bad. We killed a few warriors, and you may see a scalp hanging here or there. We burned every crop they had in the fields and destroyed what was already harvested. We burnt hut after hut, village after village. They will starve this winter by the multitudes."

---

[61] The Battle of Point Pleasant took place on October 10, 1774 at Present-day Point Pleasant West Virginia. It was a victory for the Virginia Militia and forced the Shawnee nation into a treaty that ceded to Virginia the Shawnee claims to all lands south of the Ohio River.

"Good!" Old Fed replied "What's good for the goose is good for the gander. They got our crops in the summer when they had us stockaded up inside here. Remember? I ain't forgetting. So, you really believe they are broke?

"Yes." Rice nodded. "I just don't see how a starving nation can go to war when they have nothing at home of substance. It will take a year to just rebuild their villages. Lord only knows where they will get any seed to plant come spring. They better hope King George will send them something. But I don't think the British will send anything to them with us here. They may be able to mount small raids maybe, but that will be about it I would say. We pretty much scorched the earth. [62] I'll be glad to get home tomorrow. Some normalcy will be nice for a change.

Chapter 65

A Homecoming

It felt good to set foot on his own land again Rice thought as he walked into his yard. A warm fire and a soft bed would bring comfort tonight, with this October chill in the air. And Rachael in his arms would make this homecoming so much more than any ever before.

---

[62] The Rutherford expedition basally ended at the council of war meeting held at Hiwassee. Gen Rutherford marched his troops back home a few days later over much of the same course that he used to march in the Middle Towns of the Cherokee. What he left behind was much changed. Crops were destroyed along with tools and household goods; prisoners and horses were lost by the Cherokee. Yet, as bad as that was, it paled compared to the burning of the villages. At least twenty-one Cherokee villages were laid to ash and maybe more. The Cherokee would stay allied with King George but a powerful Cherokee invasion into the southern colonies from the west was taken off of the table forever by Rutherford and his men. Much like General Sherman's march to the sea broke the Confederacy during the American Civil War, Rutherford did the same to the Cherokee eighty-eight years before.

She was truly the love of his life and this separation had confirmed his love for her. He had greatly missed her companionship, her wit, her touch and even her oddities. It seemed like years since he had last seen her, but in reality, it had only been an absence of a month and a half.

The cabin looked as solid as ever, still standing just where it should among the turning fall leaves. But it was odd not seeing Brute in the yard. It was a rare occasion for someone to get this close to the cabin without him knowing. Liberty was trotting spiritedly along the split rail fence of his lot, as he normally did at Rice's approach. "No apples in my bag today," Rice thought as he ignored the horses' nickers for a treat. His eyes were focused on the closed door of the cabin, and with each step, he knew his long homeward journey was coming to an end.

The door flung open and with a cry of "Rice" on Rachael's smiling lips she darted across the threshold. Rice caught his leaping wife around the waist with his strong hands. He pulled her in close as she placed the sweetest kiss he had ever received upon his lips. Somewhat sheepishly, he turned his attention to Jack who was standing by anxiously looking for his own wife.

"Annabel, where is she?" Jack asked, wanting the same greeting of his own.

"Around back," Rachael answered, not breaking her loving eye contact with her husband as she spoke. Her smile was something that Rice had longed for, and it was a telling one, for he could see that he had been missed. She was still as smitten with him as he was with her, such emotions cannot be hidden.

Jack wasted little time as he left his two friends still lost in their embrace. He too longed for his wife's company, and wasted no time hot footing it around the cabin to find Annabel.

Rachael's feet never touched the ground as Rice carried her back inside the open door. There in the safe walls of his home he returned her kiss with one of his own. But as he was doing so, he heard the shuffle of another's feet and caught the glimpse of a petticoat as it was exiting the cabin's back door. "Who was that?" he asked "Annabel? or your mother perhaps?"

"No. neither," Rachael replied. "It was a friend, a dear friend. We need to speak about her, but later, not at this moment. Not about anything at this time except that I have my husband back and in one piece it seems. We will speak of her concerns later. All's right with the world once again, for you are home. God has answered my prayers Rice, for here you stand. To lose a brother to the Indians was bad enough. He knew I could not bear to lose you my love. She again passionately kissed him with the emotion that could only exist between husband and wife. And Rice was losing himself in that emotion as well, but down deep he had a feeling that not all was well. Rachael was delaying in telling him something, but for the moment he did not care. He was home.

Chapter 66

A Foggy Memory

Rice proudly stood over the grave of his beloved dog. His heart ached badly, but Brute had died doing what Rice had trained him to do. It had a dignity to it in a sad way. Rachael had buried him behind

Rice's blacksmith shop. She had placed a stone at his head to mark the spot. After all, he was a noble animal that had died trying to protect her.

Rachael was now standing by Rice's side as he picked up a fallen limb that had landed on the grave during a recent passing storm. She folded her arms nervously as she watched her husband stare at the mound of dirt that capped the grave site. She raised one hand and bit her thumbnail. She was lost in deep thought. She had had this discussion hundreds of times in her mind. She had been dreading this and she was still not sure as to how to tell the whole story, or even if she should tell the whole story. Even though she knew it was not her fault she still had a sense of shame. As of now the only ones that knew of this, other than the bastard himself, was Iona and Annabel. They both had said they would tell no one. But she also knew it would be a difficult task not to tell such a terrible thing. Husbands and wives confide in one another; Annabel would tell Jack at some point. And Iona had only hatred for the McFalls. She too would find it a hard to keep quiet about another dark deed committed by a McFall. And not being able to tell of driving that knife home would be doubly hard for her. Rachael knew she could not keep this a secret for long. She also wanted to be the one to tell her husband. He needed to hear it from her and not second handed from Jack or Iona.

Rice turned to his wife and he had little trouble seeing that she was holding something back. "I understand that John shot the dog. That you and Iona struggled with him before Annabel took her shot. But what happened before that shot Rachael? Tell me. I need to know."

"He had lured me into your shop" she replied emotionally." He pushed me around some while accusing me of being unfaithful or some nonsense. I can't remember it all Rice, to tell the truth."

"But you know what he did. Tell me." Rice said while taking her hand into his own. It will be alright. Just tell me as best as you can."

She paused for a moment while shaking her head yes. A lump was building in her chest. She knew that Rice would never let this go. It was time to tell all, she thought as her brown eyes began to tear. As best as she could anyway, for it was a foggy memory.

"He raised my shift in the back" she finally said. He ran his hands over me. But that is all Rice. He did not get to do anymore; I was not soiled in any why. Iona saw to that. He only saw, nothing more. But I must confess; if not for Iona and her blade he would have taken me in the most terrible way."

Rice pulled her close and wrapped his arms around her as his heart dropped. A rush of guilt washed over him, like a brisk fall wind. Why did I not come home after that encounter with McFall in the Cherokee nations? He could not believe that John would desert a Tory militia and their Cherokee allies so soon after a battle to sneak back here and attack his enemy's wife. The McFalls where truly a despicable clan. They needed to be wiped from the world like in Bible times, he thought. The next time I see that devil will be his last. Then a rush of gratitude overcame him as he thought of Iona. She could stay here in his home as long as she wished from this day forward.

"What about your family? Do they know?" Rice asked.

"No" Rachael replied "and I do not ever want them to know, ever.

"Very well," Rice said still holding her tightly in his arms "I'll honor your wish but it will not be easy to do so." He wanted to believe his wife was telling the whole truth of the matter. His heart said to him that she had told it all as it had happened. But in the back of his mind he kept thinking of that poor woman up in Virginia. She was keeping a dark secret from her husband. Rice prayed for Rachael's peace of mind, that she was not keeping one herself.

Chapter 67

They Earned This

Rice looked up into the gray tree tops as a large Great Horned owl screeched at the top of its lungs. The bird took flight and Rice watched its midair turn as it swooped down into McFall bottom. A harvest moon was still shining down brightly on this cool night. It was one of those nights where you could see forever. And even though the cabin was still several hundred feet away, Rice could see it's every detail. He could almost see the latch on the door. Rice looked up at the full moon and by its position in the sky he placed the hour to be around the fourth hour of the new day. Two and a half more hours and the sun would be up.

Rice stepped over to Jack as both men began to take one final inspection of the condition of their weapons. Satisfied that all was well Rice looked at his friend. "You know Jack, this could very well lead to more violence. It is not too late for you to stay out of this growing feud if you want. You could stay up here and keep watch.

Jack was looking at the lock of his rifle as Rice spoke. When he had finished, Jack looked up at Rice, and gave him his answer, with nothing more than the expression on his face. The expression was a cold look of disbelief. He narrowed his eyes and with a slow shake of his head, finished with a gesture that clearly said 'come on let's go and do this'.

The two men continued down the hillside with rifles at the ready. Two years ago, Rice would have never thought that he would ever be attacking a sleeping neighbor at night, but here he was about to do the deed. Rice felt his conscious would be clear when all was said and done. The McFall's had given him little choice in the matter. They had to pay. He knew he was in the right. The law would even be on his side if Colonel Cleveland was here. And the fact that Ben was not would not change the matter, since John had gone full-fledged Tory. All of the Tories in the area were going to catch hell now that word was out that they were also fighting alongside the Cherokee as well as the British. Rice had thought about telling Ben about what had happen, but that would have led to Rachael's ordeal coming to light for all to know. If anyone ever ask why this raid was carried out, all Rice would have to say, was that John was using his father's home as a launching point to attack nearby Whigs. It would not be a lie after the indignity George and John had put Jack through that night with the tar. The plan was simple, they were going to kill George and John if they were inside. Old man McFall would not be hurt unless it was necessary. The same for Arthur or any women or children who may be inside.

Jack looked up at the chimney and saw that no smoke was rising out of the top. Maybe they had let the fire burn out during the night he thought. The inner shutters where swung shut and locked from the inside, as was customary, here on the frontier during times of alarm.

Jack pulled his tomahawk from his belt as he and Rice approached the door. No hounds were around to bark, nor even any guineas to call out an alarm. Rice pulled back the hammer of his rifle as Jack smashed the wooden latch with two downward blows from his tomahawk. Rice quickly kicked open the door, and as quick as a hammer could hit a frizzen, both men were inside. The room was totally dark, without the moonlight to light the way. Rice heard a rustling sound coming from the corner of the room. As his eyes adjusted to the darkness he saw the silhouette of a rising figure.

"Hold your ground or I'll shoot," Rice ordered.

The two men stood there for a moment to see what the other would do until John Alexander broke the silence.

"I'm going to strike a lamp so I can see who is intruding into my home at such an ungodly hour and disturbing my sleep. If you want to fire that rifle of yours, then go ahead and do so. My eyes can't take the strain of this poor light.

"Fair enough but if you try to pull a pistol you will never get off a shot" Rice warned.

Rice watch ever so closely as, John Alexander struck flint to iron to light the lamp. Jack likewise light a candle as well to reveal that the oldest of the McFall's was indeed alone.

"Where are your sons?" Rice asked.

John Alexander sat down in his chair and looked at his rifle across the room. "Damn" he proclaimed "getting too old for all of this gun play. Is Cleveland outside? I'm not talking to anyone but him."

"Well, you will have to. because he's not here. Just answer the question. Where are John and George?" Jack asked as he walked back to the doorway. "Out there somewhere in the dark hiding maybc, likc the dogs they are?"

"I haven't the slightest idea. I haven't seen any of my boys in a coon's age" the old man said defiantly. "What this all about anyway? You two still sour about not having your day in court I suppose."

"Not hardly." Rice answered. "It's gone way past that now. You know, so don't act like you don't. They are rotten to the core and they have earned this."

"Well, you got me there. They are as worthless as a wooden coin. But they are still my boys. And I'm not telling you anything. They may have earned this but not I," John Alexander said, while leaning forward onto a tabletop.

"Oh, but you are wrong there, John Alexander. You have in the past, and you will again in the future, harbor men that have done wrong to me and mine," Rice disagreed. "Not to mention Jack here, and who knows who else. You have a Tory safehaven here. And we don't aim to have one so close to our homes any longer."

"Nothing you can do about that now is there?" the old man retorted.

"Oh yes, there is." Rice replied coolly. "We can burn you out this very night."

"You can do that, but I will build back. You can count on it" John Alexander said, rising to his feet.

"You might, but if you do, know this. General Rutherford has already said that all Tory lands around here are to be consociated by the Whigs, so it appears we do seem to have the upper hand at the moment. You can take whatever you can pack on a horse. We will even let you keep that rifle so as you can make you way back East to the coast. But no powder, we can't have you taking shots at us."

John Alexander did not speak another word. He just went about the work of packing what he could; clothing, jerked meat, pots and pans and what little coin he had on hand. He had saved enough to load down two pack horses by the time the sun came up. He watched as Jack piled some straw and kindling on the floor in the center of the cabin. As Rice was about to pitch in a flaming torch, John Alexander finally spoke. "Hold on there, I built it with my own two hands, so I'll burn it as well." He took the torch from Rice's hand and flung it onto the pile. He then climbed up on his mount and said "I am grateful that you let me keep something. Ben would have burnt everything I am confident. But know this Rice Medaris. The British will not stand for this and someday they will march into this country with an army miles long. And when they do I'll be with them. Enjoy this victory today boys while you can, because it won't last long.

"We will see about that," Rice said as McFall rode away leaving his home in flames.

As Rice and Jack made their way back home, Rice pondered what the old man had just said. He was right. The British would come someday. He could only pray that the North Carolina militia could keep them at bay. The war in the backcountry was only beginning and it was becoming personal. What would spring bring?

Chapter 68

To Meet His Destiny

Patrick Ferguson stood on the deck of HMS Christopher on the 26th day of May 1777. The wind was blowing hard in his face as he looked out over the approaching wharf. Not the rolling of the ship's deck nor the loud popping of the sails overhead in the ships tall masts could distract him from New York City. He was surprised by the lack of humidity in the air. The climate was nothing like that of his plantation back in Tobago; it was more like that of his childhood home in Scotland. But it was just May, he thought.

The harbor was full with British Ships, both merchants, and of course, those of his Majesty's Royal Navy. George Washington's Rebel Army had long since been driven away from the city. But with the King's forces having suffered defeats at both Trenton and Princeton, the war was still ongoing, and Ferguson was eager to claim his part before it was won.

Lord Townshend had ordered Ferguson to raise a special rifle corps of two hundred men to introduce Ferguson's breach loading rifle into combat. Ferguson had only trained one hundred men by the time his orders came to cross the ocean. His men would not be clad in red like the traditional soldier of foot. They would be dressed in an emerald green coat that would be better suited for the forest of North America. Some of the Rebel commanders were beginning to fight in a more hit and run style that they themselves had been victim of, from the Indians for years. This was just the type of warfare that Ferguson had been training his men for. The back country may have good fighters and marksmen in hand to hand fighting, but Ferguson was confident that they would be no match for his well trained and better equipped force. He just needed a battle to prove the point.

The sound of the ship's anchor splashing into the water was a frustrating sound to Ferguson. The ship had been flagged from the shore with the news that the Christopher would have to wait for a docking spot on the busy wharf to unload its cargo and Ferguson's troops.

Patrick Ferguson was eager to meet his destiny and he was sure that his reputation was about to take another step forward, even if this ship was not. It had been a long voyage from England and he was dying to get off this ship and march into history to meet that destiny.

Chapter 69

A Different Kind of a Revolution

Rice looked up stream alongside the bank of his homestead on Warriors Creek to the mouth of his newly built water flume. This one-hundred-foot-long wooden waterway would soon power a four-foot waterwheel. Which in turn would turn the mill stone inside Rice's small but newly constructed mill house.

Rice had been using his time well during this uneventful summer. Last fall Rutherford's expedition had greatly reduced the Cherokee's war making abilities. They had to relocate and rebuild new villages, plant new crops and reorganize their livelihoods, not to mention nurse their weak back to health. Rice knew this would not last for long. He kept a watchful eye out for any Cherokee that may be heading down stream, for Dragging Canoe still drew breath. Added to that, the Shawnee were still strong in the Ohio country, and it was not unheard of for them to raid this far south, and like their native brothers, the back country Tories were in much disorder themselves, having taken a beaten at Moore's Creek Bridge and a few other small skirmishes. Rice and the Grider's had been on more than one spying excursion looking for all three groups. And praise be to God they had been uneventful. Rice and Rachael had been enjoying something of a normal life. Not only had they been improving their home, but their family would soon increase with the arrival of the couple's first newborn sometime before fall.

With a grateful heart, Rice reached out and grabbed Rachael around the waist, pulling her in for another hug. This practice was becoming a daily occurrence. Life was good, and he was relishing every moment of it.

"Ease now" she warned with a playful tap, "Don't wake him up, for he will be poking into my ribs again."

"It could be a lad I suppose," Rice replied "but she feels like a lass to me."

"And just how would you know what a lass feels like?" Rachael asked.

Rice just smiled and trotted off, without an answer, to the far end of the flume. Once there, he pulled up the end plank from its slot and watched as the water rushed inside. He walked alongside the running water as it made its way to the waterwheel. He put his hand inside and caught a drink of water with the cup of his hand. "Water never tasted so sweet!' he said as he flung his hand down to shake it dry. He watched proudly as the waterwheel began to make it first revolution. He and Rachael, happily stepped inside to see the culling mill stone began to turn. This old stone had come from Northern Germany according of Ole Fed who Rice had traded blacksmith work for, in order to purchase it.

It would grind grains such as oats, rye and barley into flour. And most importantly it would grind corn, the crop that grew best here, into corn meal. In time he would travel back East where he would buy a second mill stone. A burrstone would be needed in order to turn wheat into flour as well. Life was good for the Medaris family. Rice just hoped that it would last, now that the McFalls seemed to be gone. As he stood watching his new business, he wondered if this was a temporary peace or was the War in the backcountry really over?

Chapter 70

What Could Have Been

Patrick Ferguson was bedridden in the British field hospital near Brandywine Creek Pennsylvania. His right elbow had been stuck by a musket ball in the battle that bore the watercourse's name. He had flatly denied the head surgeon the right to amputate the now useless limb no matter what the consequences. He had endured illness and wounds before, and he still held confidence in his body's recuperative abilities.

The doctor had not sugarcoated the Major's dire condition "Either the King is going to lose a fine officer or you that limb. I, for one, would hope it will be only an arm and not the valuable man connected to it."

"Sir, he will lose neither," Ferguson replied "It's not God's will for me to lose an arm. I will leave this world whole, as a complete man, just as I came into it. Not with a stump penned up inside my sleeves or a dangling worthless mass swaying by my side. Providence will see to that. I do have one request however. Send for my aid, for if this is indeed, my great day of reckoning, I want to make out my reports. My lads performed well today. General Howe is going to have a well-documented account of their actions in the field as evidence of the superior execution of my rifle's performance. This is one report that I have long anticipated and I will not be denied the privilege of compiling it."

"No need for your man," replied the Doctor as he pulled up a chair. "I have seen the carnage from the week's work first hand. I should have the honor of hearing a firsthand account as to how it all developed. This is the bloodiest battle I have ever been associated with in all of my time as the regimental surgeon. My penmanship is adequate enough I assure you. All I require is paper and pen. You there, boy." He said to a passing aide. "Fetch me my writing matcrials. The major has duties to fulfill and I have time to spare in abundance."

"How did you receive that wound?" He asked staring down a long Scottish nose, over his low riding spectacles.

"I must admit," Ferguson replied to his countryman "I have no clue. I never saw where that shot came from. That bloody fog. We were alongside John Graves Simcoe's Company of the Queen's Rangers. I understand he took a wound as well."

"Indeed, he did," answered the doctor. "For I removed the ball from his leg as well as I did your arm. He should recover, I predict. A great number of his men were cut to pieces. They seemed to performed gallantly in spite of their losses, which is a credit to young Simcoe's command. He is another up and comer I dare say".

"As did my own men" Ferguson insisted "we had no shortage on the matter of desire, only a shortage of a clear line of fire. If only we had had the weather of three days before. I had a fine-looking rebel officer well within my reach.

"On the seventh?" inquired the good doctor.

"Yes," replied Ferguson, as a sharp pain ran up his arm, causing a grimace to cross his face.

"Then please, do tell the circumstances for I may know of whom you speak."

"I was along the Brandywine with two of my sharpshooters scouting the American lines near Chadd's Ford. We heard what turned out to be two officers approaching on horseback from the enemy's lines; one on a bay, the other on a chestnut.

The lead rider was a brilliantly clad Hussar[63], possibly a Frenchman. The second rider was most certainly a Senior Officer of the Continentals. He wore a remarkably large cocked hat. My first inclination was to fire upon them from our concealment. They would have been easy marks. But my first impulse was not proper or becoming of a British office. I then signaled my two subordinates to hold fire. I stepped into their view with my rifle leveled squarely at my foes. I loudly ordered the Hussar to step down from his mount. Only to have him shout an alarm to his fellow rider. Both men whirled around and galloped off. But the second was slower in doing so. We made eye contact and his glance was calm and steady, the look of a brave man. I could have lodged a half dozen balls in or about him before he was out of my reach, I had only to determine if I should act, but it was not pleasant to fire at the back of an unoffending individual who was acquitting himself coolly of his duty, and so I let him alone."

On hearing Ferguson's account, the Doctor removed his spectacles and with his other hand he ran his fingers along his jawline in deep thought. He looked squarely back at his patient and said.

---

63 A Hussar was a rank in the light cavalry of both the European and American armies.

"You will tell that story for the rest of your life my friend. Till the day you die, and that will be a long time from now, if you let me remove that arm.

"We have already covered this ground" replied Ferguson "You are not getting my arm. But why would I retell such an uneventful tale over and over?"

"Well, I will tell you why" replied the good doctor. "Just one short hour ago I dressed the wounds of a captured American officer. "We spoke of his commander in chief. Of how Washington likes to ride alongside his officers to scout firsthand the lay of the ground. He spoke of how Washington, only days ago, had ridden out on his bay mount Nelson [64]. He was accompanied by only one other rider. Casimir Pulaski, [65] a native of Poland. A Polish Hussar as a matter of

---

64 Nelson was a gift from Thomas Nelson, hence his name3 His was a while faced chestnut that stood at sixteen hands. He was Washington's favorite mount because of his coolness under fire. Washington rode Nelson to accept the British surrender at Yorktown, Virginia in 1781.Washington other mount used during the war was named Blueskin. Both horses were retired to Mount Vernon after the war.

65 Casimir Pulaski; born March 6, 1745 – October 11, 1779 A Polish born nobleman that was credited to be the father of the American Cavalry. He is remembered as a hero who fought for independence and freedom in both his native Poland and that of the United States during the American Revolution. He held the rear of Gen Washington's retreat at the battle of Brandywine Creek. He also took part in the Battle of Germantown and wintered at Valley Forge. He skirmished at Burlington and Little Egg Harbor both in New Jersey. In 1779 he was sent to the south where he died at the battle of Savannah Georgia while leading a cavalry charge. He has counties in Kentucky, Virginia, Tennessee, Missouri, Indiana, Arkansas, Florida, Illinois and George named in his honor.

fact. He had been recommended by that scandal, Benjamin Franklin, to Washington. My God Pattie, it was Washington himself that you had in your sights. What could have been, if only you had not have changed you mind? A shot truly heard around the world."

"Dishonor is what my reward would have been," Ferguson answered without hesitation. Brutus would have had a new companion in the annals of history. I have never seen Washington's likeness in the past and if I had, I still would have not fired upon him in that manner. There are still more battles to come. My conscious is clear, for my reputation will be made on my own terms in an honorable fashion. Washington will not be a martyr by my hand. But God help him if we ever again meet on a true field of battle, for I will not be so kind in an evenly matched situation."

Chapter 71

1777

The year of our Lord 1777 had many changes. Rice and Racheal celebrated the birth of their first child, Millie. Iona was now a full-time house guest, having taken refuge with the Medaris family. Jack and Annabel had purchased Colonel Cleveland's isolated tract of land near Deep Gap Creek, a risky business venture in many eyes. Yet it was an opportunity that a poor couple could little afford to pass up.

As for the war in the North, it dragged on with victories and losses on both sides. Fort Ticonderoga fell under siege from General John Burgoyne and his 7,800 British and Hessian forces from Quebec. General Arthur St. Clair, the American commander of the fort ordered a retreat abandoning Ticonderoga. The loss of Ticonderoga was somewhat offset by General Peter Gansevoort and Benedict Arnold's victory at the siege of Fort Stanwix inside the Mohawk Valley.

General George Washington and his British counterpart General Henry Howe meet at the Battle of Brandywine Creek in September. It was the largest and longest battle of the war. More than 30,000 men fought over eleven hours before the battle was won by Howe. Not only was this a humiliating defeat for Washington but it led to the loss of Philadelphia. Still, it could have been a war ending battle had Ferguson taken that shot at Washington. A few days later the Americans took yet another defeat when Mad Anthony Wayne was badly overrun at the Battle of Paoli.

General Horatio Gates won two crucial American victories at Freeman's Farm. Two battles fought on the same ground, weeks apart that would become known as the Battle of Saratoga. Dan Morgan and Benedict Arnold played major roles in this victory only to have the self-serving Gates take most of the credit for the much needed victory. Not only did this victory net the capture of General John Burgoyne and his army, but it also helped persuade the French to enter the war allied to the American cause.

Washington again battled with Howe at the Battle of Germantown in October. And again, Washington tasted defeat, making many in Congress believe that Gates should become the commander in chief of the Continental Army.

News was slow to travel to Warriors Creek, but Rice tried to keep up with the goings on up north as best as he could. The year had ended in a stalemate as far as Rice could see. Maybe 1778 would be the deciding year of the war and determine the outcome, hopefully one in favor of the Colonies.

Chapter 72

Pattie and Virginia

Patrick Ferguson stood in the parlor of his new home in the city of Philadelphia. He, like all the other occupying British officers, was being quartered in the finest houses that Philadelphia could offer. Any rebels that craved a new Government before the Redcoats occupation had now forfeited their homes all over the city. Chestnut Street was one of the most coveted locations in all of Philadelphia and Ferguson was granted use of one of the finer homes for the winter. Some had said that Ferguson was graced with this residence because he was not expected to live past the New Year. He had gone under the knife several times while in the city. Splinters of bone would make his right arm puss and fester. The doctors always wanted to amputate, but each time Ferguson refused, allowing only the bone fragments to be removed.

Eventually his refusals payed off, and the arm was finally healed. But it left him with a crook below the elbow, and a hand that would never again bear any weight. Out of necessity he was now forced to become left handed. He could easily fire a pistol with either hand before the wound, however it took a while for him to regain the marksmanship he had in the past, but after weeks of practice he had mastered the pistol again. However, the sword was another matter. Tonight, found him swinging away inside this elegant parlor. Weak muscles needed to be strengthened if he was ever to win another fencing match on the battlefield. He desperately needed to build up the muscles in his newly dominant arm.

In the center of the room, sitting on a royal blue sofa watching his every move was his newest mistress, Virginia Paul[66]. She was an ageing beauty, in her early forties, passing herself off as a woman of thirty-two to Pattie. She had been highly sought after as a bride while in her early twenties by many of the working class, but she craved a higher class and declined many good proposals in hopes of catching the golden ring. The greatest mistake of her life was falling in love with a young rich merchant. He had inherited a store near the docks, from his father where he could sell his West Indies merchandise. Sensing that his family was never going to allow a marriage to take place between their son and a young woman with little standing, she gave herself to him. But her time between the sheets only gained her a bastard child. He soon tired of her and abandoned both her and the baby. She was forced by circumstance to place her child in an orphanage for the poor. The only memento she had left of that child was half of a faded piece of white cloth with some red roses embroidered on it. The other half the orphanage kept to identify her daughter if she should ever be able to provide for the child. It had all happened so long ago that she had given up hope of ever reuniting with her daughter, who was now a young woman of twenty-two. Virginia often watched for her while out and about in Philadelphia, but she had no way of knowing what Peggy would look like now. Once, not long ago while on Rose Alley, she saw a beautiful young woman with dark hair and brown eyes much like her own. She was dressed well. Virginia had almost called out "Peggy" to see if the young women would stop to see who had called her name. There was no way to know if the name she had given her daughter was the one she had kept. Regardless, she did not want to spoil the fantasy that her child had a better life than the one she herself had.

---

[66] Virginia Paul's surname may have very well been Poll. There is some debate on what her true last name was. But most historians do believe she was indeed Virginia Paul.

Ferguson knew that she was older than what she claimed. She may not have been truthful when it came to her age, but she was trustworthy in every other aspect, including the bed. The British were in control of the city, but it was a tumultuous control. An American blockade was effectively keeping supplies from entering the city. There were shortages of many of the necessities and luxuries throughout the city. Virginia had a knack for getting her hands on anything that Ferguson might need. Fire wood was hard to come by, but she could always secure some before the last stick was burnt. Food was not a concern for an officer, but medical supplies were. Every church in the city was now a makeshift hospital due to this year's battles. And there too, she could come by ointments and bandages for his ever-needy arm. That was how they had met in the first place, when she was nursing at the Walnut Street church.

She watched Pattie take one last thrust into his fencing doll. She rose to her feet, but not before fixing her hair with her fingertips. She pressed her stomacher higher against her chest to further endow her already well-formed cleavage "You are becoming the man of old, my dear" she announced.

"Slowly," he replied "And much to your credit I must confess. You have helped immensely in my recovery.

"Pattie" she said, taking his arm. "What is to come of me when you muster back into the ranks? You know that I have already been deserted once by a man of mean. Please tell me that it will not happen again."

Hearing her request, Ferguson placed his sword on top of the cherry tabletop to his right. He crossed the candlelit room to answer her question. "Virginia," He said softly "You will always have a place by my side while I'm here in the Colonies, but you must know that we can never wed. Still, with that being said, I will always see to your future. From here or abroad; either way you future will be seen to. Your bad days are behind you. I am not one to destroy a mistress once a romance has ended. As for the moment, you will stay by my side. You must also know that I do harbor affectionate feelings towards you my dear. When I have the benefit of a house like this one, you will run my household. The lady of such a fine home should have fine things about her. Such as this," he said, pulling a pearl necklace from his pocket. He took her hand and opened it, slowly letting the string of pearls fall into her hand.

"And when in the field?" she asked fastening the pearls around her neck. "Not as a lowly camp follower I pray".

"No," he answered, taking her hand "But as my companion. You will be respected by my subordesence, I will see to that. As for my superiors and equals I cannot guarantee anything, but I will request it from them. And with jewelry such as this I'm sure you will receive respect."

Virginia leaned into his chest, and as he wrapped his one good arm around her waist her heart jumped for joy. Not for any love she may have for him, she had long lost the ability to love, but for a chance at a better future. She still held out hope for marriage. Pattie's time in America should be a long one, at least until the rebels were put down, and maybe even afterward.
It was possible he could be assigned to govern here. Given enough time, maybe she could change his mind and receive an offer from this Scotsman. After all, who back in Scotland would know of her past? She looked like a well to do Tory. Why not a wealthy Tory, who had lost everything in this God-awful war? How would they ever know?

As long as she was by his side, she felt she still had an opportunity to finally reach that long elusive golden ring.

Chapter 73

Portuguese Double Joe's

Iona was setting in a chair inside the Medaris cabin. She was watching Rachael hold her first born. She was patting the little girl's back after her feeding. With a few more pats, a loud burp broke the silence inside the room.

"Finally," Rachael announced as she rose to her feet. She walked over to the cradle beside Iona's feet and placed the child inside, tucking a blanket under the infant's small chin. As she walked away, Iona placed a foot on the cradle's rocker and began to rock the child with the tip of her toes. Before Racheal reached her chair, Iona began to hum a lullaby. It was a duet that Rachael usually joined in on, but tonight she had complained of a headache. As Rachael sat back down and closed her eyes, she tilted her head back and rested it on the chair's top slat. She could hear the sound of Rice's boots walking across the floor behind her. She felt Rice's fingertips on both her temples. Between the sensation of Rice's massage and the soothing sound of Iona's hum, the pain behind her eyes started to subside.

"There she goes. Off to sleep" Iona announced. "Hopefully for the night. You two are so blessed. She is such a doll. What I wouldn't give for one of my own, but that will never be,"

"I do not see why you cannot" Rachael disagreed. You have plenty of time for a child of your own.

"Doubtful" Iona replied. "And we all know why. It is sweet for you to say so, but I have a great disadvantage when its comes to drawing suitors. And tonight, I would prefer not to go down that long, dark road of conversation."

"A wig is all you need Iona," Rachael said as she opened her eyes and looked at her friend.

"And we have already covered that ground before," Iona said. "Wigs are for the wealthy, not a woman of the mountains such as I"

Rice looked down at his house guest and opened a new line of conversation with a question. "Iona, have I ever told you of my family's history? It is quite unique"

"No." Iona replied seemingly happy to move away from the topic of her missing hair. Please, do tell".

"Most around these parts wrongly believe that I have a Scottish bloodline. Perhaps from a small sept from the Highlands, long ago crushed by the McDonald clan; but I do not. You see mine is a old family name here in the Colonies. We have been here almost from the beginning of settlement here in new world. My ancestors landed at Jamestown not too long after Captain John Smith. Not from Scotland or even England for that matter, but from Portugal. Domingo Medaris was his name. A cattle baron, here to feed beef to the new world. Domingo translation to English is Sunday you understand."

"Is that so?" Iona asked with a smile.

"Yes," Rice replied and it was quite the shock to my Racheal here" he teased. "Yet this Portuguese heritage was a source of pride for my father. He kept a small piece of that heritage all of his life, and once he passed on to God's great reward, he passed it along to his children. Would you like to see it?"

"Sure, I would!" was Iona's answer.

Rice walked over and took a knee in the far corner of the cabin. There he pulled up a loose floorboard from the flooring. He reached down and pulled up a small box from the compartment below.

"Our father gave each of us three brothers five Portuguese Double Joes. Solid gold pieces with King Joao of Portugal's profile on the face. They are dated 1724 so they did not come over with Ole Domingo. I cannot say how they came to my father's hand, but he sure was proud of them, He always said if we were to part with them, to make it count. I have never seen anything worth spending them on in the past. But thinking back on it now, I did see something once in Salisbury worth parting with them for." Rice held one of them up to the candlelight to admire the coin one more time.

Iona watched Rice as he grasped one of the coins, reflecting what his father had told him all those years ago. He stopped talking, not even finishing the story of what he had seen in Salisbury.

"Well," she said after waiting another long moment. "Tell us what caught your eye."

"It was not so much an item as it was the shop itself, and what they sold inside. Wigs was the shop's merchandise. Wigs made mostly for barristers of the court, but with a coin such as this, a red wig for someone of the female persuasion would surely be no problem."

Iona sat in her chair somewhat stunned, not knowing how to respond to what she had just heard. Someone was actually being kind to her? A gold coin like this one Rice had said. Did he really mean to give her a gold coin? A coin such as this would buy much more than a wig. It would change her life, she thought as she began to tremble.

Rice reached down and took her hand into his own. He opened up her clenched fingers and placed the coin inside her hand. "Thank you for saving my beloved," he said as he closed her fingers back around the gold piece. "You saved her virtue and maybe even her life. I could hold on to this for the rest of my life and never find anything worth buying that would compare to what you saved us on that terrible day. I would even dare say that father would be pleased with my purchase here today. Thank you once again Iona. What a fool Arthur truly is!"

Chapter 74

May God Have Mercy On Their Souls

Rice stood under the shade of a massive beech tree as he watched the condemned step up onto the back of a flatbed wagon. The three had been chased down by Colonel Cleveland. They had been part of Gideon Wright's band of Tories who had the misfortune of being given orders to supply a Tory militia with new mounts. But instead of buying horseflesh, the trio and been stealing up and down the Yadkin. Ben was becoming one of, if not the most hated Whig in Western Carolina for his intolerance of anything Tory. Rice was surprised that these three had raided so deeply into Ben's jurisdiction. The only reward that raid was to net these men was the three nooses that were now hanging over their heads.

The horses that had been recaptured, were tied along a rope that was tethered between two trees. Several had already been reclaimed, and those that did not have an owner come forward to claim them, were to be auctioned off to the highest bidder after the execution. That was way Rice was here. Jack was hoping to place a winning bid in the coming auction. He and Rice always traveled together these days, not wanting to be caught alone on the roads. No word of the McFall's had come to ear in the last two years. Both knew firsthand what that clan was capable of, and both thought it was best to travel in tandem. The McFalls were not the only threat to be concerned about. The Cherokee were again hitting outlying cabins. Not at the same rate as before the Rutherford expedition, but enough to make all the settlers concerned about the safety of their families. The very fact that these three had been caught so close to home showed that the battle at Moore's Creek had not broken the Tories in North Carolina. 1778 and '79 had changed little as far as how long this war was going to last. Washington had won a hard-fought draw at The Battle of Monmouth Court House after the hard winter at Valley Forge. It may not have been an all-out victory but it showed that the American Army was improving. It was also the first battle that Patrick Ferguson had taken part in since Brandywine.

George Rogers Clarke and his Kentuckians had captured Vincennes, and in doing so was keeping the Shawnee occupied. The redcoats had captured Savannah, Georgia which was in part the cause of this resurgence of the southern Loyalist. Rice, like many of his fellow rebels in the west, was praying that Charles town would not fall to the same fate.

If that happened, Rebel lands would be confiscated and sold like this parcel of land was to be. This very track had belonged to the Tory, Colonel James Roberts. The very same Roberts that Rice had helped chase into Virginia while under Ben's command. The Rebel legislature in New Bern was taking Tory lands all over the colony by acts of law.

As Rice looked over the prisoners, he thought back to the only other hanging he had ever witnessed. These three were far less offensive than that damn rapist had been.

They had not told Ben who they were out of fear of retaliation to their families. Rice respected that. And despite the fact that they were indeed horse thieves, they did have some dignity left. Two were brothers from the way they looked, and by the way they seemed to try to keep each other's courage up with encouraging words. The third was much older, most likely the leader of the small band. The three were asked if they had any last words. And instead of giving a long condemning speech about British rule they started reciting the Lord's Prayer.

On hearing these familiar words, Rice turned and walked down the hill and away from the condemned men. That rapist had earned his rope and Rice enjoyed seeing that man's end. But this was something different. Something he did not want to see. Horse thievery was a hanging offence, but they had done this deed under orders. If not for the war, they would have been home turning sod and planting crops it seemed to Rice. War could turn an enemy into a friend and a friend into an enemy. My God have mercy on their souls.

Chapter 75

Stumbling About

Patrick Ferguson was sitting on the ground with his back propped up against a large sycamore tree. It had been a disappointing evening and he was writing a dispatch by firelight that was soon to be delivered to Sir Henry Clinton. Ferguson was in command of a three-hundred-man corps called the American Volunteers. This unit consisted of mainly New York loyalist. He also had Major Charles Cochrane's infantry, usually a branch of Tarleton's Legion, at his disposal. The troop that he was commanding was marching from Augusta Georgia to join the upcoming siege of the port of Charles Town. He and his men were the point of a larger force that was about twenty miles behind his current position here at McPherson's Plantation. The mosquito infested terrain that he had been covering was swampy and thickly wooded. He had taken possession of three bridges along his route, and had already won a few skirmishes along the way. The opposing Militia ambushes were no more than a nuisance to his progress.

But this morning the shoe was on the other foot. As luck would have it, as he was about to break camp, an old man and a young boy of no more than five years of age walked in bearing news. The old silver haired man was full of information. He had heard that his much-hated son-in-law was taking part in a planned ambush of Ferguson's men here at this plantation. The Whigs plan was to have two small ambush spots set up; one at a creek crossing a few miles north, tomorrow. And the other at a tavern about a two-hour ride to the east, today. Patrick was grateful for the information and payed the old man the price of a week's stay at the stated tavern for his troubles.

Without delay Ferguson promptly divide his troops, planning to catch both Rebel parties off guard. Major Cochrane was to overrun the Whigs at the tavern and rejoin Ferguson here tonight, and if needed, to help mop up any of the Whig militia that might still be left alive.

Ferguson's plan, as well formed as it was, soon came to a disappointing end. The Rebels had already abandoned their camp before Ferguson's approach. They had either left their campfires burning as a decoy or had simply seen Ferguson approach and had pulled out in haste. Either way, the camp was deserted.

Major Cochrane had yet to arrive and no sounds of battle had been heard coming from his direction. Ferguson believed that the Rebel's had either melted away, returning to their nearby homes, or were reorganizing for a future battle. Pattie was hoping for the later. As was his normal practice, Ferguson deployed his outlying pickets to assure that the rebels were really gone and that no attack would be launched without a warning.

As Ferguson folded his completed dispatch he heard the Call to Arms coming from his eastern pickets. He calmly placed the document into a leather carrying case and stood up, pulling his sword from its scabbard with his left hand.

A junior officer came running into camp saying that the Rebels had overrun his pickett and had killed one of his men. Before Ferguson could speak his next order, three men dashed into camp from out of the darkness with fixed bayonets. Ferguson deflected the first forward thrust of a bayonet with his sword. As he was about to drive home a killing thrust to his adversary, his eyes picked up the red sleeve of yet another charging soldier. A British soldier. Ferguson stepped back and yelled for his attacker to stand down.

It was now obvious to Ferguson, that Major Cochrane had mistaken Ferguson's American Volunteers for the enemy. And apparently, his own pickets had made the same misjudgment about Major Cochrane's advance guard.

Hearing the familiar voice of a Scotsman, Ferguson's attacker recognizes the situation, and realizing his mistake, halted his assault. Ferguson had lost his footing in the scuffle, and had stumbled backward, falling to the ground, and landing in a vulnerable and undefinable position. Another British soldier ran forward and drove his bayonet into Ferguson's left arm. It seemed that this soldier was the only one to understand that he was fighting his own commanding officers.

Ignoring the pain in his arm Ferguson rose to his feet, shouting at the top of his lungs for all to stand down. He looked across the camp and saw that Major Cochrane was giving the same order to stop this tragedy from become a major catastrophe.

Once order was restored Pattie looked at his wound. At first glance he thought that he could not have received it in a worst place. He had again been wounded in the arm, on the opposite arm from the wound he had received at the Battle of Brandywine. That one was already useless, he could ill afford to lose the use of his remaining good arm.

The surgeon was quickly summoned, and the result of his examination was one of great relief to the whole camp, for Pattie was a very popular officer. The cut was clean, doing little damage other than the actual puncture. If infection did not set in, the arm should be fine within a few weeks. All in all, the butcher's bill was light, only three men had died. But several were wounded in this act of mistaken identity.

"What will they say of us once word of this gets back to London?" Cochrane asked.

"Nothing if we win battles here in the south," Pattie replied. "However, if we lose, they will say we are two drunken fools stumbling about in the dark, killing each other".

Chapter 76

It Will Be A Hornets Nest

Rice stood inside his shop mopping his sweat soaked forehead. The combination of hot coals, and downward blows of his hammer on red iron was getting the best of him, so he stepped outside, heading to the creek to cool off. He sat down on a cool bolder at the water's edge, cupped a handful of the water, and splashed it against his red, flushed face. As the cool water ran down his cheeks, he heard the sound of approaching horses. There was little doubt about the first two riders, Jack and John Grider.
The third was William Lenoir and the fourth, bringing up the rear, was a blue coated Continental soldier. Rice stood up and walked toward the horses.

"Boys," he nodded in greeting to the first two riders as he stepped between Jack and John.

"Recognize that one there?" Jack asked, pointing to the dust covered solder.

"Anywhere," Rice answered. A smile parted his lips as he reached up and took his brother's hand. "Good to see you Massey. It's been way too long."

"Yes, way too long. So long that I didn't know how to get here on my own. I had to have these boys show me the way. It's a shame how our family has drifted in different ways, so to speak since the folks passed."

"But always on good terms," Rice replied. "I can't wait for you to meet Rachael and our children. We have two now, you know."

"I did not know about the second." Massey replied as he dismounted from his horse. Another girl?"

"Not this time. We named him Rice after me." Rice replied as he gave his brother a hug and a pat on the back. "Still it didn't take all three of these fellows to lead you here. What's afoot?"

"Charles Town has fallen," Lenoir announced. General Lincoln and his whole command are now in Lord Cornwallis' clutches".

"The Tories are already said to be mustering in. It will be a real hornet's nest. John replied. "David Fanning, Burn Foot Brown, and our old friends James Roberts and Gideon Wright will be burning and pillaging every Whig home they can."

"And we know who will be whispering in their ears and riding alongside them don't we Rice?" Jack asked.

"The McFall's" Rice answered. "They will be out to settle old scores. And that means you and me, Jack. What about John?' Rice asked referring to his other brother. "Was he still quartermaster for Charles Town?"

"Yes," Massey replied. "But thankfully, he was out of the city when the British began the siege. He is safe for the time being. As safe as any of us can be. He is out now trying to convince as many Whigs as he can to help supply rations for the Continentals. A new commander is going to have to replace General Lincoln at some point. And that army will be needing sustenance if they are going to defend against the British. You boys are worried about the Tories and rightfully so, but they are not the greatest threat any longer. The British are. The whole damn British high command is now here in the south. Sir Henry Clinton, for a while at least, Lord Cornwallis, that bastard Banastre Tarleton, Lord Rowden and Patrick Ferguson are all here. Northern Tories under Beverly Robinson from New York, along with Aquilla Price from Virginia is here with his mob. It's going to get mean down here."

"Aquilla Price!" Jack groaned, remembering the old bastard who had deceived him on that now sour land deal.

John, still mounted leaned forward on his horse and said, "The Cherokee. Don't forget about them. They will be taking advantage of this as well. You can bet on it. I'm off to Davidson Fort with dispatches. William here is off to Roundabout to fill Ben in."

"And you?" Rice asked looking at Massey."

"Quakers Meadows with dispatches for Charles McDowell."

"Well, not until you meet the Family," Rice replied.

"I would not have it any other way. Lead the way brother. I fear pleasures will be few this coming year, but this is one the war will not be denying me today. Can the lady of the house cook?"

As Rice led the way to his home, it was a bittersweet walk. It was nice to have his brother in his home, but the bad war news would dampen any good cheer that this gathering would bring.

Chapter 77

Devil at the door

Martin Davenport settled his family at the mouth of Wilson Creek off of the Johns River just in time for the Rutherford expedition in 1776. Between that time and now, he had made his reputation for being a harden Whig by fighting the Cherokee and the Tories with a strong vigorous purpose. Today was no different. He was out with the militia, miles away from this own homestead. His wife Hannah had gotten used to his absence over the years. And this evening was no different. She was working in her herb garden, unaware of the small marauding band of Tories that was coming up river.

John McFall walked his horse into Wilson Creek with his eyes set on the Davenport cabin. His flintlock was resting over his lap, at the ready. As his horse stepped out on dry land, he was flanked by two other riders, James Blevins and Samuel Stokes. These two men had met up with McFall at Cox's Mill, hoping to latch onto any Loyalist Militia they could find. McFall, trying to make a name for himself with the upper echelon among the Loyalist, had succeeded in talking these two into joining him on this raid. They had not yet addressed him as Captain, but that was as big a goal to him on this raid, as was the capture of Martin Davenport.

From her garden Hannah spotted the riders as they approached the cabin. At first she thought it was the return of her husband. But the closer the riders came to her, she realized that she was mistaken.

"William!" she cried, speaking to her eldest son of twelve "take your little brothers inside the cabin."

As McFall watched the boys run inside, he could see the fear on their faces. This led him to believe that the man of the house was absent. If Davenport was at home, they would have no need to flee, as they had. Feeling safe now, and with a rush of adrenaline, McFall rode his horse directly into the garden. He slowly turned his horse around three times deliberately stomping plants beneath his horse's hooves.

"Where is your husband this fine evening Mrs. Davenport?" he asked smugly.

"That is none of your concern," she replied calmly. "Certainly not out frightening children, as you are I assure you."

McFall smiled at her reply as he slid off his mount. She backed up a step as he approached, but then she stopped and stood her ground.

"This is the last time that I will ask nicely," he said standing close in front of her, looking down at her small frame. He was so close that he could feel her breath.

Hannah ignored his harsh request despite the fear that was building inside her. Seeing her determination, McFall realized that she was not going to reply. So, he gave her a hard shove on her chest, causing her to fall to the ground in a hard fall.

She began to crawl backwards on her hands and feet as he reached down to grab her ankles.

Seeing that this situation was quickly deteriorating, Samuel Stokes looked over to James Blevins. Blevins had the same look of disgust that Stokes knew he had on his own face. Stokes looked down at McFall and shouted, "That is quite enough John. Leave that woman alone."

McFall ignored the order at first, but when he heard the click of Stoke's rifle, he turned to his two fellow riders. "Don't let a pretty face get in the way of your better judgment Samuel. She is just like any other strumpet."

"McFall, you best use your better judgment, by looking at my face. If you think I have come all this way to watch you abused the wife of some rebel, then you are sorely mistaken. Step away or I'll end your day on a very sour note," Stokes warned.

McFall, red faced, turned away from Hannah and walked back to his horse, as mad as a hatter.

"You take our mounts on over to that pen, and tend to the saddles, and cool off some. We will take Mrs. Davenport inside.
Her husband could ride up at any time. If he does, we will take him inside before he knows what has happened. After you have unsaddled them, put the horses somewhere out of sight. We don't want to give anything away if Davenport returns."

It had been one of the longest nights in Hannah's life. She had been forced to prepare supper for this unwanted group of intruders. While she had been preparing the food, the Torics had all stayed inside the cabin. They had positioned themselves at the door and windows, just waiting to ambush her husband on his return. McFall had said very little after tending to the horses. He seemed to be pouting about the way the day had ended. Even when it came time to eat, he stayed at the window. "Keeping a lookout", he had said, but Hannah was sure it was more his wounded pride than anything else that kept him away from the table. He had barked out a few rough orders to William throughout the night. For some reason McFall had picked young William to be his new object of torment. The boy was slow to obey at first, but she kept assuring her son that it would be best to do what they were told. Soon they would tire and move on their way, because she knew that Martin would be gone for another ten days before his return. They just had to wait them out.

After the boys had eaten she quickly made them climb the ladder to the sleeping loft overhead. And once her clean up chores were finished, she too joined them in the loft. McFall had taken her and her husband's bed for the night, but not before he and Blevins had ransacked the cabin and packed away her mother silver spoons into their haversacks. Satisfied that everything of value had been found, Blevins had stretched out in front of the door and had quickly fallen asleep. His snoring gave McFall something else to complain about, but soon he too drifted off to sleep.

Stokes had placed himself at the foot of the loft ladder. He leaned his back against the lower slats and was looking straight ahead. She could not tell if he was still awake or not from her view above. All she could see was the balding spot that was developing on the top of his head. She was determined to not fall asleep herself with men like these inside her home. Once she had leaned over the top of the ladder to see what Stokes was doing, if anything. But the sound of her rolling over caught Stokes attention.

He looked up at her and said. "Go to sleep Mrs. Davenport. Not a soul is climbing this ladder tonight. You and yours are safe."

She politely thanked him, but she never did take his advice on going to sleep. But now the sun was up and she was again cooking for the Tory devils.

Stokes and Blevins where the first to arise and as they ate Hannah's eggs they began to talk over how this raid was not going as planned. The more they talked the less satisfied they seemed to become. Finally, they agreed to head back East to Cox's Mill or even Cross Creek and muster into a real militia.

"Fine then," McFall said angrily as he rose from the bed. "Boy! Get your sorry ass down here," he yelled to William who was still in the loft. "Cross Creek," he muttered to himself "Why the Hell not?"

He hurried about eating, not even taking the time to sit down. As soon as William's feet hit the floor of the cabin he ordered him to go out and saddle up the horses. William slowly exited the door, as McFall pulled on the first of his boots. Once they were both on, he announced that he was going out to make sure that boy was doing what he had been told. Hannah did not like the fact that her son was outside with McFall alone, so she took a step toward the door, but before she could reach the doorway she was stopped by Blevins. He wanted her to pack his haversack with food. Once his was filled, Stokes made the same demand as Blevins made his way outside. It took her another ten minutes to fill the second sack, but once it was done she made her way outside. McFall was already riding away with Blevins right behind. Stokes pulled himself up on his horse, nodded his head and followed suit.

"They have gone" she said to herself in relief as she watched them ford the creek again.

"William," she thought "Where is he?" She turned back to the barn and saw William walking towards her. He was moving slowly with his head down, sobbing. She could see red whelps on his legs. She pulled up the boy's night shirt and saw that the whelps went all the way up to his back and shoulders. "How did you get these William?" she asked somberly, knowing all too well as to where they had come from.

"The mean one did it. He told me to feed his horse some grain. I told him to do it himself, and he went into a rage. He cut a limb off a peach tree and whipped me smartly until the other one stopped him. I know that I should have shut up and just done it, but I just could not help myself Maw. I am sorry"

"That is alright son" Hannah [67] said, leading him to the cabin. "You handled yourself like a man. He is the one who should be sorry. Once your father hears of this, I am sure John McFall, will be more than sorry."

---

[67] Hannah Davenport did survive John McFall's home invasion but sadly she did not survive the war. It seems that she died of a good heart. She had loaned a poorer family the use of a pot to wash clothes with. Once she got the pot back she and others members of her family died of Smallpox.

Chapter 78

Another Virginia

Virginia Paul could smell the sea air in the wind as a strong gust of wind blew down Tradd Street. She was standing outside on the upper balcony of one of Charles Town finer homes; the former residence of Dr. Archibald McNeill who was now deceased. Patrick Ferguson had taken this three-story brick mansion for his southern home. Unknown to him, she was watching Patrick as he made his way down the street below. He was taking his time on his Sunday afternoon stroll, stopping to talk to fellow officers and well to do loyalist. She was positively certain that his conversations were of an official nature. But they did give him an opportunity to show off the new woman on his arm. She was a beautiful redhead of twenty-two by the name of Virginia Sal.[68]

Virginia continued to watch the two as they walked around the corner of the street and out of sight. Her eyes focused on the bay and its gray water for a moment, but then she turned and walked back into her bedchamber. Tired, she walked over to her mahogany bed and laid down and closed her eyes. Sleep would not come. She was mad at him and the other woman. But most of all she was mad at herself for making what could be a terrible mistake.

It all began last week when she was walking among the shops of Charles Town. Ferguson was in need of riding britches for the coming summer campaign. She had entered several tailor shops in search of good cloth and had found two quality shops, but both had attractive seamstress employed. They were entirely too attractive for a

---

[68] Little is known of Virginia Sal's history: some believe that her surname was Featherstone.

man with Pattie's wondering eye. Finally, she settled on a shop on Queens Street with an elderly woman as its proprietor, ensuring that when Pattie came in for his measurements, no flirtations would take place. So, on the day of Pattie's appointment Virginia saw no need to accompany him. She did not want to be overbearing with his free time if she was ever to become his wife. Ferguson made no comment after his measurement session at the shop and she was sure that all had gone well with her plan, until Virginia Sal showed up on the doorstep with the ridings britches in hand. It seemed that the old woman's apprentice was out of the shop when Virginia first made her inquiries. At first sight Virginia was concerned about Sal's presence, but once the girl spoke they diminished somewhat. She was not educated, and being so young she knew little in the ways of the world. She was the type of girl you would meet in a tavern, or even worse, a poor laundress with bad manners. Pattie would never be able to present this girl to the upper class without hurting his own standing. But late last night, all of her fears came rushing back. Ferguson had disappeared after their supper. She knew that he had not left the house, for all of his boots and shoes were accounted for. Virginia lit a candle and proceeded to the basement. As she reached the bottom of the staircase she blew out the candle and saw a crick of light was pouring out from under the door at the end of the hallway. She walked to the door on the tips of her toes and placed her ear to the wood.

"Don't worry my dear," Pattie said "you will be comfortable here."

"But in the basement? Why must I stay down here when there are three floors upstairs with so many empty rooms?" Sal asked.

"Because, this is where the servants stay, my dear," I can't bring you into the house any other way," Ferguson replied.

"I see no reasons for me to hide out down here. She is not your wife. Why must we act like she is?

"No, she is not my wife, but I do care for her. Virginia cared for me when I was wounded, like no other. She is very resourceful, and very capable of maintaining a household. You could learn a thing or two from her when it comes to domestic life. In time. I will bring you up, but for now this will have to do. Besides this does put three floors between her and us. This gives us the best possible privacy for our pleasures and pastimes. Now take off that pretty new green gown. You will have plenty of time to show it off tomorrow on our afternoon walk."

The conversation behind the door drew quite at that point, only the giggles from the other Virginia could be heard. Not wanting to hear the sounds of love making Virginia returned to her bedchamber. She needed to come up with a plan to rid herself of this other woman. Ferguson gave her little time to do so, for within the hour he entered the bedroom,

"I have a surprise for you my dear" he said as he sat on the edge of the bed, taking her hand. "I hired a servant girl today to help with the cooking and cleaning. This is too large a place for one person to maintain on their own, even one of your outstanding abilities."

"That will be of great help for now," Virginia replied as he kissed her hand. "But just how long will she be needed? Lord Cornwallis is not going to let us stay here in Charles Town for long."

"True enough." Ferguson agreed, "but until then I see no need for you to continue alone in the running of this household. Besides, I believe you will find her quite likable. You have already met her. She is the one who delivered my britches earlier in the week."

"Yes, I do remember her. She is quite attractive, but somewhat lacking in her manncrisms and wit.

"True." Ferguson agreed, "her ingredients are somewhat lacking. Not every woman possesses your charms."

Virginia thanked Pattie for his compliment with a goodnight kiss. She then watched him put out all the lights in the room. She held her smile well, but hid a feeling of contempt and disdain in her heart. Once he was in bed she placed an arm over his chest as she always did, snuggling up close to his body. She could not let this other Virginia come along and destroy all she had worked for, but how was she to stop this new bitchfoxly[69]?

Chapter 79

Moccasins On The Floor

Rachael stood outside the back door of the cabin just inside the shade that was created by the roofline overhead. It was still cool this morning, but the heat coming off her boiling black pot was breaking out sweat beads on her forehead. She had been making soap the last two days. The recipe called for last winter's wood ash, water, lye and the fat from the animals that Rice had butchered. Her finishing touch was to drop in oat straw or ground walnut shells just to give the

---

[69] Bitchfoxly is a slang term used in the 1700'for a prostitute.

smooth soap a little grit. But her favorite ingredient was lavender. She loved the smell of the beautiful purple flowers that grew under her window.

She was happy with the way her latest batch was looking. She poured it into a wooden box frame to dry and cure. She needed to go back inside to see if she could start cutting yesterday's work into fresh bars. As she stepped back inside, her eyes spotted her rifle propped up against the cabin's outer wall. But she was too busy with her work to take it inside with her every time she went in or out of the doorway.

Once inside, she checked on the still sleeping children on the bed. Little Rice was sleeping with his knees bunched up under his stomach with his little butt stuck up in the air. Millie was curled up on her side next to her brother, sucking on her thumb. Rachael reached down and pulled the little girl's thumb out of her mouth and lightly patted Rice's little behind. Smiling she returned to her work, picking up one of her wooden soap frames. She turned it upside down and gently tapped it on her tabletop. The large square of soap fell free from the frame, ready to be cut. She picked up her best knife and made a long cut across the brick of soap, within a few minutes she had cut twenty bars from the larger brick. She picked up a bar and held it to her nose. It smelled wonderful.

She began stacking the bars one on the other, so she could store them away, when she saw the light from the doorway change. Her glance went from the
tabletop to the floor where her eyes fell on a brown pair of moccasins belonging to the silent Indian who stood watching her.

She stepped back startled, but she held her composer putting on a brave face. He had not rushed her. She hoped that he would not, at least until she could reach the door and try for her rifle sitting uselessly outside.

He raised his hand, ever so slowly, and with the other pulled a white string of wampum from his belt. He placed it on the tabletop and stepped away from it.

"Fear nothing" he said to her in English "No warpaint on the face." He raised his hand and touched his chest. "Catawba people. We allied to you. Not the English. Catawba" He said once again still tapping his chest. "I fight with your man against the Cherokee. We are friendly."

"My husband?" Rachael asked. "You know Rice?"

"Yes," he nodded with a smile.

"New River!" she said, feeling relieved but still cautious about her situation. "You must be General New River, the chief."

"Yes. I am he. Is Rice with you? I would speak to him this day." New River said, looking about the cabin. His eyes stopped on the sleeping children, but he paid them no mind, for he did not want to frighten the wife of his friend any more than he already had.

"He is." She said looking over New River's shoulder at the warriors wandering about the lawn just outside her doorway. She knew that Rice was most likely inside the mill bagging feed. But she was still unsure if she should tell that to this man. He said he was New River, but she had never seen him before. How could she know for sure? Maybe he was, but maybe he was not.

New River stood there for a moment, waiting for her to tell him Rice's whereabouts when Rice suddenly walked into the room. He took New River's hand in his own in greeting, while giving his wife a reassuring look that let her know that all was well.

"What brings you to my door old friend?" Rice asked.

"We are on the path home." New River explained. "We have been out hunting to feed our people, we sometimes hunt far from the Catawba River to find enough meat to feed our children and old ones. May we rest the night here. Not all is so trusting to the Catawba as you are. They see Cherokee and Shawnee in every Indian face they see. Not a small tribe allied to the Whigs, such as we."

"Yes," Rice said" of course you and your warriors may stay. General New River is always welcome here".

"Many thanks," New River replied "I shall take your leave now and relay your welcoming permission to my hunting party."

As New River exited the door, Rice reached out and took Rachel's hand in his own. "Did your heart skip a beat?

"Yes" she said as she pulled out a chair and flopped down into it. "I may have a gray hair or two now."

That night Rice stood in his doorway looking out over his lawn. Forty warriors were camped all about his property. They had started a single fire where New River was eating his evening meal. Rice was flattered that New River had thought of him as a safe haven for the night. But like his wife he too was a little uneasy with all the warriors about. Some of the them were using English name such as John Joe,

Patrick Brown, Tom Cook and George Canty[70] but they were still Indians of a different culture with their own customs that Rice knew little about. He hoped that tonight he would learn more.

Rachael looked at her husband from beside the rear window of the cabin and said "The sunrise cannot get here quickly enough for me, husband."

"We will be just fine" Rice said "I trust New River completely."

"Then why stand by the door?" She asked.

"Oh, just observing" He replied "This is a sight that will be gone in a few short years, in my opinion. At best, theirs is a way of life doomed to fade away like a morning fog.

---

70 A Revolutionary muster roll submitted by Capt. Thomas Drennans On 21, June 1780 records a company of Catawba Indians under the command of General Thomas Sumter in the State of South Carolina for the year 1780 and discharge in the year 1781."

General New River, John Brown , Robin, Willis, "deceased killed at the Battle of Rocky Mount (his wife & child alive" Sugar, Jamey, Pinetree George, Jno Morrison, Henry White, John Cagg , Capt. Quash , Little Mick , Patrick Readhead, Billy Williams, Big Jamey, Billey Cagg, John Connor, Doctor John, Chunkey Pipe, Capt. Peter, Billey Otter, Little Aleck, John Eayrs, Peter Harris, Jacob Eayrs, Billey Readhead, John Thompson, Joue, Patrick Brown, George Cantey ,Jacob Scott , Bobb, James Eayrs,Little Stephen , Little Charley, John Celliah "Kelliah", Peter George ,George White, Jack Simmons, Billy Scott ,Young John, Tom Cook and White Men. Matthew Brown, Michael Delou and Ralph Smith.

Chapter 80

No Time For a Real Goodbye

New River's hunting party departed quickly the following morning. They had been gone no more than an hour before Rice and Rachel had a second group of visitors in so many days. Jack was leading a party of twenty men and he was leading them straight up to the porch. Many of the riders were familiar faces from General Rutherford's Cherokee Expedition. Others were such men as Absalom Baker[71], who went by Abe and Robert Bedwell,[72] both men who were neighbours and experienced fighters. There was no need to ask why they were here. It was obvious the militia had been called up.

"If it's the Indians that you are after, then all is well. It was New River and his Catawba's that you are on the trail of." Rice explained. "No Cherokee war parties are about today as far as I know."

"Well, that is something I suppose," Jack said with a weary sigh. "However, we already suspected as much. Our business is of a much larger threat than anything that Dragging Canoe could ever muster. It's the Tories again, but this time the British infantry is with them, and worst still, the Redcoats are in command. They are pushing up out of Camden. They are said to be establishing outposts all along the border between the two Carolinas. With that being said, you can

---

[71]Absalom Baker Revolutionary War pension number is S35181.

[72] Robert Bedwell Revolutionary War pension number is S16321

plainly see that this is a full out alarm. We are not the only party out spreading the word. There are several others, and we are to rendezvous at Shallow Ford tonight. We have little time"

"If you would saddle Liberty for me, it will go a bit faster" Rice said, as he turned to go back inside.

Jack nodded his head and turned Ringtail towards Rice's corral to comply with his request. But then he stopped and called out to Rachael, "Only a thirty-day enlistment this time. No need for you to worry."

Rachael was already filling her husband's haversack with what little food she had on hand as Rice entered the doorway. The look on her face told him that she knew all too well that this may not be as short a muster as Jack had said. And far more dangerous than any of the others Rice had been on in the past. They both knew battles were being fought in the East, such as at Waxhaws, where eighty-four men, just like Rice had died. Even closer to home was the battle of Ramseur's Mill [73] in which Baker, who was outside right now, had fought alongside her two brothers, Joseph and David. She understood that chaos could abound, that horror could soon be at the door of everyone she loved. He could sense the tension in his beloved by the way she moved so intently.

---

[73] Battle of Ramseur's Mill took place on June 20, 1780 in present-day Lincolnton North Carolina. The result was a Patriot victory.

Rice pulled his powder horn over his shoulder, wondering how he had stayed out of this new wave of the war as long as he had. He walked over to his two sleeping children and bent over giving each child a kiss on the cheek. Turning back, he took his haversack from Rachael and placed it over his shoulder. He wrapped both arms around her waist, looking deeply into her eyes. He put his finger under her chin and playfully tilted her head as if to say, 'We knew this was bound to happen'.

"I would feel much better if you would go to your father's with the children while I am gone," he said breaking their silence. "But if you decide not to, and fort up with the Grider's, or perhaps go to Salisbury instead, let me know by the use of a post rider. I need to know my family is safe if I am to keep my mind on what lies ahead."

"I will," she said as she leaned in for his farewell kiss. She made sure that it was a soft kiss at its beginning, but deep and hard at the end. One that would not be forgotten by either of them in the long days and nights that were to follow. A kiss without tears, one that a strong, passionate woman would deliver in a time of distress. A kiss that she would cherish and dearly hold onto, in her memories, until he came home to bring her a new one.

He reluctantly pulled away and exhaled a long breath as he exited the door with rifle in hand. As he closed the door on his cherished family, he heard her say, "Be safe out among the English, for this family needs you."

Chapter 81

He Would Know Of My Scars

Loyalist Lieutenant Anthony Allaire[74] sat at a round table in front of the open window of the Black Swan Tavern. As a member of the Loyal American Volunteers the New Yorker was stationed at the South Carolina outpost called Fort Ninety-Six. He was serving as Adjutant to Patrick Ferguson and had performed well at the siege of Charles Town and at the battle of Monck's Corner. Little was here in this small village that could hold Allaire interest. There were just over twenty homes in the whole town. This Tavern was a little better than the village's other watering hole. A few shops were located here that could supply him with an opportunity to replenish his low supplies of personal items. There were a few prostitutes as well, but he did not want to be the next man in a long line of men from the star shaped fort that was just down the road. So the lack of feminine companionship was a forgone conclusion for him at the moment.

Ferguson had finished his meal and had already departed to his quarters for the night. But before retiring for the evening he did make

---

[74] Anthony Allaire 1755-1838 kept a diary while in the south with Patrick Ferguson. In it he describes all of Ferguson's movements while in the Carolinians. His diary is considered today as one of the most detailed records of the Revolutionary War from the British point of view.

an offhand comment about an attractive beauty outside the window waiting to eat a meal like all the other patrons of the Black Swan.

"Would you consider it rude for me to invite a third female to my quarters for the evening, if you were one of my two ladies in waiting?" he asked looking at Allaire. "Most certainly so." he said himself, answering his own question with a smile. Allaire did not reply, he smiled at his commanding officer, even though he disapproved of Ferguson's polygamist life style here in the Americas. After

Ferguson had departed, Allaire allowed his own gaze to rest upon the subject of Ferguson's desire. She was striking. Odd that a woman with such an air of dignity was to be found alone, in such a place as this. He approached the lady in question and asked if she would consider it proper for her to join him at his table. She agreed, to his delight, but there was something in her manner of speaking, that told him that her social class was far below his own. But her quiet dignity and calm inner glow was too attractive not to pass the evening with. Who knew, maybe she would be a willing camp follower, one that would comfort him on the rest of this southern campaign.

"So, tell me what bring such a lady as yourself to such an outpost as this?" he asked. "Family, home, or possibly a loved one?"

"None of those things really," she replied. "I am heading for the coast."

"Alone?" he asked. "I see no escort to accompany a lady on such an undertaking"

"No." Iona replied, lying to this red-coated officer. She was amazed by the number of flirtatious conversations she had been engaged in since she had acquired her new head of hair. Astonished really, she never thought that she would ever hold another man's attention since the scalping. But Rachael's repeated statements about her winning another man's affections, seemed possible to her. More than a possibility really, more like a reality. But not a man who was allied with the savages that had ripped off her hair. She was willing for him to pay for a meal, but that was all, so tonight she would continue with her falsehood.

"My uncle and I are traveling to Charles Town on business. We plan to continue our trek in the morning."

"And where is he now?" Allaire asked.

"Resting," she replied not adding too much to the conversation now that her food was sitting in front of her on a pewter plate.

As he watched her eat, he began to doubt her story. She was eating quickly and he figured there were two possible reasons for her actions. Either she had not eaten in awhile or she was hurrying in her meal to make a quick exit from his presence. Perhaps she was a rebellious Whig. Perhaps she was in search of a protector. In his eyes, neither were good, so he stopped talking to her. A woman on a trip in the company of a family member would not behave as she was. She would be relaxed and at ease, but this woman was on edge.

As Iona bid him good evening she could sense that the tone of his voice was not as pleasant as before. He paid the bill as she walked away at a pace that made him feel she was indeed hiding something. Out the door and through the village she walked, not looking back to see if he was following. As she reached the corner of the first building down from the Black Swan she glanced back and saw no sight of him. She was relieved that she had fooled him into thinking she was not alone. But as she reached the next house, he stepped in behind her, from around the corner, pushing her roughly against the wall face first. He quickly turned her around by her shoulder and was surprises to see her wig slip to the other side of her head, revealing her ghastly scar. He stepped back as he saw the panic in her eyes. He was ashamed of his actions. What had happened to his poor women?

"My apology," he said. "Please, take your leave with all haste."

Iona readjusted the wig as a rush of anger came over her. She looked at him and said "Now you know way I am leaving. See what your Indian allies have done to me. I am running from a husband who has abandoned me to whatever fate comes my way. That is what your King as done to me."

"Your own husband abandoned you? Why?"

"Because he saw my scars" Iona replied. "Now may I go?"

"Of course, you may, my dear lady. With all God's speed."

Iona quickly hurried to her room for the night. As she made her way through the village of Ninety-Six she was overcome with joy. She had not only stood her ground when pressed this evening, but she had done so against a man. Something she could never have done while in the McFall family. She also knew that men were still attracted to her. Out there somewhere was a man who would love her in the daytime, and during the night, when she removed her wig. 'He will know of my scars', she thought, but it would not matter to him. He was out there somewhere and she was determined to find him. Determined to live out the rest of her life like any other woman, in the manner that she deserved. Life would go on and she would make it a triumph. Maybe she already had.

Chapter 82

The Tall And The Short Of It

Rice and his fellow militiamen had ridden hard the last few days. Their route had taken them well beyond Shallow Ford. They had travelled East to Salisbury then turned South to Charlottetown. Even there they did not stop until another twenty miles were behind them.

Not until they reached the camp of Major William Richardson Davie.[75] Rice was not even sure which Carolina he was in, the Northern or the Southern. All he knew for sure was that he was on the banks of Waxhaw Creek.[76] And out there somewhere was that son of a bitch, John McFall.

He had learned of McFall's presence while back at Shallow Ford on the first night. He and Jack had met Joseph Kerr, [77] a friend of Robert Bedwell. Kerr was also well acquainted with Jack's old friend, Frederick Miller, who had introduced him to Annabel. That knowledge of McFall's whereabouts was why Rice was still here. He could have been back at home by now if not for that. It was decided by the militia leaders that night, that not all of the militia should be sent to aid General Thomas Sumter's Army. Most were to stay home to prevent those old antagonist, like Gideon Wright, from running

---

[75] Major William Richardson Davie 1756-1820. One of the founding fathers of the University of North Carolina. He would become the 10th Governor of North Carolina serving from 1798 to 1799. Also, in 1799 he was appointed to serve on a peace commission to France by President John Adams.

[76] Waxhaw Creek flows in both North and South Carolina and dumps into the Catawba River.

[77] Joseph Kerr 1760- 1843 Kerr was granted a Rev. War pension of $80 per annum commencing March 4, 1831 under the Act of Congress for being a spy. His Rev. War Pension Application number is M804-1476. At this time in the war his spying had already been put to good use. His intelligence was a great help at The Battle of Williamson Plantation.

roughshod over the country. Rice and Jack chose to travel South in hopes of finding the bastard and ending this feud in the process.

McFall was stuck in Rice's craw like nothing else had ever been in his life. Seldom a day passed, without a vision entering his head, of his beloved Rachael being abused by that filth. The thought of another man seeing his wife in the way that only her husband should see her was infuriating. Sometimes Rice felt less than a man, because he had yet to settle that account. Time had passed since that day, but his need for revenge had not. John had taken advantage of the war as a way to keep himself out of Rice's reach. He had hidden among the Cherokee, and now within the ranks of the Tory militia. Perhaps now the tables would turn, and the war would work to Rice's advantage. If so, every day John McFall was getting closer to being within Rice's reach.

Joseph Kerr was a small man, even for the eighteen-year-old that he was. He had had the misfortune to be born with a right clubfoot. His ankle was twisted upside down and caused the toes of his foot to grow backwards. This disfigurement had placed his heel at the top of foot while his toes were twisted around on the underside facing the rear instead of its normal position to the front. Thus, the leg was a few inches shorter than other, so Joseph walked about with the aid of a crutch. He was not very engaging when it came to conversations within a crowd, maybe because of his young age, but in a small setting he was quite talkative, charming even. It was rumored that he was spying on the British, but he had never owned up to the accusation. However, he did seem free with information about the loyalist. It was no secret about the hatred between Rice and the

McFalls, so Joseph was eager to inform Rice that John was still with the Tories to the South. He had now joined up with the Camden District Militia. John, ever the braggart was taking credit for the murder of a Quaker by the name of Samuel Wyly[78]. It was a well-known fact that Wyly had been drawn and quartered by one of Tarleton's Captains named Christian Huck[79]in the Waxhaw valley. Few believed that John was even there, but that did not silence his boasting. It seemed that John was now an accomplished liar as well as an abuser of women and children.

As for Rice's new commander, the tall Major William Richardson Davie, Rice could not be more pleased. The Salisbury barrister was a true veteran having started out in the militia. Then having raised his own company of dragoons, he had fought in several skirmishes and had been seriously wounded at the battle of Stono Ferry [80]. Best of all no one understood the lay of the land here any better. Davie had grown up here under the care of his uncle, a

---

[78] Samuel Wyly ?-1780 His murder took place in present day Lancaster Co South Carolina.

[79] Capt. Christian Huck "The Swearing Captain" 1740-1780 He was a German born lawyer and Land speculator from Philadelphia Penn upper society. He was very loyal to the crown having fought at The Battle of Monmouth as well as several other small skirmishes before coming south. He met his just end at The Battle of Williamson Plantation also known as Huck's Defeat. He was said to have been shot through the neck during the battle while threatening his female prisoners that he had captured the day before.

[80] Battle of Stono Ferry was British victory fought near Charleston in June of 1779.

Presbyterian minister. Jack had dubbed Davie and Kerr "the tall and the short of it" Between the two of them it seemed no one understood the situation here any better, baring General New River. And that was soon to be remedied for New River was said to be heading into camp any day now.

Chapter 83

Shedding English blood

Rice was hunkered down along the roadside trying to keep out of sight. His rifle was primed and ready, just like those of all the other men scattered along Camden road near Flat Rock. Waiting in ambush was not one of his favorite pastimes in this July heat. He was also worried about Liberty, who was tied, down by the creek with the other horses. There were several young boys standing watch over the mounts, but it still made Rice a little nervous. Liberty was a fine mount and Rice did not want to lose him this far away from home. Jack was also looking over his shoulder, in the direction of Ringtail, with the same concern.

"Hope that boy is up to the task" He whispered looking at Rice. "At that age they are not always reliable."

"Indeed," Rice replied, looking down the road with a grin on his face.

"That gives us another reason to win the day I suppose."

"Like we needed another," Jack answered "You do realize that there will be an armed escort, most likely made up of regulars. British Regulars mind you, not some part-time soldier who is usually a bookkeeper when not in the militia."

"The thought has crossed my mind, but those Redcoats will make a fine target." Rice retorted in jest.

It was nice to have the fellowship of a good friend at a time like this, Rice thought to himself. It helped to ease the tension while waiting. He had been in combat before, but he had never shed English blood. That fact had not occurred to Rice until today. He understood that the colonies were at war with Great Britain, but it seemed so far away. But today it was just down the hill from where he was.

The supply train they were waiting for, was still out of sight. But the Patriots could hear the sound of its rolling wheels singing above the clinking of check lines in the distance. Major Davie had gotten word of this approaching British convoy that was to resupply the new British outpost at Hanging Rock. Most likely the work of Joseph Kerr, Rice thought.

Rice cocked his rifle as he saw the first of the mounted British soldiers ride into view. Jack was correct in his assumption, there was eight of them riding two abreast and four deep escorting the convoy. Rice picked his mark by placing the bead of his rifle on the silver gorget hanging around the first rider's neck. He squeezed the trigger as the order to fire was given. The horses of the fallen British Regulars galloped off to the right, and were quickly recovered by the Whig Militia. Rice and Jack were reloading their rifles as their fellow militiamen rushed past them from the rear. They still had loaded guns, not having discharged their weapons as of yet. They ordered the teamsters to stop their wagons or be shot likewise, with the next volley.

"Surrender or suffer the consequences!" yelled Major Davie, reinforcing the order. A few more shots were fired from down the road as two of the teamsters unsuccessfully tried to make an escape, but most of them accepted the situation and raised their hands, giving up on the fight before it really started.

Rice walked over to the Brit that he had just killed. He had flipped over backwards off his horse from the impact of Rice's shot. He had landed on his stomach and as Rice rolled him over he saw that the gorget had indeed been pierced by his shot. He thought of taking the gorget as a prize, but thought better of it. If he were to ever fall into British hands, the last thing he needed would be to enrage his enemy by possessing such a trophy.

Jack likewise had hit his mark, and was removing his victim's gorget when Rice suggested, "best let it lay, you would not want to be captured with one of these hanging around your neck. We won today, but maybe on the morrow or in a fortnight we could be the unfortunate ones in chains."

"Maybe so," Jack replied as he removed his newly won trophy. "I'll worry about that if that times ever comes. Until then, this is mine. We Scots have suffered at the hands of these bastards for generations, and today my retribution is at hand."

"So it is," Rice replied as he watched the conquering Whigs climb into the newly won wagons. "Wonder if there is any rum among the stores in those wagons?"

"Without question, but we will never pull the cork." Major Davie said as he walked by. "For the time being we need to secure our prisoners and return to camp. More Redcoats are bound to be close by. Hanging Rock is only five miles away, so we have little time to waste. We will keep the horses but the wagons will be too slow for us to haul back. They must be put to the torch along with any spirits that may be among the provisions."

"Yes Sir," Rice replied as he and Jack turned to retrieve their mounts. As the two made their way to the creek bed Jack looked at Rice with a heartbroken expression and said "That it is a damn shame. First we are deprived of our wives and now our drink as well."

Rice laughed at Jack's statement as he reached for his saddle horn. He looked over his horse's back at his friend and said, "Sadly, I cannot tell if you are serious or not."

"Hell, yes I'm serious" Jack replied with a lopsided grin that did little to convince Rice one way or the other.

"Well then, which of the two relationships are the greater loss, the wife or the drink?"

"Well sir, It is hard to say. It's like choosing between your two favorite children. Which do you prefer? You're strapping lad or you bonnie lass. I suppose it depends on the time of day," Jack chuckled. "And how dry you are."

"Now I know you are speaking in jest," Rice said as he pulled himself up onto Liberty's back.

"Well I'm glad one of us knows for sure, because I'm still torn on the debate" Jack said as he turned Ringtail around. Rice shook his head and pulled alongside Jack as the two rode up the hill together. The view from the top was quite beautiful. The sunset was lacing the darkening sky with a glorious purple and pink glow, while the flames of the burning wagons added a red tint to the lower horizon. Flying sparks and fragments of burning canvas floated in the air as the two men looked down the road. The captured Brits were riding two deep on draft horses with their hands bound behind their back. The patriots were riding alongside with rifles aimed at the prisoners, assuring that none would try to gallop off or shout out a warning into the quickly fading day. Being quite on the trail was a high priority since the trip back to camp would take the militia left of the British outpost at Hanging Rock. A second enemy outpost was also located at Rocky Mount to the West. The British Army often had mounted patrols traveling back and forth between the two outposts. Rice knew that being detected was a very real possibility.

As the hours passed the night grew darker. The sky was overcast with clouds, allowing very little light to shine on the roadside, which was a blessing, for if any British patrols were encountered, visibility would be limited. However, the poor visibility was a two-edged sword affecting both sides, it prompted Major Davie to issue orders for walking the horses instead of riding at a faster pace. This meant it would take them longer to get back to the safety of the main camp on Waxhaw Creek.

One of the men had fallen off the pace, lagging well behind the main group, presenting another problem for the Major. It was a widely known fact that he was a drunkard. He had most likely disobeyed orders, and filled his canteen with British rum and was now enjoying its aftereffects. Davie understood all too well that drunken men were easily captured, and had an inclination to talk too much when pressed. Davie was a cautious man and instead of returning the same way he had come, decided to take a lesser traveled route back. He had chosen a trail that crossed Beaver Creek instead. This route would take at least an hour longer than the original, but he felt it was for the best.

Usually Rice would have been content to ride along in the middle of the group, but tonight he rode at the front of the column. He felt safer in the middle of the line, it was more dangerous to be in the front or the rear. Major Davie knew of a plantation at the ford of the creek, and he felt that if they were to be attacked on their return it would present a fine spot for the British to take advantage of. At times, when they were in the area, they would simply enforce the Quartering Act [81] and spend the night at the plantation, either way a

British presence was possible. Being the Prudent officer that Davie was, he sent a vanguard to reconnoiter the plantation. Rice and Jack were among the vanguard, under the command of Captain Henry Pettit[82] for the mission.

Rice pulled Liberty to a stop on top of a hill and looked down at the valley plantation. No outlying camp fires was seen about the grounds. No candle light glowed from the framed windows in the house, no large amount of horses was seen in the lots. All seemed quite at first glance. Pettit rode down the hill at a slow pace and the rest of his men followed with Rice and Jack both on his right. Once at the bottom of the hill they spread out over the farmland looking for any sign of the British. Rice and Jack circled a suspicious corn crib. The moon was full but the cloud cover still lingered overhead making it hard to see. Yet nothing was seen and no shots from a British Brown Bess were heard. Satisfied that all was well, Major Pettit sent a rider back to the main column to inform Major Davie that it was safe to advance.

Rice spotted a feeding trough next to the crib so he rode Liberty over to it to see if there was any feed still inside. As his horse sniffed out the trough's contents Jack rode over to a field of waist-high corn beyond a split rail fence. He stood there for a moment and

---

[81] The Quartering Act was a law passed by the British Parliament in 1765 and again in 1774. It allowed British Troops to take housing within Inns, alehouses, private homes, Livery stables, uninhabited homes and outbuilding

[82] Henry Pettit 1763-1838 Revolutionary War pension number is W5528. He was at the Battle of Brown Oats Field

was soon joined by a fellow militiaman by the name of Carson. The air was still, but the sound of rattling corn leaves could be heard. Carson called out a command to halt but no response was forthcoming.

"A fox or raccoon?" he asked Jack.

"Possibly," Jack replied as Ringtail slowly turned his backside to the fence.

"There it is again," Carson observed "You hear that? Who goes there?" he called out forcibly, as his horse nervously moved under him.

Musket fire was his reply. A lead ball struck him square in the chest and he fell from his saddle dead as he would ever be. Jack's mount flinched wildly in a quick nervous leap as more musket balls flew past. Jack felt a sharp pain shoot through his neck as he tried to gained control of Ringtail. Rice could hear the rattle as the Redcoats rammed metal ramrods down the muzzles of their muskets. Realizing that time was short he kicked Liberty into a full out gallop and rode as fast as the horse could carry him to Jack's side. Another round of shots was fired from the cornfield as the patriot's scattered in panic. It appeared that Jack was no longer deemed a threat by the Redcoats, because their second volley had been aimed in a different direction. Rice could tell something was not right with his friend. Jack was having too much trouble controlling his horse. Rice reached over and grabbed the reins from Jack's unsteady hand. He quickly led Jack off the field of battle and into the ford of the creek. As the two reached the bank on the other side Jack said "Let go of my reins Rice. I believe that I can control him now. My wits are returning."

Rice did as he was asked, but he could see the blood flowing from his friend's wound. He pulled a cloth from his haversack to stop the bleeding, as he heard Major Davie and the rest of the main column charge into the waters of the creek as well. Another volley was fired, killing several of the captured British soldiers who were mounted on the slower moving draft horses that had been taken from the convoy early in the night. Davie gave the order for all to ride ahead and take up a defensive position at the top of the hill.

Rice was relieved to see that Jack was no longer in a daze when they made their way to the hilltop. His faculties seemed to be returning, but that wound was another matter altogether. It would need attention soon.

Rice steadied his friend from horseback, as the rest of the Patriots dismounted, forming a defensive line. Davie waited and watched for a moment. Three lanterns were seen moving about on the field below. One at the Cornfield, no doubt examining Carson's corpse. The other two, spreading out over the field. Then a call to return was heard and all three lanterns returned to the fence. No pursuit seemed to be coming. Davie looked at his men and said. "God's Providence, boys. We should have been cut to ribbons back there. Who is not among us?"

"Carson." Jack answered, slumped over.

"Any more? That is all we lost?" Davie asked again.

"And the prisoners," Colonel William Polk replied "I'm afraid they were mistaken for our rearguard and took the brunt of that last volley. God does have a sense of irony does he not?"

"Very well then. Has anyone else been hit beside Mcalpin here?" Davie asked.

"Just a graze Sir," replied an aging Patriot in his fifties while putting pressure to his bleeding earlobe.

Rice had been tending to Jack's wound while this conversation had been going on. He had a two to three-inch gash missing from his neck below the ear. He was breathing well considering the wound was so close to his throat. The flow of blood was even slowing a bit.

"Can you ride?" Rice asked as he wrapped a white neck scarf around the wound. "How weak are you?"

"You get me up there on that horse and I'll ride to kingdom come if need be old friend," Jack replied. "It will take more than this to put me down, but my ear is ringing something awful. Do I still have my rifle?"

Rice cocked his head in relief and said "Yes, Sweet Lips is secure, just be glad that you are riding on a horse and not the wings of an angel. Kingdom come could be a fast trip on the latter."

With that being said Jack was pushed into his saddle and the return ride was continued. Jack's worry now was would wound in his neck fester or heal? Only time would tell. As Rice rode alongside his friend, his thoughts were on the night's events [83]. English blood has been spilled, but so had his friend's. What would tomorrow bring?

Chapter 84

As Hard As Hickory

The sun had risen as Davie's detachment rode back in the Waxhaw Creek camp. Rice waved over two of the lads who were responsible for tending to the horses here in camp. The two were brothers from right here in the Waxhaw region. They were a little young to fight, but they were itching for the chance. They had been told by many here that if they performed their duties well, it would be only a matter of time until they could actually take part in the fighting.

"Andy! Come here boy." Rice said as he was dismounting from his Liberty. "Let your brother tend to the mounts. I need you to stay

---

[83] These two skirmishes took place hours apart on July 21 and July 22 1780. Today they are known as the skirmishes of Flat Rock and Beaver Creek Ford. Both in present day Kershaw County, South Carolina.

here with us. I may need your help. Can you stand the sight of blood boy?"

"Oh yea," the youth replied. "I've been gutting game and cattle for as long as I can recall. Maw saw to that."

"I'm not speaking of the blood of the rabbits and squirrels. I am speaking of the blood of your fellow man."

"It is all red ain't it?" Andy responded.

"Alright then," Rice said as he watched Jack sit down beside the creek bank.

Jack slowly removed Rice's scarf from around the wound, as Rice and Andy watched. The boy's eyes grew large and he did take in a long breath as Jack exposed the wound to the morning light. But to his credit, his constitution held firm.

"How does it look in the daylight?" Jack asked, tilting his head to give Rice a clearer view.

"Better than I thought, but not what I was hoping for. Your neck will be stretched awfully tight if I have to take needle and thread to you. It is a wide gap. Like I said, more than I was hoping for."

"Needle and thread won't do" Jack replied. "I saw you mend a shirt sleeve once and it was some mighty poor workmanship," he laughed, in pain.

"Well, that only leaves us a hot poker." Rice said as he looked at a nearby fire.

"Bloody hell! Don't I know it!" Jack groaned in despair. "Andy stick one in the fire before I have reservations."

Rice sat by Jack's side as they waited for the boy's return. Neither said anything during Andy's absence. Jack just sat there with hands clasped together, looking at the ground. Rice on the other hand, bowed his head and said a prayer for a steady hand. Rice looked back over his shoulder when he had finished and saw Andy coming back with a red tipped poker in his hand.

"You sure about this?" Rice asked once more.

"Just do it. Do it now."

Rice took the poker from Andy's hand and with his free hand, grasp Jack's shoulder. Jack stared straight into the eyes of young Andrew Jackson as the hot metal burned his wound closed. His eyes never broke contact with the youth and not a sound parted his lips. As Rice stepped back Jack rose to his feet, exhaling a long breath. "That is a fine good morning's work for ye'all," he said as he walked off into the camp.

"Damn," Rice said as he looked at Andy. He is as tough as an old piece of hickory."

Chapter 85

Memories Of Cockleburs

It had been a week since Jack had received his wound, and it seemed to be healing well. He was sore, and in some pain, but he had no red streaks running from the burn. Rice had been out on a few patrols, but nothing eventful had taken place. The only thing that seemed to break up the monotony of camp life was Andy Jackson and his slightly older brother Robert. The two had latched onto Jack and Rice, and as soon as their daily chores were taken care of they were always close by. They were bonded to each other as most brothers were. They would argue and fuss about the smallest of topics. Yet no grudges seem to last long between them. Mostly because the two already knew what it was like to lose a brother. Hugh, their older brother had died the year before at the battle of Stono Ferry from a heat stroke. So, if one offended the other, it was soon forgotten.

Yesterday Andy had brought in a bushel of June apples and Robert soon took to eating them right down to the core. Andy, not wanting to miss a chance to embarrass his brother, began to tell of Robert eating too many the year before and getting what Andy called the 'privy trots. After the two had bedded down for the night Robert put a few ant covered apple cores into Andy's bed roll as his revenge. Andy had awakened with red bite mark all over his legs. Rice was astonished that the boy could sleep through such a night, but he had.

Andy was rubbing some mud onto the bites in an effort to stop the itching, as Robert headed off to attend to the horses, which was his usual morning task. But today he had an extra spring in his step.

"I got to get him back somehow. Got any ideas?" Andy asked looking at Rice.

Rice smiled, as memories of his own youth came rushing back to him. "Well maybe, but you can't tell of my involvement.

"What is it?" Andy asked, "You've got something in mind. I can see it."

"What do you think?" Rice asked, looking at Jack with a devilish smile "Should I?"

"It is your good sleep that your putting at risk, not mine," Jack replied. "But it could be fun, to see how this would be plan of yours works out. Go on, tell the boy."

"Well I am not telling you to do it, I want to make that clear. I'm just telling you what happened to me as a boy. What you do with the information, you do of your own accord. Not mine. Understand?"

Andy nodded his head in agreement as Rice began his tale. "I was just a little younger than you are now I suppose. Still at my father's table, back at home. It was dark out and we were sitting by the fire, and my brother Massy looked over at me with great anticipation, asking our father for one of his ghost stories. Our father you see, was quite a storyteller and he could always put fear in my heart with his tales of haunted woods and graveyards. Massy knew that I took them way too much to heart, and took great pleasure in trying to frightened me with a goose to the ribs or some such nonsense. But on this night, he had done nothing. And once father was finished, we were off to bed. But unbeknownst to me, earlier in the evening, he had tied a knot to the corners of my quilt and had tied a string to that knot. He then ran the other end across the floor to his bed. Once in bed he let me fall asleep but not before saying that he had seen a spirit floating about the room. You can only imagine the fear that ran through me, as an unseen spirit jerked the covers from over my sleeping body."

"Oh, that will never work" Andy replied with a smile. "It is a good enough story and all, but Robert is long past the fear of apparitions going bump in the night."

"True," Rice replied "But you have yet to hear what I did to Massey in return. You see, the next day I collected a basket full of cockleburs and placed them in his bed sheets. That night, I challenged him to a race, to be the first in our beds. He ran across the room and leaped into a pile of anguish.

"Cockleburs!" Jack said as his attention was drawn to the road by an incoming mounted vanguard. "I saw some growing down by the creek yesterday!"

"That's got to be Thomas Sumter's boys," Rice said as he watched the rider's pull their horses to a stop and began to dismount. He looked at Jack with a look that said, their passing of slow days in camp was surely at an end. Word was already out about General Horatio Gates being in Hillsborough to reorganize the Southern

Department of the Continental Army. His reputation for being impatient led many to believe that by fall he would be after Lord Cornwallis just as he had Gen Burgoyne at Saratoga, New York. With that in mind, the three cocklebur conspirators walked to the road's edge and watched Thomas Sumter [84] come into view. He was clad in his old Continental uniform from two years before. He was easy to spot, being the only man in uniform among the common man dress of the Militia.

Sumter was a hard drinking, cockfighting, gambler that loved horse racing as much as he did fighting Indians. He had begun the war as a Lieutenant Colonel in the South Carolina Line. He was present at the Battle of Sullivan's Island back in 76, helped to defended Georgia from Lord Cornwallis at Savannah, and lead the Snow Campaign here in South Carolina. But, as the war shifted towards the North, in 1778 he resigned from the Continentals and retired to his home plantation on the Santee River out of boredom. However, with Tarleton's outrageous tactics in the Waxhaws being so near to his home, he felt it was no longer a time to set idly by. The British occupation had drawn Sumter out of his hiatus, by burning his home to the ground. He was fleeing from Tarleton, with his men at the time, and had to leave the charge of his home to his wife. All she could do was protest as the British burned the house. Since then Sumter had been in Salisbury, North Carolina speaking with the exiled governor of South Carolina, John Rutledge about a new command. Officially, He was appointed as the highest-ranking colonel in the South Carolina Militia but he was mostly addressed as

---

[84] Gen. Thomas Sumter 1734-1832 He died at the grand age of 97; this made him the last surviving General of the Revolution. Banastre Tarleton was the first to call Sumter "The fighting Gamecock" Fort Sumter of Civil War fame was named after Sumter soon after the War of 1812. He was a veteran of the French and Indian War.

General Sumter, even if it was an unofficial title. Once back in South Carolina he had raised over five hundred men plus he had persuaded General New River and his Catawba warriors to join his force.

"A true honest to God General" Andy said with awe. "Someday that could be me. Riding high on a horse and taking no sass from Robert, or anyone for that matter. General Andrew Jackson. Sort of roles off the tongue, don't it?"

"That it does" Jack said, giving the youth a nudge on the shoulder. "Just remember your old companions when you come into such a high position. We could use a friend in a place of authority in the future."

Rice watched as Davie and Sumter met each other, The two stood under a long fly that was pitched in front of a cabin that acted as headquarters. Davie gave his best salute as Sumter approached with hat in hand. The two extended hands for a dignified handshake before disappearing through the cabin door. They were joined by several junior officers and one small cripple.

"Battle plans" Jack observed. "I say we are attacking those outposts at Rocky Mount or Hanging Rock. Maybe even the village of Camden."

"We will find out by dusk I would say. What else could it be general?" Rice asked, looking at Andy. "Should we attend to our rifles?"

"If I had one like y'all, I sure as hell would be, "answered Jackson.

The rest of the day Rice and Jack did just that. Flints were test fired and tightened, pans were rubbed, touch holes were picked, and barrels were swabbed clean. Rice was sure that a fight was at hand. He had kept an eye on the cabin door all day. Officers had been darting in and out for hours. Rice had also noticed that Sumter's men had been given an extra supply of ammunition. New River had disappeared with his warriors, most likely out scouting an attack route. As night fell they were told that orders would be given before sunup. Rice spent the ten o'clock hour in prayer, preparing himself, if this was to be his last living night. He knew that his soul would be saved for he was a believer in Jesus Christ. The majority of his prayers were directed towards the well-being of the children and his wife.

It was hard to sleep, but Rice was trying. Finally, his eyelids grew heavy and he nodded off only to be awakened by Robert Jackson's aggravated cries of "Damn infernal Cockleburs."

Chapter 86

The First Battle Of Hanging Rock

It had been a quiet Sunday morning ride along Hanging Rock Creek, considering that there were sixty horses in the column. Major Davie was planning to make the 30th day of July, 1780 a day to remember. His command was much smaller than the five hundred under Thomas Sumter who was about to attack Rocky Mount fifteen miles to the East.

Rice was eager to take his part in the fray and felt somewhat at ease as he watched Abe Baker's mount in front of him swish its tail back and forth. The thought of the morning's good fortune gave him an optimistic view of what could lie ahead for the remainder of the day. They had not encountered any Loyalist patrols keeping watch over the approach to the Tory camp. This had not been anticipated and it was well appreciated by them all. Still, Rice knew that could change around the next bend. The Tory camp was so close by, that if an encounter took place while they were still on horseback, the sounds would definitely be heard. The element of surprise would be gone and a defeat would surely follow.

It was believed that the Hanging Rock outpost was under the command of Colonel Samuel Bryan [85]of Rowan County. He was a

---

[85] Colonel Samuel Bryan 1726-1798 In an odd twist of fate Bryan was captured in 1782 along with two other Tories. They were taken before the courts and tried in Salisbury during the March term of that year. The Lawyer who represented Bryan was none other than Maj. William R. Davie. Bryan lost the case and was found guilty of treason and was sentenced to be hanged. However, because of Bryan impeccable honor and integrity He was granted clemency by Governor Thomas Burk and lived out the rest of his peaceful life in the Yadkin Valley.

well-liked man before the war. Robert Bedwell had worked for Bryan years before, and said that Bryan had even loaned him money. Robert had admitted to Rice that he would have a hard time taking a shot at his old friend. Rice had no good advice for Robert's problem. He could only say, 'if you can save him without putting any of our lives in jeopardy that would be fine. Otherwise he would have to take that shot'.

As for Rice's own commander Major Davie's luck only needed to hold out a little longer. Rice was hoping that Gen Sumter was having the same results, most likely he was, because he had the benefit of New River's scouts; a luxury that Davie did not have. Sumter had, in theory, hatched out a well-planned attack. He was leading the other part of the two-pronged attack on the outpost of Rocky Mount where the majority of the enemy was stationed. The battle that Rice and Jack were sure to engage in was to keep the Hanging Rock Tories from coming to the larger force's aide. If all went as planned, the two most western outposts of the British would be overrun today.

Rice pulled Liberty to a stop as the column came to a halt. He dismounted, as did the rest of the men. The whole group led their horses down into a hollow to keep them out of sight. Rice and Jack had no more than tied their horse's reins when Davie motioned for the two of them to approach.

"Boys", He announced, "We are going to put those moccasins of yours to good use. The outpost is just ahead, and you two are to accompany me to see what is afoot down there. Let's go."

Rice looked at Jack and saw the same facial expression on Jack's face that no doubt was on his own. It was quite an honor to be chosen for such a detail. It was also a relief to still be engaged at the moment, and not sitting back with the other men looking at each other, and not knowing what was going on at the campsite. Rice hated sitting idly by at times like this and was grateful to still be on the move. As the three moved slowly from tree to tree in hunkered down positions, Rice saw another reason to admire his commanding officer. Most would have stayed behind and relied on a report, but not Davie. He wanted to see what the situation was for himself, even if it was dangerous, it was an admirable quality. The three finally came to a stop by a large boulder that seemed to have spring up out of the ground, the terrain was not mountainous at all here at Hanging Rock, somewhat rolling, but nothing like the name implied.

As Davie pulled a spyglass from a black leather haversack, Rice peered around the bolder. He saw a large cabin that was surrounded by Tories. About a hundred feet in front of the cabin was a poorly manned picket with only a few sentries standing guard. They seemed to be more concerned with the goings on inside the camp, than what was laying out in the surrounding tree lines. Rice was also looking for the bastard, but John McFall's face was not among the men in his line of view.

Jack, like his companions, was also taking in the view. What caught his eye was the large number of horses tied in a grove of trees. If each horse equaled one rider, then the Patriot force was heavily outnumbered, maybe as much as five to one.

Davie slid his spyglass back together, placing it inside his haversack and started back. Rice and Jack followed suit, not turning their backs on the enemy until they were out of view.

"There are way too many of them for us," Davie said once he felt they were out of earshot and could safely talk again. "We cannot take the field from them with our modest numbers, however we still have our orders to keep them at bay and off of General Sumter's back. We must do something."

"There are very few Regulars in their numbers", Rice said.

"Aye," Jack replied "a lot of Militia dressed very much like ourselves. They wear waistcoats of homespun just like us,"

"Indeed," Rice agreed. "I just saw a raw sentinel so relaxed he just let twenty or so of his own men, dressed just like us, ride up to that cabin without any ado."

"Once inside their defenses, we could simply dismount and fire a few volleys into their midst before they knew what hit them," Davie said with a wicked smile. "We can place the rest of our men in the trees to open our escape route with the additional firepower that they will provide. Maybe even pen them between us for a turkey shoot. It's unorthodox, but it could work."

"Yes Sir," Rice replied "The day could still be ours."

Nothing else was said on their return. Rice was pleased to have been part of a council of war's decision, He felt that he was truly making a contribution to the cause, and not just as a lowly private, which in reality he was, but not today.

Once back with the rest of his command Davie quickly sent out forty men to surround the unsuspecting outpost. Rice and Jack were to ride behind Davie as part of the false Tory patrol. Major Davie had ordered a wait of thirty minutes to allow the other men to take up their positions in the trees. That time passed slowly for Rice, but once he was back in the saddle, the time flew by. Now he was riding straight into the British outpost of Hanging Rock as if he was Lord Cornwallis himself.

Major Davie rode past the enemy picket without so much as a glance at the sentry on duty. He was playing his role well, as though he had done it a hundred times before, in truth he had, but in his own army. Rice did make eye contact with the Loyalist as he rode by, the unsuspecting militiaman even managed to muster a smile at Rice, as if he knew him. Rice almost felt sorry for the poor bastard, but that did not last long. Rice watched as Major Davie dismounted with his rifle in hand, seemingly at ease with the world. He looked down his column of men and ordered them to dismount, which they did. Robert Bedwell was relieved not to see Colonel Bryan standing among the Tories.

Although Rice and Jack were the masterminds behind the plan, he was pleased and surprised that the plan was working so well. Rice glanced in the opposite direction, where he spotted the majority of the enemy, gathered around the large rock formation that gave this place its name. They had given little attention to the arrival of a few inbound riders.

The Major brought Rice's attention back to the cabin with an order to present arms. The Tory militia stood by, wide mouthed as the order to fire was given. Rice emptied his rifle with a deadly shot, like so many of his companions had. The dumbfounded Tories finally comprehended that they were under attack.

Most of them were unarmed, and broke in a panic for the outer tree line, only to receive another round of deadly fire from the Patriots waiting there.

Major Davie barked out a new order to wheel about. Rice and the rest of the Whigs turned and fired a round into the main camp near the rock formation. The men gathered there broke into confusion, running out of sight down the creekbank. Jack reached down and picked up a discarded rifle from the ground. He made a nice pitch to Rice who caught the weapon in midair, Other men took Jack's lead and within a breath all of the discarded rifles left behind, about 100 stands of arms, along with sixty horses were no longer the property of King George's loyal subjects.

Major Davie made his last order of the raid, 'retreat in an orderly fashion'. Rice was soon in full gallop heading back to the Patriot camp, riding in a heavy downpour of rain that came from out of nowhere. He looked back over his shoulder and saw no pursuit. Abe Baker had called out several insults as he was riding out of the outpost, giving the victory a little more flavor for the patriots. He had been at the Waxhaw massacre and wanted it known that he would never forget that day.

Rice had no idea how many they had killed and wounded, but he did know that not a single man among his own ranks was so much as scratched. The Tories were too shocked to pursue, in spite of Abe's goating.

Rice was sure that if General Sumter had experienced half as much success as Davie had just had, this day would truly be remembered as one of the best of the entire war.

Chapter 87

Repelled But Not Done

Rice was sitting on the ground with his back against the spokes of a wagon wheel. He was dead tired. So tired that he heard little of the late evening sermon that was just preached by some unknown deacon from the Camden Regiment of Militia. It had been a long Sunday. One that he had killed on. 'How would God look upon that?' he thought. Most of the men here were ecstatic over their victory, especially Abe, but not Rice. He had broken one of God's commandments "Thou shalt not kill," and it laid hard upon his heart. The only true pleasure of the day was the grateful reaction of Andy Jackson, when he and his brother were presented with two of the captured muskets from Hanging Rock. Both of the Jackson's claimed to be well acquainted with firearms. They said they had grown up with two rifles in the family. One was back home with their mother. They had wanted to bring it with them, but she had said "two boys with only one toy was a formula for resentment." Rice was inclined to believe that was a mother's way of keeping her sons off the battlefields for a little while longer. The other rifle was somewhere unknown to them, having been lost to the family when their brother had died the year before while still in the ranks. It was most likely now in the hands of some grateful lad like themselves, in General Gate's currently forming army.

Rice closed his eyes and was almost in the first stage of sleep when the camp broke into a loud cry of huzzah. He looked at the road to see Sumter's branch of the army returning. The faces of the men were solemn and downcast. No echoing huzzah was called in returned. A defeat must have befallen them, however their ranks were still long. If they had tasted defeat it was not a complete disaster, Rice thought.

Sumter and Davie quickly went inside headquarters, no doubt to discuss the day's events. As Sumter's men dismounted they were greeted by the camp. They did not have to ask what had developed. Sumter's men were eager to talk. Captain Richard Tucker, another Camden militiaman walked over to the wagon where Rice was sitting and began to talk.

"We lost or had wounded at least twelve men today. Four are dead. Among them are Captain Andrew Neel[86] of the New Acquisition Militia. Six more wounded that I know of. Young Haynes [87]lost an eye and will forfeit his life too, before dawn I suspect. Two more are missing, believed to be captured. We invested the whole outpost upon arrival. Sumter even went as far as to ask for their surrender. But their Lt. Colonel George Turnbull refused. His defenses were strong. Rocky Mount consisted of two log houses, a loop-holed building, and an abatis with ditches placed on an eminence. That eminence commands the entire view around the outpost. If only we had had cannon. We made three attacks on that blasted place. All failed."

---

[86] Andrew Neel had two brothers that were killed in the war as well, according to family lore. Thomas Neel was killed in 1781. John Neel was only sixteen when he was killed at Hayes' Station in 1778 by Major William Cunningham's Loyalist militia.

[87] Alexander Haynes did not die from the wound. He was granted his Rev War pension in 1827 while residing in the York District of South Carolina. The Pension # is S1519

"How did Captain Neel die" asked Jack.

"Well!" answered Tucker. "He was able to push through the abatis and drive the Tories into their cabins, but he was soon killed by musketry, along with two of his men and a Catawba."

"Not New River, I pray?" asked Rice.

"No, Thankfully not," Tucker replied "That is one Indian we can ill afford to lose. But the one that died did have a Christian name. Willis. That was his name. Anyway, the British sent out a large detail, to charge with bayonets affixed. Scary as hell, I tell you. But we drove them back easily with a volley. We killed between 10 to 20 on that exchange, and tried to fire the place with torches, but that rain storm put an end to that. So, we withdrew. Not in victory nor in defeat. Repelled but not done. We were just getting acquainted, so to speak. How did you all and Major Davie fair at Hanging Rock?"

Chapter 88

One Never Knows

Another Sunday and another attack on the Hanging Rock outpost. Rice was not sure if Sumter was superstitious or just trying to catch the outpost off guard, because of the Sabbath. Either way, it did not really matter, because they were here. What difference could a week have actually made, Rice wondered? He did not know for sure, but New River and his braves had been here two days ago and had observed no significant changes in the defenses. Sumter was eager to sack one of the two outposts that he had attacked the week before. He decided Hanging Rock would be the best of the two targets to attack.

It would not be a split attack this time, his entire force was attacking today. The last six days had not been eventful, but they were active. Sumter was worried about a counter attack by the British, and for good reason. Two members of the British Legion Infantryman had been captured by New River on Monday, and with the aid of his tomahawk and his red war paint, they were eager to talk. They gave, to a man, those who were stationed at Hanging Rock.

Major John Carden was the Commanding Officer of the outpost. His Prince of Wales American Regiment was 181 men strong. They were northern Militia and well-seasoned from battles up East. The two prisoners were from the 160 manned British Legion Infantry led by Captain Kenneth McCulloch with Captain John Roussel. The North Carolina Volunteers, who took the brunt of the first attack was led by Colonel Samuel Bryan and still camped in the same place. The Royal North Carolina Regiment, being led by Major Daniel Manson was also present at Hanging Rock. Local men of the Camden's Loyalist Militia led by Colonel Henry Rugeley was also using the outpost as it's base of operations. In all, these three Loyalist Militia had a combined force of 800 men. This put the total of troops at Hanging Rock a little shy of 1200 men. Plus, reinforcements could arrive from Rocky Mount at any time.

On Wednesday. more news arrived in the form of a youth from homestead four miles East of the outpost. He had walked into camp with news of a sighting of 150 of Tarleton's Dragoons riding towards Hanging Rock, but Bloody Ban was not among them he said If true, that would raise the ante to 1400 enemy soldiers. On hearing this intelligence, Sumter thought it would be wise to split his army temporarily. He decided to take 300 men back with him to his old camp near the Catawba River. There he would gather the rest of his men who had not accompanied him to Davie's camp, leaving Davie's army at its old campsite alone. If the British were looking for his army, he saw no reason for them to catch the whole army.

Last night the Armies reunited at Land's Ford. Sumter was back and he had more men. A small Georgia Militia led by a Captain Coleman, had joined his ranks. In addition, the furnace of Colonel William Hill,[88] an Ironmaster from Allison's Creek who had supplied much needed cannonballs and swivel guns to the rebel cause, was now in ashes. Refusing to be deterred Hill had raised a company of light Dragoons, and had put them at Sumter's disposal. They had performed well at Rocky Mount and would surely to do the same today.

With Sumter's presence, one last Council of War was held by firelight. Davie argued that they should proceed without horse. He was concerned that the horses would be unruly and hard to handle during the coming battle. But Sumter strongly disagreed, fearing that if Tarleton's Dragoons where in the area horse would be needed to fend them off. The majority of the army would march the final fifteen miles on foot Sumter ruled, but Dave would lead 300 men on horseback. They could move about quickly on the field once the battle started, and they could fight by either foot or on horseback which ever was needed. Major Davie might not have wanted to take the mounts but Rice was happy that he was overruled. Liberty, like so many other men's horses, was a fine mount and Rice knew that they would be a great asset in the coming battle.

Since most of the men were on foot, the march was slow going. Rice and the other men on horseback had ridden out in the front of the

_____

[88] Colonel William Hill was born in Ireland in 1740. He had settled in South Carolina by 1762 in what is now York County. There he would build his Iron Works on his 5000-acre plantation.

column to lead the way. As ordered, they came to a halt about two miles from the outpost a little before the witching hour. Major Davie had ordered half of his men to dismount and form a line of defense in a small dry branch that ran into Hanging Rock Creek. Abe, always ready to kill another Tory or Brit, was first off, his horse and into the branch. Rice and Jack were in the half that stayed mounted until the militia arrived. They were still sitting in the saddle when the first men came marching in.

"Look at those faces" Rice said, patting Liberty's neck. "Their arses are dragging out their tracks. The only good dealing I ever had with a McFall was when I bought this horse. Otherwise, I would be down there with sore feet too.
Only a few hours till sunup," Jack said. "Looks as though they should use that time to rest up. Going to be hot if yesterday's weather holds for the morrow. Look, here comes Andy toting that musket and still strutting like a banty rooster."

"How are you holding up there Mr. Jackson?" Rice asked.

"Like a buck in the rut," the youth replied proudly for all to hear. He walked over and stood between Rice and Jack's horses, as the rest of the men on foot began looking for a place to drop to the ground and get some rest before the coming battle. Andy looked up at Rice and said in a lowered tone of voice, "To be honest, I have to admit that I do have some tension about what's to come. Nothing cowardly mind you, just concerned, that is all. Don't tell Robert, I said so though. Alright?"

"The thought never crossed my mind. There is nothing to be ashamed of. That means you are just like all the rest of us," Rice said, pointing to the rest of the men around them. "If you did not feel that way I would say you are either lying or crazy."

"You will do fine" Jack said joining in on the conversation "Stay in the ranks and do as you are told. Don't be too aggressive and do something on your own. Keep out of sight while loading and stay out of the clear while firing. If we do need to fall back, and I doubt there will be a need to do so, just keep your wits about you. Do all of that and you will be able to tell your children about the day you took Hanging Rock as a prize from Ole King George."

As Andy walked away smiling, to find his brother Robert, Rice heard the order for him to dismount along with the rest of the riders being relayed down the line. Once on the ground he pulled the saddle from Liberty's back and dropped it on the ground. He used it for a hard pillow as he laid down on his back for the night. Within twenty minutes the camp was quiet The only sound he could hear was the chirping of crickets, peeping treefrogs and the humming sound of some winged insect in the treetops overhead. He soon fell into a deep sleep. He was sleeping soundly when his shoulder was shaken lightly by Jack.

"Time to rise old friend" Jack said "How in the hell you can sleep at a time like this? I cannot understand how you can sleep so well before such a day, while I toss and turn all night.

Rice rubbed his eyes and stood up feeling refreshed, as a splash of pink was spreading low in the Eastern sky. Hours had passed in literally a wink. He slung the saddle up onto Liberty's back, and as he was cinching down the girth he looked at Jack. "I will tell you a secret, my sleep is in something of a race. If I don't fall first, then I hear you cutting logs all night. So, you see it is purely out of necessity that I drop off first."

"I have heard that from Annabel a time or two," Jack said as he pulled himself up into his own saddle. He reached over and took Rice's hand into his own and said "Just in case, ole friend."

Rice appreciated the gesture, and as the two were shaking hands he realized that Jack was really his best friend. He felt confident that this would not be their last adventure together, but then again, you never know.

Chapter 89

The Second Battle of Hanging Rock

Rice was leading his horse by the reins as he moved towards the outpost. Major Davie was walking the men, as ordered by General Sumter. The General did not want them to outpace the infantry, so everyone walked at the same pace, allowing the forces to arrive together. They were to remount when the first enemy picket came into view.

The plan of attack called for the Major's men to attack as Dragoons, this was something new to Rice. He had never fought on horseback before, and like Jack, he had no sabre to wheel about in the coming charge, only his tomahawk with its short handle. The battle plan was to be carried out in a speedy simultaneous attack from three different directions. The plan also called for no shots to be fired. The idea being that the pickets were so thinly manned that they could easily and quietly be overwhelmed.

Within the picket lines were three different Loyalties campsites. Bryan's corps would again be the first camp to be attacked, it being the most western of the three. If the pickets were overrun as planned, Bryan's men would be at the Dragoons mercy. Behind them would be the rest of General Sumter's army charging in on foot.

Rice looked to his left and saw Colonel William Hill and his Light Dragoons detachment pulling themselves into their saddles. Something was amiss for they were supposed to attack from the south end of the outpost, Either Major Davie or Colonel Hill was not in the correct position. But it was too late to reform the attack line now.

Rice mounted up and within seconds Liberty was in full gallop. The horse's hooves were making a thunderous sound as the dragoons approached. Directly in front of him, Rice saw his first Tory of the day. The sight of so many men attacking all at once put the poor man into a panic. He had dropped his rifle and was in full flight, running back towards Bryan's camp, but his horse was no match for Liberty. Rice made a downward strike with his tomahawk and heard the thudding sound of the weapon as it sank into the fleeing man's neck. Rice turned his horse around to see if any more of the Tories were still a threat. What he saw was Jack in full pursuit of another loyalist, but this man had more vigor than Rice's. He had stopped running and was presenting his rifle to fire it at Jack. As he was cocking his Brown Bess Jack threw his tomahawk. Jack's aim was true and the Tory never got a chance to pull his trigger as the hawk cut deep into his chest. Jack quickly dismounted Ringtail, collected his weapon, and was soon back in the saddle. The picket did not have a live man remaining among it. And fortunately, no enemy shots had been fired, and only two yells were called out to announce that an attack was commencing, but Rice was not convinced that they had been heard inside Bryan's camp.

One of the prisoners began to speak out in anger, but was cut off by another one saying, "For God's sake man, hold your tongue! We are at their mercy."

"Damn right," Jack agreed. "Hold that wicked tongue or I just might cut it out and feed it to one of those Catawba. I hear they like tongue"

Rice approached the one who had said not to talk and asked, "Is John McFall here about?"

"Never heard of the man" the prisoner answered.

"He is from up around the Yadkin," Rice spoke again. "Dark haired and mean tempered."

"Cannot say that I know him" replied the man once again "But there are lots of men here that I do not know".

Rice was not satisfied with the answer, but he realized this man was not likely to tell him the truth, even if he did know McFall. He moved on to their tent. Inside he found musket charges for the Brown Bess but it was too large a caliber to fit his rifle. So, he walked over to a nearby frying pan that was sitting over some red coals. Inside he found some burning meat. He picked it out and ate what little was edible before discarding the rest onto the ground. He then dropped English lead into the hot pan. As it was melting he pulled his bullet mold from his haversack. Within five minutes he and Jack had six new rounds each, and Robert Bedwell had three that could be fired back at the British. Other men were doing the same, as Sumter was in low supply of readymade balls. Bedwell had broken open a keg of rum and was taking his fill.

In the distance, shots were being fired at the enemy's second campsite. Hearing it, Rice continued on, as did Jack, having already handed his prisoner over to a detail that was assigned to such duty. They rode their horses down a steep hill past several odder rock formations, and into Hanging Rock Creek. There they dismount, and charged into the small woods that separated them from the Prince of Wales American Regiment campsite. Once on the other side, Rice took cover, alongside Jack, behind another split rail fence.

"What would young Jackson have to say about our choice of cover?" Rice asked, knowing full well they were in an exposed position.

"Damned foolhardy" Jack replied as he shot his rifle. "We should have taken to a tree instead. like Baker and Bedwell have."

Then the ground shook under their feet. The British had brought their artillery to bear on the right side of Davie's men. And just as Davie had feared, many of his men were shot down, while entangled with unruly horses.

Another field piece was about to be discharged towards Davie's men, but Rice put a well-aimed round into its gunner forehead. Jack followed suit by killing an officer that was holding a spontoon just behind the small canon. As Rice was reloading he heard a loud cry of huzzah coming from the enemy. He looked up and saw that they had fixed bayonets was charging towards the fence in the most threatening manner he had ever seen from them.

His heart raced as he brought his rifle to bear. he was sure that they could not be turned back with only his and Jack's next shots. Then, a loud volley came from the trees behind. Sumter's Militia stopped the charge as quick as it had begun. That volley was a God send to Rice and Jack, but it had completely destroyed Major John Carden's Prince of Wales American Regiment. Eighty percent of them were killed, in Rice's estimation, from what he could see. Still, the battle was far from over. As soon as the retreating survivors of the first charge made it to safety, another charging line of men broke from the trees.

Rice had never seen a member of Tarleton's legion, but he had heard of them. Their Green uniforms were a deadly calling card in this war, and they were in a dead run with bayonets fixed. They were gambling that Sumter's men would fall back at the very sight of them, but it was a poor gamble. Men like Abe Baker and Bill Alexander were eager to settle old scores, and they did exactly that with a deadly volley that met the enemy in midfield.

Rice had not fired on the Prince of Wales Regiment as they had retreated, but he had no problem doing so to these bastards. They had shown little honor throughout the war. No quarter whatsoever was ever granted by their hand. Why should he grant them something that they had never granted to anyone themselves?
He put the first of his newly molded rounds into the back of the first retreating green uniform that he saw. "You reap what you sow" yelled Abe.

The battlefield was eerily silent for the moment. Two of the camps had been engaged thus far. Both had not only been badly bloodied, but decimated by the patriot forces. All that stood between them and total victory was the third camp, and it lay just beyond the next grove of trees.

Rice was hot, tired, and thirsty but that was not going to stop him now. He pulled the plug from his canteen and took his first drink of the day. As it was going down he heard Andy Jackson[89] asking for a drink.

"Can I have a shot of that Rice? With all of this smoke in the air I have been drinking like a fish. My canteen has been empty for the greater part of the day."

Rice handed Jackson the canteen with a smile. As he was watching Andy take a drink Rice said, "It's hard work ridding the countryside of these provincial dilberries[90],"

Hearing Rice's crude comment, Andy choked on his drink.

"Yes, it surely is," he said after clearing his windpipe. "Let us finish them off,"

Jack reached over a gave Andy a gentle slap on the back. "Well boy, you may be able to fight off one of the King's Armies, but it appears you still can't hold your rum." he teased.

"Oh, I can hold it all right. Just not when Rice is cracking jokes. Did you see me picking them off from yonder trees?"

"That we did," Rice replied. "And it was deeply appreciated I assure you."

Rice looked around the field, and saw that at least half for his fellow soldiers were complaining of a lack of ammunition. They had

---

89 The Battle of Hanging Rock would be Andrew Jackson first taste of the battle. His military career would eventually led him to the White House in 1829.

90 Dilberries is an 18th century insult.

all but depleted their shot bags. Plunder was now becoming the main objective for many. Rum was for the taking and some were already getting drunk, especially those who had already partaken at the first camp like Robert Bedwell. The lure of expensive gear was even a greater temptation to the poor. With that in mind Rice turned to Andy and said. "You and your brother Robert should sit this one out. And before you begin to kick up a ruckus, let me tell you why. A lot of valuables are waiting for someone in need, to pick them up. And I know a widowed woman, like your mother, could use some of what's down there. Carden, and what's left of his men, is surely on the run. We can handle them without you boys. You all start ransacking, we will be back directly."

At that Rice and Jack entered the woods with about three hundred men for the last attack of the day. General Sumter knew what was at stake. If too much of a lapse took place the enemy could still rally. He encouraged his men forward, but only three hundred followed. What they saw in the woods were bloody trails everywhere. Even a few dying men had been left behind with the dead to face their own fates.

When the patriots reached the other side of the woods, they saw that the British regulars had formed the loyalist militia into a hollow square formation. Upon seeing Davies's approach, they fired a volley into the line. Rice could hear the buzzing of flying lead as it flew by. He quickly fell to the ground and crawled to a nearby beech tree for cover.

Major Davie called for a patriot volley in response. Rice again fired and like many around him, he again hit his mark. However, he was now down to four or five shots as his ammunition was again running low.

Sumter was well aware of the situation. He gathered his officers around for their opinions and a roll call was issued. He knew that he had taken some casualties. Major John McClure was mortally wounded early in the fight and most likely had passed by now.
He understood that his casualties were nothing like what he had inflicted upon the enemy, but he had casualties nevertheless.

Colonel Richard Winn of the Fairfield Militia, was the first to speak, "My Captain James Mitchell has been wounded. I have seen others fall as well, outside of my own men. Your Captain Bishop is dead for sure, General. As are Mecklenburg County Captains Charles McKee and George Reed. I also fear that Captain Luke Petty may have lost an arm.

Major Davie looked around and said, "There are also other officers not accounted for. I estimate we have lost fifty men for sure. However, with that being said we have inflected three times as much damage on them. We could clean them out with another engagement, but do we have enough shot to do so?"

"That is the question," Sumter announced to all "Have each man take a count of his rounds gentlemen, and get back to me as soon as you can with the numbers."

As he watched the officers debate the situation, Jack wanted at least one more shot. Not being able to resist a clear shot, he went against his better judgment and took one that ended another of Samuel Bryan's men's life. Rice too was tempted, but he passed on a few shots he otherwise would have taken if his shot supply was not so low. Abe was already out of shot, and Rice had given him two extra rounds, leaving himself very little.

As the ammunition was being counted, it was obvious that they were running too low to make that last charge into history. Major Davie suggested one last consideration. "Why not fire one last volley into them. It just may be enough to make them exit the field. If not, we still retire in victory."

"Agreed!" Sumter replied "Give the order."

Rice, along with the rest of the men, fired as the order was given. And again, it did damage, but the square held firmly in the end. By now, it was nearly one o'clock in the afternoon. Sumter was too low on ammunition, and his men were too hot, tired, and in some cases too drunk to continue the fight. He decided to withdraw and fight another day.

When the Tories saw that the Patriots were falling back. they yelled out Three Cheers for King George in defiance.

Sweat soaked, Rice turned back and looked at the Redcoats in disgust. They knew that they were soundly beaten this day. Still they acted as though holding that small patch of ground equaled a victory. 'What arrogance', he thought.

Jack looked at Rice and said, "We cannot let that be the last word of the day, can we? Come on boys let's give them three cheers for American Liberty."

As General Sumter was marching away with his wounded, and his newly won plunder from the day's victory, he reviewed the day's events. If only he had more ammunition or if so many of his undisciplined men had not gotten intoxicated on the captured rum, the third camp could have been his as well. But, still it was his victory, and everyone knew it, no matter who held the field at the end. And if

Major John Carden, the commanding officer across the way was under the illusion that he had a moral victory he was sorely mistaken. A smile parted Sumter's lips as he heard three cheers of "American Liberty" coming from Major Davie's vanguard in the rear. One last verbal volley to pierce the Tories and British ears and hearts.

As the last of the patriots were walking back through the woods, Rice and Jack were lingering behind, watching the Redcoats from a safe distance, well out of the Brown Bess's range. One British officer was calling on his men to harass the Patriot withdraw. Ten men quickly gathered around him and as he was walking towards the woods they began to follow.

Rice looked at Jack and smiled. They both presented their rifles at the same time. "I will take the officer, you the closest behind" Rice remarked to Jack.

Their shots were the last fired of the battle. With the death of two more men the Brits thought better of any pursuit. The Battle of Hanging Rock was over. As Rice and Jack was making their way back through the trees Jack looked at Rice. "That was one hell of a shot that we just made. Is it not time to give that rifle of yours a name?"

"Oh, it has one" Rice replied. "Something New River   said a while back."

After walking a few more paces without Rice revealing the name, Jack demanded, "Well, what is it?"

"Deathwind." Rice replied with a smile.

Chapter 90

Around The Cockpit

The last few days had been good for the morale of Sumter's men. Several were saddened by the loss of friends, a troubling fact of war. But, as a whole, spirits were high. They had performed well and had dealt the Tories, and best of all the British with a severe beating. The Prince of Wales American Regiment had been completely decimated. No one had stopped to count the bodies on the field but they were strewn about like wheat. Rice had heard several accounts of the battle, and the most disturbing was that of poor Captain George Reed. He had been shot in the abdomen and had doubled over in agony. Only to be pulled away by his feet, as a prisoner of war, by two scoundrels of the British Legion Infantry. He did die in their hands, but not before they had stomped on his wounds. Afterwards they abandoned his body where it laid in a badly beaten state.

On the other hand, the best account had come from Andy. The night of the battle the lad had claimed to have wounded two Tories thinking he had killed one. It was a reasonable statement that many had witnessed. But by the next day he had killed both. This morning they both were still dead but now one was a low- ranking officer. Jack had teased the boy by saying "They both were killed no doubt by a single bullet in a spectacular shot of over a hundred yards." Hearing this Andy had disappeared to the other side of camp.

But he must have liked part of Jack's jest because, that is when the range of his musket grew as far as a rifle's in his next tale.

Rice was enjoying his time here. He and the other men now had some time to catch up and talk about past campaigns and their personal lives. He and Bill Alexander got to speak for the first time since Bill had been wounded back in 76 during Rutherford's Cherokee Campaign. It was fun, but tonight would be his last in camp. His and Jack's enlistment was up and they would be heading home with the sunrise. They would be returning home in one piece by God's grace, and if not for Jack's neck wound completely unscathed. Abe and Robert's enlistment was also up, but Abe had talked Robert into enlisting into the Rowan County militia so they could continue to fight under Colonel Locke.

Tonight's entertainment and goodbyes would come around a cockpit to the sound of one of Andy's most beloved tunes. As the fiddler began to play Andy joined in on the lyrics, but added a new twist.

The royal cat shit in the shavings
The royal cat shit in the shavings
The royal cat shit in the shavings
And covered it up with his paw.

Cornwallis thought was a rasin
Cornwallis thought was a rasin
Cornwallis thought was a rasin
And tucked it away in his jaw.[91]

---

91 The original version of this song was the "black cat" not royal cat and "Old man" instead of   Cornwallis. The tune is thought to be of an Irish origin and is titled "The Black Cat Shit in The Shavings"

With the festivities growing livelier by the minute, several local men from the Camden Militia, who were gamers, had sent for their battle stag roosters. Gambling would rule the night. A match of two undefeated battle cocks would end the night's matches with a large purse for the winner.

"Betting tonight?" Jack asked as he and Rice joined the other spectators forming a human ring around the birds

"No, I am not losing a single coin on such an unpredictable event as this," Rice remarked.

"Cockfights are not unpredictable if you have an eye for it" Jack said, pointing out a black rooster being headed by its handler. "See the spur on that one's leg. It's far more prominent than any of the others. Once he has the short knife tied on that left foot; look out. He's winning tonight. And I like the position of his comb. It is high on the head. That always indicates a fighter. He is my boy for the night alright."

"You do seem to know what you are talking about. And I do wish you the best of luck, but I still think I will set this one out," Rice said as he watched the matches begin.

The birds would first be presented to their opponent while still in the hands of their handler, held so close they could almost peck at each other. Once they were turned loose all hell would break loose. They flogged each other unmercifully on the neck and head. If one was overmatched he could be dead within thirty seconds. If of equal talent, a match could last up to five minutes before the winner emerged.

While Jack had been seeking out any takers, that would accept a bet on his favorite bird among the mob, New River had joined Rice. He pointed to a red rooster. "General Sumter's bird," he said "Never bet against the General's bird. He is always a winner."

Once Jack had made his wagers he made his way back to Rice's side for the fight.
"Did you bet it all? "Rice asked.

"About half," Jack said while eagerly rubbing his chin in anticipation.

"Well, General New River is of the belief that you have placed a bet on a hack and not a fighter."

Jack leaned forward and looked around Rice at New River and said "We will see soon enough for my boy is about to square off against that red rooster. He is of equal size but he lacks the high comb".

"You do know that is General Sumter's gamecock you're up against?" Rice asked.

"I don't care if it is," Jack replied "The General can have him for supper if he wants. He will fry up in the pan right good I expect".

Once released, Jack's black made a lunge forward but missed the red entirely. The Red then jumped on the black's throat, killing him easily.

Rice looked at his friend, trying to hold back a smirk. Goods had been lost and it was not a time to be teasing a friend. But Jack's overconfidence was amusing, up to a point

"Not a word from you," Jack said in good humor. "The night is still young."

"That may be true" Rice said, walking away with New River, "But I will seek my cockfighting advice elsewhere. New River seems to know what he is talking about. If not, maybe Andy will have some pointers. Or Robert or Abe, anyone but you."

Chapter 91

Word Of The Bastard

Rice and Jack were on their way home the next morning. Charlottetown was their goal for the day's ride, with wives being the ultimate goal of the whole trip. The Battle of Hanging Rock had put the South Carolinian Tories into a less aggressive state for the time being, since Cornwallis was still on the coast. However, the North Carolina Tories were in a much better frame of mind.
Several different militias were out including Gideon Wright's. So, it was by no means a safe ride back home for two lone men.

"I tried to tell you," Jack boasted "It was just a matter of time until I had my windfall."

"So, you Say," Rice replied in mock sarcasm.

"Does my purse look fuller to you or not?" Jack asked holding it up.

"Could be rocks," Rice teased again. "They do lay all about."

"Not today," Jack contended "Money earned has a wonderful feeling, but nothing is as sweet as money won on a cockfight.

"If that smile is any indication, I will not argue the point," Rice conceded. "Who is that up ahead?" he asked looking up the road. "Ours or theirs?"

"Ours," Jack answered after a long look. "That is Bill Hays from Rutherford County. His Militia detachment was supposed to be with Colonel Isaac Shelby. I recognize his waistcoat. All of those Rutherford County boys have the same red fringe hanging from the waist. And his horse is a poor looking gray just like that one is."

"Bill Hays," Jack called to get his attention. "It's Jack, from the Yadkin. Hold fast my friend and do not shoot.

William Hays [92] walked his horse into the shade of an oak and waited for the two riders to come up. He dismounted, tied his horse, and flopped to the ground. As Rice and Jack rode up he had closed his eyes.

---

[92]   William Hays 1761-1851 Applied for his Rev, War Pension application in Warren Co Kentucky. The Application number is S37973. In it he states that after recovering from his illness he moved to Kentucky. There he would fight against the Indians alongside men such as Captain Hugh McGary, Thomas Denton and Captain's Potts, Hampton, Cooper and John Miller.

"What are you doing, Bill?" Jack asked as he rode up. "You look a little peaked. Poorly, are you?"

"That I am." Hays answered "So much so that the Captain has furloughed me in fear of Yellow Fever. You boys keep your distance. I would not have stopped at all if I did not have news, but I do."

"Do tell," Jack said while covering his mouth with his hand.

"If I'm not mistaken, was it not the McFall boys who tarred and feathered you a few years back?" Hays asked.

"That is was!" Jack said looking at Rice "But I sure do not call them boys".

"Do you want to know where those rats are?"

"We sure do!" Rice answered.

"They are with Patrick Ferguson, and they ain't alone," Hays said as he took a drink from his horn canteen. "Ferguson has put together quite the army. Last we heard, he had over 1000 man. A lot from Ninety-Six District and Long Cane, Steven's Creek too. Fair Forest has even got a Regiment."

"Those are all South Carolina boys. So that is where he has been hiding all this time! Jack exclaimed.

"That he has," Hays agreed. "You see Ferguson had gotten wind of the whereabouts of our supply wagons. And he was determined to take them. He sent out a band of militia acting as dragoons to do the task, but not the whole of his Army, you see. But instead of finding the wagons, those half assed Militia ran up on three of our boys out on patrol. They were all mounted, so they headed back to our outpost at Wofford's Iron Works [93]with hopes that the dumbasses would give chase. And sure enough, they did, right on their heels. Hell, they were so eager they road right into the middle of our camp before they knew what had happen. We shot the holy hell out of them. And that is when I saw them. It seems that Walter Gilkey has put together all of the Tory refugees from our neck of the woods into a mounted militia. John McFall was right in the thick of it, as was his brothers."

"You mean George, I assume" Rice asked?

"Yes, I mean George, but Arthur has gone Tory as well. The whole damn McFall clan has gone over.

"Was that bastard John shot?" Rice asked.

"Of course not. That slippery son of a bitch got away. We killed eight of them and captured around fifty others. Colonel Shelby beat the hell out of one of them. The next man in line talked his head off after that, that is how I came by my particulars and their

---

[93] The Battle of Wofford's Iron Works took place on August 8, 1780 in present day Spartanburg Co South Carolina. Patriot   militia under Colonel Elijah Clarke of Georgia and Isaac Shelby of North Carolina defeated Capt. James Dunlap's Tory force of mounted Loyalist militia.

numbers," Hays said. "But if you boys are after revenge you are heading to the right place. If I was a betting man, I would say that Gates and Cornwallis are going to tangle fairly soon. General Gates is said to be reforming what is left of the Continental Army at Charlottetown. He should be heading South by now, or maybe to the East. I would also wager that Cornwallis will have Major Ferguson and his whores close by when the two meets. I know that I would anyway."

Rice knew what he was going to do. That bastard had been eating at him for years. And this was the first real word of him in all that time. Rice looked at Jack and asked, "Another enlistment?"

Jack nodded saying, "Reckoning is at hand."

"You boys ride on without me," Hays said after a rib shaking cough. "The only person I would wish this infliction on would be McFall, or perhaps Tarleton himself."

Chapter 92

The Tent City

What Rice saw at Cox's Mill was a lot different then what he was use to. This army was much bigger than the one Gen Rutherford had raised. This tent city held thirty-two hundred men in arms and

Next, in the order of attack, was Bryan's Camp itself. He would most likely be using the cabin as his headquarters. Rice put Liberty's reins into his mouth as he rode into the enemy camp. He was holding his pistol in one hand and his tomahawk in the other. His eye fell upon a white canvas tent. He shot the first man that appeared from the tent's open flap with his pistol. The next he killed with a throw of his tomahawk. He then dismounted and pulled his rifle from his saddle. He raised it to his shoulder and held it in a firing position as he scanned the camp for another target. The Tories were highly disorganized and unprepared for such a swift attack. Some were already asking for quarter, having fallen to their knees with raised hand in surrender. Abe Baker ignored one such request, killing a red headed brute of a man that had scalps hanging from his belt. Other were running away toward the other two Tory camps.

Jack was holding three prisoners at bay with his rifle, as Rice looked towards the cabin. New River and his braves were ramming the cabin door open with a split rail that they had pulled from a nearby fence. With one last thrust the door was knocked open. As Rice approached the cabin he heard a few shots coming from inside, quickly followed by the Catawba's war cries. Rice looked into the open door and saw four bloodied corpses lying on the floor without scalps. The Indians were eating some bacon that the dead had been about to have for breakfast. New River was busy trying on a dead officer's red coat. With all dead inside, Rice stepped back out and gather his and Jack's horses and led them to Jack as he continued to hold his prisoners at gunpoint. While he had their attention, Jack was giving the Tories an earful.

"This is how you defend an outpost?" Jack asked "All the talk I hear is about how undisciplined our Militia is, and how inapt we are. Circumstances say otherwise today boys."

countless camp followers and teamsters. It was one large mass of humanity with still more soldiers to arrive.

The Continental forces were impressive by themselves. They have been led by Major General Johann-Alexander von Robaii, Baron DeKalb, Gate's second. A German by birth. But he had made his good reputation in the French army. Like so many other European generals, he liked the American cause and had volunteered his services to General Washington for a good wage. He had marched south from Philadelphia back in April with the Maryland Brigadiers. This was even before General Gates had arrived in the south. He had been holding defensive positions until Gates had taken command on his arrival.

The Maryland 1st Brigade, led by Brigadier General William Smallwood contained five regiments, equaling nearly one half of General Sumter's Army itself. The 2nd Maryland Brigade, led by Brigadier General Mordecai Gist was even large then the 1st. There was also a Delaware contingent of Continental's, under the command of Lt. Colonel Joseph Vaughan, a North Carolina Light Infantry troop led by Major John Armstrong, and Surry County's own Captain James Freeman. The Cavalry, led by Count Nicholas Dietrick, Baron von Ottendorf, was an all-German lot of Dragoons made up into three Troops, added to which, South Carolina had provided a Mounted Infantry led by Major Thomas Pinckney.

The Continental Artillery was just as impressive. It contained Companies from Maryland and Virginia. They had been in North Carolina since early June. It was this unit that demonstrated another difference between life in the militia and the Continental line, discipline. One of their ranks had broken a rule. He was tied to a wheel of a canon, shirtless, being flogged by the whip for all to see as Rice and Jack rode by. It was hard to watch and Rice was relieved when he was out of sight of such a reminder of military discipline.

The left side of the camp was held for the North Carolina Militia. Virginia and South Carolina both had Regiments of Militia on the march to be at the disposal of this Grand Army, as Gates was calling it, but they were yet to arrive. Rice's home unit from North Carolina was already present, and Rice saw many a familiar face. The whole was under the command of Major General Richard Caswell and his Adjutant General, Colonel John Sitgreaves and Aide-de-Camp William Haley.

Rice was somewhat surprised to see that his old commander of the 1776 Cherokee War, Brigadier General Griffith Rutherford was not in full command of the militia. But he had long given up on trying to understand Military politics. However, Rutherford was present, commanding the Salisbury District Brigade of Militia.

Orange County had two different Regiments of Militia. One under Lt. Colonel Thomas Farmer, and the other under Colonel John Collier. Other county militias were also present. Anson, Burke, Guilford, Lincoln, Mecklenburg, Washington and Richmond. Rowan was under Colonel Francis Locke who Rice liked and was pleased to see in that position. The Surry County Regiment was being led by Colonel Martin Armstrong, who had accompanied Rice on the chase of the Tory James Roberts, into Virginia. But what was truly disheartening was the fact That Ole Roundabout was not commanding the Wilkes County Regiment. Rice and Jack had nothing against the man that was, Drury Ledbetter, but how in the hell Ben Cleveland was not be here was baffling. Even more disappointing was the fact that not one single Grider was here either. Keeping the Indians in check was possibly was the only reason Rice could come up with. Maybe his beloved Rachael was at Fort Grider under their protection.

Since Ben was not with the Wilkes County boys, it made the decision to join Colonel Lock's militia a lot easier for Rice and Jack, they had come down with Robert and Abe who had been under Lock in the past. So now all they had to do was let the next page of this war play out and hopefully it would lead them to the McFall's in the coming days.

Chapter 93

The Battle of Camden

As soon as Lord Cornwallis got reports of Sumter's victory at Hanging Rock he departed Charlestown for Camden. His small but fleet escort made the 140-mile trip in three days, to join his Army at Camden. Speed was of the essence in his objective to keep a secure hold on the growing village. He knew that General Gates would be eager to organize his new command and put them in the field. He also needed to keep Sumter's Militia from doing any more harm until that time. He was of the opinion that Gates would try to strike quickly, like he did at The Battle of Saratoga. But this time the situation was somewhat reversed. At Saratoga, the British under General John Burgoyne, had marched out of Canada into New York. They were the ones who had just finished a long trek and was ill supplied. This time Gates would have the tired hungry Army. Neither North or South Carolina had made proper preparations to feed the Continentals. On the other hand, The British had been well supplied and rested while posted in Camden. Cornwallis was determined to take advantage of that fact.

Upon arriving, Cornwallis went directly to the home of Joseph Kershaw who had founded Camden over twenty years before. Kershaw was an unbending Whig who had helped influence New River and his Catawba's to become allies with the Patriots. He had also lead militia, at the Battle of Stono River the year before. And this very year, he had established The Kershaw Militia, who had just taken part in the victory at Hanging Rock although, not under his command. His whereabouts was unknown to Cornwallis, most likely with Gates, he estimated. As Lord Cornwallis walked through Kershaw's three story Georgian style mansion he could not keep from smiling. The fool was sure to never set foot in this grand home ever again, the Lord chuckled.

As Cornwallis entered what was certainly Kershaw's study, He walked behind a one-hundred year old mahogany desk. There he pulled a blue silk covered wingback chair away from the desk. He sat down in the chair and stretched his long legs out on top of the smooth, well cared for desktop. He looked around the room and thought that if he were to keep this mansion in British hands, he needed to go over the strengths of his troops. Lt. Colonel James Webster had already prepared a report of the troops and it was laying on top of the desk. Focusing his attention to the job ahead, he picked up the paper before him and read,

Report to Sir Lord Cornwallis by Lt. Colonel Webster of the 33rd Regiment of Foot

The Royal Welsh Fusiliers, 23rd of foot could muster	292 men
The of 33rd Regiment of Foot	238 men
The 71[s] Fraser's Highlanders	354 men
Volunteers of Ireland led by Colonel Francis, Lord Rawdon	303 men
16th Regiment of Foot Light Infantry	78 men
The British Legion led by Lt. Colonel Banastre Tarleton	306 men
North Carolina, Loyalist Militia led by Col. Sam Bryan	202 men
Royal North Carolina Regiment	62 men
Royal Regiment of Artillery with 12 guns	19 men
New York Volunteers, 3rd Battalion	271 men
The 16th Regiment of Foot Light Infantry	78 men
The Prince of Wales American Regiment	66 men

Total men in arms 2471

Lt. Colonel Webster's address to Lord Cornwallis

Sir, I suggest that The Prince of Wales American Regiment should not enter the field due to high casualties sustained at Hanging Rock.

Lord Cornwallis understood that he was out numbered. Reports indicated that if General Gates should attack with his full complement of men, he would have between five or six thousand men in the field. It would be a dangerous fight to engage. Cornwallis could not allow himself to be outflanked in the battle. Such an outcome would be like a ruination from God. Still, a retreat back to Charlestown would allow Gates even more time to recruit and improve his already strong situation.

Cornwallis also knew that the majority of Gates Army was undisciplined militia, at best. They would flinch, he felt if pushed hard by the finest, and most disciplined Army in the world. He dispatched a rider to inform Major Ferguson who was raiding in the south to return to Camden at once. With his thirteen-hundred men Cornwallis was confident he would win the day and show the world that General Gates was no better commander than Washington, who Cornwallis had already defeated more than once. Cornwallis made his decision. He would march out of Camden and meet the Rebels. Hopefully, he could catch them in the Gum swamps that was seven and half miles out from Camden.

Rice and Jack were appreciating life in the Militia much more than they ever had in the past. General Horatio Gates was seeing to that. Old Granny Gates, as he was now being called by his men was truly a pompous ass. Ever decision the man made seemed to fly against every piece of advice he was receiving from his staff. He would take the most difficult route, when told another was easier. He would march the men when they needed rest. His men were becoming exhausted, not a good situation for an army yet to see battle. He had abandoned two brass cannons when DeKalb had advised otherwise. Rice was unsure of Gates reasoning. Perhaps he was doing all this for a purpose known only to him since he was a proven winner of battles in this war. But now, after seeing him in action, Rice wondered if maybe that victory at Saratoga was just pure, dumb luck. Jack was already convinced that that was indeed the case.

Luckily, they had been able to get some sleep at Mask's Ferry on the Peedee River. The water was high that night, and the crossing was very slow. Rice and Jack had been close to the front and were able to take advantage of the time by stealing some much-needed sleep.

While at the Peedee, Gates had gotten word that Hanging Rock and Rocky Mount had been abandoned by the British. Gates believed that Cornwallis was retreating to the coast, or maybe as far south as Georgia.

Rice could understand why, if that was the case, because of the food shortage that the whole countryside was gripped in.
Sumter was having a hard time feeding his small army. Cornwallis would be having the same problem, especially with Francis Marion harassing his supply lines. The question Rice thought, was just how much food was in Camden? It had to be better than the green peaches and molasses that he had been eating for way too long. Jack was feeling poorly yesterday after eating, and today they had both passed on another helping of sticky peaches, hoping that the Virginia militia

that was a day behind would soon arrive with beef. But again, Gates had pushed on, marching eighteen miles that day and nineteen the next. Rice was also having concerns for Liberty's wellbeing. Feed was a mere memory to the horse's stomach.

Colonel Francis Locke was well aware of this situation as well. With the Maryland and Delaware Continentals being slow of foot, Locke, had given leave for his men to go out to graze their horses on whatever they could find. Gates disapproved of the practice, but allowed it once he understood that he could not keep the militia from doing so, if that was their wish. The militia was full of men like Abe, so he had little choice. Gates was becoming very frustrated with the independent minded militias. He considered the major reason for their liberal state of mind, was the presence of their camp followers. Women and even children were following his army in great numbers, in order to stay close to their husbands and fathers. It was nothing unusual, but still, he considered it a great drain on his troops. Gates was also aware that some of his men were coming down sick, and saw a chance to rid himself of both the sick and the camp followers. He ordered both groups to be sent back North to Charlottetown under an armed escort. About half of the Camp follows took the opportunity to have a roof over head back at Charlottetown, but the other half stayed with the Army, to Gates great displeasure.

In addition, Gates had other concerns. Patrols of his cavalry had spotted a line of British infantry around Little Lynches Creek. In response Gates sent John Butler's Hillsborough Militia, but the Redcoats disappeared into the woods before their arrival.

Gates put his Army in full pursuit but they could not catch up with the retreating Brits, feeding his frustration even more.

With every step forward, the countryside was becoming more familiar to Rice. They had passed through Sumter's old campsite and even Hanging Rock. It was peaceful this time. Rice and Jack took the time to stop in the small creek that was just below the rock formation. The sound of the water trickling around their horse's feet was pleasing to the ear. It was satisfying that they had liberated such a wonderful place. It was so different now with the enemy gone.

Gates finally gave up the chase by halting his Army at Rugeley Mill, a Tory stronghold in the past. It was the property of Colonel Henry Rugeley. Gates made good use of its log barns, mill, and house for two days. Tonight, would be their last night here.

"Hell, we should have just stayed with the old Gamecock," Jack said in references to Thomas Sumter. I understand they are coming down the West bank of the Wateree River to cut off the route to Ninety-Six. Bet they are chewing meat not this poor mush. Basking in the sun they are."

"I suppose" Rice replied, staring into a fire. "But our situation will change for the better once we are in Camden. It's only thirteen miles away, I've been told. It would indeed be a sad note if Sumter were to engage Ferguson while we are stuck here. Sometimes, I think The Bastard has a sinister presence watching over him."

"Could be," Jack agreed. "John does seem to be a step ahead at times. But his judgment day is coming. If not in this world, then the next."

"I Just hope I'm there to see it happen," Rice said as he stood up.

"Do you really believe that Cornwallis is not going to engage us at some point?" Jack asked "A lot of folk around here do. Granny must. He sent two cannons to Sumter and some of the Continentals."

"No. I don't," Rice answered. "You ever seen or heard of the King's men running for long? Those are Redcoats out there, that we will be fighting tomorrow. They could be a rearguard. Or perhaps a new outpost like the one back at Hanging Rock was. But then again, it could be Cornwallis's whole army. If we are lucky maybe even Ferguson and we can end this tomorrow."

"Will it end it for you if that is the case? I mean the war won't end with John McFall's death," Jack said looking into Rice's eyes.

"I Don't know for sure," Rice answered as he ran a hand over the length of his rifle. "I'll have to wait and see. You know that I support the War, but John has become the driving force for me being here lately. I just don't know if I have had my fill or not. It is a hard thing to predict."

"Well, ponder while you can" Jack said, pulling his hat down over his eyes. "We will be on our way before the sun says good morning."

It was still dark when General Gates put his Grand Army into motion in the predawn hours of August 16, 1780. He was not completely sure that Cornwallis was out there, but he was about to find out.

What peaceful feelings Rice had experienced at Hanging Rock was now long gone. Gates had put his plan into motion a little after midnight. Rice, Jack and all of the other men under Colonel Locke's command was marching over the ford of the Gum Swamp when shots were heard miles up ahead. The American advance guard was entangled with Lord Cornwallis' advance troops.

A few volleys were exchanged and both parties fell back to the safety of their own lines. As the sun popped over the horizon it was evident that Cornwallis' full force was just down the wooded road ahead.

A battle formation was arranged by Gates. He and DeKalb would make a stand in the center, alongside the North Carolina and Virginia Militias. This would put Rice on the road, and on foot. He and Colonel Locke would not be part of the cavalry. Liberty and the other mounts would not see this battle. To Rice's left was Gen Mordecai Gist and his Maryland Continentals. To their left was the Delaware Line. Seven artillery pieces were placed close to the road, since marshland was on both sides of the Waxhaw Road. Gates had keep the 1st Maryland Continentals and Rutherford's Militia in reserve under General Smallwood.

Across from Rice, standing in his way, was Lt. Colonel Webster and the 33rd Regiment of Foot, Lord Cornwallis's very best. The Royal Welsh Fusiliers was to their right flank; another of his best. To their rear was the 71st Highlanders, who were held in the highest esteem. Artillery was placed between the two, with Banastre Tarleton and his dragoons to have a free reign to fight wherever needed; especially if a retreat occurred. Cornwallis' very best was staring at Gates most inexperienced men. The North Carolinians were all good with a gun, and had fought well against the Indians, but they have never seen a European Army fighting in formation.

The American Artillery opened the battle with a barrage that tore into the 33rd, doing great damage. As the British answered with their own barrage, Rice watched as Gates moved among the men. Rice could not hear what was being said, but he seemed to be encouraging them. He was showing his courage, but Rice was wondering why Gates had not yet given the order to advance. Then Rice realized why! After his speech, that few had heard, Gates had disappeared to the rear with the Marylanders. However, DeKalb did remain in the front.

Rice was eager to attack, but he was waiting for the order to be drummed out. As he was standing shoulder to shoulder with the rest of Colonel Locke's men he watched as a few Virginians rushed forward into the smoke-filled field. The cannon fire from both sides was producing a great amount of smoke, and it was hard to see what was happening. But as the wind blew across the field Rice could see that the Virginians were no match for the British bayonets.

Suddenly, as one, the whole of the Virginia Militia broke ranks and began to flee in total panic. Rice heard a loud cry of 'huzzah', and as he looked across the field, he saw another wave of Redcoats charging. Jack did not wait for an order; he shouldered his rifle and made smoke roll. Rice discharged his rifle as well. Rice saw his Welsh mark fall to the ground, but this man's death did nothing to stop the charge. At this point, many of Colonel Locke's men also turned tail and ran to the rear, some not even taking the time for at least one volley. Others, like Robert ran after taking a shot, but not staying to see its outcome.

Jack, still holding his ground, looked at Rice with a fearful expression that Rice had never seen on his friend's face before. Rice wanted to take a second shot, but was sure that if he and Jack did, they would soon be overrun and killed. Instead of taking the risky shot, Rice reached over grabbing Jack's arm and yelled, "Fall back. Now".

A British volley came sailing past as the two turned and ran. Men were falling to the left and to the right of Rice as he ran. He was sure that Abe was one of them. Rice was amazed that neither he nor Jack had not been hit. A captain, unknown to Rice, was trying to stop some of the fleeing men, in order to send a volley into the charging enemy. Rice had reloaded his rifle while on the run, so he stopped running and took a place inside the captain's line. Half of the men around him fell before the volley could be fired. The captain was dead, so Rice shot his rifle, killing a Highlander, this time. He again took to his heels, and as he was running, he could not believe that this American Army was already defeated, however they appeared to be. He looked for Jack, but he was nowhere to be seen. The Militia was in complete disorder and confusion was everywhere. A gut wrenching feeling hit Rice all at once. Was Jack dead? He prayed they were only separated.

Rice heard the sound of horse's hoofs rumbling over the ground. He looked over his shoulder to see a green coated Dragoon of Tarleton's hacking into a Virginian who was unarmed and on foot. Rice pulled his pistol and knocked the dragoon from his saddle with a shot of only ten yards. A second Dragoon turned his mount towards Rice with a raised sword in hand. Rice stood his ground as the dragoon approach at full gallop. Rice let the horse get just a few feet away before he dove to the ground in a rolling fall. As the dragoon rode by, the swing of his sword cut only air. Rice rose to his feet, to the sound of a Patriot volley coming from God, he was sure. It killed and maimed enough of the green coated opponents to slow their charge. Rice looked at his lock, and saw that the flint was gone. He had lost it in the fall, and now his rifle was useless.

Rice looked across the road to see that the Continentals were still holding ground, but taking a bad beating in the process. DeKalb was wounded but still giving orders to continue the fight. Rice ran across the road only to see another bayonet charge coming from the British. With his rifle not in firing order, Rice retreated until he reached the already deserted American battery. He only then looked back to see that the Continentals were in complete defeat as DeKalb was now dead and Gates was nowhere to be seen.

'The horses,' Rice thought, 'Maybe Jack has gotten back to the mounts. General Gates could be reforming and the horses tied in the woods could be the rallying point for a final stand'.

Rice kept falling back, as so many others were. He made his way to where the supply wagons were. They too had been abandoned. He had hoped to get a flint from one, but with the British hot on his heels, he could not afford the time to search for one.
He came to a heartbreaking decision. He needed a working gun, and as much as he hated to do it, he had to abandon his rifle. He dropped it were he stood in hopes he could come back for it after the battle was over. He spotted the body of a fellow Militiaman. This poor fellow still had a strong grip on his rifle, and it was still clutched in his hand. It was very much like Rice's own weapon, curly maple stock and all. It even looked to be a fifty caliber. Rice picked it up to reload, and sure enough the fifty-caliber ball from Rice's shot bag fit into the barrel.

To his right, a group of seven or eight Continentals were being cut down by more Dragoons. "Those bastards never give quarter" Rice said out loud. He turned and took to the trees in an effort to get back to the horses. Other groups of survivors were being attacked in the woods. It seemed the dragoons would not bother with a single man when they could chase down a group, at least not yet. Rice avoided other clusters of men as he was running through the woods, for just that reason. But one occasion he did spot one lone dragoon riding near the swamp. It was a mistake that the dragoon would never make again. Rice put a shot through the man's chest as he had pulled his horse to a stop in order to reload his pistol. The old owner of this new rifle sure did have the sights set to Rice's liking. Rice   reloaded again, and continued his escape

As the morning hours passed, the sounds of gunfire began to die down. Sweat was running down the side of Rice's face as he reached the spot where the horses had been left the night before. He was completely drained and the fact that Liberty was not here made matters so much worse. Only two horses were here and they were both dead, having been shot by the British. Rice, feeling outright fatigued dropped under an ash tree. This damned day had been unforgiving. Not only had he lost his rifle, but now his horses as well. The battle was definitely lost. He was purposely not thinking of Jack's whereabouts. The thought of losing Jack was just too much for him to fathom at the moment.

As he leaned his head back against the tree trunk, he heard the sound of approaching horses. He quickly moved around the back side of his tree, putting a rifle bead on the front rider.

"Do not shoot!" William Tipton[94] announced from atop his horse "We are militia. Patriot militia from Virginia. Are you Rice?"

Rice stepped from behind the safety of his tree after hearing his name called. John McFall had taught him a hard lesson on exposing himself in such instances, but this man somehow knew his name, and

---

[94] William Tipton 1754-1837 was a Virginia Militiamen who after the war settled in Montgomery County Kentucky. He is the main character in my first novel Redskins and Lobsterbacks.

that made him feel it was worth the risk. "How did you know who I am?" Rice asked.

"I don't know you." William answered "But some fellow from down the road a ways does. I am William Tipton, and this is my brother Joshua."

"What was that fellow's name?" William asked looking to his brother.

"Jack," Joshua replied. "He said you two are brothers. He is down the road about four or five miles with a couple of horses and he says one of them is yours. He is asking everyone he sees about you. Said you got split up early on in the battle. He's been looking for you ever since.

Rice stood there for a moment absorbing what he just heard. Jack was telling people that they were brothers. Quite the complement, Rice thought. They were indeed more than friends. "Yes" Rice replied "We are, of sorts.

"Good then," William said looking at the youngest of his party "Samuel, let Rice have the use of Fly and we will take him to retrieve his horse. We missed the biggest part of the battle ourselves." He said looking at Rice. "All we have gotten out of the day was a dragoon and this here mount that Joshua is on."

Rice took Fly's reins and pulled himself up onto the horse's back as William continued to talk. He was unsteady on top of the horse being very dehydrated from his retreat.

"Got three brothers myself" William said as he handed a full canteen of water to Rice. "I can understand why Jack was so eager to find you. As a matter of fact, we are here to meet up with one my brothers. Thomas Tipton of the Virginia Line, you know him?"

Rice shook his head no as he drank greedily from the canteen. "Sorry, I'm afraid not" he said handing the canteen back. "And I have no clue as to when, or even if, this army will ever gather again. You may find it difficult to locate your brother. General Gates' Grand Army is no more."

Chapter 94

The Aftermath

It had been two days since the disaster at the Gum Swamps of Camden. Rice was more than happy to again pull himself up into Liberty's saddle. For a while there, he thought that his prized horse was lost forever.

He would never forget the look on Jack's face as he rode in on Tipton's old horse. Jack tried to play it coy, but for that brief moment Rice could see a joyful relief wash over his friend. The two shook hands as a smile parted Rice's lips. "Lost track of you there for a while, brother."

"I just said that, thinking they would put more effort into their inquiries. There were a lot of men out there looking for each other. But two brothers trying to reunite would make my request for help in finding you more memorable, I hoped" Jack replied reluctantly. "It seemed to work."

"Indeed," Rice said with a smile. "They say blood is thicker than water, but it is the heart that pumps the blood."

The conversation then moved to what was to be done. Tipton and his men were going on to Hillsborough in hopes that the Continentals would regroup there. Rice and Jack had had enough of Gates' leadership. Home was an easy decision for the two.

Today, the outcome of the battle was becoming clearer. It was obvious that it was a defeat. The entire wagon train of supplies was lost. Even more disheartening was the loss of the artillery. Cornwallis would have the use of them now.

Rice was glad that they were no longer being pursued by Tarleton's men. They had stopped their pursuit at Hanging Rock. With them no longer around, Rice could stop and talk to other survivors of the battle and trade details. Captain Peter Jacquett of the Delaware Blues, had relayed to Jack that General Gates had abandoned the field of battle as soon as the

North Carolina Militia had faltered. He even went as far as to use the word desertion. He had also spoken of the death of his friend Captain John Rhodes, another member of the Blues. The Continentals had lost a great many men in this battle, the Baron DeKalb, being the most prominent. Others included Lt. Nathan Williams, Captain Edward Duvall, and Captain Matthew Elbon to just name a few.

William Ledford, a Rowan County militiaman had told Rice that General Rutherford [95]was taken prisoner alongside Colonel Joseph Kershaw [96]. Rice feared that General Rutherford could face execution for having destroyed the Cherokee Nation who was bound to the crown. It would take weeks to find out for sure who was dead and missing. From what Rice had gathered he was sure that seven hundred to a thousand of his fellow soldiers were either dead or missing, with Abe included in that number.

---

[95] Griffith Rutherford received two wounds at the Battle of Camden before being captured. One, a slash of a saber to the head. The other was a gunshot wound to the leg. His wounds were treated in Camden by the British. Once well enough to travel, he was transferred to Charleston before ending up in a prison ship in St. Augustine Florida. In June of 1781 he was released in a prisoner exchange. He then returned to the militia and continued to harass the Loyalist of North Carolina. In 1782 he again attacked the Cherokee Nation in what would be his last military engagement

[96] Colonel Joseph Kershaw was captured at Camden and imprisoned on the Island of Barbados. There, as a prisoner of war, he mortgaged his landholdings in South Carolina for the American war effort. However, after the war the new American government could never afford to reimburse Kershaw. This put a great financial strain on him for the rest of his life.

General Gates, if you could still call him a general had completely destroyed in one day, any advantage that men such as DeKalb, Sumter, Davie and Marion had taken a year to build. Was the South beaten for good after this battle? Rice doubted that was the case, but morale was at a crushing low. This was the first time that Rice had tasted defeat and it was bitter.

Another disturbing fact was that the local Tories would soon be feeling their oats. John McFall was still out there with Ferguson. They will almost certainly come calling soon now, with General Gates defeated. Was General Washington going to come South with a new army, or perhaps another general? Rice could not answer, but he did know that Ben Cleveland was still here. He also knew that the mountains were full of fighting men like the Grider's, Shelby's, and McDowell's. If they had any say left in this war, it would be far from over. No matter what was to come, at this point, Rice just needed to get home.

Chapter 95

Skirmishes, Hangings And A Little Hope

Patrick Ferguson had missed the Battle of Camden. The day of the battle, he was at Mobley's Meeting House, which was a good two day's travel from Camden. General Sumter, with his men, had been marching down the Wateree River as ordered. This put him in a very vulnerable position between Ferguson and Cornwallis' two armies. The next day, Ferguson stopped at the Winn plantation when an express rider arrived from the battlefield with word of Gates' defeat. In addition to this glorious news, the courier had new orders for Ferguson. Sumter had the only Rebel army still fighting in the region. Ferguson was to pursue the Gamecock with all due vigor. Banastre Tarleton had the same orders and was riding from the victory at Camden. Between the two of them they were to crush Sumter like a bug.

Banastre Tarleton got to Sumter first. Sumter had little choice, but to retreat after Gates's debacle. He had pushed his men hard for two days before stopping his retreat where Fishing Creek ran into the Catawba River. At noon Tarleton's dragoons, who were riding double having shared their mounts with infantry, caught Sumter off guard. Many of the Patriots were swimming in the river. Others cooking their first hot meal in days. Still other were drinking and becoming drunk. Sumter himself was curled up, sleeping wrapped in a blanket, under a wagon without his shirt and boots. The attack was as swift as any of Tarleton's other victories.

One hundred and fifty of Sumter's men were cut to pieces within minutes. They had foolishly placed their muskets all together on one side of their camp. With no weaponry, they were no match for the bloodthirsty dragoons. Tarleton even recaptured the prisoners from the Battle of Hanging Rock that Rice had helped capture. The only drawback of the skirmish, was the fact that Sumter had managed to escape on a saddleless horse.

John McFall reached down and grabbed the collar of a young man whose hands were locked in irons. He roughly jerked him up out of his sitting position and onto his bare feet. He gave his prisoner a hard push in the back.

"Come on boy let's go. Lieutenant Allaire is waiting."

"What about my boots?" the prisoner asked.

"The dead don't need boots boy," McFall replied, enjoying himself. Spirits were high among the American Provincial Volunteer Militia that was being led by Major Patrick Ferguson, with none more so than the McFall's.

As the two made their way across the green of the Winn plantation, Smith, the prisoner spotted a carriage in front of the Winn House. He looked at the surrounding mob and he could see that these militiamen truly hated him. It was in their eyes, and he had little hope if they were to decide his fate. He hoped that Major Ferguson was the reasonable man that he had heard he was. As he was being pushed along, the front door of the house opened, and out walked a beautiful young woman. She was dressed in a gold striped petticoat with floral bed jacket. As she stepped into the green carriage Smith was again pushed by McFall. "Observe while you can boy, that is the last bonny lass you will ever see."

Smith looked back over his shoulder as he walked past. What he saw next was Patrick Ferguson in his finest uniform exiting the house. He had a second beauty on his arm. This one's attire was just as elegant as the first; a light green satin petticoat and matching bed jacket. Ferguson never looked at Smith. He just took the woman's hand and said. "Virginia my dear, Lord Cornwallis is in for a treat tonight. You are as stunning as ever."

At that statement, Smith's heart sank. He now knew Ferguson would not be involved in his upcoming trial. Walter Gilkey took Smith's other arm and presented him to lieutenant Allaire who was standing under an oak tree. Smith tried to compose himself as the carriage pulled away for its trip to Camden, his only hope of a fair trial leaving with it.

"This is the man," McFall said. "He was with us under Lt. Colonel John Hamilton at the Battle of Stono Ferry. He had taken a sworn oath to the King. And in doing so, he misleads all into thinking he was one of us. He had put himself under the King's protection and good graces. And now we find him a rebel, riding as one of William Hill's dogs. He is a man of poor conviction, and his actions take away all of his rights as a loyal subject of the King."

"That Sir, is treason" Walter Gilkey said forcefully, pulling on Smith ear "A hanging offense here in the Carolinas. Maybe we should just cut off his ear to begin with."

Allaire looked around at the mob for a moment and then replied "Do with him as you wish, only a fool would take up with a Rebel Militia now,"

"Do I not get a say in this matter?" Smith [97] asked.

McFall looked at the condemned man and said, "Not in this world. Perhaps in the next. Come on boys let's get a rope."

Meanwhile back in the Ninety-Six District at Musgrove's Mill, Colonel Isaac Shelby's small force made up of several militias, defeated a Tory outpost. It was under the command of Lt. Colonel Alexander Innis, who was shot from his horse during the battle. Shelby's mountaineers pushed the Tories back across the Enerone River, killing 61 men and wounded 94 and taking 79 prisoners in the process. With this small victory, a new Patriot Army was born. The Battle of Musgrove's Mill helped to put some hope back in the hearts of all Whigs.

Chapter 96

Ever the Opportunist

Rachael Medaris, like her surroundings was beautiful, and consistent in her habits. She had married, ran a household, and bore children. Along with Rice, she had her whole life's work invested in her homestead. She loved her home and it was hard to stay away, but she had done just that in Rice's absence. First, she had stayed at Fort

---

[97] Lieutenant Anthony Allaire recorded Smith's hanging at the Winn Plantation in his diary but he failed to record Smith's Christian name.

Grider. As time passed and nothing bad had happened, she moved back into her father's home. John and Val Grider, had been spying over the countryside and had seen no sign of any Cherokee presence. Still, they had advised against her leaving the Fort. They had pointed out that Tories were still a threat. Even with that being said, Rachael was determined to surround herself with family, and to be in more familiar surroundings. She knew all too well of the Tory threat, having experienced it in the past. However, this time the situation was much different. The McFall's had not been seen in the Yadkin vicinity for two years. Ever since Colonel Francis Locke's victory at Ramseur's Mill, the Tories here in the west seemed more subdued. The worst of the lot were now being detained in the goal in Salisbury. In addition to that, she had always felt safe in her father's home. It was a blockhouse and David was there, just having mustered out of General Caswell's service.

Her time there was comforting. Even a married daughter need motherly advice at times. She and her mother enjoyed each other's company and what grandparent did not want to spend more time with their grandchildren. Charles, her father, was still a capable man with his rifle, and that made Rachael feel very safe. Her days at her childhood home had been far better than those in Old Fed's Fort. Her mind often lingered on Rice, and his well-being. But her parents and the children's needs helped to keep her time occupied and her days full. At night, she and David would talk like old cronies. David would avoid talking about his involvement at the Battle of Moncks Corner, for her benefit, because of Rice. Instead they spoke of their youth and of Jeremiah's past deeds. Sometimes she thought that he just might walk through the door and take his place at the table with them. Of course, that could never happen, now that he had passed.

Tonight, they were sitting outside watching the sunset. She was snapping some green beans while he was pushing his knife over a whet rock. She stood up from her chair and was going back inside when she saw a golden glow lying low in the Eastern sky. She turned and looked back to the West to see that the pink sunset was almost out of view. As she looked back to the East, her heart tightened in her chest as she said. "Oh, dear Lord, David, someone has burned my home."

David slid his knife back into its sheath and ran to the corral. Within minutes he had saddled his horse and was off to Fort Grider. He told Rachael the he was going to give the alarm of this new Tory theart that was raiding and burning on Warriors Creek; perhaps they would be caught if the Grider's could gather enough men in time.

Rachael stood in the dark watching as he rode away. She could still see the fire in the distance, but it was fading. 'I just can't sit here and do nothing,' she thought to herself. 'Perhaps I can save something.' She quickly saddled her father's horse and mounted up. As she rode out of the empty corral she looked at her parent's door. They were still inside, unaware of what was happening, and they needed to be told. She trotted the horse over and called thru the doorway, "Tories father! Tories are about and burning."

Charles come out of the cabin with an inquisitive look, only to see his headstrong daughter ride off into the night with his last remaining mount. He called for her to stop, but she never heard his pleas of "Where are you going and what are you thinking?"

Colonel Gideon Wright was sitting just inside the Medaris cabin door watching Rice's mill and blacksmith shop as they burned to the ground. He had sixteen men with him and he planned to raise more in the coming days. He knew that Rice, like so many others around the Yadkin were away with the Whig militia. This was a wonderful opportunity for him to strike. If the cats were away, then he would gladly play the mouse that played. But his game would be a harsh one, if they were disloyal to the King, then property would be forfeit. His brother Hezekiah, was down by the creek bank, in hiding with the rest of the men. They were lying in ambush, waiting for any Whig militia that might ride into his trap. Gideon was hoping that Captain Daniel Smith, who the Grider's had taken up with as Indian spies, would soon ride to his demise. Gidden had told his brother that if a single rider was to approach the house not to fire. That he and the two men with him inside could deal with a small threat themselves.

The two buildings were now nearly consumed by the flames. One wall of the mill was still standing. All that was left of the shop was a skeleton of the back wall. Soon both would be laid to ash.

Gideon cocked the hammer of his pistol as a rider rode into the cabin yard. He could see Rachel's figure well from where he sat. The glow of the fire was dying but he had no problem seeing that she was a woman in its light. He watched quietly as she dismounted. She stood by the lathered horse and watched as the last wall of the mill collapsed. Then she looked at the dark cabin for a moment. She took a few steps towards her home, but then she hesitated. He could see that she was having second thoughts about approaching. She seemed to be unarmed. He could see well enough that she did not have a rifle, but a knife or perhaps that old Queen Anne pistol of hers could be at hand. He had seen Rachael twice before. Once at Mulberry Fields, and the other in Salisbury. Both times she had carried herself well, and he had heard of her even keel during the Cherokee attack upon Grider's. He did not want to hurt her, but no woman was going to end his days either. If he had to shoot her, he would. He continued to watch as she turned back to her horse. He could not just let her ride away so he called out. "Mrs. Medaris, please stay where you are. It's Colonel Wright, you have no more to fear, if you do as you are told, my dear."

Rachael slowly turned back to the cabin knowing that she was once again at the mercy of a Tory. She needed to be strong, and was determined to do so. But she also needed to be smart about it. If she seemed weak, only God knew what would happen to her. If she was too forceful she could receive backlash for her daring. She said nothing as Gideon approached.

"Do you have a weapon of any sort?" he asked

"No," was the short response.

"Grand then' Gideon said as he came to a stop only two feet away "Tell me Mrs. Medaris, why are you here alone tonight?"

Rachael pondered the question for a moment, shaking her head as she looked into his eyes. "For the life of me Colonel, I have no clue. I saw the flames coming from my home, and come without really thinking of what I was doing. And for that moment of lapse in judgement, I am in your hands. I do pray that they are noble hands, that I find myself in."

"They are indeed Madame, for I am no ruffian. I Suppose that you were at your father's and came running to save what you could."

"I was," She answered "Something to that effect. Is his home the next to be burned?"

"No" Gideon said as he took the reins of her horse from her hand. "Your father has not taken up arms against the King. Why would I burn him out? But Rice, on the other hand. We both know where he is, as we speak. That is if he is still among the living. You have gotten word of General Gates's defeat by now have you not?"

Rachael stood stock still, dumbfounded for a moment. Was he telling the truth? Was he trustworthy?

"I am the bearer of bad news, I see. I cannot tell you if Rice is dead or not, but I can relay that the North Carolina Militia took a beating at Camden. If your husband is among the dead then you have my condolences. However, with that being said, I fear I must put your cabin to the torch."

"Why?" Rachael asked through tear filled eyes.

"Madam, it is a well-known fact that Rice burnt the McFall's out. Turnabout is fair play, is it not? I have little choice in the matter. Protocol demands it from me I am afraid."

"Yes, you do have a choice," she pleaded, taking his arm "If what you say is true and Rice is no more, than I am a widowed woman, with two fatherless children. If you burn this little cabin you are no better than Tarleton or Burnfoot Brown. Without the mill, you have already taken away my livelihood, but if you burn my home you may as well kill me now."

Gideon Wright was not known to be a sympathetic man. Expressing kindness to the enemy was not something that was done often. But here tonight with the smell of ash and hot coals still in the air, Rachael had reached the man's better character.

"In an odd way, your poor circumstance is in your favor tonight madam". Gideon said uncharacteristically. "The war is certainly over with Gates' defeat here in the south. I see no need to increase your suffering. Madam, you home will stand".

Rachael did not know how to act. She had just save her home, but could it still be a home for her if Rice was indeed dead? One thing she did know was that this could be a chance to rid the countryside of Wright presence for the moment. "Sir, thank you very much for the great kindness you have shown me tonight. I cannot express enough gratitude. However, I can return one good deed for another. Colonel, you must go at once. My brother is at this moment bringing Captain Smith and his eighty-man force to do battle with you."

"Where? Here?" Gideon asked sharply.

"No," Rachael, ever the opportunist lied. "They plan to ambush you at Shallow Ford in two days' time. They are hoping that you will stay here for another day or two. That will give them enough time to beat you to the ford. But if you leave tonight they will not be able to catch up with you. You can cross the river with ease, but only if you go now. I am not lying to you sir, this is not a falsehood."

"How do you know their numbers?" Gideon asked.

"The Griders," Rachael replied.

"Very well then Madam, until we meet again, I wish you the best," was Gideon's closing statement.

Rachael walked inside the cabin door numbly, as the Tories mounted up. She pulled up Rice's favorite chair and sat down in it as they rode away.
She could not take any pride in the fact that she had fooled Gideon into believing her story of Captain Smith and his eighty men. She knew that there was no more than ten men at Fort Grider. If they had ridden into her yard, Gideon Wright would have won the day. No, all that she could think of now as her tears began to flow, was of Rice and his wellbeing. Was he alive or not? She could only pray. And wait.

Chapter 97

From the Ashes

Rice and Jack had been separated for a few hours now. Jack was certain that Annabelle would still be at Fort Grider. Rice on the other hand, knew the nature of his wife, and was sure she was long gone. Possibly to her father's and very likely back at home. The waters of Warriors Creek never looked better as he and Liberty crossed it this afternoon. Home was close now, just upstream a few miles. He was looking forward to his family's company. He enjoyed watching his children play about. And he greatly missed Rachael. Her long dark hair hanging over her exposed shoulder was a sight that only he had seen. A view that he needed to see, and had not in such a long time.

He pulled his horse to a stop as he looked down at the ground. The dirt path that lead to his home had been well traveled in the last few days. Too well traveled for such a isolated cabin. The tracks showed that the horses had been shod. This mostly ruled out Indians, unless they had been stolen from some trader or from a homestead. Militia was a better guess, but whose? Ben's he hoped. Surely the Tories had not already taken advantage of Gates's defeat.

He kicked Liberty's side to set him at a faster gate. As the wind blew from the direction of home he could smell the faint scent of smoke. He looked at the bend in the path where he should be able to see the roofline of the mill, but it was not there to be seen. It was evident that something very wrong had taken place in the last few days. He could feel the anxiety building in his chest as the path widen into his yard. The shop was gone as well as the mill, but the cabin was still standing. His three cows were dead, having been shot, but thank God, no human bodies were lying on the grounds.

He jumped from the saddle with rifle in hand and ran inside the cabin as quickly as he could. It seemed to be in good order, but a few things were missing. A small silver cup of his mothers was not in its place on the mantel. A small mirror was missing from the wall. He opened the door that lead out back. He called out for Rachael as he stepped through the doorway, and to his great relief, he heard her voice say his name. She stepped around the corner of the far end of the cabin with her arms full of firewood. She dropped it where she stood and tearfully fell into his arms "Praise to the Lord!" she cried. "God has seen fit to keep us together a while longer. I just knew that you were safe and not in some shallow grave, but I have been sick with worry."

"What are you speaking of?" Rice asked. "Of course, I am not in my grave. You are the one that was in danger, it seems to me. Who did this? How are the children? How are you? Were you here when it happened? Tell me!"

"Yes, I was here, and yes, the children are fine' She answered happily as she held him away from her, before crushing him to her again. Nothing had ever felt so good to her as having him in her arms again. "Come, Let us go back inside and I will tell you everything. Believe me when I tell you it could have been a lot worse. We are all safe and together again now, by God's good grace. and that is what matters the most. What they took can be replaced, you cannot. Thank God that you are home."

Chapter 98

With Fire And Sword

Patrick Ferguson's time in Camden was short. His evening with Lord Cornwallis was pleasant enough. The food was very fine and a dance capped off the night's festivities. His two Virginia's were quite the talk of the evening. Even with his disabled arm, he took a few turns around the ballroom floor, displaying his two mistresses for all to see. However, his new orders were not as pleasant or exciting. He had hoped to stay with the main army, but the continentals, though soundly beaten, seemed to be reorganizing. Gates was trying to save his career, but most felt that he would soon be replaced by Nathaniel Green. Ferguson had missed his chance with Gates, but hoped to see action against Green soon. Instead, he was to subdue the Carolina backcountry by defeating Shelby, who had to abandon his attack on Fort Ninety-six. He was to march Northwest and crush the last of the rebel holdouts. The dregs of mankind, in his eyes. His Majesty had the prison ship Eske[98] anchored in the harbor of Charlestown, and Ferguson was more than willing to fill it with Shelby's men.

His path to victory would crisscross several times from Fair Forest, to Mitchell's Creek, to Cedar Springs, onto Wofford's Iron

---

98 Several Whig prisoners who were captured at the Battle of Lindley's Mill was imprisoned aboard The HMS Eske.

Works. The march rarely missed a day without some sort of gun play. The rebel barbarians would appear, fire, and then disappear again. But they would suffer for their bad deeds. One such sufferer was a rebel from Cedar Springs, who had his arm amputated by a blacksmith using a shoemaker's knife and some carpenters' saws. On the seventh of September, Ferguson marched into North Carolina by crossing Buck Creek, stopping that evening at Gilbert Town[99]. Here he took up quarters and used the small town of crude cabins as his outpost. Virginia Paul, as resourceful as ever, quickly won over the favor of the hospitable Sara Gilbert. She was the wife of town founder William Gilbert. Virginia was sure that the Gilbert cabin was large enough to accommodate Pattie, herself and the other Virginia. This would be their home until this God-awful tour ended. Anything was better than that baggage wagon they had been living out of.

Ferguson was now sitting at his desk rereading the proclamation he had just written. It was short and to the point, and was to be delivered to Colonel Isaac Shelby. It read,

Officers on the Western waters, You must desist at once from this foolhardy opposition to the British army, and take protection under His Majesty King George III standard by taking a renewed loyalty oath to the crown. If not, I will march my army over the mountains, hang your leaders, and lay your countryside to waste with fire and sword.

Major Patrick Ferguson, of the American Volunteers Provincials

---

[99] Gilbert Town no longer exist. It was three miles north of the current town of Rutherfordton, North Carolina.

Being satisfied with his choice of wording, Ferguson looked at George McFall who was standing by the door and said, "Bring in the prisoner." As McFall exited the room, Ferguson looked at Lt. Anthony Allaire and complained, "What is that Cumberworld [100] doing here again? I told you to rid him of this duty."

"I did sir, unfortunately this new man is the first one's brother. I will see that he too is reassigned."

"Good." Ferguson said was he was sealing the wax on the folded document. "He is unnerving to Virginia."

McFall opened the door and pushed Samuel Phillips into the room. Phillips had been captured at the Battle of Musgrove Mill as a member of Shelby's Militia. He was still in irons. Ferguson lifted his stamp from the hot glob of red wax and looked at Phillips. "I understand that you are familiar with the Shelby's. Is that the case?"

"Yes" Phillips replied "He is a neighbor."

"Then you know the way to where he is," Ferguson, said as he looked at the irons. "If you want out of those and are quick to the challenge, you may be my courier. So, are you my man?"

"That I am," Phillips replied as he raised his hands and presented them to McFall who held the key to the lock.

"Very well then, you are paroled, but heed this," Ferguson said firmly. "If you fall into my hands again you will be executed on the spot."

---

[100] Cumberworld a 18th century insult meaning someone who was useless and inept.

Samuel Phillips rode out of Gilbert Town on a fast bay horse with Ferguson's threat safely tucked inside a saddlebag. He would be over the Blue Ridge by tomorrow night. Ferguson did not expect a complete collapse of the Rebel militia with a mere threat, but he could reduce their numbers with one. Time would tell if he was correct or not.

Once Phillips had delivered Ferguson's threat, Isaac Shelby was quick to flee his home on the lower Settlements of the Holston River. It was more than evident to Shelby that the Over the Mountain men needed to stand as one force. Samuel Phillips delivered far more than what Ferguson wanted. Being a prisoner held among the Loyalist, he knew the size of Ferguson's force and was more than willing to tell all that he knew of Ferguson's men. Shelby took that information to the Nolichucky settlements were Colonel John Sevier lived. There, the two Colonels would hatch out a plan of attack to deal with this coming invasion.

Chapter 99

The Heroes Of Congress

John McFall was feeling his oats. He had been counting the days for years, until he could return to his beloved home in the mountains. And what a triumphant homecoming it was going to be. This was exactly how he wanted to take back what was rightfully his. He was not returning with hat in hand, but as a conquering soldier of old. The Western Carolina Loyalist were finally having their day. Those who had not enlisted were doing the King's work in other ways, supplying food and supplies and even better, intelligence.

Major Ferguson had received word from one of his spies that Colonel Charles McDowell was commanding a band of Rebels from Burke and Rutherford counties. They were somewhere along the Western waters of the Catawba River. They would be no match for such a force as Ferguson's. John was convinced that Quaker Meadows was their destination and it would be the first link in a long chain of British victories this fall. However, what McFall and Ferguson did not know was that McDowell had spying eyes as well. He too knew that Ferguson was approaching. McDowell also understood that his men were far too few in number to stop the Scotsman's invasion. But an ambush from Bedford's Hill along Cane Creek could slow his advance, and possibly keep him on this side of the Blue Ridge for a little while longer.

Captain James Dunlap [101] of the King's American Regiment was the first to walk his horse out of the creek bed at Cowan's Ford. The water level was low and did not even wet his feet as he crossed. He turned his horse off the roadway, and stood by the creekside on a small mound. He watched as his men rode by. He glanced around, looking at the thick tree cover that was on both sides of the valley. As the last of his men rode out of the creek he looked back across the water to see Captain Walter Gilkey's horse take its first step into the creek. Gilkey's horse spooked and rose up on its back legs as the

---

[101] Capt. James Dunlap a native of New Jersey, had come south with Ferguson. He was a member of the Queen's Ranger that was reassigned to Ferguson new corps. While still in the East he took part in the Battles of Brandywine and Monmouth and the attack on the Hancock House in Salem Massachusetts. There he mistakenly killed a group of Tories along with the Patriot garrison stationed there. In the South, he was in the Battles of Wofford's Iron Works and at Earl's Ford, another engagement fought and won against Colonel Charles McDowell. McDowell took much criticism for his actions there.

sound of gunshots filled the air. Dunlap turned his mount to face the rebel fire as a round struck his leg in the thigh. A second shot fired by a fighting Quaker by the name of James Blair hit his side just above the hip, knocking him out of the saddle to the ground. Gilkey, having regained control of his horse, rushed across the ford. He saw a Whig reloading his rifle behind a fallen cherry tree. As he was pulling his ramrod from his rifle, Gilkey put a well-aimed shot into James Hemphill's chest.

John McFall raced by Gilkey on horseback, in full out pursuit of one of the retreating rebels, William Dysart. Dysart having already emptied his rifle had seen the mad dash that the loyalist was making across the shallow water. They were coming in full charge. He knew that he, and some of his fellow militiamen, had made a grave mistake in dismounting before the volley had been fired.

McFall leaped from his horse and drove a killing tomahawk blow into Dysart's neck. He pulled his knife free, and with one quick slice and a strong yank he rose with Dysart's red scalp in his hand. Lt. Anthony Allaire galloped by as McFall was waving his trophy high overhead. Allaire soon outpaced four other fleeing Whigs who were also on foot. He turned his horse about in front of them and pulled his saber. The mere threat he offered was enough to allow him to capture all four. As they stood there with raised hands, Allaire begin to mock them. "You are a brave lot, I must say. The heroes of Congress you truly are."

McFall, now joined by his brother George walked over and grabbed one of the prisoners, Edward Harris by his neck. "Where is your camp?" he asked.

Harris said nothing in reply, causing McFall to fly into a rage "You look thirsty to me. They say the best drinking water his down deep. Let's go see."

At that they pushed Harris to the creek's edge and plunged his head under the water. His legs began to kick for the lack of air as another prisoner called out. "We have no camp. We are of a flying camp, never staying the same place as the night before."

"I have my doubts about that," McFall answered. "See any fish down there, boy?"

"Alright pull him out of the water. The camp is not far, just be on the other side of South Mountain at its foot."

Hearing this McFall's released Harris, who struggled to get to his feet. As he stood there, he began to cough up the muddy creek water.

Ferguson was pleased to hear that seventeen of McDowell's men were captured along with twelve horses that day at the skirmish of Cain Creek [102]. McDowell used the chance to retreat across the Blue Ridge. Ferguson followed in pursuit for about five miles, but then returned to Gilbert Town with what was sure to be the first of many victories of this fall campaign. He was now even more confident that if this was the best resistance that the Whig's could muster the Crown would again, have control of this unruly mob within a week.

---

[102] The battle of Cane Creek took place September 12, 1780 in Burke County North Carolina. Dysart and Hemphill were the only deaths of the battle for the Patriots. The loyalist Militia, lost only Colonel. Vezey Husbands of Burke County.

Chapter 100

He Has No Clue As To Who We Are

Rice and Jack was once again notching logs. They were determined to rebuild the mill and blacksmith shop before winter arrived. With every swing of his ax Rice marveled at his Rachael's bravery. Rice was so very proud of his wife, if not for her heroism everything would have been lost. She had taken a great gamble in coming here that night. In truth, he would not have approved of her actions at the time. He could have rebuilt the cabin just as easily as the other buildings. He could never replace her, and even though Gideon Wright had destroyed much of his property, Rice did respect him in one way. He had taken pity on a vulnerable woman when many other would not have. He had shown mercy when others in this war had not.

As the two continued their work, Duchess rose to her feet with raised hackles on the back of her neck. The dog was looking towards the road, growing a low rumble that eventually broke into a bark. Rice reached for his rifle and took a place behind the log with Jack. Both had cocked hammers, waiting to see who was approaching, and had sounded the dog's alarm.

It was Ben Cleveland swaying ever so gently back in forth in his saddle. His ever-growing frame was dressed in a blue waistcoat that was so dark it was almost black. His tri-cornered hat was decorated with his black cockade that indicated this was not a social visit. He was leading a column of men that included his brother Robert, William Lenoir, Martin and Jacob Grider, and Rachael's brother David among others. He rode up to Rice, scanning the grounds. "Rice my boy! It is a damn shame, but it could have been a lot worse than this. But I suppose that I do not have to tell you that. It was Gideon and his crew I understand. I do wish that we could have been here that night instead of over at Court House of Wilkes raising men. We got so bored there we had a sham battle[103] late one night just to keep my boys sharp and on their toes. I would have much rather preferred to have been here, dealing with Gideon. He seems to enjoy inflicting harm when we are the most vulnerable with Cornwallis being so close in Charlottetown."

"That he does" Rice answered as Rachael walked out of the cabin door.

"Rachael my dear," Ben said upon seeing her "You have my compliments. I understand from Davi, here, that you alone stood toe to toe with Gideon Wright the other night. Well done my dear. I could see on the day that I wed you to Rice, that he had won a fine lady. Your conduct keeps proving my impressions to be right"

Ole Roundabout turned back to Rice and said, "Well, if vengeance is what you want, we are your vessel to get it."

"Has Wright been seen?" Jack asked.

"No," Ben replied "I do believe he has disbanded for the moment. To see what our reaction to Ferguson's scare tactics will be."

"What scare tactics?" Rice asked.

_____

[103] Elihu Ayres recorded this "Sham or mock battle" in his 1834 Rev. War pension application. The pension number is R335.

"Pretty much the same as what happened here. Except he plans to hang me in the processes." Ben cried in a mocking laugh. "That arrogant bastard was ignorant enough to send a message to all of us backwater folk, as he likes to calls us. Either run to the King's standard or take an ass beating. He has no clue as to who we are. Under the King's standard! What protection has the King ever given us way out here? We were the ones who drove off the Indians, not his troops. If the law is broken we handle it, not the King. Plenty of trees around here."

"So, Ferguson is already in North Carolina. Then what is to be done with him?" asked Jack. "Is there a plan?"

"Yes, he is in Gilbert Town," Cleveland replied. "We are taking the fight to him. Shelby and Sevier are rendezvousing at Sycamore Shoals with MacDowell's Rutherford County boys. William Campbell, who has been corresponding with me and the others, is supposed to be coming down from Virginia with more militia."

"And as for us, we are on his sour scent, we are going to meet up with the Over the mountain men at Quaker Meadows," Martin chimed in "You boys coming? John and George McFall are sure to be among them. This will be one more chance for you to set thing right on that old score."

Rice was reluctant to leave Rachael so soon after what had just happened. He hesitated in answering the question. No one would call him a coward if he passed on going. After all of the fighting he had done in the last few years he had already made his reputation. He looked at his wife, but before he could speak she said. "Of course, he is going, we still have a home to protect."

Chapter 101

Ferguson's Chivalry

Virginia Paul reached over the flames in the fireplace and pulled the black kettle of food away from the heat. She reached in with a wooden dipper and scooped up two full helping of beef stew. She poured them over two biscuit halves, one after the other. She walked across the lower room of the Gilbert home, and presented the pewter plate to Pattie.

"Well my Gallant officer, how was your day?" She asked.

"Pleasant enough, considering my long ride," Ferguson answered as he took a mug of ale from the other Virginia's hand. "We were out subduing a few of the Whig leaders today."

"Do tell us," Virginia Sal pleaded as she sat at Pattie's left, thus putting a Virginia on either side of the Scotsman.

"Very well," Pattie replied as he propped his feet up on a stool in front of William Gilbert's best winged backed chair. "The world never ceases to amaze in this wild country. We were up what the locals call Crooked Creek. A man named Captain Thomas Lytle has a very beautiful, but crude plantation up there. He made his reputation by manning the western forts and keeping the Cherokee in tow. Of course, he was absent, like many of the rebels these days."

"So, it was a wasted outing?" Sal asked stroking her long hair.

"No, not by any means," Pattie said, watching her. "That is where the amazement came about. On our arrival I hailed the house, and to my surprise, out walked what I would describe as the second most handsome woman in all of North Carolina."

"Who being the first would be the better question," Virginia Paul said with a flirtatious smile.

"Why you my dear," Pattie replied.

At that statement, a jealous Virginia Sal stood up and stormed across the room, only to have Pattie call for her to stop. "My dear, if you do not wish to hear the remainder of my tale, then please check on Captain Dunlap. I am sure he could use some assistance, in his condition". Sal never looked back, but she did stop and after he had spoken, she left the room without a word.

Virginia looked at Pattie and let out a long sigh, "One less in the bed tonight. I hope the rest of your tale is worth her absence."

"The sight of Miss Lytle's curtsy was well worth it. She was very well dressed and she had a fine ladies beaver hat. You would have liked it," Pattie answered. "She has a presences very much like your own. I told her to have her husband come in and take an oath to the King. She bravely discussed the situation with me, I fear he will not come in. I then gave her my compliments and retired."

Virginia nodded her head and said "It is fortunate for Mrs. Lytle that you are a far better man then say, Banastre Tarleton for instance. He would have ravished her on the spot if she is half the beauty you say she is. I have heard of his bragging in the past of such situations."

"I dare say that you are correct," Pattie agreed. "He is a vile man. I have often wondered what would happen to that man if he were ever captured by the Rebels. Most likely chopped up like a rack of beef by a half- starved butcher."

"Oh, enough about Tarleton and his antics. What about your plans for this day and the morrow?" Virginia asked.

"Jon Hampton's trial." Pattie replied "If he comes in at all. He said he would, on his honor. If he does come in I will be lenient. If not, he will hang in time."

The next morning Patrick Ferguson did indeed preside over the case of Jonathan Hampton, who had been appointed by the Rebel government as Justice of the Peace, and from that illegal office had been performing criminal marriages. Once again, Ferguson showed his chivalrous side by paroling Hampton. The ruling disgusted Captain James Dunlap, who hated the Hampton family
 for reasons known only to himself. He had killed Hampton's brother in the battle of Earle's Ford, yet he still wanted more blood from their family. As he dragged himself out of the Gilbert cabin on his crutches he cussed with every step.

Chapter 102

Rendezvous At Sycamore Shoals

With word of Ferguson's threat rapidly circulating throughout Western Carolina, a great number of Burke County Whigs had little choice but to flee their homes and retreat across the Blue Ridge. Shelby and Sevier had called for Sycamore Shoals to be the rallying point for the march to meet the enemy. They were not disappointed in the turnout, for over one thousand men had gathered on the banks of the Watauga on the appointed day of September 25. Refugees were pouring in daily, well before the twenty fifth. Wives and children had come with the men out of necessity, as displaced refugees. Even the women of the most western settlements, who had not yet been threatened, came to see their loved ones a while longer, and to be there to see them off with one last embrace and to wish them a speedy return. Once they had all gathered together, it reminded many of the elderly of their youth in their old Scottish clans. Stories of abuse, thievery, hanging and the burning of homes were told by many. Their stories of villainy included the usual names of Tarleton, Fanning, and Wright. But with Patrick Ferguson's arrival a new list was emerging. Men such as James Dunlap, Abraham De Peyster, Thomas "Burn Foot" Brown and Ambrose Mills were now becoming hated men as well. Even old neighbors were now becoming more abusive and violent to one another. The McFall's were not alone in their actions anymore, Walter Gilkey was earning a bad reputation as well. However, James Dunlap in particular, had enraged the most. He had taken a fancy to a beautiful young lady by the name of Mary McRae. She had shown little to no interest in his advances, and soon afterwards had disappeared, having been kidnapped by Dunlap. All of these outrages, and more served to strengthen everyone's resolve. It was obvious to all that such outrages needed to be dealt with. Everyone's safety and livelihood depended on the upcoming battle's outcome.

If they were victorious, life would on, and little would change, but defeat would turn their world upside down. The choices offered them were to either bow to the King, or travel north into Kentucky to fight another day. Or worse, go South by the riverways and become a subject of the Spanish Crown.

That night, the good Reverend Samuel Doak[104] of the Watauga settlement, preached "My countrymen, you are about to set out on an expedition which is full of hardships and dangers, but one in which the Almighty will attend you. The Mother Country has her grip upon you, these American colonies, and takes that for which our fathers planted their homes in the wilderness. Our liberty. Taxation without representation and the quartering of soldiers in the homes of our people without their consent are evidence that the crown of England would take from its American Subjects the last vestiges of Freedom. Your brethren across the mountains are crying like Macedonia unto your help. God forbid that you should refuse to hear and answer their call; but the call of your brethren is not your only plight. The enemy is marching hither to destroy your homes. Brave men, you are not unacquainted with battle. Your hands have already been taught to war and your fingers to fight. You have wrested these beautiful valleys of the Holston and Watauga from the savage hand. Will you tarry now until the other enemy carries fire and sword to your very doors? No, it shall not be. Go forth then in the strength of your manhood to the aid of your brethren, the defense of your liberty and the protection of your homes. And may the God of Justice be with you and give you victory. Let us pray. 'Almighty and gracious God! Thou hast been the refuge and strength of Thy people in all ages. In time of sorest need we have learned to come to Thee - our Rock and our Fortress. Thou knowest the dangers and snares that surround us on march and in battle. Thou knowest the dangers that constantly threaten the humble, but well-beloved homes, which Thy servants have left behind them. Oh, in Thine infinite mercy, save us from the cruel hand of the savage, and of tyranny. Save the unprotected homes while fathers and husbands and sons are far away fighting for freedom and helping the oppressed. Thou, who promised to protect the sparrow in its flight,

---

[104] Samuel Doak 1749-1830 Presbyterian minister and founder of the school "Academy of Liberty Hall" that would become Washington and Lee University. 347

keep ceaseless watch, by day and by night, over our loved ones. The helpless women and little children, we commit to Thy care. Thou wilt not leave them or forsake them in times of loneliness and anxiety and terror. Oh, God of Battle, arise in Thy might. Avenge the slaughter of Thy people. Confound those who plot for our destruction. Crown this mighty effort with victory, and smite those who exalt themselves against liberty and justice and truth. Help us as good soldiers to wield the sword of the Lord and Gideon. Amen."

The next morning, after several hundred tearful farewell hugs, the Over the Mountain Men where on the march. Quaker Meadows would be the next rendezvous location. This first leg of the march to Gilbert Town would be the most difficult. The mountain tops could be snow covered if the weather turned bad. And it did. The old hunting and Indian trails which they must follow, were in some places covered knee deep in snow for the men not on horseback. But the snow soon became the least of their concerns. It was discovered that two men, James Crawford and Samuel Chambers, who many thought to be Tories at heart, had disappeared. Would they go back home, or to Ferguson with word of their approach? As they neared Gillespie Gap, all thoughts turned to the deserters and their intentions, remembering that Francis Marion had been ambushed inside that gap back in 1761, by the Indians. Every man knew it was a great place for an ambush and were on alert, but this army passed through untouched. Two days later an exhausted militia marched into Quaker Meadows.

Chapter 103

Three Rousing Calls Of Huzzah

Colonel Charles McDowell and his brother, Major Joseph McDowell were the co-owners of Quaker Meadows. Their plantation was to be the temporary home of this frontier army for the next few days. All of the commanders here had done well in raising their militia's and gathering here at the same time. But were the numbers enough to win a battle against a leader as well regarded as Patrick Ferguson? With General Rutherford locked away in irons in Charlestown's harbor, having been captured at the Battle of Camden, a new chain of commanded needed to be established. Charles McDowell was the highest-ranking militia officer in the Colony, making him the leading candidate by protocol.

All of this reorganization had put the plantation abuzz as Benjamin Cleveland lead three hundred and fifty more men from Wilkes and Surry Counties onto its grounds. As they rode through camp they were greeted with three rousing calls of 'huzzah' from Shelby's men. Sevier's troops soon followed suit, as if the two militias were dueling each other in their salute to the newcomers. While Rice's ride here had been a long, taxing, three-day ride from Fort Grider, it was still not as far as that of Ole Roundabout. While he and his men were still at William Lenoir' new Fort [105] a wounded courier by the name of James Blair [106], who had been shot from a wooded cliff by a cowardly

---

[105] This is Fort Defiance in Lenoir North Carolina.

[106] James Blair 1761-1839 was in the battles of Pacolet River, Sumter's Defeat, Cane Creek, Kings Mountain, Blackstock's Plantation, Hampton Plantation, Ramsour's Mill and the siege of Augusta. After the war he lived in the Pendleton District South Carolina (now this district is part of Georgia), Ray Co Tennessee and in Franklin and

Tory, had arrived with another express from Colonel McDowell. It was urging Cleveland to come in all haste. Ole Roundabout complied, stopping along the way at Fort Grider, where Rice joined his company, but the journey was not without a cost. While in the same vicinity where Blair was shot, Larkin Cleveland, a brother to Ben was shot in the thigh. This added to the stressfulness of the ride, and also to everyone's fatigue. This grand greeting had put some energy back into Rice's tired bones. It sent a tingle up his spine and it made his hair stand on end with pride. Even Colonel William Campbell's Virginians called the salute.

Rice once again, recognized many faces among the men who were already here. This war was always in need of soldiers, and it seemed at every critical moment, the same men would rise to the challenge. Camden had certainly been a defeat, but it had not broken their desire for freedom .

As nightfall came upon Quaker Meadows the temperature fell as well. Fires were kindled and fueled by the split rails from the fences that ran around the plantation. The McDowell's had come to the conclusion, that if this army lost to Ferguson he would definitely seize Quaker Meadows. It was in their best interest to have a healthy army in order to fight him off, one that was not cold at night. Joseph had even gone so far as to say he would burn every building on the place, before he would let some damned Tory like Gideon Wright or Samuel Bryan move into his home, if the war was lost.

As Rice looked around the fire he came to realize this was not just a group of men pulled together to merely fight a common foe.

Habersham counties Georgia. He was a state Legislator in Georgia. His sister would marry John Grider in 1781.

They were family, in both blood and friendship, such as he and his brother-in-law David. The McDowell's were even distant cousin to his wife Rachel. His good friends Martin and Jacob Grider was here doing their part, while John and Val were out roaming from one frontier fort to the other, keeping the Indians at bay back home. Jeremiah's old companions from his Kentucky days, Robert and Samuel Tate were sitting right across from Rice. Earlier in the day, they had told   how well Rachael's brother Jeremiah had died that night on Tate's Creek. And of course, Jack was always close by in bad times such as these.

Rice stood up and stretched his back in a arch to relieve his aching muscles. As he was sitting back down, he spotted Robert Bedwell walk past with another man. Rice called out for him to come and join the group. Rice's eyes grew large as he realized who Robert's companion was. "Why Abe Baker, is that you or is your spirit out haunting tonight? I could have sworn that I saw you fall at Camden."

"You did," Abe replied "But as you can see it was not a fatal shot, nicked in the ankle was all. Those bastards hauled me to Camden in one of our captured wagons. Said they were going to make me take that oath to the King once I was well. That was all I needed to hear. I hopped out of Camden that night."

"No one stopped you on your way back?" Jack asked

"Oh yah, but I told them I was one of Samuel Bryan's Loyalist. Just out for a walk, recouping." Abe said smiling. "I tell you boys they ain't all that smart in Camden."

"What does that say about Gates then?" Martin asked with a smile. He ain't too sharp of a knife either, is he?"

"No, he is not, and I for one do not want to go down that dark road under his orders ever again. So, do you boys really think that Colonel McDowell is up for this command?" Robert asked. "He is a good man and all, but Earle's Ford and Cain Creek did not turn out too well now did they? Cornwallis is said to be marching to Salisbury. At this point, we cannot afford for another Camden to take place."

"Why? Do Shelby and Sevier have doubts about Colonel McDowell?" Martin asked, pushing his hat back.

"Yes, they do," Abe answered. "They are of the opinion that Ferguson and Dunlap have his number, so to speak. Ferguson has always been a good step ahead of the Colonel."

"So does Ben," Rice said, looking toward the McDowell cabin. "He said as much last evening. He was hoping that someone other than the colonel would take command. But he was not sure how to go about changing it. Something like that could disband our young army before we get a chance to meet Ferguson at Gilbert Town. I believe that Ole Roundabout is partial to Colonel Shelby. He was the one who got us all in motion in the first place."

"Time will tell I suppose," Robert said, "I understand that a council of war is going to be held in the morning. If they make a change it will fly through this camp like the women of the Yadkin Valley talks about me."

"Now why would any woman speak about you?" Abe asked.

"Why my name says it all. Don't you know that? Bedwell! It says all that any women ever needs to know."

As the men groaned at Robert's statement, Rice rose to his feet and walked away from the fire. He patted Abe's back on his way out and said "Glad to see you well again old friend, but I do feel for you if Robert is the best you can do in the way of companionship."

The next morning the Council of War was held under a grand old oak tree. Shelby, Sevier, the McDowell brothers, Campbell, and Ben were all present.

"Gentlemen," Charles McDowell opened. "All of us, every man here has faced the enemy on more than one occasion. I have the fullest confidence in all here today. But with that being said, I truly believe that we need a commander-in- chief. And since we are made up of troops from more than one Colony it would be wise to have General Gates appoint us a commanding officer for the Continentals. That would avoid any disputes that may arise in the future among our men."

"That will take valuable time," Shelby replied. "Gilbert Town is only fifteen or twenty miles away. As far as we know, Ferguson is as yet unaware of us. But that could change at any time."

"True," Ben agreed. "He could even attack us here while we wait for Gates' man to arrive."

"I see your point," McDowell replied. "However, I still think it would be prudent to do so. Let me suggest this. What if I was to ride to Gates and make the request in person. I know the roads well and can be back in little time."

"I agree with that," Sevier said looking at McDowell "But we still need a commander in the meantime. With you being gone, we should select a man still here among us. He will of course, step down on your return."

"Then I nominate Colonel Campbell," Shelby spoke up looking at the tall silent Virginian. "You have marched your men the furthest, and I understand that you have previously been in the Virginia Line. Colonel Sevier here, has already been burdened with raising funds for this expedition. I am sure that you would not mind if Colonel Campbell shared the load in this way for the time being."

"I do not," agreed Sevier.

Colonel Campbell looked at Shelby and said "Sir I have one request, that being a word in private."

"Very well,' Colonel Shelby answered. "Lead the way."

The two men walked away a few hundred feet before speaking again. Campbell broke the silence. "Colonel Shelby, I'm truly flattered by your confidence in my abilities. However, this expedition has been under your direction from the beginning. Should it not be you that has full command?"

"Perhaps" Shelby replied. "But I am a junior officer to McDowell. Some of his men may not take a liking to me being in charge over him. You understand as well as I do, we cannot wait here any longer. As soon as Charles is on the road to Gates, we will march out after Ferguson. When that happens, I want Joseph McDowell and his men with us. If you take command, that will ensure good morale and camaraderie between all parties. We need no petty jealousies between our North Carolinian troops. What do you say, Sir?"

William Campbell removed his hand from the handle of his Scottish grandfather's broadsword, which he had carried at Culloden, and took Isaac Shelby's hand into his own and said "Colonel Shelby, it will be my honor."

Chapter 104

What!

Patrick Ferguson was sitting at the head of William Gilbert's table, eating his noon time meal. He was enjoying every juicy bite of his rare steak. One of Colonel Ambrose Mills' patrols had had the good fortune to discover a young steer that belonged to some unknown Whig. This unfortunate fellow had tried to hide his beef unsuccessfully. behind Brittain Church [107] As Ferguson stuck his two-pronged fork into his steak, he looked at Captain Abraham DePeyster and Lt. Allaire at the other end of the table. He watched Allaire, as his eyes followed Virginia Sal's hips as she left the room. Allaire quickly dropped his eyes back to his plate after seeing Ferguson had noticed his stare.

"Lieutenant, you should have wooed that lovely creature away from Ninety-Six when you had the chance." Ferguson laughed. "Romantic relations are quite the challenge in this Rebel infested valley I understand."

"Perhaps, she was really quite remarkable," Allaire said remembering Iona "Far superior to the inhabitants here. These

[107] Brittain Church is of the Presbyterian Denomination. It was Established in 1768. It's congregation still exist and is meeting in its third building in Rutherfordton North Carolina.

settlements are composed of the most violent Rebels I have ever seen, particularly the young ladies. [108]"

Ferguson smiled and nodded his head. He took another bite, and as he chewed, his tone took on a more serious note. "Any word on Elijah Clarke's retreat from his failed siege of Augusta? [109] We should be able to bring him to justice as soon as we learn of his whereabouts."

"Nothing definite," DePeyster replied, concentrating on his own steak. "Any day though, I assume. They have pretty much scattered to the winds with all the hangings of their captured comrades that have taken place in Georgia. I have learned that the noose can be quite the tool."

Ferguson paused from his meal, looking at his second in command and said, "I find that hard to believe, Sir. I have given leave to a large number of our local troops, in hopes that by now, one of them would return with some good intelligence concerning his whereabouts."

"Well Sir," Allaire announced "it could be that we have news of his location just outside the door. Two buck skinners are here, and they say they have information that we will fine to be useful. Shall I have them brought in? They have handed over their weapons, and

---

[108] A quote from Lieutenant Allaire diary on 9-18-1780.

[109] This was the first of two sieges carried out by General Andrew Pickens and Colonel Clarke on the city of Augusta Georgia. The first was a failure. However, the second in 1781 was a success.

have been checked by the guards for your safety. Do you want to see them yourself or should I deal with them?"

"No, bring them in and let us hear what they have to say," Ferguson replied.

Allaire stood up, walked over to the door and said, "Bring them in." As he returned to his place at the table, James Crawford and Samuel Chambers entered the room. Ferguson watched as the two approached, and addressed Crawford, since Chambers was little more than a lad. "So, what is the purpose of your presence here today?"

"We have news you might find interesting," Crawford replied.

"From where?" asked Ferguson as he picked up his pewter cup. "Are you from Ninety- Six?"

"No, from over The Blue Ridge. We just came through Gillespie Gap."

Ferguson took a drink and said "So, you are here because of my proclamation. I suppose that you want to take the oath?"

"Not hardly sir" Replied Crawford nervously. "We are the King men for sure and we will take your oath if that is what you want. But that is not way we are here. We were in Colonel Sevier's militia."

"Never heard of him," Ferguson replied.

"Well Sir, I am not surprised that you have no knowledge of Colonel Sevier, but he certainly knows about you. If I may be so bold, knowing the caliber of man you are, it occurs to me that you would be more than willing to reward two such loyal servants of the King as us, with whatever bounty you see fit."

"What!" Ferguson roared as he came to his feet. "You demand payment for information while there are others here who freely give their allegiance, loyalty, time, and even their lives to stop this rebellion." Ferguson shouted, pounding his fist against the table. "Bounty, you say. I will give you the same bounty given to Clarke's men. A noose. Once you have swung, your young counterpart here will surely be willing to impart his information more freely."

"Oh, please sir, you misunderstand me." Crawford pleaded. "We have traveled many difficult miles to bring you this information out of our loyalty. The heart of the matter is that Colonel Sevier, along with Colonel Shelby, and Colonel McDowell are marching an Army of one thousand men to engage you at this very spot. Gilbert Town is to be their destination."

"Yes Sir, that they are," Chambers confirmed, "They should be at Quaker Meadows by now. For that is their last rendezvous. There they are to meet up with some Virginia Militia, we think."

"One thousand men only Fifteen miles away!" DePeyster exclaimed as he rushed to put on his hat. "They could be here by tomorrow night. Shall we make a stand from the top of the hill [110] where we are camped? The ground is high."

Ferguson again looked at Crawford and said, "Are you sure about that number?"

---

[110] This hill today is known as Ferguson's Hill. It is located in Rutherfordton North Carolina.

"Yes Sir. At least one thousand, could be more, for Ben Cleveland is said to be on the way here from the Yadkin River as well. Sir, I say this with all due respect, but they saw that proclamation of yours as an insult to their manhood. A piss on the back, so to speak. Men are mustering in daily out of anger. We thought it only prudent to bring this information to you."

Ferguson looked back at DePeyster and coolly said. "Send out riders to give the alarm to all on furlough to return as soon as possible. We will countermarch until we are at full force. Then we will give your Colonel Sevier his fame in the form of a sound defeat and a deep grave."

Chapter 105

Rousing Words

Rice was standing between Jack and Martin Grider with the butt of his rifle resting on the ground. His fingers locked around the curly maple stock of his gun, like all the other men standing around him. They were here at the Gap of South Mountain only sixteen miles away from Gilbert Town. Tomorrow they would meet the enemy. Confidence was high among the men. They, like Rice, had been in this situation many times in the past. Only brave men were here now, the cowardly had long since been weeded out of this crop. But they also knew that the same could be said of the Tory Army that they would face in the morning. Patrick Ferguson had earned his nickname as "The Bulldog" for a reason. And for that very reason Ole Roundabout had requested that the troops form a tightly knit circle around him. Not just his men, but every man of this newly formed army of the frontier was to stand at attention.

Benjamin Cleveland, being the large man that he was, slowly paced back and forth giving everyone the time that they needed to gain a spot in the circle once it was formed, and for the chatter to die down. Rice looked back over his shoulder to see David, Abe, and John Spelts [111] taking their places in the circle that was becoming six to eight men deep in places. Rice turned back to Cleveland, remembering his own wedding that Ben had performed. How he had asked for patience that day on account of his lack of speaking abilities to a large mass of people. How all of that had changed over the years.

Ben was joined by the other officers once the ring was formed. Colonels Campbell, Shelby, Sevier, and Joseph McDowell along with Major Joseph Winston, who had come down from Surry County with his men, were all present. Seeing that all was ready, Ben began to speak. His voice was loud and strong and carried well in the cool October night air.

"Now, my brave fellows, I have come to tell you the news. The enemy is at hand and we must up and at them. Now is the time for every man of you to do his country a priceless service. Such as shall lead your children to exault in the fact that their fathers were the conquerors of Ferguson. When the pinch comes, I shall be with you. But if any of you shrink from sharing in the battle and the glory, you now have the opportunity of backing out and leaving. You shall have a few minutes for considering the matter."

---

[111] John Spelts better known as "Continental Jack" was interviewed by Lyman Draper and if not for his testimony the King Mountain speeches would have never been recorded.

At that Ben placed his hands behind his back, and waited for an exit that he knew down deep would never come. As he stood there Major McDowell spoke a few words of his own. "Well, my good fellows what kind of a story will you, who back out, have to relate when you get home. Leaving your brave comrades to fight the battle and gain the victory?"

"You have all been informed of the offer," Shelby said stepping forward with his hands resting upon the butt of the pistol hanging from his belt." Those who desire to back out, step back three paces to the rear."

Rice stood proudly by, as not a man accepted the offer. He looked to the left and then to the right and saw no movement around the ring. With a rush of pride charging up inside of him he yelled out a cry of 'HAZZAH' at the top of his lungs, along with every other man in the army. Once the cheer had died down, Isaac Shelby spoke again. "I am heartily glad to see you, to a man, resolve to meet and fight your country's foes. When we encounter the enemy, don't wait for the word of command. Let each one of you be your own officer, and do the very best you can. Take every care you can of yourselves and availing yourselves of every advantage that chance may throw in your way. If in the woods, shelter yourselves and give them Indian play. Advance from tree to tree pressing the enemy and killing and disabling all you can. Your officer will shrink from no danger. They will be constantly with you and at the moment the enemy give way, be on the alert and strictly obey orders.

Ben again addressed the men with a few parting words. "We are to be ready to march in three hours. Prepare two meals for your haversacks. And once that is done and before our feet splash into Cain Creek, each of you shall receive a portion of rum." Once again another cheer rang out into the night air.

At that moment, fourteen miles South of Gilbert Town, along the waters of the Broad River, Patrick Ferguson had halted his countermarch at Denard's Ford. He was angry and bitterly disappointed at the speed of his furloughed men's return. So, in an effort to boost his numbers, he had taken his pen in hand and by lantern light he had begun to write, but after a few lines he wadded up the paper not satisfied with his first draft.

On seeing his difficulties, Virginia Paul walked up behind him and placed a hand on his shoulder. "What is the matter?" she asked.

"I struggle to find the best way to inspire these men to come back to camp. The reluctance they exhibit to return to their ranks is beyond my comprehension. They have to know that they are needed. What would motivate their swift return?"

"Their manhood," She replied. "The poor have little else to lose. And what is the greatest possession of all men? The woman by his side. Play upon that and the safety of their children and they should return in droves."

Pattie placed his arm around Virginia's hip and pulled her into his lap. "You my dear, are truly a treasure." And with her advice squarely embedded in his brain he began to write.

Denard's Ford, Broad River, Tryon County, October 3, 1780

Gentlemen, Unless you wish to be eat up by an inundation of barbarians, who have begun by murdering an unarmed son before the aged father, and afterwards lopped off his arms, [112] *and who by their shocking cruelties and irregularities, give the best proof of their cowardice and want of discipline; I say, if you wish to be pinioned, robbed, and murdered, and see your wives and daughters, in four days, abused by the dregs of mankind—in short, if you wish or deserve to live, and bear the name of men, grasp your arms in a moment and run to camp. The Back Water men have crossed the mountains; McDowell, Hampton* [113] *, Shelby and Cleveland are at their head, so that you know what you have to depend upon. If you choose to be degraded forever and ever by a set of mongrels, say so at once, and let your women turn their backs upon you, and look out for real men to protect them.*

PAT. FERGUSON, Major 71st Regiment

---

[112] In a letter to Lord Cornwallis' Ferguson attributed the "lopping off of arms" part of his proclamation to a band of men serving under Colonel Benjamin Cleveland.

[113] Colonel Andrew Hampton of the Rutherford County North Carolina Militia.

Chapter 106

Vengeance Will Run Rampant

Colonel William Campbell the new official commanding officer of The Over The Mountain Army, quickly demonstrated that he was indeed a wise choice for the job. Rather than march blindly off into the unknown, he was using his mounted men as scouts. With the majority of Ben Cleveland's men on horseback, Rice found himself in the scouting party that was to approach Gilbert Town. The scouting party had run into a few Whigs that had been in Gilbert Town within the past week. One old man had been extremely helpful. He had lost every chicken in his coop to those 'thieving bastards', as he put it, and according to his information, Ferguson had his men camped on top of a hill West of the town. Some town's people had even christened it Ferguson Hill. He, like many other people, had endured much hardship from the Loyalist, and was more than happy to tell all that they knew of Ferguson's whereabouts. From what Rice had gathered, he was sure that Ferguson always camped on high ground, a practice that would guarantee a difficult task ahead when taking Ferguson Hill.

Rice walked Liberty out of the waters of Cathy's Creek. Gilbert Town stood on a small eminence above the creek in the distance. He could see smoke coming from the cabins chimney tops. He pulled his horse to a stop as Jack and David rode up beside him, along with Captain Richard Allen.

"Gilbert Town," Rice said, nodding towards the village. "Kind of quiet though."

"That old man did say that his troops was stationed on top of that ridge somewhere," Allen reminded Rice, looking to the West. "Let us circle around that way and see what is afoot."

Rice put his horse into motion alongside the others. They followed the creek bank for about two miles. There, they turned and rode up the hill. The landscape was well wooded, and they could only see a few hundred feet ahead of them as they rode along through the woods. Suddenly, the foul scent of rot hung very strong in the air, and they soon found the source of the stench. Four or five carcasses of butchered cattle, still lying where they had been killed, to feed Ferguson's troops. Rice and the others knew that their campsite had to be close by. Continuing on, they found a small meadow that had had every blade of grass eaten away. This was obviously where the horses had been kept. Beyond the well worn meadow was the empty campsite. Fire pits were dug all around the grounds, with blackened ash and the remnants of unburned logs still in the pits.

"Damnation!" parted Allen's lips as he gazed down into the village below. "The fox has left its den. Where the hell are they?"

That being said, Allen kicked his horse's sides and rode down the hill into Gilbert Town. At his approach, he was meet by a small party of the town's residents with the news that Ferguson was, indeed, long gone, for two full days now. All that was left of his men was one soldier, guarding over the wounded Major Dunlap, inside the Gilbert cabin. Rice, along with Captain Allen was disappointed, but knew that the chase was just beginning. Colonel Campbell needed to be told of the current situation, so the scouts turned back North in full gallop, to relay the news of Gilbert Town's evacuation. But, as chance would have it, at Cane Creek they met a Whig party just in from South Carolina being led by a Captain Gillispie. Gillispie had not seen Ferguson on his retreat but was willing to join up with the Over the Mountain Men once he was told of Dunlap being wounded and still laid up in Gilbert Town. He and Captain Allen agreed that Gillispie would ride back to Gilbert Town and there secure Dunlap, while Allen continued on to Colonel Campbell with the news. Rice and the others gave Gillispie not a second thought as they rode away.

A few hours later, Sarah Gilbert was outside her home, drawing a pail of water from her well when Captain Gillispie rode up.

From his horse, he politely removed his hat and said. "Mrs. Gilbert, I presume. I understand that Major Dunlap is under your good care."

"He is," she replied, nodding her head.

"May I speak with him?" Gillispie asked, holding up a black leather dispatch case. "I am in possession of his new orders from Major Ferguson.

"Of Course, you may. Go on inside he is on the second floor still abed I am afraid."

"His Guard?" Gillispie asked as he dismounted.

"Just inside the door," she replied again.

Gillispie coolly walked across the yard followed by his men and entered the cabin. Once inside he saw the lone guard standing at his post at the bottom of the staircase. Their eyes met, and even though they both were in the Militia, and dressed very much the same, the Tory instinctively knew that a group of Whigs had just entered the room. As the only sentry left behind, and with no sure knowledge of the identity of the man before him, he hesitated, and gave no resistance as Gillispie walked up the first few steps. It was a mistake the guard would have little time to regret, for before the captain had reached the top step, two of his men had cut the guard's throat and was dragging him out the back door.

Gillispie entered Dunlap's room, to see the Major setting up in bed, bare chested. His crutches leaned against the cabin wall, with his green Queen Rangers coat hanging on his bedpost.

"Where is Mary McRea?" Gillispie asked in a tone so low it was almost a whisper.

"In heaven." Dunlap replied coldly.

Gillispie stood there without a word, looking down at Dunlap. His eyes narrowed, as a lump built in his chest, pressing down hard upon his heart. He nodded his head a few times, and without breaking eye contact he pulled his pistol from his belt and shot Dunlap [114] in the chest. He turned and walked out of the cabin. He sat atop his horse, watching as his men threw the body of the dead guard into a nearby fire pit. Once they all were remounted, he rode out of Gilbert Town having just revenged the death of his missing fiancée.

---

[114] James Dunlap was a very hard man to kill it seems. This Captain Gillispie whose given name we do not know, rode away believing he had killed the murderer of his fiancee. However, Dunlap survived the shooting and was smuggled out of Gilbert Town before the Over The Mountain Men could arrive. Dunlap would go on to fight in the Ninety-Six district of South Carolina the following year. He would be shot again in what is current day Abbeville County, at the Battle of Beattie's Mill on March 23, 1781. Oddly, once again being wounded, he was again returned to Gilbert Town as a POW. While there another Whig learned of his presence and with the help of another shooter charged into Dunlap's room and shot him while in bed. You would think this would have ended his life. However according to a witness, Captain Daniel Cozens, a fellow POW, Dunlap again survived. His fellow prisoners tended to his wounds and within a few hours Dunlap was again consciousness but in agony. The following day a Whig by the name of Arthur Cobb came into the room and on seeing a live James Dunlap, pulled his pistol and shot him in the head finally putting him out of his misery. According to Cozen the Whig/ Major Evan Shelby was receiving treatment inside the same hospital as Dunlap, but never lifted a finger to help the Queen's Ranger in any of these shootings.

Chapter 107

The Game Of Cat And Mouse

John McFall was lying on the bank of the Broad River about twenty-five miles East of Denard's Ford. It was a dark night and a heavy dew had fallen on his backside as he was sprawled out on the ground. He and his two brothers, George and Arthur were waiting in ambush like the rest of Ferguson's men. But in his eyes, they were waiting for the wrong army.

"Who in the hell put that Colonel Clarke burr under Pattie's ass?" He asked Arthur. "We had the high ground at Gilbert Town and what did we do? Turned ass and ran, that's what."

"It's a game of cat and mouse," Arthur said, trying to console his hot-headed brother. "Ferguson is just be systematic. First Clarke and his boys, then our old friend Ben Cleveland."

"Well I would have rather have it the other way around!" John barked. "Once Rice Medairs is six feet under, the happier I will be. They would have never made it up that hill, if Pattie would have had the guts to stand our ground" We could be back home at Paw's old place by now".

"Even if you are right about that, you cannot say with any certainty, whether Rice is with Cleveland or not," Arthur reasoned.

"Oh Hell, yes he is! Those two are as thick as thieves" John replied. What do you say about it George?"

"Oh aye, they are out there all right. And you can bet that son of a bitch Jack is with them as well" George agreed.

John raised his head and drew a long breath of air into his nostrils. "Smell that foulness? It is Medaris for sure," he said

after he exhaled. The three began to laugh together, and a rare occasion it was, for most of the time they were at each other's throats.

"Shut your mouths." Lt. Allaire said as he crawled up between the brothers. "Talking while waiting in ambush could get the three of you a flogging," he whispered. "If someone other than you had acted in such a senseless manner, and had not performed as well as you three have, I would take a pound of flesh from them myself. Enjoy God's canopy that is overhead tonight. Tomorrow will be here soon enough."

John McFall spent the rest of the night on the cold damp ground, shivering and cursing Patrick Ferguson under his breath. For when the sun rose and drew high overhead, not a single Rebel had passed before the Loyalist. "A day and a half wasted," McFall grumbled.

Colonel William Campbell was also playing a game of cat and mouse. He could not let the fact that Ferguson was now aware of his pursuit put a damper on the hopes of his frontier army. Gilbert Town was soon left behind for that very reason. He, like Ferguson, had crossed the Broad River at Denard's Ford, but not being satisfied, had pushed on to the Green River ford. Here, he and the other commanders held another council of war. In order to play the game well, it was decided that two major decisions needed to be made. The first and the most difficult was to guess the route that Patrick Ferguson would take on his retreat. As Isaac Shelby saw it Ferguson, had two options. Either head South and make a run for Fort Ninety-Six or go North to meet up with Lord Cornwallis in Charlottetown. Ninety-Six would be the best bet if Ferguson was concerned about his back-water foes. The roads would be easier to travel. The inhabitants had more Tory leanings, and the star-shaped fort at Ninety-Six was thought to be impregnable. There he would also have the help of Lt. Colonel John Cruger's militia. But Shelby also knew that Ferguson was stubborn, and that no British Officer preferred to run when they could stand and fight. While still in Gilbert Town, it was made obvious to Colonel Campbell by the locals, that Ferguson

still had hopes of catching Clarke and his Georgia Militia. This would also point towards Ferguson heading for Ninety-Six. On the other hand, Ferguson could be heading North to rendezvous with Lord Cornwallis. Together they could turn West and fight Campbell's army. But Colonel Sevier was under the impression that Cornwallis was eyeing the new Continental commander, General Greene who was soon to take over command from General Gates. Shelby had pointed out that Cornwallis could still send aide to Ferguson, simply by reinforcing him with someone like Bloody Ban Tarleton. Earlier in the evening a courier by the name of Lacey had ridden into camp. He claimed to be a Whig from Colonel William Hill's dragoons, who were some twenty miles away. His news was that Ferguson was moving East, away from Ninety-Six. But, was he to be trusted? He claimed to have been at the battle of Hanging Rock, and that somebody here had surely seen him there. He eventually won some trust with his argument, but not from everyone. In the end, after all debates, Campbell decided to head for the Cowpens in South Carolina. Colonel James Williams was to join the army there with his four hundred South Carolinians. The Cowpens was close enough to the two Carolina borders, so if the mountain men needed to shift to the North it could still be done from there.

The second decision that needed to be made, was whether or not to leave the men on foot behind, here at the ford. They were slowing down the chase, however Campbell decided that, for the time being, they would continue on with the march, at least to the Cowpens.

Chapter 108

LIES CAN BE A TOOL

Joseph Kerr looked back over his shoulder as he tied his horse's reins around a small ash tree on the bank of King's Creek. He reached down and picked up a hand full of dry dust from under the ash and rubbed it into his hands. Once again, taking a handful

of the dirt, he soiled his arms and neck. When he was finished, he felt that his dirty skin matched up well with his hole ridden, drop front breeches and the completely worn out waistcoat that he was wearing. His desired look of a beggar was completed with torn stockings and a buckle missing from his right shoe. It being worn on his good foot. He laughed to himself as he pulled a crutch from a sack hanging over the rump of his mount. He placed the top of the crutch under his armpit and hobbled into the loyalist friendly plantation of Peter Quinn.

Patrick Ferguson had halted his countermarch from the Tate Plantation to Peter Quinn's this morning, and in doing so, gave the patriot spy the perfect opportunity to evaluate Ferguson's numbers. Kerr made good use of the split rail fence that bordered the lane of the plantation as he made his way into camp. He would stop and rest every few feet the closer that he got to the two sentries standing guard at the picket line.

"You are the King's men are you not?" he called out as he propped himself up against the fence, as if the life was drained from his weak body.

"Of course, we are!" was the reply Arthur McFall gave.

"Praise the Lord! I do not think that I could withstand another run in with those damned, treacherous, scallywags of Cleveland's" Joseph lied. "Those bastards have robbed me blind. And a man in my station in life as little to take, I can well testify."

"Cleveland's men you say?" John McFall asked angrily. "Where and when did you see them?"

"At Quaker Meadows about a week ago" Joseph lied again. "Said they were going to stay there for some time.

They took my horse and all of my vittles as well. Could I possibly get some food? My belly button is rubbing a hole in my backbone. It's been a few days since any meat has gone down this gullet"

"I don't see why not," Arthur answered."

"That can wait," John interrupted. "Rice Medaris. You ever heard of him?"

"Ever heard of him? He was the one who stole my shoe," Joseph replied, pointing to his twisted foot. "What kind of a man would steal one shoe and the buckle off the other? He said, that I did not need it because I cannot put any weight on it in the first place. I tell you what. My feet get cold at night just like the next man's does. Told him as much, but you see what effect it had on the thief. None whatsoever."

"You do not have to tell me about that man," John replied "He burned out my father a few years ago."

"Not surprising," Joseph said having found his way into the Loyalist's good graces. Kerr was looking for a way to win the trust of one of Ferguson's men, and John's hatred for Rice appeared to be Kerr's way in. He made up lie after lie to keep John appeased as they walked through the camp. And when John was not cussing Rice, Joseph was counting heads and horses. He got a good idea of how much food they had on hand from one of Ferguson's mistresses, who had taken pity on him after John had finally tired of Joseph company. But best of all, Virginia Sal had told him to not to worry, that Pattie had been in correspondence with Lord Cornwallis and he was sure that Cornwallis would send more troops within the week, four hundred in number. Maybe even Tarleton's Dragoons. Plus, he had also sent a dispatch to the star fort at Ninety-Six with a request for more men from Lt. Colonel Cruger. While his information was all well and good, Kerr felt that the Whig commanders that were heading for the Cowpens already had a good handle on the size of Ferguson's Army, and how full his baggage wagons were. The one thing that they were lacking, and needed to know, was where Ferguson was heading next. Luckily for him, young Virginia Sal also revealed that secret in her efforts to calm this poor misfortunate, who was terrified at the thought of falling into Whig hands again. Ferguson had been told of a wooded plateau nearby, called by the locals, as King's Mountain. There, from its top, Pattie was going to wait for his reinforcements. Once they arrived, he would march to meet the Backwater men on a field of battle of his choosing. With that victory, Virginia told her dirty friend, the rebellion in the West would be crushed, and all those loyal to the crown would once again have the upper hand.

"Fear not" She had told him "The reckoning is coming."

Later that night, when most were asleep, Joseph Kerr slowly hobbled out of camp. Once he had made his way past the outer pickets, the speed of his pace quickened. As soon as he was mounted, he was off to the Cowpens, with news that could very well change the outcome of the war.

Chapter 109

At The Cowpens

It was at nine o'clock when Rice reached up and grabbed the horn of his saddle and pulled himself up onto Liberty's back. He looked out over the dark pasture, that had become known as the Cowpens. It was owned was a Tory named Hiram Saunders. The field was abuzz with movement, as it had been all afternoon. Campfires were glowing in the night as if they were lightening bugs illuminating the sky. The Over the Mountain Army had grown to around fourteen hundred men. Fourteen hundred tired and hungry men. But now, they all had full stomachs instead of empty ones, thanks to Saunders.

This morning Saunders had been pulled from his bed after being awakened by a hard slap to the side of his head. He had been questioned by Colonel Campbell as to whether or not Ferguson had been this way in the last few days. Saunders was quick to answer any questions that were asked. He had little choice in the matter, because if he was slow in answering another slap was swiftly administered. He had said that he had not seen Ferguson, nor did he have any idea as to his whereabouts. He had even gone so far as to say that if the Whigs could fine one track of a loyalist horse's hoof, then Colonel Cleveland could burn his house down around his ears. Ben had made no promises that he would not do just that. However, he did mention that twenty-five to fifty head of beef donated to the cause of liberty, would go a long way in keeping his home from going up in flames. Saunders, being in the cattle business, was always fattening his beef with grain. That meant fields of corn were nearby and would furnish a good food source for the Mountaineer's horses who were becoming very lean. Tonight, had been something of a feast, thanks to Saunders newly found Whig enthusiasm.

Rice looked over at Jack who was pulling the last strip of meat from the wooden stake that had held the meat over the flames while it was cooking.

"Is that the last of our supper?" Rice asked,

"It is." Jack replied not taking his eyes off of the prize.

"Well, I hope it burns your mouth then," Rice teased.

Jack laughed as he mounted Ringtail, happily chewing away on his last mouthful. Once squarely on his mount Jack said, "May as well enjoy it. Who known, it could very well be my last. You know as well as I do, some of us ain't coming back."

Rice nodded his head, and looked at all of the men standing around on foot. "I sure do wish that all of these boys were coming with us. But Shelby is right. Not all of these horses are in good enough shape to continue. Ben said that we are down to nine hundred good mounts. It truly is a shame that we did not get to them at Gilbert

Town when we were at full force. But they should catch up to us tomorrow evening."

"Yes," Jack replied "But if Young Kerr's information is correct, we are only thirty miles or so away from the prize. One night's ride away from the McFall's and perhaps an ending to their sorry lives."

"Hopefully," Rice answered, looking up at the fading stars in the West. "But we both know that this is a much bigger issue than just them. Life, liberty, prosperity, and even the fates of our children and families depend on this issue. If we are to be men, how can we not respond to such a threat as the Scotsman's?"

"I know" Jack replied smiling "I too have a wife at home, as well as a new country to be won. Imagine that! A new country. But why not let the McFall's be the gravy on tomorrow's work?"

"Indeed." Rice said still looking at the western sky. "Do you think that the good Lord would think less of us if we prayed for that rain to hold off? I mean to ask for a prayer so that we can kill our fellow man?"

"He has his plans for us already set, I imagine. Maybe a rain will hurt them more than us. But it sure would not hurt to have the Lord's blessing. Pray for our safety instead," Jack said, also looking at the sky.

"I cannot see too many stars up there, with all of the cloud cover. Yes, it's going to rain on our heads for sure tonight. Let's keep Mrs. Mary Patton's powder [115] dry a few more hours, 'eh brother."

Chapter 110

The Battle Of King's Mountain

It had been raining outside of Patrick Ferguson's tent for most of the night. It was still raining this morning as he stood just outside of the tent's open flap at the top of King's Mountain. His mood was as dark as the sky overhead. He had been waiting for days now, for a reply from Lord Cornwallis. Ferguson had sent a dispatch addressed to his lordship, who was still only fifty miles away in Charlottetown. It was plain enough to relay the situation. "I am on my march toward you, by a road leading from Cherokee Ford, North of Kings Mountain." Ferguson had written "Three or four hundred good

---

[115] Mary McKeehan Patton 1751-1836 was a gunpowder manufacturer. She had learned her trade from her father while living in Pennsylvania. After she married she and her husband went into the business. Her powder mill was on the waters of Powder Creek in what is now Carter County Tennessee. She provided 500 Lbs. of gunpowder for the Over The Mountain Men.

soldiers, part dragoons, would finish the business. Something must be done soon. This is their last push in this quarter, and they are extremely desolate and cowed."

Once Ferguson had laid eyes upon the six-hundred-yard long ridge, he was sure that this would be the place to wait for reinforcements. In the meantime, he would defend the high ground. He saw no need to build any defensive works. The slope running up King's Mountain was well wooded, and in addition, it was well endowed with rock formations. He felt these natural defenses were adequate. He did have the baggage train brought up to the top of the summit, where they were placed in a circular formation around the campsite as a barricade. In addition, he had a picket line set up a quarter of a mile out from the foot of the ridge. Pattie was very confident that he could withstand any assault that the Backwater dregs could muster. If they were foolish enough to attack this strong position, he was sure one volley and a bayonet charge would win the day. Cold steel always won when it came to disobedient rebels, who were without a point at the end of their rifles. Ferguson's confidence was confirmed to Cornwallis in his message the day before. "I have arrived today at Kings Mountain. I have taken a post, from where I do not think I can be forced by a stronger army than the one that is against us."

Yet, as confident as he was, he could not understand why his Lordship was so slow in responding to his request for more men [116]. He had said as much to Virginia Paul the night before. Cornwallis had

---

[116] What Ferguson did not know, was that at the time both Lord Cornwallis and Banastre Tarleton were sick Cornwallis with a bad fall cold, Tarleton with a high fever. Both were neglecting their duties due to their illnesses.

been cold to Ferguson in the past, but he was sure that the needs of the campaign would outweigh any animosity Cornwallis held for him now. Virginia had her doubts about that, but Pattie was quick to cut her off on the matter. He may not be one of his Lordship's favorites, but he was a British office in need. Cornwallis would surely come through in the end. Yet, deep in his heart Ferguson knew, that if he had not been denied the use of his breach loading rifles, he would not have needed to be reinforced in the first place. Its design may have been expensive, but it would save on manpower, and thus it's expense would be less of an issue. The topic was still a great source of aggravation to him.

Virginia walked to the tent opening, and looked out at Ferguson as he stood in the light drizzle, lost in his thoughts. "Standing in the rain will not make it stop or your reinforcements arrive any quicker," She said holding out his red and white checkered frock coat.

"What does that mean?" he snapped. "Do I sense sarcasm in your tone?"

"Maybe," She replied "You know how I feel about our predicament. Why not break camp and march on to CharlotteTown?"

Pattie wheeled about, with gritted teeth and blazing eyes that told her that he was not going to stand for such talk. "It will be a sorry state in Denmark when a British officer takes advice from a lowly whore, such as yourself!" he announced cruelly.

"What? Is that how you see me after all of this time?" she cried. "Year after year of devotion. All of the nursing of your wounds. Following you from one campaign to another. Living in huts and out of wagons, not to mention wet tents. That is how you see me? Never mind my putting up with that other woman, who is fast asleep in the back of that wagon, while I am here, trying to help you."

Ferguson stepped forward and placed one hand over her mouth roughly, while the other gripped the back side of her head, stopping her from speaking. "Virginia, you are a tart. And even a tart as lovely as you, must know that becoming my wife is nothing more than a fantasy for someone in your station. I told you as much from the beginning. If matrimony is what you desire I suggest that you find it elsewhere. Once back on the coast we will end this arrangement, if not sooner." He jerked the coat out of her hand and spun her around. He unclasped the pearl necklace from around her neck and put it in his vest pocket to officially end their relationship. He then walked away to meet with his second in command, Captain DePeyster without a backwards glance.

Across the ridgetop, a smile parted the lips of John McFall as he watched Ferguson's dispute with one of his ladies. He could hear the sound of their arguing voices, but he could not make out the words from such a distance.

'Serves him right. Flaunting about two women such as that', McFall thought to himself. 'Maybe the Bulldog is not quite the cock-of-the-walk that he led everyone to believe.'

Feeling malicious joy at Ferguson's expense, McFall turned his attention to a young girl of fifteen or so, who had just entered camp. His thieving eyes fell on a basket handle laying in the crook of her arm. Tucked down under a blue cloth on top of the basket was what had to be fried chicken from the way it smelled. "What do you have there, young lady?" he asked as she walked by?

"A meal of chicken for a gallant officer of the King," she replied smiling.

"Captain John McFall, at your service," He replied, stepping out from under his lean to hut with hat in hand, then to her surprise, he abruptly pulled the basket off her arm.

"I was told that an officer would pay for such a meal!" she said as he sat back down under his hut.

"Were you, now?" McFall said, just before taking his first bite of the chicken's thigh. "Perhaps from Cleveland's buffoons, but not in this army."

Eight miles away at Solomon Beason's homestead Rice was off his horse. His legs were sore and his back was tight from so many long cold hours in the saddle. He was walking around Liberty in an effort to loosen up his aching muscles, and to warm himself in the process. He looked at his equally worn out horse who was still wet from the rain. Rice was becoming concerned about the condition of

Liberty's forelock as well. He had wrapped his rifle with an oiled cloth early in the night. Now he was wrapping over it with an old hunting shirt to keep the rain out. Early this morning, as

the sun was coming up, the frontier army again crossed the Broad River at Cherokee Ford. River crossings were always a tough task when it came to keeping rifles dry. One misstep of your horse and you were dunked underwater with a rifle that would not fire for hours. Still, somehow not a single rider took a plunge, which was quite a credit to the army's horseflesh. The horses had to have been wearing down after such a long ride, but you would have never known it by the way they crossed the river's rising waters. Once everyone was across Colonels Campbell, Sevier and even Ben, could see that a heavy toll was showing on the mounts and riders alike. Perhaps a halt to the march would be smart, at least an hour or so. However, Isaac Shelby would have none of that. "I will not stop until nightfall, if I have to follow Ferguson into Cornwallis's very lines!" he roared. So the pursuit carried on to Beason front door.

Rice could see fear in Beason eyes as the long, rain-soaked line of determined frontiersmen surrounded his home. Ben walked up to Beason's barn door and looked inside, seeing no livestock. He walked over to where Beason now walked among the mass of men on his farm.

"Well Sir, either you have been robbed by Ferguson, or you have donated to the crown's cause," Ben said looking at Beason. "Which is it?"

"Neither one," he answered. "Once I learned of his presence, I had my boys take them off into the woods and out of harm's way."

"So, we are close to catching the Scott!" Ben exclaimed. But, before you tell us what you know, I want to tell you something. I know what you are. I have hanged many a sour lot over the last few years who clung to the King when they should not have. And every now and then your name would come up as a sympathizer to the crown. On other occasions, you have been said to be a rebel like us. You blow about like the wind. You are not a Whig, you are not a Tory. Whoever has the upper hand at the moment has your

allegiance. Well today you are falling off that fence, one way or the other. If you steer us wrong in what you are about to say, I will ride back here, and have you hanged inside that very barn. Now back to my question: Where is Ferguson?"

Beason looked to the East and said "That way, no more the eight miles away. You can count on my honesty and patriotism today."

Jack looked at Rice, and with a satisfied smile on his tired face, he said. "If that man has ever told the truth, it was today. I believe that the threat of Ben's noose can get more of the truth out of a man, than having him place a hand on the bible."

"I believe so," Rice replied as he pulled himself back into his saddle. 'Seeing one's end can deliver some clarity, even from a Tory."

Once the horses were back in motion the conversation ended. The pace of the ride was a fast gate. The road between the Cowpens and Charlottetown was in good condition considering that it was muddy. Every rider was pushing his horse to the limit. Rice admired all of the horses among his ranks, but Roebuck, Ben's mount was carrying the largest man in all of this army. To the horse's credit he matched step for step with every other horse in the chase. With all urgency, The Over The Mountain Men rode up on another homestead. Rice watched as Colonel Campbell interrogated the Tory owner. The man was reluctant with his responses. It was obvious that he was not eager to relay any useful information. He would shake his head, no while raising the palms of his hands with every denial. Feeling that he was just wasting time, Colonel Campbell returned to the road. There, just outside of the entrance to the Tory's lane, Campbell encountered the young lady that had lost her fried chicken to McFall earlier in the day. She was most likely the daughter of the uncooperative Tory he had just spoken to. She looked at Campbell and asked "How many are there of you?"

"Enough to whip Ferguson if we can find him," Campbell boasted.

She stood there for a moment as if she was in deep thought. Campbell looked down at her from his saddle as she was pondering what to say, if anything. She looked up at him as if she was about to speak, but she hesitated in uncertainty. Campbell gave her a pleading glance that he hoped would appeal to her. Remembering how rudely McFall had treated her, she turned and pointed to Little Kings Mountain and said "He is on that hill."

Campbell nodded his head, raised his hand, and tipped his hat. "Thank you my dear," he addressed her, and rode away.

Virginia Paul was so furious at Pattie that she still could not face him. She was not even sure that she wanted to after his cruel and crude comments. Even the fact that the sun had finally broken through the day's gloom, could not lift her spirits. After her early morning argument with him, she had walked off the ridgetop during a downpour. Her straw hat did little to keep her head dry. She made her way down to Kings Creek and took some shelter from the rain under a large chestnut tree to gather her thoughts. She and Pattie had spoken harshly to one another in the past, but this time was different. It had cut deep into her soul, and for the first time she felt that he truly was about to end their relationship. Strangely, for some reason she did not really mind if that was to be her fate with him. Charlottetown was not that far away. If need to be, that was as good a place to start anew as anywhere else she supposed. Why reconcile with a man who saw her as a tart? She knew that he would soon be returning to his tent. She would make her way back up to the top of King's Mountain and see if he had cooled any in her absence. If he had, perhaps all could return to normal. If not, then goodbye it would be. It was not as though she loved him. She knew that her life would go on either way. The golden ring, that she had long chased after, was losing it shine.

It was a little before three o'clock in the afternoon when Rice took a torn piece of white paper and tucked it into his hat. This was to distinguish friend from foe in the coming battle. The Tories on top of the King's Mountain usually wore evergreen twigs in their headgear. They would have only a few in uniform as well. It would be a subtle distinction between men dressed very much in the same manner, but on opposite sides of the battle. Rice looked around at the serious men standing beside him with pride. Jack was picking at the touch hole of his rifle, having twice already done so to Rice's. Martin and Val Grider were standing together with heads bowed in prayer. Abe Baker and Robert Bedwell were sharing a canteen of rum, telling tall tales between long tugs at the canteen's spout. David was pulling a cleaning cloth from the barrel of his rifle, laughing with Abe and Robert. Rice realized he was seeing a man standing were a young boy had stood at the beginning of the war. There were hundreds of stories being played out here. Every man had his own reason for his presence here. Martin Davenport, like Rice, had a hatred for the McFall's. Three brothers[117] by the surname of Benge, were here as patriots, but also looking for their half-brother Bob, who had grown up as a Cherokee. John Adair[118] was here for no other reason than that he hated all things British. John Crockett[119] was here to avenge the death of his father who was killed in a British backed attack by Dragging

[117] David 1760-1854, Obadiah 1763-1846 and William Benge? -1780. William would die at the battle of Kings Mountain.

[118] John Adair 1757-1840. Already a veteran of the battles of Williamson's Plantation, Rocky Mount and Hanging Rock. He would go on to fight at the Cowpens and Eutaw Springs among other battles. He would become a governor of Kentucky and a General in the War of 1812 playing a major role at the battle of New Orleans. He and Andrew Jackson almost had a duel over the reports that Jackson made after the battle, downplaying Adair's Kentuckians who performed well in the center of the American lines.

[119] John Crockett 1753 -1834 was the father of Davy Crockett of the Alamo fame.

Canoe. Rice had a love for all of his fellow militiamen, and it was not just Colonel Cleveland's men either, it was for the whole army. It was a growing bond that he could not deny. His heart was already aching for the men who would surely die in the coming hours. That would make the outcome of this battle even more significant. They would not die in vain if the battle was won, and he like all the men around him, was willing to die if his death would insure that victory.

In all reality, the battle had already begun. Colonel Shelby had handpicked a small but well-seasoned party of woodsmen to sneak up on Ferguson's outer picket. They moved so well through the woods that they were able to kill and capture the entire picket line without firing a single shot. Ferguson still had no clue of the pressing danger just down the hill from him.

As Rice pulled his knife and began to push it's point over his whetstone to keep its edge in good order, he heard the familiar voice of Ole Roundabout, encouraging the men. He was telling them the plan of action that was about to unfold. "My brave boys," He said "The bear as fallen into our trap, and he is so blind that he still doesn't know it. Our plan is a simple one. We have enough men to completely surround the mountain that stands before us. We are to simultaneously charge up that hill, and put an end to all of Ferguson's vile threats for all times."

He walked over to Rice, and placed a hand on his back. He looked down at the ground and pressed down on a pile of golden tree leaves. They made no sound as he pushed all of his great weight upon them. "It was a damned rain last night, but it is a God send today, 'eh Rice?"

"Yes, Sir" Rice replied "They will never hear us coming. At least, until we fire that first volley I pray. What is the order of battle Colonel?"

Ben pointed ahead and said "See that split in the road. It encircles the whole ridge. There, we are to split our forces into two wings. We are to stay on this side, going all the way down to the ridge's end. Shelby is to attack this end, with William Candler, Ben Roebuck and James Hawthorn's boys between us and Shelby. On our other flank will be the Lincoln County Militia, led by Lt. Colonel Frederick Hambright. On the Eastern side, Sevier, Campbell, McDowell and Winston will complete the circle around

the Tories". Upon completion of his orders, Ben pulled himself up onto Roebuck's back and ordered his men into motion.

Back on top of Kings Mountain, Patrick Ferguson was engaged in the everyday duties of a commanding officer. He had spoken to his surgeon, Dr. Uzal Johnson about the condition of his men, and he was also waiting for a report from his outward pickets that was overdue. Captain Abraham DePeyster had been taking an inventory of the baggage wagons, with the help of Arthur McFall. He was about to report his finding when he heard the yells of Isaac Shelby's men charging up the hill. He turned to Ferguson and said, "Those sounds are ominous. Those are the damned, yelling boys from The Battle of Musgrove Mill!"

John and George McFall each grabbed a musket, as the Loyalist drummer began to beat out the call to arms. As they cleared their lean-to on the North ridge, John looked at his brother, as he was fixing his bayonet and said ,"By God, our day of reckoning is finally at hand. I do pray that is fat assed Ben Cleveland coming up that ridge to meet his death. What in the hell are they thinking, attacking us while we are holding the high ground? They are doomed for sure. Ignorant bastards. We will decimate them and have the run of the country." The confident McFalls took their place inside a firing line that was being organized by Lt. Allaire. They held their fire until Allaire gave the order from atop of his horse. Smoke filled the air as the volley was sent flying down the hillside. John was enjoying the thought of his round slamming into a charging Whig's chest. As he was reloading his rifle,he fervently wished it would be Rice's. His wild laughs were evident to the fact.

Shelby's men fell to the ground or took to the nearest trees when the volley was heard. They regained their footing and continued on up the steep hillside not having a man among them hit. Many were about to return fire but Shelby ordered for them to hold off. "Not yet," He yelled. "Press on to your places and your fire will not be wasted." His men did as they were told as another volley came flying down from the top. The second effort by Allaire's line was again high.

This time the patriots returned fire. John McFall lost his smile as a fellow Yadkin Valley Tory, fell on the far side of George. His name was Branson[120] and he had received a ball in the thigh.

Ferguson, like Allaire had mounted his horse. Hearing the patriot's fire in mass, he knew they were now vulnerable to the bayonet charge. Their grooved rifle barrel dictated being slower to reload. He reached for his silver whistle that always hung from around his neck. He placed it in his mouth and blow out the signal that ordered the charge for his men to descend the hill. Ferguson watched as his men cried out "Huzzah" and ran down the hill in one mass to put the blade to the rebels. Out of the corner of his eye, Pattie saw Virginia making her return to camp. She was running up the hill holding the hems of her skirt and shift in her hand as she ran. As she made a leaping dive under one of the baggage wagons to safety, he thought to himself. 'What a magnificent woman. If only she had breading." With that in mind, he made his way down the hill behind his men.

On the opposite side of Kings Mountain, directly across from Shelby's position, Colonel Campbell had already put his men into motion with a cry of "Here they are, my brave boys. Shoot like hell and fight like devils." With that said, they took off up the hillside to commence the fighting. Their war cries gained the attention of DePeyster. He wheeled about, with a company of New Jersey Loyalist, to defend the other side of Kings Mountain.

---

[120]   Branson was not killed by the shot. That night he would lay on the battlefield where he was found by his brother-in-law, Captain James Withrow who was a Patriot. Branson begged for help only to have Withrow to walk away and say "Look to your friends for help".

Back on Colonel Shelby's side of the battle, his men where reloading when they saw the approaching bayonet charge being led by Allaire. They quickly gave way and began to retreat back down the mountainside. John took great pride in the sight of so many Whigs turning en masse. "Run! Like the cowards you are," he yelled as Allaire rode by in full gallop. He had drawn his sword, and was chasing down one of the rebels who was slow of foot. With one slash of Allaire's sword, the rebel was decapitated. He pulled his horse to a stop, and turned back to his men, trotting his mount over the lifeless corpse of his victim. Ferguson was pleased with the results of the charge. He ordered his men to turn back to the crest of the hill, and prepare for another Whig assault, providing there were enough of them left to mount one. The high ground was his ground, and he was not going to relinquish it.

Colonel Cleveland was still leading his men to the far side of the mountain, and Rice could hear the sounds of the battle in the distance. He looked at Jack with great frustration on his face. They, and all of Ben's other men, were bogged down in a wetland at the base of the mountain. The day's early morning rains had made the ground very swampy. The horses were balking in the mud, and the men had dismounted to pull them along. Rice's feet were sinking down into mud up over his ankles with every step. Pulling himself from the mud was a big enough chore in itself, without the added effort to keep Liberty moving ahead. David had even gotten stuck at one point due of the mud's suction. It took a helping hand from Rice to free him from the gritty mud. "Damn it to hell, it will be over before we get there!" yelled Martin Grider to his brother Val, as they all heard another series of gunfire come from the battlefield. Colonel Shelby would not yield the field to one mere threat of the bayonet. The gunfire that Rice and the others heard was Colonel Shelby, leading his men back up the hill. His words were "Now boys, quickly reload your rifles and let us advance upon them and give them another hail of fire." Ferguson would indeed have to defend the hill again.

Virginia, still under the baggage wagon, ducked her head as she heard several rounds of Rebel fire slam into the top of the wagon's wooden slats. Knowing that she was now in a more vulnerable position than before, she again took to her heels. She made the twenty-yard dash to Pattie's tent unscathed. There, she found a panic-stricken Virginia Sal. She was clinging to one of Pattie's muskets in a complete state of hysteria. She was pacing the tent in pure panic. Virginia pulled her rival to the ground as a ball passed through the tent fabric, just a few feet away from where she stood.

"Come on," she cried we cannot stay here any longer. Drop that gun and come down the hill with me. I doubt they will shoot two fleeing women if we are unarmed."

"No!" Sal retorted. "I am not leaving Pattie. You may run out on him, but I will not. This is my chance to prove my worth to him."

"Well, you can stay here and die if you wish, but I am going down this hill to safety." Virginia announced as she peered out of the tent's flap. She could see John McFall running to the opposite side of the ridge top. He was drawing little to no fire as he ran, so Virginia followed after him at a dead run. As she was running away, she heard the other Virginia call to her from the rear to stop and come back. Virginia looked back over her shoulder while hunching down low to see Sal dart from the tent with the musket still in hand. She made only four steps until a shot struck her back and tore through her breast on the other side of her body. Virginia turned away, feeling pity for Sal for the first time since the two had met. Virginia continued on downhill, making a sharp turn in her escape route, and entered the trees in a full-out run.

Rice tied Liberty's reins around a young sapling, having finally made his way through the swamp. Its sticky mud had cost them fifteen valuable minutes. He grabbed his rifle as Ben began to speak.

"My brave fellows, we have beaten the Tories in the past, and we can beat them again. They are all cowards. If they had the spirit of men they would join with their fellow citizens in supporting the independence of our country. When you are engaged, you are not to wait for the word of command from me. I will show you by my example how to fight. I can undertake no more. Every man must consider himself an officer and act from his own judgment. Fire as quickly as you can and stand your ground as long as you can. When you can do no better, get behind trees or retreat, but I beg you not to run off. If we are repulsed, let us make a point of returning and renewing the fight.

Perhaps we may have better luck on a second attempt than the first. If any of you are afraid, such shall have leave to retire and they are requested immediately to take themselves off."

Rice looked at Jack and reached out and shook his hand as if they were parting for the last time in life. He pulled Jack in close turning the handshake into a heartfelt hug. Jake slapped Rice's back and pulled away by saying "See you up yonder, one way or the other I suppose. If not the ridgetop then in the Almighty's Kingdom, but I would prefer the ridgetop for now."

Rice smiled and nodded his head as he made his first step up the hillside. It was well wooded and it would provide protection for both sides of the fight. The trees ranged in size, some as large as four feet around, and the canopy overhead was so dense that little sunlight could make its way to the ground. There was little under growth to slow the march uphill, as Rice first made his way to an oak tree for cover, then to an ash, and from there on to a hickory. There, Cleveland's men met their first volley of the day. Rice could hear and even see the bullets as they ripped through the tree leaves overhead. He could hear the sound of twigs snapping as the shots flew harmlessly by. The smoke from the Tory volley gave away their position. Rice presented his rifle and took careful aim as he pulled his set trigger. Then with the slightest tap of his trigger finger he entered the battle by splitting open the head of a Tory fifty feet away. The whole of Ben's men began to fire as well, just as he had requested, on their own accord. Their days and years in the woods was evident by the number of kills they were making with each shot. Rice reloaded and bolted on up the hillside as the first line of the Tory defense melted away before his eyes. They were retreating in masse, but one turned in his flight, and took a shot at Ben. Rice's heart dropped as he saw Roebuck, Ben's beloved horse, fall to the ground. Rice and Jack both ran to Ben's side and helped him to his feet. "I am fine," he said, pulling his pistol from his belt. "Go on boys. I will be along as soon as my other horse is brought up from the rear. Keep on them, like the hounds on the fox."

Jack looked at Ben and asked enthusiastically, "Did you see who was at the head of that command?

"That I did boy! Now go on, and send Aquila Price to the hereafter." Ben ordered.

As Rice and Jack turned to head up the hill, Ole Roundabout pulled his horn from off his saddle and blew it to announce that he needed his second mount brought up from the foot of the hill.

Back on top, Patrick Ferguson was trying to keep control over his men, many of them were losing heart. The Fair Forest Regiment was having a hard time with Colonel John Sevier's wing. One of its Captains had gone so far as to raise a white flag. Once having seen it flapping in the wind, Ferguson promptly rode his horse over to the offending flag and cut its pole with one hack from his sword. He looked down at his subordinate and said. "The next time I see you wave a surrender flag, by God I'll cut you in half. Lieutenant Allaire has already beaten off a wing of the enemy.[121] We will do the same, or die trying. If you think that they will give quarter you are sadly mistaken. Now fight to your last."

John McFall rested his musket on top of a fallen log, and took aim as one of his former neighbors raced up the hillside. He had

---

[121] This is in reference to Allaire having chased off Colonel Campbell on his first attack up the hill. Like Shelby, he too rallied his troops and was again charging back up the side of Kings Mountain.

Thomas Biecknell squarely in his sights. He pulled the trigger and as the smoke cleared he saw that he had not missed his mark. He quickly reloaded as he saw Jack Mcalpin dart from trcc to tree. IIe waited for his best view to take Jack down. When the moment came, he shot again. This time, it was a miss. All he had done was put Jack behind the trunk of a chestnut tree, thankful that the shot had only cut a hole through the tails of his frock coat and not into his flesh. John began to cuss the inaccurate musket that the Loyalist were making him use. If only he had had his rifle, Jack wound now be dead at the base of that tree. He angrily rose to his feet, and retreated up the hill to reload again. He swore that his next shot would not go awry.

Ben had made his way back to the front of his men who were now over half way up ridge. He was again on foot, having already lost his second mount of the day. It too, had been shot out from under him just a moments ago. He now, like his men was shooting from tree to tree.

Rice had just reloaded and was looking up hill when he saw four Tories running at him in full charge with fixed bayonets. He fired his rifle in defense, killing the man in the center of the charge. David and Martin put two more of Rice's would be killers down with well-aimed shots as they climbed upward, off to Rice's left about hundred feet behind him. Rice pulled his tomahawk, and with a downward blow of his blade, deflected his adversary's bayonet that was thrust towards his midsection. Its point jobbed into the ground at Rice feet, as he stepped forward and buried his tomahawk into the Tory's shoulder at the base of his neck. He withdrew the weapon, looking back at his brother-in-law. He raised the bloody blade to the tip of his hat, giving David and Martin a warrior's salute for the well-aimed shots that had just saved his life.

Around the curve of the mountain Captain Joel Lewis, of the Surry County, North Carolina Militia, was making his way up the hill as part of Major Joseph Winston's wing. His offhand thumb was tightly tied in a blood-soaked rag. The tip of that thumb had been shot off just a few minutes before. He was hunkered down beside a large rock when he spotted movement above. He watched intensely until he realized that the person approaching him was a woman. He leaned his back against the rock and whispered to his subordinate John McQueen[122], the hushing sound of "shshsh."

As Virginia walked by, Lewis reached out, grabbing her arm, and pulled her behind the rock. He looked at her for a moment pinning her arms over her head. "If I were to let you go, you would not try to run off, or even worse, wield a knife from under your garments, would you?"

"Hardly," she replied shaking her head. "I just want off of this God forsaken hill and out of these woods. And to prove the point, I

---

[122] John McQueen recorded this event in his Estill County Kentucky Rev. War Pension application. The application number is S30577. Captain Joel Lewis' Pension application number is W780.

will give you some valuable information. Pattie Ferguson is directly above you. He is dressed in a red and white checkered frock coat. Do you hear that whistle blowing? That is your Scotsman. Bring him down and the day will be yours." As her words escaped her and filled the air she had a slight amount of regret rush through her. She had just betrayed a man that she had hoped to marry. Yet he had turned on her earlier. So, in her eyes, he was reaping what he had sown.

Walter Gilkey had been watching Virginia, as she descended the hill. He was yet to fire from his position behind a walnut tree. He was hoping that the attractive women fleeing the battlefield would cause a Whig to expose himself when otherwise he would not. When Virginia had disappeared behind the rock he was beginning to think that may not be the case. He waited for a while longer until Virginia again stepped into view. She had taken no more than three steps down the hill when Lewis also stepped away from the rock. He was running up the hill as Gilkey squeezed his trigger. The lead ball struck Lewis in the thigh, causing him to tumble down the hill. Gilkey, pleased with his shot, retreated back up the hill as the Rebels below took to cover. Gilkey again found a favorable firing spot behind a rock formation. He was reloading from its cover when Aquila Price, the Virginia Tory rushed behind the same rocks. "Is there a way to break through their lines on this side?" asked the heavily breathing older man.

"Not as of yet. I had to fall back here just a moment ago." Gilkey replied as he fired off another shot. "Why? Are things that bad on the other side of the mountain?"

"Hell yes!" Price almost screamed at Gilkey. "Ferguson has already put down two attempts to strike a surrender flag. He is under the impression that no quarter is to be given by that damned Isaac Shelby. I saw two of my men killed with white handkerchiefs tied to their ramrods. Their killers only yelled "Give them "Buford's play"[123] in response. Quarter is to be rare today it seems. Are you sure that this could not be the way out?" Price asked again franticly.

"No, maybe with another bayonet charge, but it will take more men than what I see here now." Gilkey surmised. Price did not respond, just turned and retreated back up the hill in hopes of finding another escape route.

Rice took a knee as a lead ball slammed into the bark of a poplar tree right above his head. From this low position, he could now see the crest of the mountain for the first time. The Tories were becoming thinner with also most every shot the patriots took, and it was taking a toll on Ferguson's Army. They were becoming desperate, and in so doing, they were also becoming more savage like. But it was enthusiasm that was being felt by the Patriots. They could see and feel that the battle was turning in their favor. Adrenaline was pumping into both armies, at the same time, but for very different reasons. One could sense victory, the other annihilation. Emotions were running high everywhere. Some of the Patriots had seen family members fall, others had heard of a family member being killed. One such, was Charles Bowen who had lost his

---

[123] This was in reference to Tarleton not give quarter to Colonel Abraham Buford's troops at the battle of the Waxhaws. Buford was also the countersign password the Over the Mountain men used during the Battle of Kings Mountain.

brother Reece. This had caused a thirst for blood to send Charles into a state of temporary madness, fighting like a wild animal.

Back on top of the eminence, Patrick Ferguson looked out across the clearing from atop of his white stallion. His men had been pushed all the way across the mountaintop. The corpses of their fellow soldiers lying in woods along the mountainside, across the flat hilltop, and lying among the baggage wagons, had marked the path of their retreat. They were gathering into the most northern corner of the mountain top. He could not believe that his army was in total defeat. He had already consoled himself three or four times by telling himself, "If only I were allowed to have my breech loading rifle, the outcome would have been much different." But he knew that was a moot point now. Victory was lost, but perhaps not all. Escape was still a possibility, he hoped. He would have DePeyster hold the front line with his men on foot, while his own cavalry would rush downhill cutting a path through the rebels for the rest to follow as best as they could. Ferguson was flanked by two of his serving officers, Major Daniel Plummer of the Fair Forest Militia, and Vezey Husband of the Burke County, North Carolina Loyalist. The three watched as most of the cavalry was shot from their horses before reaching the tree line. With one last hope for escape Ferguson put his horse into motion.

Rice glanced to his right as Jack discharged his rifle at a Tory on horseback. His eyes grew large as he looked up hill after having taken his shot. He looked at Rice and pointed to the top of the hill with great agitation. Rice looked up and saw Ferguson approaching with drawn sword in hand. Rice shouldered his rifle and was taking a bead on the red and white checks of Ferguson's coat, but before he could discharge his rifle, Ferguson was blown from his saddle. He had been hit by seven or eight balls with one to the head. His foot was still stuck in the stirrup as his horse drug him down the hill. Rice took careful aim at Husband's back as he was trying to turn his mount around. And as soon as the rifle was discharged, Husband tumbled forward over the horse's head dead to the world. Plummer fared a bit better, as Martin Grider only wounded him with a shot to the hip[124].

Rice charged on up the hill, as Ben called for one last push to win the day. As he reached the summit, he saw Whig after Whig shooting into what was left of Ferguson's troops. Some of the Tories were being murdered, having dropped their guns but being killed anyway, by men such as the enraged Charles Bowen. Other Loyalist, true to their nature were still fighting to the end. A group with tomahawks in hand had caught Rice's attention. One in particular among them, none other than John McFall. He was still alive, and still fighting to the end. Rice shouldered his rifle and took aim at his longtime nemesis. As he pulled back the hammer, he saw that his flint was missing. Having fired so many shots in the past hour, the flint had loosened and fallen out on his last shot at Husband. He dropped his rifle and in a full run, he charged at McFall with tomahawk drawn. To his left, he saw Ben being knocked to the ground by Bowen, who had no idea that his new prey was one of his own. Ben cried out the counterword of "Buford" yet Bowen continued the fight. Rice had little choice, either let Ben Cleveland die, or continue on for McFall. He reached down and grabbed the crazed Bowen's tomahawk and held him until he regained his senses. Ben cried out "Buford" again and this time the word sunk into Bowen memory. His face relaxed as he stepped away from Ben[125]. Once Ben was back on his feet Rice,

---

[124] Plummer owned at least two tracts of land in the area of Fair Forest, all of which was confiscated after the War. He would move to Florida after the war.

[125] Charles Bowen recorded this event in his Revolutionary War pension

returned his attention to McFall. Each saw the other at the same moment. Within a few steps, they were upon each other, rolling on the ground in what would surely be the last moment of one of their lives. Rice broke free from their grip and rose to his feet, as did the bastard but Rice had a handful of McFalls hair in his hand. But in their struggle, he had lost his tomahawk. As McFall came forward with his hawk raised, Rice pulled his knife. They lunged at each other with Rice blocking McFall's downward blow with his forearm. Although Rice had deflected the attempted chop, the blade did cut his cheek. Rice quickly stepped aside and around McFall as his attacking momentum pulled him forward. Rice grabbed McFall from behind, around his neck and put his knife at his throat, as Joseph McDowell grabbed Rice's arm demanding that the battle was over, and quarter was now to be given. Rice's eyes looked at McDowell and then at Jack's as other men gathered around to see how this long feud would end.

"Go on! Cut his damned throat" Jack yelled as McFall stopped his struggling.

"Yes, go on and cut it." McFall smirked as he spoke into Rice's ear. "Become a murdered as well as an abuser of women. Your blasphemy will be completed with one jerk, sending your soul to hell. Do it, if you have the guts. Burn in hell."

application. His application number is S16055.

Rice pushed the bastard to the ground, without making the cut. He walked away as McFall was relaying a profanity laced cuss between sobs and laughs. The Battle of King's Mountain was over[126].

Chapter 111

The Night Of

Rice's eyes were red and watery. He was not sure what was the reason for their bad condition. Maybe it was from lack of sleep, he had gone two full days now without any. Or it could have been from the smoke-filled air during the battle. Either way, they were itchy and tired. He had crawled under one of the Tory's baggage wagons with Jack and the Grider brothers, in hope of getting some sleep once it was dark. The battle had been exhausting. Fighting uphill was no easy chore, especially after such a long and wet ride from the Cowpens. But sleep was hard to come by, with all that was racing through his tired mind. Every time he shut his eyes he could see McFall's warped face. Deep down, part of him had wished that he had taken Jack's advice, and cut the wretched bastard's throat. But then he would think

---

[126] The Battle of Kings Mountain did not end the American Revolution but it was a turning point in the war. The British lost a valuable commander in Ferguson, and it gave the Americans hope that they could still win the war. It was the first in a long chain of events that would lead to ultimate victory. Daniel Morgan would win the Battle of the Cowpens, Nathaniel Greene would win the race to the Dan River, and in doing so cause Lord Cornwallis to retire to the coast and the port city of Yorktown. Greene would also perform well at the battle of Guilford Courthouse, winning a draw. Finally, Washington would lay siege to Yorktown and capture Cornwallis and in essence, win the War.

of what the bible said in Romans 12 verse 19, *"Do not take revenge, my dear friends. But leave room for God's wrath, for it is written "It is mine to avenge. I will repay says the Lord."* McFall was a true test to that verse, and Rice was still wrestling with his pride, and what God would have him do.

He was trying to dwell on the good parts of the day. Ferguson was no more. He would never step foot inside North Carolina again. No homes would be burnt by his hand. No hanging of friends would be done by the Scotsman. This was a total victory that would be hailed all over the colonies. And a defeat that would be cussed overseas in London.

Rice, like many others, had gone to gaze upon the body of Ferguson after the battle. He had nine different wounds to the body, and one to the head. Much of his belonging had been stripped from his body. Even his mistress Virginia, who herself was still a prisoner, came to his corpse and took something. In her case, it was a necklace from his pocket, that she claimed was hers in the first place. She expressed little emotion while doing so. Other trophies of war were soon divided. Colonel Shelby would take one of Ferguson's two silver whistles. Colonel Campbell kept Ferguson's correspondence. Colonel Sevier took a silk sash off the body. Samuel Talbot, a lowly private, who was one of the first to reach Ferguson, took his pistols. Joseph McDowell took china dinner plates and cups from Ferguson's wagon. A silver watch was the prize of one of Samuel Lacey's men. Strips of clothing was even divided up. But, perhaps the best of all went to "Ole Roundabout", Ben Cleveland. He was granted Ferguson's stallion to replace Roebuck, who had died in the battle. Once everything of value was taken, Ferguson's body was kicked and beaten viciously, and as one final insult, urinated upon. Rice did not stay for that crude display. At last, Ferguson was wrapped in a tanned cowhide and buried with Virginia Sal, a woman that he would not marry in life, but would lay with forever in death.

Ferguson was the only member of his army to be laid to rest. The rest would lay where they fell, one hundred and fifty-seven in all. One hundred and sixty-three more wounded men would cry out most of the night for water and assistance. None ever came. The only doctor at the battle was the loyalist, Dr. Uzal Johnson and he was forced to tend to the Whigs that were wounded, sixty-four in number. He dressed their wounds as best as he could, and gave them rum to drink to help with the pain. William Lenoir was one of the wounded, as was Colonel Sevier's brother Robert, who was feared to be dying, as was Colonel James Williams. Johnson could do nothing for the twenty-some-odd that had died among the mountain men. Among the fallen was Major William Chronicle, and Captain John Mattocks. Rice had seen two of his fellow Wilkes county men fall, Daniel Siske and Captain Thomas Bicknell. They would be missed.

Exhausted, Rice finally drifted off to sleep. The army was heading back West in the morning, and he would need his rest. It would be a long, dangerous, trek. The prisoners, almost seven hundred in number would have to be watched along the road, and even worse, where was Bloody Tarleton and his dragoons?

Chapter 112

The Unsettled Mind

John McFall was carrying two captured muskets, one over each shoulder as he marched away from King's Mountain as a prisoner of war. The flints had been removed of course, so he could not do any harm to the Patriots guarding the column. The top of the mountain behind the two armies was still smoke covered. All of Ferguson's baggage wagons had been put to the torch. It was a shame that they had been burnt. They could have been useful in the coming days, but they would have slowed the return march home. And with Cornwallis so close by, a swift retreat was of the utmost importance. The horse litters carrying the wounded were slow enough.

The prisoners were already starting rumors with their talk of Tarleton's dragoons being only a few miles away. Many of them had family inside the Patriot militias. Walter Gilkey was one of the first to start the propaganda war between the two sides. He was lying to his Whig, brother Samuel about Cornwallis' whereabouts. Other prisoners soon took to the same story, and in truth it was playing on the patriots' minds. Rice was happy to see that the men left behind at The Cowpens on foot, had marched on toward the battlefield, and was met up with at Cherokee Ford. They were too late to take part in the battle itself, but they would be a great help when it came to keeping the prisoners under control, and their added guns would also be needed if Tarleton were to attack. Many of the loyalist were still very cocky early this morning, considering they had been soundly defeated. But that soon came to a rapid halt. Some of the worst agitators had been dragged from the lines into the woods. A shot would be heard, and only the guards would return out of the trees. At other times, a Whig would come back with a blood covered blade on his tomahawk, but always alone. This put a fear into the captured Tories, especially those among DePeyster's New Jersey Volunteers. They had long heard that the backwater men were just as savage as the Indians, if not more so. The roadside killings confirmed that to them in many ways, but to the Whigs defense, those that were falling victim had commented atrocities themselves, and was using the war as a way to justify their wicked acts. Rice was pondering the idea of pulling McFall from the line. He knew that Martin Davenport would be more than willing to assist, but he also knew that it would be a murderous act, something that he would have to live with throughout his life, and then account for on his final judgment day. So, he kept clear of the McFall brothers to keep his temptation at bay. Colonel Campbell had ordered early this morning, that if they were attacked, that the prisoners should be fired upon at first chance. That could give Rice an excuse to indulge in his fantasy of ending the bastard's life, but at what cost. He and John had exchanged looks once. McFall had made a taunting gesture with his eyes during the exchange, however Rice chose to ignore it for the moment. Night would fall soon and what happened in the dark was not always seen.

Darkness fell on the deserted plantation of a Tory by the name of Matthew Faldron, as the army marched onto its lawn. Rails had been pulled from its fences and poles taken from its barns to fuel the night fires. Colonel Campbell had ordered outer picket lines to be set up, and well manned, standing almost shoulder to shoulder. The Waxhaws had been a hard lesson learned and its disastrous outcome would not be repeated tonight if an attack were to come. Sweet potatoes were frantically dug for a much-needed meal. Two days without food was a enemy in itself. Rice and his friends did not let the sweet potatoes cool before eating them. If the roof of the mouth was burned, so be it. Afterwards, Martin and Val were back to telling tales. Jack was contentedly listening to their stories while stretched out on his back looking up at the stars. David was fast asleep. Rice was laying at the group's edge, looking toward where the prisoners was being held. He looked back at his friends, and without a word he slipped off into the night. Elihu Ayres was standing guard over the McFall's as Rice walked up. Arthur was nursing a broken arm, having been shot below the elbow in the battle. George had a cut across his nose. John was sitting on the ground, without stretched legs, and folded arms. He had come through the battle unscathed. Rice had made Ayres a pair of door hinges no more than a month ago, and was in good standing with the man.

"I need to speak with that one alone." Rice said, pointing his rifle at John.

"I thought as much," replied Ayres. "Take him down by that creek bank. No one will be the wiser."

"Here we go," McFall said as he rose to his feet. "I am somewhat surprised that it took this long.

Rice could hear the other two McFall's protesting as they walked away. Ayres seemed to know what the outcome was going to be as he gave John a parting gesture of "Farewell, you bastard." Rice walked about ten feet behind John, wondering how this was going to turn out himself. He could feel the hatred building in him with every step he took into the darkness. He and John had hated each other for years, with each being elusive to the other for so long.

It was almost surreal to think that the end of their feud was finally coming to an end.

"Are we going to get our feet wet?" John asked as they reached the water's edge. "Or am I to die with dry feet tonight."

"I suppose that depends on you John," Rice answered.

"Do not give me any of those self-righteous falsehoods of yours tonight!" John replied. "You hate my very being and for that you are going to end my days tonight. So, don't act like you are not going to kill me. No lies this time."

"I have never lied to you before, John. Why would you think I would do any different tonight?"

"You have stolen and burned everything I have ever had!" John said through gritted teeth. "Why would you not lie?"

"Ture, I did burn your father's place, but that was on account of your actions, not mine. Your bad deeds demanded that response. I had little choice in the matter, but I have never stolen from you John. God known it and you do as well."

"You never stole from me?" McFall cried in a loud voice. "You never stole from me? You took my very heart! My very heart, you took! I don't give a good damn about that old man's cabin, never did. But Rachael! Rachael is another matter altogether."

"She was never yours, John! Where did you get this insane idea?"

"Oh, she was one night, wasn't she?" the bastard replied with an insane cackle. "My what a taste she was."

"Watch it!" Rice said stepping forward with his rifle raised, "You are on thin ice and hell is under the water."

"Hit a nerve, did I?" John asked. "Aw, that is almost as sweet as her. Almost."

"She told me about that." Rice said still levelling his rifle at John's chest. 'She said you leered a lustful gaze, but that was all. Iona saw to that did she not?"

"That bitch!" John whispered angrily. "If I ever get my hands on her! I pray that you and that bitch will soon know the fiery pit."

"Hit a nerve, did I" Rice replied as he pulled back the hammer of his rifle.

"You know. I almost hit a deadly nerve back on the Tuckasegee River. That very night I wrapped that sorry rifle around an oak for flashing in the pan the way it did" John complained. "I have cussed and damned that day ever since. Why God would spare a devil such as you, I have no clue. Demons must watch over you."

"I have said the same of you, believe me," Rice said shouldering his rifle and bring it to bear on McFall's chest. "Has God hardened my heart? I feel that he has when it comes to you John. If I pull this trigger, will I be doing his work?"

"Don't do it Rice," Jack said stepping from out of the darkness. "He deserves it all right, but I don't know about in this way. Back at the battle, yes, but not like this. Then, you would have killed something that is totally vile but in battle. I know you Rice. If you do it on this night, it will stay with you like a well dug in tick. For years, you will be wondering if it was just or not, to kill this bastard. When you stand before the Lord you will already have enough sins to atone for. Hell, just like all of us will. Do not let this be another. Be true to your honesty. Tonight, there is talk going around camp of a trial in the days to come. Ben is pressing hard for it. He is sure to have this snake among the accused. Let the noose do its work. Keep your hands clean of this filth. Do you remember Richard Tucker,[127] who told us while we were in camp about what happened at the Battle of Rocky Mount?   Well, he was captured at Camden, and he was hanged, and in front of Lord Cornwallis they say. Without a trail, they hanged him. There are some awful mad men back in our camp who wants blood in retaliation. Let John here, be their vengeance."

Red faced with anger, Rice lowered his rifle and walked away. "You take him back Jack. I would surely kill him if I have to," Rice predicted.

As he walked away, Rice again heard McFall's foul cursing fill the air. His rage was beyond madness. His was truly an unsettled mind. Rice was coming to believe that John McFall was something of a demon. Even in defeat, and in chains, he could not contain his wickedness.

---

[127] Captain Richard Tucker was hanged along with at least four other men; they being John Miles, Josiah Gayle, Eleazer Smith and Samuel Andrews. The execution took place between the 13 Aug and the 6 Sept in Camden South Carolina.

Chapter 113

Judgement

The next morning the march home continued, but for only two miles. Colonel Williams had died and was buried with honors. For the rest of the day the wounded was tended to and everyone took a well-earned rest. Then the march again renewed. The morale of the patriots was growing with every mile while the Tories were dying with every step. Escape attempts was become more common in the last few days. Many had gotten away, but once a prisoner was recaptured it was seldom that he was not put to death. Colonel Campbell did not approve of such consequence but he did tolerate it. He was afraid of losing control over his undisciplined army, so he indulged them on the matter. His men wanted accountability for all of the atrocities that had been carried out on their Whig families and friends. After the Battle of Camden, the British and Tories had hanged Whigs from Camden all the way South to Fort Ninety-Six,[128] and as far West as Salisbury. Now that the Patriot Army had come to a halt, about ten miles Northeast of Gilbert Town, at Aaron Bickerstaff's plantation they were demanding justice. Bickerstaff was a loyalist who had just lost his life fighting under Ferguson at King's Mountain. His home had now become a makeshift courtroom.

---

[128] Eleven Whig prisoners were hanged at Fort Ninety-Six a few days after the Battle of King's Mountain. It was in retaliation to the Over the Mountain Men's victory.

With Ben being an acting magistrate, he was in charge of holding the court with a few other Whigs acting as judges but Ben was to be the voice of the court. Abraham DePeyster was quick to protest Cleveland appointment. He complained on the grounds of bias and prejudice, citing that it was natural for Cleveland to be so, as his brother had been badly wounded on the march to the battle. "That is a bad omen for the accused" he had stated. But Martin Grider reminded him that he had no authority in these proceedings. Hearing DePeyster's concerns, Martin walked over to the small oak table that was being used as Ben's bench. There he picked up a glass goblet. "Those were mighty stirring words, Captain. It was truly touching." He raised his glass in toast and said, "To the Tory officers. My they all be hanged."

Ambrose Mills, Arthur Grimes, Robert Wilson, James Chitwood, Thomas Lafferty, John Bibby, Augustine Hobbs, and Walter Gilkey had all been found guilty, along with twenty-two others. Mills was judged guilty for encouraging the Cherokee to attack both North and South Carolina. Grimes, for being the leader of a group of highwaymen and horse thieves. Wilson and Hobbs, for hanging prisoners at Fort Ninety-Six. Chitwood and Bibby, were charged and found guilty of murder. Lafferty for embezzlement against several of Colonel McDowell's men. Gilkey, for shooting a boy in the arm after interrogating him about his father's whereabouts. Many of the condemned had supporters among the gathering crowd watching the proceeding. Word of the battle had spread throughout the countryside. Many loyalists had come to see what was to happen to the prisoners. Wives and children, fathers and mothers, watched helplessly as their loved ones stood before the very men that they had sworn to kill just weeks before. Some were overcome with verdicts of innocence when they did come down, proving Lt. Allaire's statement that these proceedings were "an infamous mock jury" to be a falsehood.

Jack walked over to Rice and leaned on his rifle barrel as he watched Aquila Price being led in front of the court. Price's hat was in his hand, as he played his well-rehearsed role of a modest man, hardly the cocky land swindler that he was known to be.

"Are you going to be a witness?" Asked Rice. "Ben would surely call on you to do so."

"I pray I get to do so," Jack replied "That man stole years' worth of work from me in one fell swoop. Justice will be served if I can speak of his foul deeds. "

Ben looked down at Price with raised eyebrows and said. "Colonel Aquilia Price, you have the look of a man who would pick a pocket on a dark night, or a sunny day for that matter. This will be short work. You have stolen from one of my very best men, Jack, standing right there. You have pressed men into the King's service against their wishes. That is a well-known fact. In order to speed these proceedings along, I proclaim that you are found guilty sir, of said crimes. You have a date with a rope."

Rice looked at Jack. as the mob around the court erupted in an approving cheer and said, "Damn! That was short, but sweet. How does it make you feel?"

"Good." Jack replied, as he locked eyes on Price. Both men had hard expressions, but Price's was also inquisitive.

"I declare, Rice" Jack remarked. "I believe that he does not even remember me. He has wronged so many, he cannot keep us all straight in his mind."

Next, George McFall was led before the court. He was downtrodden in his behavior. He had nervously been rubbing a scab on his nose, left from an old battle wound that was yet to heal, while watching Price's time in front of the bench. He had rubbed it so hard, that it was now bleeding. He looked around at the stern face of the court and began to beg for leniency. "I have only been a good soldier for the King. My conduct has been nothing but honorable."

"Save your breath George." Ben said looking him in the eye. "Have you not forgotten our long ride to Salisbury? Does tar not come to your mind boy? This one is to hang as well. Take him away."

Ben turned his attention to Arthur McFall as he was lead before the bench. Ben clutched his hands together as he

stared at his onetime savior. Arthur was smart enough to hold his tongue when Ben began to speak. "What a fall you have taken Arthur. How is it, that I find this court facing a man who has fought bravely by my side, even going so far as to save my very life, to now be on the wrong side of this bloody war. I heard of a wilderness divorce being executed by your hand. How you could have tuned out a wife such as Iona, I have no clue, but as much as I disapprove of that sad affair, I cannot hang a man for losing interest in his wife. I also see that you still carry a wound in your arm that most likely will remind you for years to come of the choice you made. However, there is more than one side to every man. Over the years, I have seen you choose a different path than your wilder brothers. You always were the voice of reason for the McFall clan. I wonder if the tragedy of Iona's misfortune unhinged your mind. You have changed from the man you once were. Maybe it is time for the old Arthur to return. If I were to free you, would you take an oath, not to bear arms against any of us ever again?"

"I would gladly take such an oath!" Arthur replied, greatly relieved.

"Very well." Ben replied "I suppose a wound as such as that will serve as punishment enough. With that being said, you do not want to find yourself before me ever again. Leniency I will do once, but not twice."

Rice watched with gritted teeth as John McFall was lead before the court, but the bastard was not focused on Ben. His eyes were fixed on Rice, as if he were a haunting ghost that would never leave McFall alone. His expression did not waver as Joseph McDowell[129] began speak on McFall's behalf "This man stood with General Rutherford,

---

[129] Joseph McDowell of Pleasant Gardens acted as the defiance lawyer for all of the accused Tories on trial .

on the 1776 Cherokee expedition, as a spy and scout. He should receive some reward for that deed."

Ben looked at McDowell and said, "Sir, I am afraid that you have the wrong brother in mind. It was Arthur, not John with us in the Cherokee towns. John here is a noted Tory. That man went to the house of Martin Davenport, one of my best soldiers, when he was away from home fighting for his country. He insulted his wife and whipped his child. He also played a role in the tar and feathering of another of my men. Such man ought not to be allowed to live. I am sure that Martin will be more than willing to testify to these offending facts."

As Davenport began to tell of John's unwanted visit to his home, the sun began to fade. John finally looked away from Rice, having just delivered the most evil stare that Rice had ever seen. McFall began to hum, "God save the King" knowing that God would not save him this day. It was one last act of defiance to the men he hated most in the world. His humming became so loud that Rice was sure that the bastard could not have heard Ben announce his guilt. And as he was being led away, he began to dance a fast jig to his humming. He was the last of the thirty men to be found guilty and sentenced to death by hanging. A hoard of weeping wives and children of the North and South Carolina Tories had come to the camp. Their pleas and begging had taken some of the fire out of the Whigs hearts. Leniency became the practice of the court, once the most dangerous of the Tories had been condemned. The executions were to be carried out later tonight, and Rice was relieved that John McFall's was among them.

Chapter 114

The Gallows Oak

It had been a short hour for John McFall since the judgment had come down. Arthur had come to console his two brothers. George, unappreciative as ever was mad at the fact that his brother was walking away with his life, while he was to swing. His rant was as foul mouthed as any he had spat in the past.

He had damned Arthur for his good fortune. He had even gone as far as to say, that he hoped that Arthur's bad arm would soon rot off. On the other hand, John did not hold any hard feelings about Arthur's good fortune. He had even bequeathed a few personal items he had stored away back at Ninety-Six to his surviving brother. Yet, he was quick to hush Arthur's talk about his salvation. He was resigned to the fact that he was hell bound, and he knew that repentance was not his way. He had too much hatred in his heart and it was buried too deep to give it up. But he did have one request, as he pulled his brother close, to hear his last plea.

"When you are free, no matter when that will be. I want you to look up two of my old friends. They could be at Ninety-Six. If not try Cross Creek. They are brothers themselves. One a large tall man that goes by Big Harp. The other, much smaller, is Little Harp. Find them, and tell them of Rice's evil deeds. How he was the ruination of my life. Have them do to him the same as we have done to the Hill family on Leepers Creek. They will understand what that means, even if you don't. One last thing, do not trust them, and do not stay in their company any longer than necessary. They can turn on anyone, at any moment. Relay my request and move on quickly afterwards."

"Very well," Arthur replied. "Consider it done. But I cannot stay here and watch my two brothers die tonight. So, this is our goodbye. I hope that you understand and forgive me for going, but my eyes and my soul could not bear it"

"Fair enough," John answered as it began to sprinkle a light rain from above, "But don't forget what I said about the Harps. It is my dying wish."

"I will not forget," Arthur assured him. "Consider it done." He turned around and walked off into the darkness, but

he had no intentions of relaying John's message to the Harps[130]. If he could not save his brother though salvation, he could let him exit this world with the thought that he would still have victory over Rice. That victory would never come to pass, but in John's last moments it

---

[130] The Harp brothers are said to be America's first serial killers. Micajah or "Big Harp" was the leader of the two. Wiley "Little Harp" the younger. They were said to be Loyalist during the War. They killed as many as fifty people after the war was over in Kentucky, Illinois, Mississippi and Tennessee before being killed themselves by vigilantes.

would be a truth that he could hold onto. Maybe he could draw strength from it and die well.

Pine tar torches lead the way to a oak tree that was to be the gallows. The tree had a strong limb that was long enough to hang three men at one time. John, George and Price were to be the second group to be hanged. They watched as Mills, Chitwood and Wilson were placed on three horses with their hands bound behind their backs. Samuel and Thomas Scott[131] two of Campbell's Virginians who had fought well in the battle led the horses under the tree. Samuel had been one of Ben's fellow judges during the trial. Chitwood proclaimed that the whole process was illegal, but held his composure. As Samuel Scott roughly placed the noose around his neck he said. "Maybe so. But you will still be dead, now want you?" He walked around in front of the horse and lead it away from the tree as the mob began to cheer. Their fall was short and lacked the force to snap their necks. They hung there for a while kicking and choking as they died. Their dying breaths could be seen, floating in the cold air as their lives came to an end.

Rice watched the McFalls as the first three were being executed. John showed little emotion on his face, but Rice could see his chest moving rapidly with every breath. His breaths were short and erratic, as the onlookers let out a cheer while the condemned swung in midair. George began to sob, as the dead were having the nooses removed from around their necks.

---

[131] Samuel and Thomas Scott Revolutionary War pensions numbers are R9307 and R9313 respectively.

Jack looked at Rice and said, "That is one hell of a way to go, but they were the ones who started the hangings in the first place. Old man Price sure is squirming over there while waiting his turn."

Outraged, DePeyster and Allaire both began to protest, but were quickly shouted down by the Whigs. Rice overheard Allaire[132] say "They died like Romans" to DePeyster. However, Rice saw nothing noble about these men. Besides what was ever noble about a Roman?

John looked at Rice as he was being led under the gallows tree[133]. Once he was in the saddle, he again looked back, trying to hide his fear with an unconvincing smile. He said something to Thomas Scott. Rice watched as young Scott approached. "That one wants a word with you." He said "something about setting things right between you two. It is up to you if you want to grant his wish or not. I for one, would not mind to hear one last lie from that one before he dangles. It could be memorable." Scott replied inquisitively. "It could be amusing. If not, we will go on with our task and shut him up with the drop."

Against his better judgment Rice, walk over to the horse. McFall's eyes were watery and red and he was biting his lower lip to keep it from quivering. Then a smile parted his mouth. "Vengeance is

---

[132] From Allaire's diary.

[133] The spot of the hangings has a historical roadside marker to indicate where they took place. It is on Whitesides Road, South from Morganton, North Carolina in Burke County.

coming your way Rice. I will not see it, but it is coming all the same. My reach goes beyond the grave. "

"I doubt that very much John, it is hard to get things done in hell. If I were you I would be getting right with the Lord." With that said Rice, turned and walked away as the horse was pull out from under the most despicable man he would ever know.

Chapter 115

Peace and Contentment

Rice was walking down Tradd Street with Rachael's arm locked through his own. The city of Charles Town was now in American hands. Since the Battle of King's Mountain, the war had taken a favorable turn for the Americans. Cornwallis had been captured along with eight thousand men at the Siege of Yorktown. General Greene had proven why he was Washington's favorite, by push what was left of the British into this city. They had evacuated its harbor back on December the fourteenth in the year of our Lord seventeen hundred and eighty-two. The Union Jack was no longer flying anywhere in the Carolinas.

As the couple were walking Rice looked at his best girl as he now called Rachael. She was as beautiful as ever, and on this special occasion her attire was almost a matched to her beauty. She was stunning in her light green gown that they had just purchased here in the city. Rice looked down at his new brass shoe buckles. They had a nice shine to them. His blue waistcoat was clean. His new black stockings felt good on his feet. His appearance was a far cry from what he had looked like at King's Mountain, he thought to himself. That day was one of the most important days he would ever see, because of it, he would have far more enjoyable days to come in the future, he was sure of it. That day paled to his wedding day, and on the days his children had come into this world. It was an important day for a very different reason. It had assured that his offspring would never be ruled by a foreign power. He was very proud that he could say that he was at that battle with men like Jack, David, the Griders, Ole Roundabout, and all the others who had stormed up that wooded hillside.

Jack had teased Rice about this grand ball he and Rachael were about to attend for the next few hours. He, like Rice, was here in the city performing his last duties of the war. They were to protect the city for one more week, then they were to return home

in peace. Peacetime was something hard to imagine for Rice. Not having to worry about Redcoats or Tories was a wonderful thing. The Cherokee would be a small threat compared to what they once were. And best of all, the McFalls were gone. Rice would never have to deal with them ever again, he thought, as he looked at Rachael whose hand was still intertwined in his arm. He was so proud of her. She had endured so much during this war. When it had begun she was a mere girl, and now she was the mature women that he loved so deeply.

"I must say Rice it is quite nice to have a brother in law, such as mine. Massey's high position as Quartermaster of a city such as this is a blessing. We would have never darted such a door as this one without his help," Rachael said as their destination came into view.

"Very true" Rice said in agreement. "But I believe that this war has changed that forever. One's position, from now on will be earned, instead of appointed by a monarchy. The rich will always have an advantage, but not like before the war. I think that now everyone will have the chance to make their own destiny. We can set our sites on whatever we want, and have no one to stop us but ourselves. The war assured us of that. But enough talk of war. Rachel, what do you think of this city that we have been in for the last two months? Would you like to stay here and take up residence?"

"Oh, it is wonderful alright. The cobblestone streets are nice, but sometime very dirty and busy. The sea air blowing in off the ocean is sweet to the senses, but so is the mountain breeze back home. The ocean is vast, but our rivers are beautiful and clear and taste so good. All the palmetto trees here are nice as well, but they lack the shade of the chestnut's around our home. So no, I am content with what we have and am looking forward to going home. I dearly love the mountains. They will always be home. But I will miss their grand homes and their wonderfully colorful wallpapers and paints.

"Good" Rice said as he opened the door to the former residence of Major Patrick Ferguson for the evening's ball.

"I was hoping that you would say something like that. So maybe, just maybe, in our next house we will find a wall for you to hang some wallpaper. Life is going to be grand from here on out. I predict peace and contentment along with a few trials as always, and then heaven."

The End

Author's Notes

The American Revolution has always fascinated me. It was such an extraordinary period of time. The fact that thirteen colonies could pull together and defeat the most powerful nation in the world was quite an achievement. That victory announced to the world, that America was destined to become a superpower in the coming years. And time did prove that announcement to be correct.

There were so many fascinating people, with great stories throughout the war, and Rice and Rachael Medaris had one of those stories. He was not a famous man by any means. But he played a part in one of the war's most important battles when he fought his way up that hillside at King's Mountain. I will always fondly remember the first time I visited the battlefield and walked up the same hill that Rice had fought on. It gives one such pride to walk the same steps as your ancestor. It was such an awesome feeling it is hard to put into words. It was hair raising for me and I experienced the same feelings at Hanging Rock and Camden when I was there as well. What a life my fifth great-grandfather lived.

Rice died on July 22,1824. Rachael lived until at least 1850. That was the year she applied for Rice's Revolutionary War pension. Much of this book is based on that document and others like it. His pension number is R6685, if anyone would like to look it up. The document tells of Rice being in the 1776 Cherokee War and in the battles of Hanging Rock and Camden, which she calls the battle of "Gum Springs", another name for the Battle of Camden. And of course, of him being at the Battle of King's Mountain and lastly, his stay in Charleston, South Carolina as the war was coming to a close. Rachael was ninety five years old when she gave the deposition. She showed that she was still sharp at such an advanced age. She could still remember what battles he was in, and in what years they took place. She even knew who his commanding officers were. She did fail to mention the two skirmishes at Flat Rock and Beaver Creek Ford. This could have been due to the fact that both were small in nature and that Rice did not make a big deal of them.

But we know that Rice was there, because he was under the command of Major Davie at that time, when he orchestrated those two skirmishes.

Rice and Rachael would go on to have eight children together and lived out their lives in western North Carolina in Wilkes, Caldwell and Burke counties and finally in Rachael's case, Buncombe County. One cannot know for sure, but they seemed to have had a good and happy marriage together, and a life that they could have taken pride in. I know that many of their descendants are very proud of them. I can truly say that my mother, brothers, sons and nephews all fall into that category.

John Grider, another of my ancestral Grandfathers also survived the war. He applied for his Revolutionary War pension in Adair County, Kentucky. His pension Number is W358. He and his wife Isabell Blair, had a son named James, who would marry Rice's daughter Sarah, in Kentucky, in about 1804. This family line would eventually lead to me, through my mother Sue Cox Roberts' pedigree. All of the other Grider men also survived the war. Their pension numbers are as follows, Jacob's W3980, Valentine's W11082, Martin's S31078.

Benjamin Cleveland's war did not end at King's Mountain. A band of Tories under Captain William Riddle would kidnap Cleveland at Wolf's Den in retaliation for the hanging at Bickerstaff Plantation. Cleveland's men rescued Ole Roundabout and captured Riddle and two other men in the process. I have often wondered if this was another act of the war that Rachael forgot to mention about Rice being involved with. All three of the prisoners were hanged from the same tree, "The Tory Oak," a historic landmark, that stood behind the old Wilkes County courthouse until its death. Cleveland moved after the war, to South Carolina where he would die in 1806 in Oconee County.

Griffith Rutherford was exchanged for another prisoner in 1781 and released from Castillo De San Marcos, a fort in St. Augustine Florida. He would go on to besiege British held Wilmington, North Carolina. And in 1782 he again attacked the Cherokee in Tennessee and Georgia.

William Richardson Davie would go on to fight at the battle of Charlotte in September of 1780. He then served under General Nathanael Greene. After the war, he became the Governor of North Carolina.

Isaac Shelby and John Sevier would both go on to be Governors of Kentucky and Tennessee respectively. William Campbell would fight at the Battle of Guilford Courthouse, only to die of a heart attack on August 22, 1781.

As for Rice's best friend Jack McAlpin, and his wife Annabel, they exist only in my head. I needed a strong character to help the story along, and Jack provided that for me. He and Annabel are the only fictitious characters in the book with main rolls. "Sorry to all of you Jack lovers out there."

General New River, the Catawba chief was very much a real man. He was the Catawba ruler from 1776 to 1802. He was born circa 1725 and died in 1804 at New Town. After the British victory at Camden, New River evacuated the Lancaster County, South Carolina, Catawba village of Old town. He took his people to the mountains of Virginia for safety. When He lead them back the following year, they found their villages had been destroyed in their exile. However, they did rebuild Old town and later constructed New Town in Kings Bottom. UNC Archeologist have made several digs at General New Rivers and his wife Sally's home. Their cabin was well stocked with kitchen utensil, even flow blue china. One of New River's old pistols was found. The Catawba Nation was one of the very few Indian tribes that held onto their lands. New River's decisions to ally with the Whigs was instrumental in saving their homeland.

Land leases from the 1760's were honored because of that decision. Those land leases would lead to a Catawba Reservation, that the Catawba control to this day.

As for Dragging Canoe and the Cherokee they would suffer two more major defeats at the hand of the whites. One led by Isaac Shelby in 1779 and another in 1781 by John Sevier. By 1782, Dragging Canoe was again attacking the settlements in Tennessee and Kentucky. Dragging Canoe never did submit, he died performing a war dance on February 29, 1792. Most likely from a heart attack. He was 54 years old.

Bloody Fellow, along with Young Tassel led a war party against Gillespie's Fort, below the mouth of the Little Tennessee River, killing 28 people in 1788. He would fight along with Dragging Canoe to the end.

Doublehead would go down in history as the Cherokee version of Benedict Arnold. In 1807 he was selling Cherokee land without council approval. For that he was murdered by his own people.

Bob Benge, "The Bench" was the most feared Cherokee warrior of all times. It is said that he took over forty scalps in battle.

On April 6, 1794 he was ambushed and killed in what is now Wise County Virginia. Benge's Gap, in Wise County is named after him.

As for the loyalist, Colonel Gideon Wright's war ended at the Battle of Shallow Ford on Oct 14, 1780. He was defeated by Major Joseph Cloyd of Virginia and by the North Carolina Militia led by several captains, among them, Captain Salathiel Martin and Captain Richard Allen, both of whom Rice had served with at various times during the war. Gideon fled the battlefield to the safety of Charleston, where he died on August 9, 1782.

Arthur McFall would go on to wed two other wives after divorcing his first. He lived out the rest of his life as a hunter. He seemed to be well liked, despite the fact that he had abandoned his first wife, and his Tory background. He died in 1839 in Mitchell County North Carolina. As for Iona McFall, nothing is known of her. Not even what her given name was. I gave her the name Iona, because I needed her to have a first name for the storyline in the book. I do pray that her life ended well, but we will never know. Jacob Grider spoke of her in his pension application, but he could not remember her first name.

Virginia Paul's fate is just as cloudy as was Mrs. McFall's. We do know that she was released by the Over the Mountain Men a few days after the battle. She was said to have made her way to Charlotte in hopes of meeting up with the British Army there. Maybe she found that elusive husband in their ranks.

Like Jack, Aquilla Price is fictitious. A carryover character from my first novel Redskins and Lobsterbacks.

Lt. Anthony Allaire, Captain Abraham DePeyster, and Dr. Uzal Johnson all made their escape from the Over The Mountain Men on November 2. However, the escape was a few days late, in Johnson's case. Colonel Cleveland gave him a good thrashing over a prisoner. They made their way to safety by going to Fort Ninety-Six. While on their escape route they stayed two days with Colbert Blair, John Grider's future Father in law and my sixth Great Grandfather. They stayed in his fodder house because of heavy rains. He even guided them a few miles to their next guide, a Mr. Rider. After the war both Allaire and De Peyster moved to New Brunswick Canada. Johnson continued to practice medicine in New Jersey.

With the Battle of King's Mountain being the climax of my second historical novel, I would like to end with a quote about the battle. "That memorable victory was the joyful annunciation of the turn of the tide of success; which terminated the Revolutionary War with a seal of Independence." President Thomas Jefferson.

Made in the USA
Columbia, SC
07 August 2023

21233987R00293